THE ORPHAN'S DREAM

Mirabel Cutler was raised by her father to be a lady. But when he dies suddenly Mirabel finds herself cast out on the street by her ruthless stepmother. She is taken to a place of refuge by charismatic sea captain Jack Starke. But the haven turns out to be a house of ill-repute. Here she catches the eye of Hubert Kettle. Mirabel has fallen in love with Jack Starke, but when she hears that his ship has foundered and all were lost, she accepts Hubert's offer of marriage. Mirabel is determined to make the best of her life, until her life is thrown into turmoil once more.

THE ORPHAN'S DREAM

THE ORPHAN'S DREAM

by

Dilly Court

Magna Large Print Books
Long Preston, North Yorkshire,
BD23 4ND, England.

British Library Cataloguing in Publication Data.

Court, Dilly
        The orphan's dream.

        A catalogue record of this book is
        available from the British Library

        ISBN   978-0-7505-4247-0

First published in Great Britain by Century in 2015

Magna Large Print is an imprint of Library Magna Books Ltd.

Printed and bound in Great Britain by
T.J. (International) Ltd., Cornwall, PL28 8RW

For Jonathan, Sarah and Sophie, with love

Chapter One

Catherine Court, Great Tower Hill, London, 1881

The locals called the house Cutler's Castle, and it was not intended as a compliment. Mirabel was painfully aware of the fact that her father was not the most popular man in the City, having acquired his wealth by sharp trading and a ruthless desire to put his rivals out of business. Jumped-up Jacob Cutler was one of his more repeatable nicknames, and if people were polite to his face Mirabel knew that they laughed at him behind his back. Her father's cock-of-the-walk attitude and boastful nature were unlikely to endear him to his neighbours or the other city merchants, and Mirabel had realised long ago that this was why they were shunned socially.

She hitched her basket over her arm and let herself in through one of the wrought-iron gates which separated the court from Seething Lane at one end and Trinity Square at the other. Their intended purpose was to keep out thieves and vagrants, but at times Mirabel felt as though they had been designed to create a prison for the residents, herself in particular. Her weekly excursions to help at the soup kitchen were her one way of escaping from a life bounded by her father's strict rules.

9

She headed for the house which had been her home for almost as long as she could remember. Cutler's Castle dominated the Georgian terraces in a way befitting a man of considerable means. Double-fronted, with a porch supported by ornate Corinthian columns, it satisfied Jacob's desire to show off. He employed a cook, a maid of all work and Septimus Wiley, a manservant who varied his duties between valet and butler and ruled his small empire with ruthless disregard for the feelings of others. But Wiley had a weakness: Mirabel had discovered that he was a secret drinker, imbibing his master's best brandy at every possible opportunity. How he managed to conceal his drunken state from her father she was at a loss to know. She had tried to warn Jacob about his employee's shortcomings, but her father's refusal to take her seriously made her wonder if the despicable Wiley held some sway over him. He seemed to get away with behaviour that would not be tolerated in any other household, and he treated her with barely concealed contempt. Wiley in his black tailcoat with his stick-thin arms and legs put her in mind of a spider, spinning his web, ready to strike at any moment.

She was about to knock on the door when she saw Harriet Humble emerge from the house opposite with her maid in tow, as well as a small boy whose duty was to carry his mistress's purchases home at the end of her frequent shopping expeditions. Mrs Humble's husband was a prosperous gun maker with premises in Thames Street, and if she chose to out-rival Jacob with her spendthrift ways he always managed to outdo her in a spectacular fashion, which was unlikely to win their friendship. The Humbles were pleasant enough and passed the time of day with Mirabel, but had little to say on the rare occasions when she was with her father.

'Good afternoon, Mrs Humble.' Mirabel nodded and smiled.

'Good afternoon, Miss Cutler.' Harriet acknowledged her with a pitying look and walked on, but then she paused and came to a halt, turning to stare at Mirabel with her head on one side and a calculating expression on her doughy features. 'I see your father has a new companion, Miss Cutler.'

'I beg your pardon, ma'am?'

'Such a handsome woman,' Harriet continued slyly. 'I'm sure you must have met her on many occasions. They seem quite a devoted couple, and I've been told that it's some time since your mother passed away.'

'My mother died when I was five,' Mirabel said coldly. 'I think you're mistaken, Mrs Humble. My father comes in contact with many people in his business capacity.'

Harriet shrugged her plump shoulders. 'I daresay you're right, Miss Cutler. But she is a very handsome woman and I should think she's quite a lot younger than your father, and if she's in trade, well...' She allowed the sentence to hang like a cobweb, floating in the air.

'I'm sure I don't know what you mean.' Mirabel raised her hand to knock on the door.

'I imagine that you'll find out soon enough, Miss Cutler. Come, Mary, don't dawdle or we'll

11

be late.'

Harriet seemed determined to have the last word, and she marched off with her entourage trotting along at her heels like well-trained puppies. Mary looked back and stuck her tongue out at Mirabel and the boy copied her, cocking a snook.

Mirabel raised her hand once more and rapped on the lion's head doorknocker. She waited for a moment but no one came. She knocked again, and finally she heard footsteps and the door was wrenched open. Wiley peered at her, bleary-eyed. 'Oh, it's you.' He turned on his heel and staggered off along the narrow hallway, leaving the door swinging on its hinges. He headed for the stairs which led down to the basement kitchen and the tiny room he had commandeered for himself, styling it as the butler's pantry when in truth it was little more than a glorified store cupboard.

Mirabel said nothing. She closed the front door and made her way up the winding staircase to her bedroom on the second floor. For all its width the house was relatively narrow in depth. There were only two rooms on each floor, although these were large and well-proportioned with front aspects and uninspiring views of the houses opposite. The exception to this was the top floor which was divided into much smaller rooms, one for Cook and another for Flossie, the maid of all work, a boxroom, and finally, and most important to Mirabel, was her own special room, her dreaming place. Spending hours in solitary confinement had been a punishment meted out by her ill-tempered governess, but the attic room had become a place

12

of sanctuary. Here she would sit on the window seat and look out over the rooftops to the spire of All Hallows Church and the vast expanse of sky. It was here that she would escape into a world inhabited by handsome princes who fought fiery dragons in order to win the hand of a princess, who coincidentally bore a strong resemblance to her. Then as she grew older her dreams altered and she imagined herself travelling the world, visiting foreign countries where the sun shone every day and there were no peasouper fogs, drenching rain or the bone-chilling cold of an English winter.

She smiled as she took off her bonnet and shawl and laid them on a boudoir chair placed between the two tall windows. Her room, like every other part of the house was decorated lavishly. The rose-patterned wallpaper and curtains matched the coverlet on her bed. The delicate pink of the flowers was repeated in the upholstery on the chairs and the dressing-table stool, and in the rugs which were scattered about on the polished wooden floorboards. It was unashamed luxury, but Mirabel could remember the time before her father fought his way out of poverty, using whatever means came to hand.

She had been born in a room at the top of a warehouse in Shad Thames overlooking Butler's Wharf on the south bank of the mighty river, and that was where she had spent the first five years of her life. The scent of roasting coffee beans and spices had the power to take her back to those days when her father had been a humble clerk, working for the rich merchant who owned the building and several ships which traded with the Americas. The small family had scraped by on his meagre wages, frequently going hungry, and more often than not she had gone barefoot even in the coldest weather. Then, as if by a miracle, everything had changed. The merchant had died, some said in suspicious circumstances, leaving the warehouse and his entire business to his clerk, Jacob Cutler. They had risen in the world, but too late to save her mother from the dreaded consumptive disease that claimed so many lives. It was then that Jacob had purchased the house in Catherine Court, and Mirabel's life had changed, seemingly for the better. Acting on a whim, her father had decided that she should be educated as befitted a young lady of means, and Miss Barton had been employed to act as governess. Mirabel's days of freedom had ended abruptly.

Miss Barton was a termagant who inhabited the schoolroom, sleeping on a truckle bed concealed behind a curtain, and she ruled every aspect of her charge's life from the moment Mirabel awoke in the morning until she retired to bed at night. She ordered her meals, chose her clothes, organised her lessons and never let her out of doors unaccompanied. Any hint of rebellion was quickly and thoroughly crushed, and if Mirabel did not mend her ways immediately her rebellious conduct was reported to her father. Jacob was not a patient man, and he gave Miss Barton leave to deal with his daughter as she saw fit. Going without supper was the least of the punishments meted out, and caning was used for more serious offences, such as not having a handkerchief or falling asleep during lessons. But Miss Barton's favourite form of correction was to lock Mirabel in the attic for hours on end. Poor Betty Barton, Mirabel thought with a wry grin, if only she knew that her efforts to terrorise and subdue her charge had all been in vain. The attic had become her friend, the spiders her companions, and the mice might at any time be turned into horses to pull a carriage provided by a good fairy, who trans-formed her into a beautiful princess with a wave of her wand. It was a quiet place away from the hurly-burly of the city streets and the sounds of the river that continued day and night. It was a place to dream. It was Mirabel's own private place.

'You were a silly child,' she said out loud, taking a seat at the dressing table. Her reflection smiled back at her as she shook the pins from her long dark hair, so that it cascaded around her shoul-ders in a shining cape, blue-black as the coal brought upriver by the Thames barges. Her smile faded and she frowned. What right had she to be discontented with her lot when there were people barely a stone's throw away who were literally starving to death? The gaunt faces and wasted limbs of those who queued for food in the soup kitchen would haunt her dreams tonight. The bowls of thin broth provided just enough nourishment to keep them from starvation, but some of the unfortunates Mirabel had seen earlier that day must surely be hovering on the edge of disaster, especially the children. She could still smell the stench of unwashed bodies which were tortured by parasites and scarred by skin diseases. She shuddered, twisting her hair into a chignon at the back of her neck and securing it in a net. Compared to the standards of the poor, who lived and died on the streets, she had no cause to complain.

She was about to get up when someone tapped on the door. 'Yes, who is it?'

Flossie burst into the room, her round face flushed and her pale blue eyes shining with excitement. 'You're to come downstairs immediately, miss. The master says so.'

'I'll be down in a minute.' Mirabel was used to Flossie's wild flights of fancy and over-dramatic behaviour.

'No, miss. Please come now. I'll be in for it if you don't.'

Mirabel shot her a curious glance. 'What's the matter? Why so urgent? I didn't even know that my father was at home.'

'He just arrived, miss. He brought...' Flossie hesitated, biting her lip. 'He brought a guest. You're to come now, please.'

'Very well.' Mirabel rose from her seat and followed the girl down the stairs to the first floor. She was taken by surprise when Flossie stopped outside the drawing room, which was only used on special occasions, and was about to point out her mistake when the maid's timid knock was answered by Jacob Cutler's curt instruction to enter. Flossie opened the door and stood aside to allow Mirabel to pass, but instead of bowing out like a well-trained servant she hovered in the doorway, gawping at the occupants, open-mouthed.

'Thank you, Flossie,' Mirabel murmured. 'That will be all.'

Reluctantly Flossie withdrew, and Jacob jumped up from his seat, greeting his daughter with a beaming smile. 'My dear, I want you to meet a very special lady.' He held his hand out to the woman who was reclining on the sofa. 'This is my fiancée, Ernestine Mutton, and these are her two delightful daughters, Charity and Prudence.'

'It's Moo-ton,' Ernestine said, emphasising the syllables. 'Moo-ton, Jacob. How many times do I have to tell you?' She tempered the words with a coquettish smile. 'What are men like? Aren't they all just little boys at heart, needing a good woman to take care of them?' She extended a plump white hand. 'I hope to be your stepmama very shortly, Mirabel my dear.'

Mirabel stared at her dumbstruck. Harriet Humble's words came back to her with a force that took her breath away. Ernestine Mutton, or however she chose to pronounce her name, was a good twenty years Jacob's junior, plump and brassy, and her lips were suspiciously red, as were her round cheeks.

'Say something,' Jacob hissed, poking Mirabel in the ribs.

'Cat got your tongue, dearie?' Ernestine prompted. 'I daresay she's too overcome with joy to speak, Jake my love.'

Jake! Mirabel turned to her father and was astonished to see that he had not taken offence. In fact he was grinning like an idiot, and it seemed in that instant that a stranger had inhabited her father's body. 'You are a one, Ernestine my precious,' he said, chuckling.

'Ma, can we go now?' The elder of the two

17

children, a girl of about fourteen who would un-doubtedly grow up to be the image of her mother, spoke in a nasal whining voice that set Mirabel's nerves on edge but seemed to have the reverse effect on Ernestine, who put her arm around her daughter and gave her a hug.

'I'm sorry, lambkin. I should introduce you to your new sister.'

'And me, Ma. You're always forgetting me.' The younger child, whom Mirabel judged to be about twelve, nudged her sister in the ribs.

Charity yelped with pain. 'You little beast.'

Ernestine continued to smile benignly. 'Now now, my darlings don't be naughty.' She looked up at Mirabel with a steely glint in her grey eyes. 'Charity is my eldest and Prudence is my baby.'

'Oh, Ma!' Prudence pouted ominously. 'Don't say such things. I ain't a baby.'

'Yes you are,' Charity said spitefully. 'You are a big baby. Just look at you. Your eyes are full of tears. You're going to cry. You'll do anything to get your own way.' She turned to her mother. 'Tell her off, Ma. Don't let her make a fuss.'

Jacob cleared his throat. 'Now now, my dears. Let your mama have a bit of peace, or I'll...'

Ernestine released Charity and hauled herself to her feet, her plump bosom heaving above her tight stays. 'Or you'll what, Jacob? Do you dare to threaten my girls?'

Mirabel waited for her father to explode with rage and tell the awful woman and her equally awful daughters to leave, but he seemed to shrink beneath the force of his fiancée's wrath, and he positively cowered before her. 'I'm sorry, my love.

I didn't mean it to sound that way.' He shot a sideways glance at Mirabel. 'Ring the bell for Flossie. We'll have some refreshments. Whatever my ladies wish for will be granted.'

Mirabel made a move towards the door. 'I'll go to the kitchen and make sure Cook understands, Pa.' She hurried from the room, unable to stand it any longer.

Cook was hacking at a loaf of bread, cutting it into thick slices that were more suitable for a navvy's dinner than afternoon tea. She glared at Mirabel as if daring her to criticise her efforts. 'Whatever next?'

'Have you any jam, Mrs James? I'm sure Pa's guests would appreciate something sweet.'

'Flossie, take a look in the larder. See if there's any jam left in the pot, and fetch the fruit cake. I put a meat cover over it to keep it away from the blooming mice.' Cook tossed a cloth at Flossie who was staring into space, having gone off in one of her trance-like states. 'Do you hear me, you stupid girl?'

She came back to reality with a start. 'Yes, Cook.'

'That Mutton woman's been here before, Miss Mirabel,' Cook said gloomily. 'She only comes when you're at the soup kitchen, or if you've gone to market. Seems to me that something ain't right, if you know what I mean.'

'I'm sure she's a very nice person when you get to know her.' Mirabel tried to sound convincing, but her first impression of Ernestine had not been favourable.

Flossie bounded out of the cupboard like a jack-in-the-box. 'The cake's gone. Not a crumb left and only one pot of jam.'

Mirabel caught Cook's eye and had the grace to blush. 'I'm sorry. I forgot to mention that I took the cake for the poor children at the soup kitchen.'

'Really, Miss Mirabel, whatever next?' Mrs James puffed out her cheeks. 'You'd see us all starve in order to feed those who ought to do an honest day's work to pay for their vittles like the rest of us.'

'Not even a crumb left,' Flossie said sadly. 'I'm partial to a slice of fruit cake.' She handed the jam pot to Cook, receiving a stinging blow round the ear for her pains.

'If I thought you'd pinched it you'd be in for trouble, my girl.'

'No, Cook, it weren't me,' Flossie howled. 'It was her, she said so.'

'It was indeed, Mrs James. Flossie isn't to blame.'

'It wouldn't be the first time. That useless creature loves anything sweet.' Cook peered into the jam pot. 'If you've had your finger round the rim I'll give you what for, Flossie my girl.'

'Let me help you,' Mirabel said, stepping in quickly. 'I'll butter the bread if you'll make the tea. Bread and jam will have to do; after all, we weren't prepared for guests.'

'Guests?' Mrs James dropped the bread knife with a derisive snort. 'That one will have her feet beneath the table before you can say Jack Robinson. I've met her sort before.'

Cook's words proved to be prophetic. Within a fortnight Jacob and Ernestine were married by special licence in All Hallows Church, which was only a short walk from Catherine Court. The small party arrived back at the house to dine off the cold collation which Cook had laid out in the dining room. Jacob presided over the meal, seated as usual at the head, and Ernestine took Mirabel's former place at the far end of the table. Mirabel was reduced to sitting next to Charity, with Prudence on the opposite side of the table, pulling faces at them both. Wiley had greeted Ernestine with an obsequious bow, bending so low that Mirabel thought he might topple over or snap in two. However, he managed to right himself and offered his congratulations to the happy couple. At the table he hovered between Jacob and Ernestine, pouring the wine and making sure that their glasses were topped up. Jacob's cheeks flushed dark red and Mirabel was alarmed. She was used to her father's variable moods, but she had never seen him in such high spirits, and she was afraid that at any moment he might burst a blood vessel. He kept raising his glass to his bride and the more he drank the more lewd his suggestions became, until Ernestine shot him a warning glance. 'Remember the children, Jake my dear.'

He choked on a mouthful of cold chicken, gulped and swallowed, washing it down with yet more wine. 'Of course, my pet. Wiley, fetch another bottle from the cellar.' He stared at Mirabel, frowning. 'There's no need to look so disapproving, daughter. You should be happy for me. You're acting as if you're at a funeral and not a wedding

21

breakfast. What's the matter with you, girl?'

'I'm sorry, Pa. I have a headache. May I be excused?'

'No, you may not.' Ernestine's voice rose to a shriek. 'It's obvious that you're jealous and your pretty little nose has been put out of joint, but you'd better get over it because that's the way things are from now on.'

Stung by the unfairness of this remark, Mirabel shook her head. 'I'm not jealous, ma'am. If I thought my pa would be happy with you I'd be overjoyed.'

Ernestine's mouth worked soundlessly and her bosom heaved. 'You little bitch,' she said angrily. 'Jake, are you going to allow your daughter to speak to me in such a manner?'

'You'd slap me for being so cheeky, and I'd deserve it, Ma,' Charity said piously.

'We wouldn't get away with it so why does she?' Prudence added, smirking.

Wiley hovered over Ernestine with the wine bottle clasped in his hand. 'More wine, ma'am?'

Ernestine brushed his offer aside, rising angrily to her feet. 'Are you going to speak to her, Jake, or will you leave it up to me to discipline your daughter?'

He signalled to Wiley. 'I'll have some more wine.'

'Don't you think you've had enough, Pa?' Mirabel asked anxiously. She could see the whole matter getting out of hand, fuelled by Wiley's unsubtle attempts to get both his master and his new mistress the worse for drink, although what he hoped to gain by it was anybody's guess. Wiley shot her a menacing glance as he moved swiftly to refill Jacob's glass, but she chose to ignore him.

'Mind your own business, girl,' Ernestine snapped. 'If you can't keep a civil tongue in your head, I suggest you leave the table.'

Mirabel pushed her chair back and stood up. 'I'm going to my room.'

'No,' Ernestine said sharply. 'Things are going to be different from now on.' She turned to her husband, eyes narrowed. 'Tell her, Jacob.'

He downed the wine in his glass in one greedy gulp. 'This was supposed to be a celebration, my love.'

'It might have been had you sorted things out with your daughter before we wed. I see I'll have to do it instead.'

'What haven't you told me?' Mirabel looked from one to the other. Her father lowered his head, staring into his empty glass.

Ernestine leaned back in her chair, a triumphant smile hovering on her painted lips. 'There have of necessity been changes. You have two younger sisters now, and each of them must have a room of her own. Charity has been given your bedchamber and the schoolroom will be made comfortable for Prudence.'

'You can't do that,' Mirabel cried angrily. 'Pa, tell her that it's my room.'

Wiley stood behind his master, folding his hands behind his back. He stood stiffly to attention but his eyes glittered with malice as they rested on Mirabel. She knew that she had made an enemy of him by reporting his drinking habit to her father, even though he had chosen not to discipline his employee.

'Ernestine is right, my pet.' Jacob slurred the words, and he seemed to have difficulty fixing his gaze on his daughter's face. 'Quite right. The girls should have rooms of their own.'

'But what about me?' Mirabel demanded. 'You can't expect me to sleep with the servants. I won't allow it.'

Ernestine rose to her feet. 'Won't allow it? Just who do you think you are, miss? I'm the lady of the house now and you'll do as I say. Your things have been moved to the attic, where I'm told you spent many hours as a child, so you'll feel quite at home. That is so, isn't it, Jake, my love?'

Chapter Two

Despite the fierce exchange of words that followed, there was nothing Mirabel could do to alter the situation. She slammed out of the dining room and raced upstairs, but Wiley followed her, catching up with her as she tried to gain access to her bedroom. 'It's locked, miss, and I have the only other key.'

She spun round to face him, recoiling as she caught a whiff of his sour breath. 'This has nothing to do with you, Wiley. Give it to me.'

He shook his head, a sly grin creasing his thin face into a mocking mask. 'You've no authority in this house now, miss. I'd advise you to do as your stepmother says.' He moved closer, pinning her to the door without actually touching her body. 'Perhaps this will teach you not to cross Septimus Wiley.'

'I don't know what you're talking about.' She faced him squarely even though she was quaking inwardly.

'I'd advise you to watch your tongue in the future, miss. Telling your father that I helped myself to his cognac was not a friendly action, and I take exception to being branded a thief.'

'But you are a thief, and now you're trying to intimidate me. I'll have you sacked, Wiley. My father won't allow such behaviour in a servant.'

He moved a fraction closer so that she could feel the heat from his body. 'He won't sack me, Miss Cutler. I know too much.'

'What do you mean by that?' Her heart was thudding against her tightly laced stays, but she managed to keep her voice level and she faced him unblinking. The man was a liar as well as a bully and he must be stopped, but she needed to know the reason for his outrageous behaviour.

'Wouldn't you like to know? But I'm not going to tell you – not yet, anyway. We'll keep that for another time, but let's say I saw what went on in the warehouse, and I know what happened to old man Pendleton.' His mirthless laughter echoed off the high ceiling, coming back to mock them both as they stood locked in silent combat.

Mirabel felt the hackles rise on the back of her neck and a shiver ran down her spine. Fear turned to anger and she gave him a mighty shove, catching him unawares, and he staggered backwards, righting himself against the curve of the balustrade. 'You little bitch.'

She tossed her head. 'I'll tell my father what you just said. You won't be laughing then.'

'Now you listen to me, Miss Cutler.' He righted himself, his eyes narrowed to dark slits and his lips drawn into a tight line. 'One word out of place and your father will swing from a hangman's noose.'

'You're lying.'

Wiley opened his mouth to reply, but at the sound of footsteps on the stairs his whole demeanour changed. He bowed and backed away. 'I think you'll find everything to your liking in your new bedchamber, miss.'

Charity and Prudence came bounding up the stairs with their skirts bunched up above their knees. Charity came to a sudden halt. 'That's my room, not yours. Ma said so and your pa agreed. You're not to let her in, Wiley.'

'And the other room is mine.' Prudence ran to the door, extending her arms in a dramatic gesture to block the entrance. 'You can't come in here. I won't let you.'

'You two are spoilt brats,' Mirabel said coldly. 'Make the most of your room, Charity, because you won't have it for long. I'll sort this out later.' Ignoring Wiley she left them and made her way up the next flight of stairs, although she had no intention of letting the matter rest. She would wait until her father had sobered up and choose a moment when she could catch him on his own. He must have been blinded by passion for his bride to have agreed to such a thing, but he would soon see the woman he had married for what she really was.

The top landing, in contrast to the lower floors,

was uncarpeted and shabby. When Jacob had sent in the workmen to renovate the old building no one had thought to redecorate the servants' quarters. It was clean, Mrs James had seen to that, or rather Flossie had been set to sweep down the cobwebs and scrub the floors, but the paintwork was the original blue-grey, and the once pristine whitewashed ceilings had dulled to ochre with the passing of time.

Mirabel let herself into her dreaming place. If she had hoped it might have been transformed into a boudoir fit for the eldest daughter of the house she would have been disappointed. As it was she was barely surprised to see a truckle bed abandoned in the middle of the floor, with the entire contents of the clothes press in her old room piled upon it, together with some threadbare blankets, a patched coverlet and a couple of pillows. The only other furniture was the wooden rocking chair which had always been there, and the trunk where she kept the few treasures she possessed away from the prying eyes of Miss Barton. These included a painted paper fan, a string of blue glass beads and several hair combs, which were the only things she had to remind her of her mother. There was Sukey, her rag doll with an embroidered face and yellow woollen hair, and there were books purchased from second-hand stalls in the market. None of them were in very good condition, but all were loved and well read, especially those on foreign travel.

Mirabel was about to investigate in case anyone had tampered with her belongings when Charity and Prudence burst into the room. They stopped, staring around wide-eyed. 'Ma put you in your place all right,' Charity said with a spiteful twist of her lips. 'This is where you belong.'

'Yes,' Prudence added, giggling. 'There'll be spiders and rats, and it's probably haunted too.'

'Get out.' Mirabel made a move towards them, holding on to her temper but only just. 'Go away and don't come up here again.'

'You can't tell us what to do.' Charity shuffled a step closer. 'This is our home now and Ma makes the rules.'

'Yes,' echoed Prudence, following her sister's example. 'Ma does.'

'Out.' Mirabel advanced on them with her hands fisted and they fled, screaming for their mother as they hurtled down the stairs. Mirabel slammed the door and turned the key in the lock.

She had to wait for two days to snatch a moment alone with her father, but Jacob was not in a talkative mood. 'But Pa,' she cried in desperation. 'You can't mean me to live like this. Why am I relegated to the attic? Couldn't the girls share the schoolroom?'

He looked away, staring at the windowpanes as if the raindrops sliding down the glass were the most interesting sight ever. 'You'll have to take it up with your stepmother, Mirabel.'

'She's the one who put me there in the first place. You're the head of the house, Pa. Tell her, please.'

Jacob rose from his seat at the dining table where he had been taking a late breakfast. 'I have to get to the counting house before nine. If I allow Williams to handle things on his own he'll be giving credit to people who can well afford to pay on the nail for their purchases.'

'Please, Pa,' Mirabel said, following him to the door. 'It's not much to ask to have my old room back.'

His answer was lost as the door opened and Ernestine swept into the room, but her smile was banished by a frown when she saw Mirabel. 'What has she said to you, Jacob?'

He kissed her on the cheek. 'I'm in a rush, my love. We'll speak about it when I return from business this evening.' He hurried across the hall to where Wiley stood, holding his master's hat and cane. 'Good man, Wiley. Is the carriage outside?'

'It's waiting in Seething Lane, sir.' He moved to open the front door, an obsequious smile pasted on his thin features.

'Good man. Look after the ladies while I'm away.' Jacob hurried outside with Wiley hurrying after him clutching an umbrella.

Ernestine pinched Mirabel's arm. 'Your father will do as I say, so don't think you can go behind my back to get what you want.'

'Why are you doing this?' Mirabel turned to face her, ignoring the pain where Ernestine's fingers had bruised her tender flesh. 'What have I done to make you hate me?'

'You may think that you come first in your father's affections, but you don't. You're nothing now, and the sooner you're out of my house the better.'

'This is my home. You can't simply throw me out.'

'Why aren't you married? You're twenty-one, so I'm told, practically an old maid, and I don't want a spinster daughter interfering with my life.'

Mirabel stared at her aghast. 'What a nasty mind you have, stepmother. I can't see what my father ever saw in you.'

'That just shows how little you know about men. They're like putty in a clever woman's hands. You just have to know how to handle them.'

'I pity you, ma'am. He'll see through you one day and then it will be you and your horrible daughters who are out on the street.' Mirabel was about to walk away when Ernestine caught her by the sleeve.

'I haven't finished with you yet.'

'What do you want now? Haven't you done enough already?'

'I've decided that your expensive education shouldn't go to waste. I want you to teach my girls how to be ladies. You'll pass on everything your governess taught you.' Ernestine's lips curved into a smile, but her eyes glittered like chips of green glass. 'They have the looks and I want them to have the polish that will catch them rich husbands. You might not know how to please men, but you can leave that part of their education up to me.'

'I won't do it.'

Charity was sullen and Prudence struggled with her lessons, spending more time moping and complaining than she did paying attention to the work Mirabel had set for her. Without the authority to discipline them in any way, Mirabel knew from the start that any effort on her part would be

30

wasted. She had begged her father to intercede on her behalf, but he seemed unable or unwilling to argue with his wife, and Ernestine appeared to revel in her newly acquired position of power.

The saving grace for Mirabel was that lessons were conducted in the morning and she was able to escape from the house after luncheon each day. Volunteers were always needed at the soup kitchen in Crispin Street, and it was the one place where she felt welcome. With a white mobcap covering her hair and a clean pinafore to protect her plainest gown, she was an anonymous helper and part of a cheerful group of women who gave their time willingly in order to help the poor and needy. Most of her efforts involved peeling potatoes, carrots and turnips or chopping onions, which made her eyes sting painfully and caused tears to pour down her cheeks. She had been doing this one afternoon, alone in the scullery attached to the larger kitchen, when the door leading to the back yard opened and a stranger sauntered into the room. He stared at her, eyebrows raised. 'What's the matter? Why are you crying?'

'It's the onions,' she murmured, sniffing as she wiped her eyes on the back of her hand, taking in his appearance with a puzzled frown. He was not the usual type of vagabond who turned up in search of a free meal. His clothes might not be those of a city gentleman or a respectable clerk, but they were reasonably clean, and although casual his waxed jacket with its leather collar and cuffs was of good quality, as were his oddly dandyish waistcoat and check trousers. Even so, there was something louche in his attitude, with an underlying hint of danger which was both frightening and strangely exciting.

He regarded her unsmiling, his forehead creased into frown lines. 'You're not the usual girl.'

'Who were you looking for? Maybe I know her.'

'Why is a young lady like you doing the work of a skivvy?'

She recoiled at his tone. 'What has it to do with you?'

An appreciative glint flickered in his startlingly blue eyes, but was replaced by a suspicious lowering of his brow. 'All right, hostilities over, I'll introduce myself.' He whipped off his soft felt hat with a flourish and a mocking bow. 'Jack Starke.'

'Mirabel Cutler.' She scooped up the onions and dropped them into the large iron stewpot, adding the carrots and potatoes to the small amount of chopped beef and several handfuls of oats. 'I think you'd better go. The lady who organises the soup kitchen doesn't approve of gentlemen callers.'

He threw back his head and laughed. 'I've never been called a gentleman before. You're obviously new to this area, Miss Cutler.'

She glanced anxiously at the doorway leading into the main kitchen, which had been left ajar. 'Shh,' she said, holding her finger to her lips. 'You'll get me thrown out.'

'Considering you're doing this for nothing I don't think they'd be so stupid. Anyway, I'm well known round here.'

She lifted the pan with difficulty. 'Move out of the way, please. I need to get this onto the range or the soup won't be ready in time for supper.'

'You'll drop it,' he said, moving swiftly to take it

from her. 'Let me.' He carried it through into the kitchen.

Mirabel hurried after him. 'I'm sorry, Mrs Hamilton. This person barged in before I had a chance to stop him.'

Adela Hamilton was seated at one of the trestle tables with a quill pen in her hand and an open ledger spread out before her. She looked up and to Mirabel's astonishment her severe expression melted into a smile of welcome. 'I wasn't expecting to see you again, Jack.'

'I've no quarrel with the Hamiltons, Adela. Edric and I parted company on amicable terms.'

'My brother-in-law is a weak fool, and you are a rogue.' She rose to her feet. 'Put the pan on the fire and come and sit down. Mirabel will make us a cup of tea.'

Mirabel shot a withering glance in Jack's direction as she lifted the simmering kettle from the hob, receiving a disarming smile in return. She made the tea, but she could not resist the temptation to look over her shoulder, and was surprised to see him seated at the table with the casual air of someone who regularly took tea with the wife of a City alderman. Her curiosity aroused, Mirabel served them in silence.

'Thank you, my dear,' Adela said, smiling. 'Won't you join us?'

'I think perhaps I'd better clean up the scullery,' Mirabel said hastily. 'I'll take my tea with me.'

She was about to walk away when Jack reached out to catch her by the sleeve. 'Sit down and take tea with us. This isn't slave labour.'

'Indeed not.' Adela nodded her head, causing

33

her tight grey curls to bounce like springs on either side of her plump cheeks. 'You've worked hard, Mirabel. I'm sure the clearing up can wait a few minutes.'

Despite her reservations Mirabel was intrigued by the stranger, who did not seem the sort of person that a lady like Mrs Hamilton would want to associate with. She pulled up a chair and sat down. 'You were looking for someone, Mr Starke. Perhaps Mrs Hamilton could help you.'

'It's Captain Starke if you insist on formality.' He regarded her with a lazy smile. 'I doubt if Mrs Hamilton would remember Gertie.'

'If you're referring to Gertrude Tinker, I shall never forget her.' Adela puckered her lips into a disapproving moue. 'She was no better than she should be, and I sent her packing. You oughtn't to associate with women of the street, Jack.'

He put his hand in his pocket and pulled out a small package wrapped in brown paper which he pushed across the table. 'There are many things that none of us should do, Adela, but we are human after all.'

She snatched the parcel and slipped it into her reticule. 'You're a rogue, and you'll probably end up in Newgate.'

'I expect you're right. But you haven't answered my question. Do you know where I can find young Gertie?'

Adela shook her head. 'I don't encourage gentlemen to associate with such women.'

'I know where she lives.' The words tumbled from Mirabel's lips.

'And how does a well brought up young lady

34

like you know about such things?' Adela demanded.

'Never mind the sermon.' Jack fixed Mirabel with a piercing stare. 'I don't care how you know; just tell me where I can find the girl.'

'Don't encourage him,' Adele said angrily.

Despite her better judgement Mirabel could not tear her gaze away. There was something hypnotic in the way he looked at her which compelled her to tell the truth. 'We used to chat sometimes when we were washing the pots and pans. She lodges in Black Dog Alley.'

'And where is that?'

Adela pushed her teacup away, slopping some of the liquid onto the ledger. 'This has gone far enough. I won't have you using this charitable institution to satisfy your carnal needs, Captain Starke.'

He gave her a lopsided grin which for some reason Mirabel could not understand only enhanced his easygoing charm, and this made him even more intriguing. 'My taste doesn't run to skinny little girls, Adela, and even if it did that's not why I need to find Gertie. I'm afraid I have bad news for her.'

'It's an alley off Seething Lane, in between Green Arbour Court and Black Raven Court. It's quite near where I live.' Mirabel felt the colour rush to her cheeks as they both turned to look at her. 'I could show you where it is,' she added shyly.

'Excellent. Are you finished now?'

Mirabel cast a sideways glance at Adela, who was not looking too pleased. 'The soup is on, Mrs Hamilton. I only need to clear up in the scullery and I'm done for the day.'

'Very well,' Adela said reluctantly. 'I suppose the others will be here soon.'

Mirabel returned to the scullery. Having left everything as it should be she took off her mobcap and was about to put on her bonnet when she sensed she was being watched. She turned to see Jack standing in the doorway, staring at her. 'It seems a crime to cover such lovely hair with caps and bonnets.'

'I'm ready,' she said, choosing to ignore the compliment. 'Do you still want me to take you to Black Dog Alley? It's a rough area.'

'I'll look after you, Miss Cutler.'

'Thank you, but I can take care of myself.' She tied the ribbons in a bow and slipped her shawl around her shoulders.

Black Dog Alley was as its name suggested dark and ferocious. Little daylight penetrated between the closely packed rows of semi-derelict buildings. The stench was suffocating and night soil had been tossed into the gulley which ran down the middle of the cobbled street, where it lay festering in the heat of the afternoon. Flies swarmed in dense clouds, and semi-naked children fought over the tiniest scraps of vegetable matter they found rotting in the gutter.

Holding her handkerchief over her mouth and nose in an attempt to escape the worst of the smells, Mirabel glanced at Jack. 'Do you still want to see this person?'

'Lead on,' he said cheerfully. 'I've been in worse places than this abroad.'

'I don't envy you.' She lifted her skirts and trod carefully, avoiding as much of the detritus as possible. 'It's number six. I think that's what she told me.'

He strode on ahead of her, counting the buildings on their right. 'This one.' He stopped outside a narrow, three-storey house with a front door that had been kicked in at some point. The bottom timbers were splintered and some of them were missing. A skinny ginger cat shot through the large gap with a dead rat in its mouth, brushing past Mirabel and disappearing in a flash of spiky orange fur with a gang of boys racing after it. Undeterred, Jack raised his hand and hammered on the door, which flew open of its own accord. He stepped inside, turning to Mirabel with a questioning look. 'You'd best come in. It's not safe to loiter out there.'

She did not argue. It would have been satisfying to refuse and walk away, but she did not fancy her chances of escaping from Black Dog Alley unmolested. An almost new straw bonnet would fetch a few pennies in the market, and so would her lacy woollen shawl. Out of the corner of her eye she could see a group of slatternly women standing in a doorway opposite, and they were watching her closely. Given the slightest opportunity she knew they would descend upon her, and she might be stripped naked and sent on her way barefoot. She had witnessed such an attack on an unfortunate young servant girl who had tried to take a short cut between Great Tower Hill and Seething Lane. The police had been informed, but there was little they could do. The residents of the teeming courts and alleys protected their own and it was a brave or foolhardy officer of the law who ventured there alone, or even in pairs.

Mirabel followed him inside, closing what was left of the door behind her. 'She might not be here. Have you thought of that?'

He shrugged his shoulders. 'I imagine she sleeps in the daylight hours. Her trade is at night.' He moved swiftly to the rear of the building. Mirabel followed, taking care not to tread on rotten floorboards, and stepping over great gaps where they had crumbled to dust. She remembered Gertie, who had been found soliciting on the streets around the Tower of London and brought to the soup kitchen by a bearded gentleman who had founded a Christian mission in the East End. Half starved and little more than a child, Gertie had been taken in, bathed and clothed in garments from the charity barrel, and allowed to sleep in a corner of the kitchen. She had been earning her keep by washing pots and pans in the scullery when Mirabel had first met her, and Mirabel had struck up a friendship with the girl, who was only a few years her junior.

'She told me she had a brother,' Mirabel said worriedly. 'But he was away at sea for a year or two at a time. I wonder if he knows she's reduced to living like this.'

'I don't suppose you know which room is hers?'

'No, I don't.'

He knocked on several doors without receiving a reply. When they reached the end of the corridor he tried again. 'Gertie Tinker. It's Captain Jack. I need to talk to you.'

Mirabel waited anxiously. It was obvious that the news he had to give the poor girl was not good. 'Maybe she's gone out to buy food. Or perhaps she's found work.'

Jack followed Mirabel's gaze as she stared in horror at the crumbling plasterwork which revealed the skeletal remains of the framework of laths, and there were cracks in the ceiling, which appeared to be in imminent danger of collapsing on them. 'If she hasn't had any success she'll be desperate for money,' he said, frowning.

'I thought she received an allotment from the ship owners.'

'Her brother jumped ship in Rio. She won't have received anything for months.' He raised his fist and beat on the wooden panels until they shook. 'If you're in there, Gertie, open up. I need to talk to you.'

'Jumped ship?' Mirabel moved a little closer. 'Why did he do that?'

Jack held up his hand. 'I heard someone moving about.' He took a step backwards and the door opened just a crack. 'I need to talk to you, Gertie.'

Chapter Three

The door opened a little more. 'Captain Starke?'

'Yes, it's me. Can I come in, Gertie?'

'Who's that with you?'

'Mirabel Cutler. We used to work together at the soup kitchen. Do you remember me, Gertie?'

The door opened to reveal a small figure, wraith thin and wearing nothing but a ragged nightgown. She wrapped her skinny arms around her body, slanting a wary look at Jack. 'I thought you was the rent collector, but now I know you. You're Cap'n Starke, so where's me money? I ain't had nothing for months.'

'If you'll let us in I'll explain.'

There was an impatient edge to Jack's voice that grated on Mirabel's nerves. Overcome with pity for the girl, who looked to be in an even worse state than when she had been found wandering the streets, Mirabel slipped past Jack and took off her shawl, placing it around Gertie's shoulders. 'You do remember me, don't you?'

'Of course I do. I ain't lost me wits, miss.'

Mirabel led her into the tiny, squalid room, where light filtered dimly through a small window high up on an outside wall. Unfurnished except for a pile of ragged bedding in one corner and a single wooden chair, it was more like a prison cell than a place fit for habitation.

Jack followed them in, brushing a large cobweb off his hat. 'Did your brother know you'd sunk to this, Gertie?'

'We had a better room when Bodger was home, but I couldn't afford to keep it on when he went back to sea.' Gertie sank down on the chair which rocked dangerously, one leg being shorter than the others. She huddled in the shawl, shivering violently.

Mirabel laid her hand on Gertie's forehead. 'She's burning up with fever. I can't say I'm surprised. This is a terrible place.'

40

'It's all right for you,' Gertie said angrily. 'You live in Cutler's Castle. I know all about you, miss. You used to talk nice and friendly, but then you went home at night to live in luxury.'

'Cutler's Castle?' Jack raised an eyebrow. 'Really? You live in a castle, Miss Cutler?'

'Don't be silly. Of course I don't, and even if I did it hardly matters. This poor girl is sick and she looks as if she hasn't had a proper meal in weeks.'

'Oy! Don't talk about me like I weren't here. I got a bit of a chill, that's all.' Gertie gave Jack a sideways glance beneath her pale eyelashes. 'If you gives me Bodger's pay I could better meself, Cap'n.'

Jack put his hand in his pocket and took out a small leather pouch, pressing it into her outstretched hand. 'This is yours by rights, but there won't be any more for a while. I'm sorry to tell you that Bodger jumped ship in Rio and we had to sail without him.'

'Jumped ship?' Gertie's pale faced turned a sickly green. 'He wouldn't. Not Bodger.' She slid to the floor in a dead faint.

'Damn! I suppose I should have seen that coming.' Jack stared at Gertie's inert body, pushing his hat to the back of his head. 'Why do women always pass out at the most inopportune moment?'

'Why are men so tactless?' Mirabel countered angrily. 'You could see that she's ill. Couldn't you have broken the news more gently?' She went down on her knees. 'Gertie, it's all right.' She chafed the small, cold hands. 'You mustn't worry.

41

We'll take care of you.'

'Leave me out of this. I've done my bit.' Jack scooped up the purse and the coins that had fallen onto the floor. 'This money will keep her off the streets for a while, but after that it's up to her.'

Mirabel looked up at him, frowning. 'Is that all you can say? You didn't look after her brother very well.'

He leaned over, peering at Gertie who was beginning to regain consciousness. 'Make her comfortable and we'll go. I've got other business to attend to.'

'What? You'd leave her in this dreadful place when she's sick and helpless? Haven't you any human decency?'

'For God's sake, woman. What do you want me to do?'

Mirabel scrambled to her feet. 'For a start you can lift her onto the chair.'

He thrust the leather pouch into her hand. 'All right, but then I'm leaving. You can stay if you've a mind to, but I've done my duty.'

Ignoring him, Mirabel turned her attention to Gertie who had opened her eyes and was staring at her dazedly. 'You're all right now. We won't leave until you feel better.'

Gertie groaned and bowed her head, clasping her hands to her face. Her shoulders heaved. 'Poor Bodger. He was a good chap.'

'See what you've done?' Mirabel said angrily. 'She thinks her brother is dead. Tell her it's not true.'

Jack ran his hand through his hair, eyeing Mirabel with a mixture of exasperation and amusement. 'You'd make a good boatswain, Miss Cutler.' He held up both hands in a gesture of appeasement. 'All right, don't look daggers at me.' He turned to Gertie with a sympathetic smile. 'Bodger was very much alive when I last saw him,' he said gently. 'I've no doubt he'll make his way home eventually.'

Gertie raised a tear-stained face. 'Do you think so, Cap'n?'

'I know so, Gertie.'

Her head lolled onto her shoulder and once again her eyes closed. Mirabel moved quickly to prevent her from sliding off the chair. 'We can't leave her here. She's in no condition to look after herself.'

'She's not my responsibility or yours. We'll put her to bed and make her comfortable, and that's it as far as I'm concerned.'

'And the kindly souls we saw loitering outside will come and nurse her back to health? Is that what you think, Captain Starke?'

'It's Jack to my friends.' He held a finger to his lips. 'Don't say it, Miss Cutler. I know when I'm beaten.'

'You know full well that she'll be robbed blind and left to suffer alone. She could die in this horrible little room and no one would be any the wiser.'

'So are you saying you'll stay here until she recovers? Or are you going to take her back to your castle and look after her there?'

'You are such a cynical man, Jack Starke. There are people who do things for others without wanting to be paid for their services.'

'There are plenty of fools in this world, but I'm not one of them.' He opened the door. 'Are you coming, or do I have to leave you here?'

'I'm coming and you're going to pick Gertie up and carry her to my house, which isn't too far away.' Once again she spoke without giving herself time to think, but there did not seem to be any alternative and her conscience would not allow her to abandon a sick girl. Ernestine had taken her daughters to the dressmaker where Mirabel knew from experience they would spend hours poring over fashion plates, discussing the latest styles and going through the possible choices of materials, no doubt squabbling over each item. Jacob would not be home until it was time for dinner. He had taken to spending long hours in his office, longer Mirabel suspected than was strictly necessary, but the dingy counting house close to St Katharine's dock was probably a great deal more peaceful than a house crowded with argumentative females. She had spoken hastily but her quick mind was already formulating a plan. Wiley would be cloistered in his cubbyhole, drinking her father's brandy, and Mrs James would be taking advantage of a quiet time and napping in her room, as would Flossie, who seemed to be half asleep at the best of times.

'Are you sure about this?' Jack demanded, frowning. 'The girl might have something catching.'

'I'm sure I've had almost all the diseases the city has to offer, apart from cholera and typhoid, but I don't think she has either of those. If you're prepared to carry her, we'll take her to Cutler's Castle.'

As Mirabel had hoped, there was no one in the kitchen. Wiley was nowhere in sight, but even though the door of the butler's pantry was closed Mirabel could still smell the fumes of alcohol. She motioned Jack to follow her as she made her way up the back stairs, pausing in the entrance hall with her head on one side as she listened for sounds of life, but all was quiet. She beckoned to him. 'Are you all right to carry her up to the top floor?'

'Isn't that where the servants sleep? Not that I'm accustomed to living in a castle.'

'That's not funny. I wish Gertie hadn't told you about that silly name.' She glanced anxiously at the unconscious girl. 'I hope she doesn't come round until we're in my room.'

'You sleep with the servants?'

His look of genuine surprise made her regret her decision to allow him into the house, but it was only momentary. Putting pride aside she led the way to her dreaming place.

Jack laid Gertie on the bed and straightened up, stretching his back and shoulder muscles. 'She might be frail but I wouldn't care to carry her much further.' He looked round slowly, taking in the details of the comfortless room. 'Are you sure you're the daughter of the house and not a maid-servant?'

'Not that it's any business of yours, but my father is Jacob Cutler.'

'And he treats you like this?' His lips twitched and his eyes twinkled. 'Have you done something wicked and this is your punishment?'

'If you must know, this is my stepmother's idea of keeping me in my place. She has two daughters who come before me in everything.' Once again she had spoken without thinking. She was angry with herself and even angrier with him for drawing the truth from her with seemingly no effort. 'But it doesn't matter. I'm quite happy up here on my own.'

Gertie stirred and uttered a low moan.

'I think you'd better go.' Mirabel moved to open the door, taking a quick look outside in case Cook or Flossie happened to have risen from their beds. 'Please don't make a noise. I'd never hear the last of it if you were seen leaving the house.'

He tipped his hat and the laughter returned to his eyes. 'I wouldn't want to compromise your good name, Miss Cutler.' His smile faded. 'And I'm sorry you find yourself in such a position. You deserve better.' He was about to leave, but he paused for a moment staring at her with an inscrutable expression. 'Goodbye, Mirabel.'

She closed the door and the room seemed suddenly smaller without his presence, but he was gone now and they were unlikely to meet again. Moving swiftly to the window she knelt on the cushions, looking down on the street below, and waited until she saw him emerge from the porch. It seemed typical of him that he let himself out through the front door instead of creeping down the back stairs to the basement. She watched him swaggering along the cobbled court towards Great Tower Hill as if he owned the world, and she experienced a pang of envy for his freedom to come and go as he pleased. Their acquaintance had been brief and fraught with arguments, and yet she would have liked to know him better. It would be wonderful to hear of his travels around the world, and to learn about the places that she longed to visit but never would.

A soft moan from the bed brought her back to reality. Gertie was feverish and her nightgown was drenched with sweat. With little experience of nursing sick people, other than tending to her father when he suffered the crippling pain of gout after an excess of food and wine, Mirabel followed her instincts. She went downstairs to fill a ewer with water from the pump in the back yard. Cook and Flossie had not yet put in an appearance and she took the opportunity to fill a bowl with some of the porridge left from breakfast, which in all likelihood had been put aside for Flossie's supper. She watered it down so that it formed a thin gruel and on her way upstairs she stopped at the linen cupboard to collect a clean towel.

It took almost an hour, but eventually Mirabel managed to wash most of the grime from Gertie's emaciated body, and dressed her in a clean night-gown. It was a difficult process with Gertie unable to help in any way, but the cool water seemed to revive her a little, and she even managed to swallow a few spoonfuls of the gruel. Exhausted by her efforts, Mirabel sat back on her heels with a sigh of relief, but she knew that this was only the beginning. How she was going to take care of a sick girl and keep her presence in the house a secret was something she had not yet worked out. If Ernestine or the girls discovered Gertie's presence there would be repercussions, and Mirabel suspected that her stepmother would take delight in throwing both her and Gertie out on the street. She had, she realised, little faith in her father's ability to stand up against Ernestine's forceful nature.

That night Mirabel slept on the floor, waking at the slightest sound and raising herself to give Gertie sips of water. At breakfast next morning Charity drew attention to the dark circles under Mirabel's eyes, and Prudence was quick to add her voice. 'My bed is so comfortable,' she said slyly. 'I sleep like a princess. What about you, Charity?'

'I love my room.' Charity darted a spiteful look in Mirabel's direction. 'And my bed is better than yours, Prudence Mutton.'

'Moo-ton,' Ernestine said automatically. 'I should hope you are both very grateful to your dear stepfather for giving you such a lovely home.' She blew a kiss to Jacob, who was attempting to hide behind his newspaper. 'Did you hear me, husband?'

Jacob folded the paper and laid it on the table. 'Whatever you say, dearest.' He rose from his seat. 'I'm late for work.'

'My darling, it's your business. You employ people to do the work for you.' Ernestine puffed out her chest. 'You do as you please.'

'That's not how business is run, my love,' Jacob said mildly. He left the table, pausing by Mirabel's chair. 'You do look tired, my dear. Are you quite comfortable on the top floor?'

'I'm fine, thank you, Pa.' Mirabel smiled valiantly even though every bone in her body ached from sleeping on the hard floorboards.

'Perhaps your girls could share a room, Ernestine...' Jacob faltered, and came to a halt beneath his wife's stony stare. 'It was just an idea.'

'And a very silly one,' Ernestine snapped. 'Mirabel has had her chance to find a rich husband so it doesn't matter if she has bags under her eyes, but my little girls have their whole lives in front of them. I intend them to marry well, and no man wants a wife who looks as though she's been up all night weeping.'

Charity and Prudence sniggered, hiding behind their damask table napkins, and Jacob opened his mouth as if to protest, but Mirabel rose quickly from the table. 'I'm quite content the way things are, Pa. You mustn't worry about me.' She turned to face Ernestine, holding her head high. 'But I am a bit tired, stepmother. There will be no lessons this morning as I have a headache. If the girls wish to work alone I'll set them a poem to learn.'

'Jacob, did you hear that?' Ernestine cried angrily, but Jacob had fled leaving the door to swing shut behind him. She pointed a shaking finger at Mirabel. 'Don't try my patience too often or you'll be sorry. I'm mistress of this house now and you're only here on sufferance. The sooner I find a husband for you the better.'

Mirabel met her stepmother's angry gaze with a steady look. 'Say what you like, but you can't make me do anything I don't want to, and that includes marrying someone just to please you. As to your stupid and over-indulged daughters, I think you'd better find another governess, because I'm done with trying to instil learning into their wooden heads.'

Ernestine snatched up the hand bell and rang it. 'Wiley, come here I need you.'

Mirabel left the room, ignoring Wiley as she passed him in the hall. She had done it at last. She had stood up to her stepmother, but at what cost to herself? At this moment she did not care, but she knew her rebellion would not go unpunished. She made her way upstairs to tend to Gertie, and found her still feverish and calling out for her errant brother. The heat beneath the roof was already stifling and would get worse towards midday, and the smell of the sickroom seemed to permeate everything. Mirabel let up the sash, but the stench from the river and the surrounding manufactories made her close it again. A trapped fly hurled itself against the window and she opened it a crack to release the insect, watching it soar into the air. How wonderful to be free, she thought, turning back to Gertie who had begun to moan. 'Hush, my dear. It's all right, you're safe now.'

Gertie quietened at the sound of Mirabel's voice, but they both jumped when someone hammered on the door. 'Who's there?' Mirabel demanded angrily.

'Ma says you're to stop behaving like a spoilt brat and come downstairs to the schoolroom, or she'll want to know the reason why.' Charity did not disguise her pleasure in passing on the message.

'I'm not coming, and that's that.'

'But you must.' Charity sounded less sure of herself. 'Ma will have a fit if you don't do as she says.'

'Go away, Charity.'

'I'll tell her what you said. She won't be pleased.'

'She never is,' Mirabel muttered as Charity's footsteps faded into the distance. She sat back, wondering who Ernestine would send next in an attempt to bully her into submission. She did not have long to wait. The sound of a heavy tread outside her door was followed by Wiley's booming voice.

'Miss Mirabel, I have a request from Mrs Cutler.'

'The answer is still no, Wiley.'

'Your father will be informed of your behaviour.'

Mirabel laid a soothing hand on Gertie's forehead. 'Do what you like. I don't care.'

'You've been warned, miss.'

She leapt to her feet and ran to the door. 'Don't threaten me, Wiley. You're little better than a thief. I'll tell Pa that you're still stealing his wine, and if he doesn't believe me I'll go to the police.'

'You can't prove anything against me.'

'Maybe not, but I suspect you have a shady past. Would it stand up to scrutiny by an officer of the law?'

'I could ruin your father, and make your life unbearable. Don't meddle with things you don't understand.'

Gertie uttered a wild cry and Mirabel hurried back to her side, murmuring softly in an attempt to quieten her.

'Who's in there with you?' Wiley banged on the door. 'Open up at once, Miss Mirabel.'

'There's no one here but me. I banged my head on a rafter. Go away, Wiley. Leave me alone.' She

51

could hear him swearing as he left, but with the danger passed even for a short while she heaved a sigh of relief. 'You nearly gave the game away then, Gertie. What am I going to do with you?'

She sat on the floor beside the bed, hoping that Ernestine would give up her efforts to flush her out of her room, but now their mutual animus was out in the open and she realised that nothing would be the same. Ernestine had been looking for an opportunity to rid herself of her stepdaughter and Mirabel knew she had given her the perfect excuse. With Wiley on her side Ernestine had an even greater advantage; Jacob would crumble beneath their combined pressure.

Time seemed to have stood still in the stuffy attic room. Mirabel bathed Gertie with cold water in an attempt to bring down the fever, but there was little else she could do. The ewer was almost empty and the slop bucket had to be taken downstairs to be emptied in the privy. Mirabel had grown used to seeing to her own needs since being consigned to the top floor, but now she was trapped until such time as her stepmother decided to leave the house. With Gertie sleeping fitfully, she took up her position at the window and eventually her patience was rewarded by the sight of Ernestine and her daughters emerging from the porch, making their way towards Seething Lane. She waited for a while longer, giving Wiley time to settle down with the brandy bottle, and then she seized her chance.

Mrs James was up to her elbows in flour but she stopped rolling out the pastry to stare at Mirabel. 'What a commotion you caused, miss.

We thought that the mistress was going to have a seizure she carried on so, and those girls of hers were shouting and screaming fit to bust.'

'Is Wiley in his room, Cook?'

'Where else would he be when the master and mistress are out? That man is a drunken sot, but he gets away with it.'

'I know he does, and I don't understand it any more than you do.' Mirabel moved to the range and lifted the lid on a large saucepan. 'That smells delicious. I'll take a bowl up to my room, and some bread and butter.' She took a dish from the dresser and filled it with soup. 'And I need some laudanum. Do you know where Mrs Cutler keeps it?'

'Are you poorly, Miss Mirabel?'

'It's nothing more than a headache. A couple of drops of laudanum will make it go away.'

'Yes, miss, of course. I don't know if the mistress has any in her room. You could ask Flossie, she does the cleaning upstairs.'

'I'll do that. Where is she now?'

'I sent her out to get some onions from the market, but she should be back any minute, that's if she hasn't stopped to gossip with someone. She'll be the death of me.'

'You manage magnificently,' Mirabel said, smiling. 'And this soup will set me up for the rest of the day.'

'I could put some dinner on a tray for you, miss. I daresay you won't be feeling up to taking your meal with the mistress and her hellcats. Begging your pardon, I shouldn't say such things, I know.'

'It's the truth, Mrs James. You can't be blamed for speaking your mind, and dinner in my room would be just the thing.'

'Flossie will bring it up to you.' Mrs James tapped the side of her nose and winked. 'We got to stick together with that woman in charge.'

Mirabel put the bowl of soup on a tray, together with a chunk of bread and a pat of butter. 'Will you send Flossie up with the slop bucket? I've emptied it but I need to take the pitcher of water up to my room.'

'Yes, of course, miss.'

'And if she can find the laudanum she could bring that too.'

'I'll see that she does. It's a relief to know that you are on our side, Miss Mirabel, but I don't know how long I can stand working for that woman.'

Gertie responded quickly to the laudanum, giving Mirabel the opportunity to leave her, safe in the knowledge that she would sleep peacefully for a couple of hours. She slipped out of the house un-noticed and made her way to Crispin Street. With no particular plan in mind she had vague hopes of seeking help from Mrs Hamilton, who was well known for her charitable works. Mirabel did not think that Gertie's life hung in the balance; she would recover from her illness with good care, but keeping her hidden in the attic room was not an option. Sooner or later her presence would be discovered and Mirabel was under no illusions when it came to her stepmother. She was well aware that her days living under her father's roof were numbered. In defying Ernestine openly she had sealed her own fate.

She stopped outside the shabby building which housed the soup kitchen, staring up at the crudely painted sign offering a welcome to the poor and destitute. The main entrance was still locked and a queue of ragged people, including many children, stretched some way down the street. Mirabel let herself in at the side entrance.

Chapter Four

'There you are, Mirabel. We thought you weren't coming today.' Lillian Marjoribanks thrust an apron into Mirabel's hands and a welcoming smile brightened her flushed face. 'You're just in time to help serve the hungry hordes.'

'I'm sorry I'm late. I was detained.' Mirabel looked round hopefully. 'Is Mrs Hamilton in today?'

'Not yet.' Lillian thrust a ladle into her hand. 'They're opening the doors; get ready for the rush.'

Mirabel lifted the lid from the pan of soup and dipped the ladle, ready to serve the first person who shambled in from the street bringing with him the odours of the unwashed. They lined up, clutching their bowls, old and young alike, men, women and children all with one thing in common: the need to take nourishment or to face a slow and painful death by starvation. Mirabel had to wait until after the first rush had been served to continue the conversation. 'Do you think that Mrs Hamilton will be in later?'

Lillian shook her head. 'I don't know. She didn't say.' She shot a curious glance in Mirabel's direction. 'Is there anything I can do to help?'

'No, thank you.' Mirabel turned her attention to the next in line and found herself looking into Jack Starke's blue eyes. 'Oh, it's you.'

'Such an enthusiastic greeting,' he said, chuckling.

'If you don't want soup you'd better make way for those who do.' She had not meant to be rude, but his unexpected arrival had thrown her into a state of confusion. 'I'm sorry,' she added apologetically. 'But as you can see I'm rather busy.'

'We have a mutual friend, Miss Cutler. I came to enquire about her well-being.'

'I really can't talk now. Please move on,' Mirabel said in a low voice. She could feel Lillian's curious gaze boring into the back of her head.

'I'm in no hurry. I'll wait until you've finished here.' Jack tipped his hat to Lillian, treating her to his most disarming smile.

Mirabel shot a sideways glance at her and saw that the older woman was blushing. 'Have you no shame?' she murmured, trying not to laugh.

'None at all.' Jack stood aside as an elderly man sidled up to the counter clutching a tin mug. 'You have a customer, Miss Cutler.' He strolled off to sit at a table on the far side of the room.

Mirabel's hand shook as she served the soup. She was at a loss to understand why the sudden appearance of a man she barely knew could have such an effect on her, but she found her eyes drawn to him whenever there was a momentary lull. She forced herself to concentrate, breathing a sigh of relief when the session ended.

'Your friend is still here,' Lillian said, jerking her head in Jack's direction. 'I don't think he's the type of gentleman you ought to be associating with, Mirabel. If you know what I mean.'

'No, I don't think I do, Mrs Marjoribanks.'

Lillian sucked in her cheeks and pursed her lips. 'I believe he associates with fallen women. I'll say no more, but be careful, my dear.'

'Thank you, ma'am. I'll bear that in mind.' Mirabel hurried over to the table where Jack was waiting for her. He was slouched in a chair with his feet up, and his hat pushed to the back of his head at a rakish angle. 'I've just been warned against you,' she said, perching on a wooden bench opposite him. 'Mrs Marjoribanks seems to think that I shouldn't associate with someone like you.'

'And she's probably right in general, but I can assure you that you're quite safe with me.'

'Oh!' She struggled to think of a suitable response, but the mocking gleam in his eyes made it difficult to think of a suitable reply and for once she was at a loss for words.

'I was concerned about Bodger's sister, and I wondered how you were managing.'

'It's difficult,' she admitted reluctantly. 'I came here hoping to see Mrs Hamilton. I thought she might be able to give me some advice.'

'I don't see what Adela could do to help.'

'I thought perhaps she'd know of a charitable institution that would look after Gertie until she's well again. I don't think she's sick enough to go to hospital, but she mustn't go back to that awful room in Black Dog Alley.'

'Now there I agree with you, and I think I might be able to help.'

'You do?'

'Don't look so surprised. I'm not all bad. What state is Gertie in now? Could she be moved?'

'I dosed her with laudanum so she should still be asleep, but I must get back before she wakes. She might be scared and call out for me, and that would ruin everything.'

'You haven't told your parents about her then?'

'Good heavens, no. Pa might be all right with it but my stepmother would be furious. I really should be going.'

'I'll accompany you.'

Seized by a feeling of panic at the thought of how Ernestine would react to a visit from Captain Jack Starke, Mirabel shook her head. 'No, you won't. I mean, thank you, but that would only make things worse. Heaven knows what would happen if you were seen with me.'

'My reputation must have gone ahead of me,' he said with a wry smile. 'But you need to remove Gertie from your house and find her a safe haven where she'll be nursed back to health. Am I right?'

'Yes, of course.'

'Then I'll help you, but I'd best leave it until late this evening. I'll come when the servants have gone to bed and move Gertie to a place of safety. Do you agree?'

'I suppose so,' she said doubtfully. 'But where

will you take her?'

'You'll have to trust me, but I do know some kind-hearted people who wouldn't turn her away. I suppose I owe it to Boatswain Tinker to look after his little sister.'

'You are a strange man,' Mirabel said, rising to her feet. 'I never know whether you're serious or if you're laughing at me.'

He slid his feet to the ground and stood up. 'I'm deadly serious at this moment, Miss Cutler. If you look out of your window at midnight you'll see me loitering beneath the street lamp, and if I'm seen people will simply assume that you have an admirer. Does that bother you?'

'My stepmother would provide you with a ladder if she thought I was about to elope. She's already threatened to marry me off to anyone who'll have me.'

'She sounds like a lovely lady. I can't wait to make her acquaintance.' He tipped his hat. 'Until tonight, Miss Cutler.'

'Thank you, Captain Starke. I'm truly grateful.'

'That's quite all right, Miss Cutler, but in the circumstances I think we could drop the formalities. You may call me Jack if I'm allowed to call you Mirabel; it's such a pretty name.'

She turned her head away so that he could not see she was blushing. 'All right, Jack. I'll see you at midnight.'

The house was in total silence except for the ticking of the grandfather clock in the entrance hall, and the whirr followed by the booming chime on the hour. With her door slightly ajar Mirabel counted the strokes. Midnight – the witching hour. She shivered, but it was excitement and not fear that made her pulses race. She closed the door softly and hurried to the window, kneeling on the seat to throw up the sash and lean out. The gas lamp hanging from the adjacent house created a pool of sulphurous yellow light on the paving stones, but there was no sign of Captain Starke. A black and white cat strolled into view but something caused it to stop and arch its back before racing off into the darkness. And then she saw him.

Jack looked up and doffed his hat with a theatrical bow. 'It's all a game to you, isn't it,' Mirabel muttered, torn between irritation and the desire to burst out laughing at his antics. She closed the window and crept out of her room, tiptoeing barefoot along the narrow corridor so that she did not disturb Cook or Flossie. She quickened her pace and hurried downstairs to admit Jack.

'You came,' she whispered. 'I wasn't sure you would.'

'I'm a man of my word.'

'We'll have to be very quiet.'

'That goes without saying. Lead on and let's get this done.'

She picked up her skirts and headed for the stairs. 'The fifth one up creaks if you step in the middle.'

'I'll bear that in mind.'

Avoiding the tread that might give them away, Mirabel ran lightly up the stairs with Jack following close behind. She could feel his warm breath on the back of her neck and caught the heady masculine scent of bay rum – crushed bay leaves, citrus, cinnamon and cloves – combined with a hint of Havana cigar smoke and the warm leather of his jacket. She had to take a deep breath in order to concentrate on the task in hand as she entered her room, acutely conscious of his presence in her own special place. The feeling that she had stepped into one of her dreams was overpowering, but this was real and a soft groan from the bed made her move to comfort Gertie. 'It's all right. I'm here and so is Captain Starke. We're going to take you to a much nicer place where you'll be looked after until you're well again.'

Jack scooped Gertie up in his arms. 'I've got a cab waiting in Seething Lane. I'll make sure she's all right, so don't worry about her.'

'You're not thinking of going without me, are you?' Mirabel slipped her feet into her shoes and snatched up a shawl, draping it around her shoulders. 'I want to see where you're taking her.'

He hesitated. 'It's not the sort of place you'd want to go.'

'I'm not sure I like that sound of that. I'm definitely coming with you.'

'All right, if you must. The cab won't wait for ever so we'd best hurry.'

She followed him out of the room, pausing only to lock the door and put the key in her pocket.

The drive through the gas-lit streets was like entering the underworld. Mirabel had grown up in the city, but had never ventured out at this time of night. Inert bodies huddled in doorways, either asleep or dead drunk or even deceased, it was impossible to tell. Prostitutes lingered on street corners, offering their services to any man who passed their way, and quick couplings were taking place in the shadows. Mirabel knew these things happened, but rarely had she witnessed such an overt display of animal lust. Drunks fell out of the pubs along the way, some of them weaving their way homeward or back to their ships, while others were involved in brawls or were set upon by the gangs who roamed the streets on the lookout for the unwary, robbing them of everything they had, including their clothes. Mirabel turned her head away at the sight of a semi-naked man staggering along the pavement with blood oozing from cuts on his head and face. She shifted Gertie's head from her shoulder, cradling the sleeping girl in her arms. 'This is a terrible place,' she whispered.

'It's like any big city at night,' Jack said casually. 'This is nothing compared to some places I've visited abroad.'

Mirabel stared out of the window. 'That child can't be more than nine or ten years old,' she cried, horrified. 'The old woman is exhibiting her like an animal in the market.'

'That's probably her mother or her grand-mother. It's a harsh world if you're poor, Mirabel.'

She shook her head. 'It's on my doorstep and yet I knew nothing of it. I thought the lives of the beggars who come to the soup kitchen were bad enough, but this is a living hell.'

'We're here,' Jack said as the hackney carriage drew to a halt. 'It's best if you wait in the cab. I'll take Gertie inside and then I'll see you home.'

'I'm coming in. I want to see what sort of place

this is.'

He opened the door and lifted Gertie gently in his arms. 'Suit yourself, but don't say I didn't warn you.' He climbed out, leaving Mirabel to manage on her own.

The street was thronged with people going about their business as if it were noon on market day. Every other building seemed to be a pub, and the sound of drunken singing, raucous laughter and raised voices was accompanied by the smashing of glass and splintering of wood as fights broke out. Bruised and bloodied men were ejected with force through open doors, landing sprawled in the gutter along with the rats and feral cats. Jack carried Gertie into a house that blazed with lights. The front door was wedged open and a burly man stood at the top of the steps with his muscular arms folded across his chest and a pugnacious set to his jaw. His expression did not alter, but he seemed to know Jack and moved aside to let him in.

Even as Mirabel stepped over the threshold she realised that this was no ordinary establishment. The gaudy red and gold wallpaper in the entrance hall and the brass candle sconces set between dozens of long mirrors created an ambience of opulence verging on vulgarity. The air was heady with a mixture of cheap perfume, cigar smoke and wine. It was unlike any other place she had ever seen, and unless she was very much mistaken this was a brothel. Any doubts she had were dispelled by the appearance of a tall, slender woman wearing an emerald-silk gown lavishly trimmed with bugle beads and quite shockingly low cut. She might once have been quite lovely, but her painted cheeks and lips could not replicate the bloom of youth. Her hazel eyes held a world-weary expression that lightened momentarily when she saw Jack and darkened almost instantly, as if she were afraid to allow human emotions to interfere with business.

'Zilla, my dear. How lovely you look tonight.' Jack inclined his head, smiling.

'Don't try to soft-soap me, Jack Starke. I'm doing you a big favour taking this skinny little rabbit of a girl under my wing.' Zilla touched Gertie's cheek with the tip of her forefinger. 'She looks terrible. Which gutter did you pluck her from?'

'Excuse me,' Mirabel said angrily. 'I didn't agree to this, Jack.'

'Didn't you tell this person what you had in mind?' Zilla shook her head. 'You always were a fool when it came to a pretty face, Jack Starke.'

Mirabel faced him angrily. 'I thought you had a refuge in mind for the poor girl. Leaving her in a brothel isn't going to improve her lot.'

'A brothel?' Zilla gave her a withering look. 'This is a private club, where gentlemen relax and enjoy the company of young women.'

'It's still a brothel,' Mirabel insisted. 'We've just rescued this girl from a life on the streets. She needs to recuperate in pleasant surroundings with people who'll treat her kindly.'

Zilla stood arms akimbo, glaring at Mirabel. 'And what makes you think she won't get that here?'

'That's enough, ladies,' Jack said firmly. 'Mira-

64

bel, this lady is Zilla Grace, one of my oldest friends. A better person you'll go a long way to meet. Zilla, this young puritan is Mirabel Cutler. Her heart is in the right place but she's led a sheltered existence, and apparently can't tell the difference between a genuine kind heart and a money-grubbing wanton.'

Zilla's angry expression melted into a smile. 'You always were good with words, Jack, as well as other things which we won't mention in front of a well-bred young lady.'

'Laugh at me if you like.' Mirabel drew herself up to her full height, finding to her annoyance that she was still half a head shorter than Zilla. 'But I'm not leaving Gertie to be sold to the highest bidder like that poor child I just saw.'

'My dear, you have a very odd idea of how I run my house,' Zilla said with a humourless chuckle. 'My girls are willing participants in the activities here. No one is forced to do anything they don't want to, and I've only agreed to take Gertie in as a favour to an old friend. She can stay here until she regains her health and strength. After that it's up to her or to you, as you seem to have taken charge of her life. Are you related in some way?'

Taken aback, Mirabel shook her head. 'No. I don't really know her.'

'Zilla will take good care of Gertie,' Jack said easily. 'And now I'd really like to put her down. Where do you want her, my love?'

'If her guardian angel agrees, I'll put her in the back room. It's next to mine and I can keep an eye on her.'

Mirabel looked from one to the other, frown-

65

ing. It was not difficult to work out the relationship between Jack and Zilla. She had disliked the woman the moment she clapped eyes on her. 'I'm not sure about this.'

'For God's sake, stop looking down your nose at me. I'm a businesswoman first and foremost,' Zilla said angrily. 'My girls aren't slaves. They come and go as they please, and they're well treated. Your little friend will be looked after.'

Mirabel opened her mouth to argue but at that moment Gertie uttered a moan. 'This is getting us nowhere,' Jack said impatiently. 'She might be small but I'm getting cramp. Lead on, Zilla.'

She hesitated for a moment, glaring at Mirabel, and then seeming to relent she led the way down a long passageway to a door at the far end. Mirabel followed them, not knowing quite what to expect. She had read lurid descriptions of houses of ill repute in penny dreadful novels she had borrowed from Cook, who was addicted to them. She was vaguely disappointed to enter a comfortable parlour such as might be found in any middle-class home, the only difference being that there was a bed in one corner, but otherwise it was tastefully furnished with a chintz-covered sofa and armchairs and the windows were draped in matching fabric. Zilla lit an oil lamp and placed it on a table close to the bed. 'It's quiet in here. She won't be disturbed.'

Mirabel watched anxiously as Jack laid Gertie on the mattress. 'She'll wake up when the laudanum wears off. She'll be scared when she realises she's not with me.'

'I'm perfectly capable of looking after her.' Zilla

66

drew the covers up to Gertie's chin, stooping to brush a lock of hair off the girl's face. 'I promise you that she'll be well cared for.'

Jack placed his hands around Zilla's slim waist and twirled her round to face him, planting a kiss on her full lips. 'Thank you, my love.'

With the recoil of a snake she raised her hand and slapped his face, leaving scarlet imprints of her fingers. 'That's for taking me for granted, Jack Starke.'

Mirabel held her breath, waiting for Jack to react, but he released Zilla, grinning ruefully as he rubbed his cheek. 'You're still the same firebrand you always were, Zilla my darling.'

'I'm nobody's darling.' She smiled and brushed his lips with a kiss. 'Don't ever assume you can be free and easy with me. My favours are not bestowed lightly.'

'You loved me once.'

'Long ago, Jack. That was a long time ago.'

He nodded his head. 'You still pack a punch, Zilla.'

Mirabel tugged at his sleeve. 'Perhaps we should leave now?'

'That's the first sensible thing you've said.' Zilla moved to the door and opened it. 'I suppose you'll be leaving port soon, Captain?'

'I haven't as yet found a cargo, but I can't afford to have the ship lying idle for long.'

'You'll come again before you set sail?'

'It's a promise. We'll see ourselves out, Zilla.'

'Thank you for taking Gertie in,' Mirabel said, pausing in the doorway. 'I am grateful.'

'So you should be. I'm not running a charity.'

'I'd like to visit her if I may.'

Zilla put her head on one side, curling her lip. 'You would dare to be seen visiting such a place?'

'What do you take me for, Miss Grace?'

'To be perfectly frank I think you're a spoilt little rich girl who's never done a hard day's work in her life.'

'That's not fair, Zilla.' Jack laid his hand on Mirabel's shoulder. 'You don't know anything of this girl's life.'

'I see you have a champion, Miss Cutler.'

'I can speak for myself. You're welcome to your opinion, but you're wrong. Goodbye, Miss Grace. I'll call tomorrow to see how Gertie is doing.' She walked away with as much dignity as she could muster.

The cabby was about to drive off as they emerged from the house but he stopped when he spotted Jack, and drew the horses to a halt. 'I thought you was never coming, guv.'

Jack tossed him a coin. 'Great Tower Hill, cabby.' He opened the door for Mirabel and climbed in beside her. 'Zilla's a good woman but you don't want to get on the wrong side of her. I've seen her throw grown men bodily from the premises if they misbehaved.'

'You were lovers?'

'What sort of question is that? I thought you were a well-brought-up young woman.'

'I was born in a warehouse loft in Shad Thames. My father wasn't always in the position he is now.'

'And my past relationship with Zilla doesn't please you?'

'You're answering my question with questions.'

'All right. Although it's really none of your business – Zilla and I were together for a long time.'

'What happened?'

'We grew apart. She didn't like me being away at sea for months at a time, sometimes a year or more, and Zilla isn't a woman who likes to be tied down.'

'But you're still in love with her?'

'I'm still fond of her, but we strike sparks off each other and that's not a comfortable relationship.'

'I see.'

He turned his head to look into her eyes. 'Do you? I wonder.'

She looked away. 'Thank you for helping me with Gertie. I don't suppose we'll meet again, unless you happen to be visiting Miss Grace's establishment at the same time as me.'

'That's a thought.'

They lapsed into silence and Mirabel stared out of the window with unseeing eyes. She was exhausted both physically and mentally. The events of the evening seemed suddenly unreal, and at any moment she might wake up to find herself in the dreaming place. She hoped that Gertie would not be too scared when she opened her eyes to find Zilla Grace staring down at her, but for now at least there was nothing more that she could do for the girl.

It seemed hardly any time at all before the cabby pulled up outside the entrance to Catherine Court. 'Wait here,' Jack said as he helped Mirabel alight. 'I'll be right back.'

'Yes, guv. You said that last time, but some of us

69

has homes to go to.'

'I'll just see the young lady to her front door and I'll be back.' Jack opened the gate and followed Mirabel into the court. 'Will you be all right?'

'They were all asleep when I left. No one will be any the wiser.' Mirabel opened her reticule and took out the key, but before she had a chance to put it in the lock the door opened and light flooded into the porch.

'What time do you call this?' Jacob demanded angrily. 'Where have you been?'

'Who's that with you?' Ernestine peered over her husband's shoulder. 'She's been with a man, the little trollop. I told you she was up to no good, Jake my love. I think she's had him in her room and that's why it's always locked. I heard moans coming from there. She's been whoring in our home, my love. What do you say to that?'

'I don't believe it. Not my little girl.' Jacob stared at Mirabel with tears in his eyes, but his expression hardened when he saw Jack. 'What's the meaning of this? Who are you, sir?'

'It's not what it looks like, Pa,' Mirabel said hastily. 'I can explain, if you'll give me a chance.'

'Guilty,' Ernestine cried, pointing a shaking finger at Mirabel. 'She's been playing you for a fool, Jacob.'

He raised his hand as if to strike his daughter, but Jack stepped forward, catching hold of his arm. 'You're mistaken, sir. Your daughter has done no wrong.'

'You would say that,' Ernestine shrieked. 'Look at him, husband. He's a seafarer if ever I saw one. He's a seducer of young women and she's fallen

70

for his sweet talk. I won't have her in the house corrupting my innocent daughters.'

'I – I...' Jacob clutched his hand to his chest and fell to his knees.

Chapter Five

'This is your fault, you harlot.' Ernestine went down on her knees beside her husband, who had lapsed into unconsciousness. She turned to Charity who had appeared in the doorway wearing nothing but her nightgown. 'Don't stand there looking stupid, girl. Fetch Wiley. He'll know what to do.'

'Yes, Ma.' Charity fled.

'He needs a doctor.' Mirabel choked on a sob. 'Pa, speak to me.' She moved closer to her father, but Ernestine gave her a vicious shove.

'Get away from him. This is your fault. You caused this to happen. Where's that bloody man? Wiley, I need you.'

Jack leaned over to feel Jacob's pulse. He shook his head. 'I'm afraid it's too late.'

'What?' Ernestine stared up at him, her mouth working soundlessly.

'No.' Mirabel covered her face with her hands and would have fallen to her knees if Jack had not supported her. 'Pa, I'm s-so s-sorry.'

'It wasn't your fault,' Jack said firmly. 'Judging by the look of him and his choleric nature, I'd say it could have happened at any time.'

Ernestine rose to her feet, pointing a shaking finger at Mirabel. 'She did this. She killed her own father and widowed me, the little bitch.'

Overcome with grief and too distraught to argue, Mirabel leaned against Jack and sobbed. 'I killed my pa.'

'That's nonsense. His uncontrollable temper was probably the cause, or at least a part of it.'

Ernestine turned at the sound of hurried footsteps. 'Wiley, the master has been took ill.'

He emerged from the house, wrapping his dressing robe around his skinny body, his hair tousled and his eyes bloodshot with drink. 'He was all right at dinner time. What happened?' He went down on one knee, holding his hand over Jacob's mouth and nose. 'He's a goner, ma'am. Dead as a doornail.'

'She killed him,' Ernestine cried shrilly. 'That slut of a daughter and her fancy man are responsible for this outrage.'

Wiley shot a wary glance in Jack's direction. 'Someone ought to fetch the doctor.'

'Then I suggest you go,' Jack said calmly. 'I take it you're in Mr Cutler's employ.'

'I was his right-hand man. I could set the paving stones on fire if I told you the things I know about Jacob Cutler.'

'Shut up, you stupid man.' Ernestine rounded on him, her eyes bulging from their sockets. 'You'll keep a civil tongue in your head or you'll leave now without a character.'

'I don't think you'd do anything so ill-judged, ma'am.' Wiley held her gaze with a contemptuous curl of his thin lips. 'I'll get myself dressed and then I'll go for the doctor, but I leave you to deal with her.' He jerked his head in Mirabel's direction. Pushing Charity aside, he re-entered the house.

Mirabel dashed her tears away with a shaking hand. 'We can't leave him lying in the porch. We must take him indoors.'

'I'll need some help,' Jack murmured. 'He's a big man.'

'You won't lay a finger on him.' Ernestine stepped over Jacob's body, forcing Mirabel to move away. 'You're not welcome in my house, Mirabel Cutler.'

'This is my home too,' Mirabel said dazedly. 'You can't throw me out.'

'Oh yes I can. This house and everything in it belongs to me now. Your father agreed to change his will, naming me as sole benefactor. You can go to hell as far as I'm concerned. Leave here now and I never want to see your face again.'

Jack stepped in between them. 'You can't do that. The girl has just lost her father. Have you no respect for the dead?'

'My Jake would be alive now but for the pair of you. You killed him as surely as if you'd stuck a knife in his heart.'

'That's not true,' Mirabel cried passionately. 'I loved my pa in spite of the way he's treated me since you got your vicious claws into him.'

'Don't let her speak to you like that, Ma.' Charity hovered in the doorway, with Prudence hanging on to her hand. 'Make her go away. I never took to her.'

'Charity, go upstairs to the attic room and throw

73

all her stuff out of the window. She's leaving now in the company of her fancy man.'

'Madam, have a heart.' Jack spoke quietly, but Mirabel could see the muscles in his jaw tightening and his fists were clenched at his sides.

'My door is locked.' Mirabel controlled her voice with difficulty. She was beyond anger, and despite the shock of seeing her father collapse and die, she was in command of her emotions. 'And I have the key. I won't allow you to touch my things.'

'Won't allow?' Ernestine thrust her face closer to Mirabel's. 'You have no rights here, lady. You'll leave this instant, with or without your things, and I'll make Wiley break the door down and have a bonfire with what's left.'

'That's harsh even for you, ma'am.' Jack's eyes flashed angrily but he kept his voice low and his hand sought Mirabel's, giving it an encouraging squeeze. 'At least allow Miss Cutler to take what is hers.'

'Don't let her in, Ma,' Prudence cried gleefully. 'I've been dying to see in her room. She's probably got all sorts of things hidden away up there.'

Mirabel knelt down beside her father's body, stroking his cheek with her fingertips. 'Goodbye, Pa. I'm so sorry.'

'Get up, you trollop. Be off with you.'

Mirabel leaned over and kissed Jacob's rapidly cooling cheek before rising to face her stepmother. 'I'd rather live anywhere than under your roof, but I will go to my room and take what's mine. You can't stop me.'

Ernestine barred her way. 'Over my dead body

as well as your father's.'

'We'll see about that, madam.' Jack placed his arms around her ample waist and lifted her out of the way. 'Go and get what's yours, Mirabel. I'll make sure this woman doesn't molest you.'

'I'll have you up for assault,' Ernestine shrieked, kicking out with her feet, but Jack had her in a firm grip.

'Keep still and stop that noise unless you want all your neighbours to come running.'

Charity and Prudence huddled together wide-eyed and trembling, neither daring to follow Mirabel as she made her way upstairs to the room where she had dreamed away her childhood. Now those dreams were shattered and she was alone and unprepared to face a world from which she had been sheltered all her life. Hardly knowing what she was doing she grabbed a carpet bag and stuffed it with as many of her plainest clothes as it would hold. She emptied the box of the few things she had of her mother's and laid them reverently on the top of the bag, leaving behind the fine dresses and dainty shoes that her father had bought for her. She would have to start life anew, abandoning her identity as Miss Cutler of Cutler's Castle. Dazed and numbed with grief, she made her way downstairs.

The cabby stared down at them with a mixture of curiosity and relief. 'I dunno what's going on, guv. But I'll have to charge you double the fare for the wait I've had.'

'You'll get your money. Back to Tenter Street, please.'

Mirabel paused with one foot on the step. 'No, Jack. You can't take me to that place. I won't go there.'

'Perhaps you'd rather sleep in a shop doorway or on the steps of St Paul's.'

'No, but...'

'Is there someone you know who would take you in? Have you any relatives in London?'

'No, there's no one.'

'As I said, Tenter Street, cabby.' Jack helped her into the carriage and climbed in beside her. 'Zilla will give you a bed for the night, and you'll be there for Gertie when she wakes up.'

She thought for a moment, desperation making her bold. 'Where do you stay when your ship is in port?'

'On board. It's no place for a woman.'

'I wasn't asking you to take me in,' she said icily. 'I can look after myself, but I don't want to be beholden to that woman.'

'Unless you've a better idea there's not much choice, and Zilla is all right. You just have to know how to handle her.'

Mirabel shot him a sideways glance. 'I'm not the one who had my face slapped.'

'Touché,' he said, chuckling. 'Don't worry about Zilla. She's got a heart of gold beneath that steely exterior.'

'Just one night,' Zilla said as she ushered Mirabel into the room where Gertie lay sleeping. 'You'll have to take the sofa.'

'Thank you, Miss Grace. I'm much obliged to you.' Jack had left her at the door, handing her over to Zilla as if she were an orphan discovered wandering the streets.

'I know what you think of me and my establishment, Miss Cutler. You made that very clear. I'm doing this as a favour to an old friend, and tomorrow you'll have to make your own arrangements.'

'I understand.' Mirabel sank down on the nearest chair. 'I'm truly grateful to you, Miss Grace.'

'It's Zilla. No one calls me Miss Grace.' Zilla gave her a calculating look. 'You need to sleep. I'll send a girl in with some blankets and a pillow. Make yourself comfortable – you won't be disturbed unless Gertie wakes up, but I've given her a hefty dose of laudanum so she should sleep until morning.'

'Thank you, Zilla.' Mirabel managed a weary smile.

'Don't thank me. This was Jack's idea.' Zilla left the room, closing the door behind her.

Mirabel sat very still. Shock and disbelief had set in the moment she left Catherine Court, but the reality of her situation was slowly beginning to dawn on her. She was alone in the world, penniless and virtually friendless. If Wiley had planned her downfall he must be rejoicing now even though he had lost his mentor, and Ernestine would be triumphant. Mirabel had suspected all along that her stepmother was in love with Jacob Cutler's money, and cared nothing for the man himself. She was now the sole owner of Cutler's Castle and Jacob's fortune would be hers to spend as she pleased.

A timid tap on the door made her turn with a start. 'Come in.'

'I brought your bedding, miss.' Barely visible

77

beneath a pile of blankets, the maidservant put it down with an audible sigh of relief. 'Shall I make up a bed for you, miss?'

'No, thank you. I can do it myself.'

'Yes, miss.' The girl backed towards the doorway. 'Miss Zilla said to ask if there was anything you wanted.'

Mirabel smiled tiredly and shook her head. 'I've everything I need, thank you.' She waited until the girl had gone, undressed and lay down on the makeshift bed. She left a candle burning in case Gertie should wake up and be afraid in the dark, and she closed her eyes.

She awakened to the sound of someone calling her, and at first she thought she was at home in her own room, but when she opened her eyes she realised that this was far from the truth. The memory of what had happened last night came flooding back, taking her breath away. It was true. It had not been a dreadful nightmare – her father was dead and Ernestine had taken everything. She sat up, realising that the faint voice belonged to Gertie, and she raised herself from the sofa. 'It's all right. I'm here.' She made her way to the window and drew back the curtains, allowing a fractured shaft of hazy sunlight to filter through the grimy windowpanes.

Gertie lifted her head, peering dazedly at her. 'I'm thirsty.'

Despite her own worries, Mirabel experienced a feeling of intense relief. Gertie was over the worst of the fever. She went to the table and filled a glass with water from a jug that Zilla had provided, taking it to the bed and holding it to Gertie's parched lips. 'Take small sips.'

Gertie sank back on the bed. 'Where are we, miss?'

'It's a long story, but you're safe here and you'll be well cared for.'

'You ain't going to leave me, are you?'

'No, of course not.' Mirabel made an effort to sound positive. The truth was she had no idea what she was going to do next, but she could hardly admit that to a sick girl. It was going to be difficult enough to explain why they were living in a brothel in the roughest part of town. Time enough for that when Gertie regained her strength.

Mirabel dressed quickly. She was about to tell her patient that she was going to ask Zilla if they could have some breakfast when she realised that Gertie had gone back to sleep. She let herself out of the room and knocked on the parlour door, but there was no response. It was only then she realised that the house was in silence and that the ladies of the night must still be asleep. She found the back stairs and went down to the kitchen.

The young maidservant who had brought her the bedding was poking the fire in the range, and she spun round at the sound of Mirabel's footsteps, brandishing the poker like a weapon. Her frightened expression was wiped away by a smile. 'Oh, it's you, miss.'

'Who did you think it was?' Mirabel asked curiously.

'I dunno. Sometimes we gets a stray gent wandering into the kitchen on the excuse of wanting something or other.'

'You looked scared.'

'You made me jump, that's all.'

Mirabel was not certain she believed her. 'What's your name?'

'It's Lizzie, miss.'

'Well, Lizzie, I was wondering if I could have a cup of tea and something to eat. I'll need a jug of warm water too.'

'You can have what you like. Cook is in bed with one of her heads, although between you and me I think she took to the gin bottle last evening.'

'Does she do that often?'

'More often than not, miss.' Lizzie gave the fire a final poke and flames licked up round the coals. 'Thank God for that. I thought the bugger was going to go out on me.' She clapped her hand to her mouth, blushing. 'Excuse the language, miss. I was forgetting meself.'

'What can I do to help?'

'You're from above stairs, miss. You don't belong down here.' Lizzie seemed genuinely shocked.

'I'm here on sufferance, if you know what I mean.'

'I'm afraid I don't, miss.'

'Well, I'm not exactly a guest and I don't work here, so while I'm under Miss Zilla's roof I'll do my bit to help.' Mirabel glanced round the untidy kitchen. Pots and pans were strewn on the table as well as the remains of last night's supper. 'I'm sure you could do with a hand, especially if Cook is indisposed.'

'If that means dead drunk, then yes, she is. I wouldn't say no to a bit of help. I have to get the water boilers filled so that the girls upstairs can take their baths, and when they wake up they'll all want tea and toast and I dunno how I'll manage.'

'Do you mean to tell me that it's just you and Cook to look after everyone here?'

'Lord, no, miss. There's the charwoman, but she's taking out the night soil ready for collection and she does all the heavy work. Then there's Edna and Florrie who come in to clean the upstairs rooms, but they don't start until late morning. There's not much point them turning up to find all the sluts still in bed, and some of them are all-nighters, if you get my meaning.'

It did not take a great leap of imagination to work out what Lizzie meant by all-nighters. 'What needs doing next? I could tidy up a bit.'

'I don't suppose you can make bread, can you?'

'No, I'm afraid I can't cook.'

'Can you make tea?'

'Yes, I can do that.'

Lizzie put down the poker, staring at her open-mouthed. 'What's a lady like you doing in the kitchen of a bawdy house?'

It was a question that Mirabel had difficulty in answering. Quite how fate had turned on her and left her with virtually nothing was something she could not explain, even to herself. 'Never mind that now, just tell me how I might help you, Lizzie. But first I think we could both do with a cup of tea and something to eat.'

After a quick breakfast Mirabel hefted pails of water from the pump in the back yard and filled the two large tanks on either side of the range, a task which Lizzie said she had to do several times

81

a day in order to satisfy the needs of the women above stairs. In between forays into the yard Mirabel went to check on Gertie, who had recovered sufficiently to sit up and drink some weak tea, but had no appetite for food. Mirabel left her, promising to return as soon as she could.

During a brief respite she sat at the table sharing a slice of rather stale seed cake and drinking tea with Lizzie. Cook's snores could still be heard from the room next to the scullery, which according to Lizzie was windowless and small, although she herself slept on a rug by the range. Mirabel was beginning to realise that not all servants were so generously treated as Cook and Flossie who had space and privacy in Cutler's Castle. 'What will you do when the ladies want food?' Mirabel asked curiously. 'I mean what will you do if Cook doesn't wake up in time to prepare a meal?'

'I dunno. I expects Miss Zilla will send out for pies, but she'll be in a foul mood afterwards. She always threatens to sack Cook when this happens, but she never does.'

Mirabel absorbed this in silence. So Zilla had a softer side to her nature; she kept it well hidden, but Jack must have seen something in her to love. She sighed, wondering if she would ever see him again. Their chance meeting in the soup kitchen had changed her life forever, and she must have seemed prudish and ungrateful when he had tried to help her, but she was now in Zilla's debt. She frowned thoughtfully. The experience she had gained helping to feed the poor and needy might enable her to pay for her night's lodgings. She rose from the table. 'There is one thing I can cook, Lizzie. I know how to make soup. Would that help?'

Lizzie jumped to her feet, eyes shining. 'It would be the answer to my prayers, miss. Cook's too, I imagine. Miss Zilla might have a soft spot for the old girl but there's only so much she'll stand. You wouldn't want to see her when she loses her temper.'

'I'll need onions, carrots, turnips and some meat and the biggest saucepan you've got.'

'I'll have a look in the meat safe outside. You'll find the vegetables in the larder.'

Zilla walked into the kitchen, coming to a sudden halt as she sniffed the savoury aroma of stew simmering in the large, soot-blackened pan. 'Where's Cook?'

Lizzie jumped to attention, clasping her hands tightly behind her back. 'If you please, Miss Zilla, Cook ain't too well.'

Zilla stared at Mirabel. 'What are you doing down here?'

'I thought I could help out in return for the night's lodging,' Mirabel said hastily.

'You can cook?'

'Not exactly. I learned how to make stew in the soup kitchen.'

Zilla threw back her head and laughed. 'So you're one of those well-intentioned ladies who give their time to charity. Now that's funny.' She walked over to the range and lifted the lid on the pan. 'It smells good.' She reached for a ladle, dipped and tasted. 'It's not bad. I had you down as a spoiled darling, no use to anyone, unless they wanted a woman purely for her looks, but I see there's more to you.'

'I won't outstay my welcome,' Mirabel said with dignity. 'Thank you for allowing me to stay last night, but I'll be on my way.'

'And where will you go?' Zilla demanded, handing the ladle to Lizzie. 'It's no good looking for Jack; his ship sailed on the tide.'

'He didn't say he was leaving.'

'Oh dear, do I hear the sound of a heart breaking?' Zilla gave her a mocking smile. 'He does that to women. He has this fatal charm which he uses to his full advantage, and then, like all seafarers, he sails away into the sunset. Or in Jack's case it was into a fiery dawn. I waved him goodbye.'

Mirabel averted her gaze, staring down at the flagstone floor. She had not intended to go looking for him, but perhaps, if she were being honest, she had hoped he might check to see that she was all right.

'Can't she stay, Miss Grace?' Lizzie asked anxiously. 'She's worked really hard this morning, and I dunno how I'd have managed if she hadn't been here.' She clapped her hand over her mouth. 'I meant to say it was only because Cook was taken poorly...'

'Dead drunk, you mean.' Zilla's eyes narrowed. 'Tell her if she does this one more time I'll send her to the workhouse. I can't run my establishment unless I have people I can rely upon.' She turned to Mirabel, eyeing her up and down. 'I could do with a smart upstairs maid. Edna and Florrie are common girls with strong arms and they do the heavy work, but a good-looking parlour maid might be an asset.'

'Thank you, but I'd prefer to seek employment elsewhere.' Mirabel headed for the door. 'I'll collect my things.'

'Wait.' Zilla's command echoed round the kitchen. 'You might look down on us for providing a service to men who are more than willing to pay, but who else would employ someone who has no training in domestic duties, or anything else as far as I can see? What are you fit for, Mirabel Cutler?'

'I don't know, but I'm not prepared to sleep with men for money.'

'My dear, I don't doubt that you're a virgin, and although some of my gentlemen would pay handsomely to deflower you, I doubt if they'd find it an enjoyable experience. You haven't the talent to make a man lust for you.'

Even though she felt her cheeks redden, it was anger as well as embarrassment that roiled in Mirabel's belly. 'You know nothing about me, Miss Zilla.'

'I'm a woman of the world and I know people. You would make a good wife for a missionary or a dull little clergyman, but you aren't the sort to set men's loins aflame with desire.'

'I leave that to people like you.' Mirabel hesitated, knowing that she had gone too far. 'I'm sorry, that was rude of me, especially when you've been kind enough to take us in.'

Zilla gave her a deprecating look. 'I don't do things out of kindness. If I did a favour it was for an old friend and not for you.'

Chastened, Mirabel nodded her head. 'I'll leave now, but Gertie is still unwell. I can't take her with me.'

'Don't be a fool. Where would you go, and what would you do?'

'I have friends who help in the soup kitchen. I'm sure they'll assist me in finding a suitable position.'

'Are you really? Do you think those good ladies will rally round to help a maiden in distress? They'll make sympathetic noises but they won't invite you into their homes, and they definitely wouldn't allow you within a hundred yards of their husbands and sons.'

'I'm not asking to be taken in,' Mirabel said angrily. 'All I want is to earn my living.'

Zilla shot a warning glance in Lizzie's direction. 'Get on with your work, girl.' She turned her head to give Mirabel an appraising look. 'Come upstairs to my parlour. I think I may have the solution to your problem.'

Chapter Six

Mirabel hesitated outside the iron gates which separated Catherine Court from Great Tower Hill. She had not intended to return home, but she needed to know when her father's funeral was to take place. He had spoiled and bullied her according to his moods, and had allowed a scheming woman to turn him against his own daughter, but he was still her father. It seemed hypocritical to say her last goodbyes in the house of God for Jacob

Cutler had never been a churchgoer. She doubted if he had a religious bone in his body, but he deserved a show of respect and she was not going to allow her stepmother to frighten her away.

She had planned her visit for a time most likely to coincide with the absence of Ernestine and her daughters. Zilla had grudgingly allowed her an hour off from her new position as parlourmaid, and she had flung a shawl over her black poplin dress and swapped her white frilled mobcap for her old straw bonnet.

She opened the gate and entered the narrow court where the sun's rays only managed to squeeze between the tall buildings when it was high in the sky at midsummer, but now with autumn fast approaching the shadows had deepened and it was cool in the shade. Mirabel made her way down the area steps to the basement kitchen.

Cook was in her rocking chair by the range with her cap askew and her mouth open as she dozed by the fire, even though it was a warm day outside and sweat was running down her plump cheeks. Flossie was washing up in the scullery but she rushed into the kitchen at the sound of the door opening. She threw up her hands in surprise. 'Miss Mirabel. You ain't supposed to be here.'

Mirabel laid her finger on her lips. 'Shh, Flossie. Don't wake Cook. Is Wiley around?'

'He's above stairs, miss. He's taken to sitting in the drawing room when the mistress is out. He's got too big for his boots if you ask me. He thinks he's master of the house now the old master has passed away.'

'That's why I came, Flossie.' Mirabel moved closer, lowering her voice. 'Do you know when my father's funeral is to take place?'

'Tomorrow, miss. All Hallows Church. You aren't thinking of going, are you?'

'I must. He was my father and nothing is going to keep me away.'

'It was that Wiley what poisoned his mind against you. Him and her above stairs are thick as thieves. I reckon they planned it all along.'

'You'd better be careful what you say, Flossie. You don't want to get on the wrong side of Mrs Cutler.'

'Cook and me reckons she'll be Mrs Wiley afore long.' Flossie glanced at the stairs as if expecting to see Wiley lurking in the shadows. 'He's got his eye on her fortune.'

'No. I can't believe that. Why would she want a man like him when she's a woman of independent means? She's got what she set out to get.'

'He whispers things in her ear and she goes quite pale. I seen it meself when I take their dinner up to them. He sits by her side at table and holds her hand. Sometimes she smiles and tosses her head like a girl and at other times she looks scared. He's up to something, mark my words, miss.'

Mirabel shivered despite the oppressive heat in the room. 'It's none of my business now. After today I'll never set foot in this house again.'

'That you won't, Miss Mirabel Cutler.' The sound of Wiley's voice awakened Cook from her slumbers with a start, and caused Flossie to scamper into the scullery and slam the door. He came slowly down the stairs. 'So you couldn't keep away from your old home.'

'I just wanted to know when my father's funeral is due to take place.' Mirabel faced him squarely. He might frighten the servants and have some kind of hold over Ernestine but she was not scared of him. He was a loathsome creature and she felt nothing but contempt for him.

'You are not welcome here and you'll keep away from the funeral.'

'He was my father and I will be there.'

Cook struggled to her feet. 'I was just resting my eyes, Mr Wiley. I wasn't asleep.'

'You'd better buck up your ideas, you idle old slut, or you'll be looking for another position.' Wiley gave her a withering look. 'Clean up this mess and start preparing dinner. I've a fancy for steak pie.'

'But Mr Wiley, I was going to roast a leg of lamb.'

'Steak pie or you can pack your bags.' He turned to Mirabel with a malicious grin. 'I can see by your mode of dress that you're in service. You've come down in the world.'

'What I do is no concern of yours, Wiley. Just tell me the time of the funeral service and I'll be gone from here. You won't see me again.'

'Don't you want your fine clothes, Miss Mirabel?' He clasped his hands together as if in prayer. 'Dear me, I was forgetting you don't need them now.'

'You sold them, Mr Wiley,' Cook muttered. 'She couldn't have them even if she wanted them.'

'That's enough from you, woman.' Wiley moved

89

swiftly to open the door leading into the area. 'You'd best leave now, Miss Cutler. The funeral is at eleven o'clock tomorrow morning, but take my advice and stay away.'

'I don't know why my father put such faith in you.' Mirabel stepped outside but he followed her and caught her by the arm.

'You think you're so high and mighty, well let me tell you something. Your pa was a bad 'un through and through. He was lucky he didn't end up with a noose round his neck, dancing a Newgate hornpipe.'

She snatched her arm free from his grasp. 'I won't listen to this.' She covered her ears, but he pulled her hands away.

'Your pa wheedled his way into Cyrus Pendleton's good books and then he did for him. That's how he came into his fortune and that's why you was brought up a lady.'

She stared at him in horror. 'That's a wicked lie. My pa wouldn't do a thing like that.'

'It's the truth. Your stepmother believed me, and now I've got her just where I want her. When we marry the money and this house will be mine.'

'You're an evil man, Wiley. I don't believe a word you say.'

He thrust his face close to hers. 'You may not, but others will. I'll blacken the name of Cutler so that you'll be shunned by decent people. Who would employ the daughter of a man who gained his fortune by murdering his employer and taking over his business? You'd end up an old maid picking oakum in the workhouse.'

She recoiled at the smell of bad breath and stale

alcohol. 'I won't listen to this.'

'That's right, run away, and don't come back. You're not welcome here.'

'I'll take what's mine. I want what's left of my possessions.'

'Too late, Miss Cutler. I cleared the attic and the stall holders in Petticoat Lane were pleased to take the lot. I daresay you could buy some of the things back, at a price.'

If she had doubted Wiley's words she realised that he had been telling the truth when she found her best gown displayed on a market stall, together with several of her bonnets and her fur-trimmed mantle. Her boots and shoes were for sale further along the street and two women were fighting over her favourite lace-trimmed nightgown. Mirabel walked on. Even if she had had enough money to redeem her clothes she would have resisted the temptation. They were part of her old life and she must look to the future, there was nothing to be gained by living in the past.

She attended the church next day, sitting in the back pew as far away from Ernestine and her girls as was possible. Wiley was there as well as Cook and Flossie, who was snivelling into her handkerchief. The ceremony was brief and the interment was to be at Brookwood Cemetery. The glass-sided hearse was waiting outside, and the coal-black horses pawed the ground with their mourning plumes waving in the cool breeze.

'Are you a member of the funeral party, miss?' The solemn-faced undertaker eyed her curiously.

'No she ain't. She can't afford the rail fare.'

91

Ernestine walked off, heading towards the second carriage with her daughters tagging along with obvious reluctance. Prudence stuck her tongue out at Mirabel but Charity chose to ignore her. Wiley strode past with his nose in the air. He was dressed like a gentleman, although Mirabel suspected that his suit had been hired for the occasion, but she recognised the silver-topped ebony cane he carried as being her father's favourite. It was plain to see that he had assumed the position of head of the house even before his old master was laid to rest. Mirabel stood stiffly erect, chin up and determined not to let them see that she was close to tears. 'Goodbye, Pa,' she whispered as the horses moved forward at the coachman's command, heading towards the London Necropolis railway station where the party would board the special train to Brookwood Cemetery.

She stood motionless, watching until they were out of sight. It was farewell to her old life, she realised with a sigh, and now she was truly alone and virtually penniless until Zilla chose to pay her the small wage they had agreed. Her home for the foreseeable future was a brothel in Tenter Street.

Zilla looked up from her desk as Mirabel entered the parlour. 'I can't keep on calling you Mirabel,' she said thoughtfully. 'It's too grand a name for a parlourmaid.'

'Yes, Miss Zilla.'

'You needn't put on that humble air with me, because I see through you as if you were a pane of glass, Miss Cutler. You look down on me and my girls.'

'That's not true,' Mirabel said, stung by the unfairness of this remark. She had been with Zilla for a month and had done her job to the best of her ability. The hours were long, and she often found herself helping in the kitchen when Cook had imbibed too freely. At any time of the day or night she might be called upon to clear up spilled wine or food, broken glass or overflowing chamber pots. It was not a job for the squeamish or anyone with a delicate constitution. In four short weeks Mirabel had learned more about the intimate amorous dealing of men and women than she had in her whole life. She doubted whether there was anything much that would shock her now.

'Well, it doesn't matter to me what you think. As long as you do your work and keep yourself to yourself I'm content to keep you on.'

'Thank you.'

'But from now on I'll call you Mabel, which is more fitting for a servant.'

'Will that be all, Miss Zilla?'

'Not quite.' Zilla leaned back in her chair. 'Gertie is completely recovered now, isn't she?'

'It's taken a long time, but yes, I'd say she is quite well now.'

'And there's still no news of her brother?'

'I'm afraid not.'

'I've told you before that I'm not a charity and I meant it. Gertie will have to work or she'll have to find somewhere else to live.'

'What exactly had you in mind?'

'To put it bluntly, she was a prostitute before she came to me and I can make use of her talents. Some gentlemen have a fancy for the waiflike creatures, while others prefer more meat on the bones of their women. Am I shocking you, Mabel?'

'After the things I've seen here I don't think anything will ever shock me again.'

Zilla nodded, eyeing her thoughtfully. 'You're a good-looking woman and you have a well-rounded figure. You could earn a lot of money if you chose to.'

'No.' Mirabel shook her head. 'I'm willing to work hard, but not that. Never that.'

'Oh, very well. Don't make a song and dance about it. But there is something you could do which might benefit you.'

'Which is?'

'I have an old and respected client who is, shall we say, rather past the age when he enjoys the carnal delights of my girls, but he still appreciates the good things in life. Am I making myself clear?'

'I'm afraid not. What are you suggesting?'

'This gentleman is very rich and quite eccentric, which is why he still likes to come here even if he doesn't avail himself of all that's on offer. I think he is lonely and he likes pretty women, but he needs someone who can converse with him on an equal level.'

'I'm still not quite clear what you want me to do.'

'You could engage him in conversation and provide a sympathetic ear when he wishes to talk about himself and his passion for flowers.'

'Flowers.' Mirabel stared at her in surprise. 'He likes flowers?'

'He is an orchid collector and very wealthy. As far as I can tell he has devoted his whole life since leaving the army to travelling the world in search of rare specimens. I find it a terrible bore, but you must hang on his every word.'

'I think I would find it very interesting.'

'As I thought, you are a strange young woman. You and he might do well together, but you would have to look the part. He might not want a woman in the physical sense, but he has eyes in his head and he appreciates beauty. When you're suitably dressed I believe you will look quite presentable.'

'I've nothing to wear.'

Zilla shrugged her slender shoulders. 'You need not worry about that, Mabel. I've already sent for my dressmaker and she will make you a gown. All I ask is that you keep him entertained, for which I'll pay you according to how satisfied he is with your company.'

'But if I agree to do this would I still be a parlourmaid?'

'That goes without saying. You carry on as usual except for the evenings when Mr Kettle requests your presence. Assuming he takes to you in the first place, of course, although I pride myself on being a good judge of character. What do you say?'

Mirabel thought quickly. 'I'll do it, but only if you make it clear to the gentleman what my duties will be.'

'That's settled then.' Zilla opened the ledger and picked up a quill pen. 'You may go, Mabel. Send Gertie to me now. I'll deal with her next.'

Mirabel found things to do in the entrance hall, dusting and then polishing the brass candle sconces while she waited for Gertie to emerge from Zilla's parlour. She caught up with her just as she was about to enter the room they had been sharing since they arrived in Tenter Street. 'Well?' she demanded. 'What did she say to you?'

Gertie turned away but not before Mirabel had seen the tears sparkling on the tips of her long eyelashes. She followed Gertie into their room, closing the door so that no one would overhear their conversation. 'Zilla told you that she wants you to work for her, didn't she?'

Gertie sank down on her bed. 'I knew it was coming. I'm well now and she's been good to me. I'd have ended up in the workhouse if you hadn't brought me here.'

'We both might have had that fate.' Mirabel sat down beside her. 'You don't have to do this if you don't want to.'

'Of course I do. What choice have I got?'

'You could go into service. I've done it and I hadn't any training.'

'I was a scullery maid until the master's son tried to get me into his bed. His mother caught us and blamed me for trying to seduce her precious boy. I was sacked and sent away without a character. Who'd take me on now?'

'Zilla would give you a reference.' Mirabel met Gertie's quizzical gaze and they both dissolved into giggles. 'Perhaps that wasn't such a good idea.'

Gertie's cheerful smile faded. 'I might have died but for Zilla. I owe her, Mirabel. I didn't have any choice but to agree to her terms.'

'I'm so sorry.' Mirabel gave Gertie's hand a

gentle squeeze. 'I know that Zilla's very strict with the gentlemen clients, but you must speak to the other girls and they'll help you. They're all nice apart from Winnie. I don't trust her at all, but you don't have to have anything to do with her.'

'It's nothing I haven't done before, but I thought I'd left all that behind me.'

'I have a plan, Gertie. As soon as I've saved up enough money I'm leaving and renting a room of my own. Then I'll look for work, any sort of work where I can earn enough to live on, and you'll come with me.'

'Really? Would you do that for me?'

'Of course I would. We've come this far together.'

'And one day Bodger will turn up,' Gertie said eagerly. 'I know he will. He's not dead. I'm sure I'd feel it in my heart if anything bad had happened to him.'

Mirabel jumped to her feet at the sound of the doorbell. 'I have to go. We'll talk more later.'

'I dunno about that. I'm to have my own room. Zilla said so. We won't be able to have a natter afore we go to sleep.'

'I'm sure we'll snatch time in the day.' Mirabel hurried from the room and ran the length of the hall to open the front door.

'I'm Miss Standish, Miss Grace's sewing woman.'

Mirabel stood aside. 'Please come in.'

'I'm to measure up a young lady for a gown.'

'That will be me, Miss Standish. I'll take you to Miss Grace and no doubt she'll tell you what she has in mind.'

The gown fitted perfectly. Mirabel studied her reflection in the tallest of the mirrors that lined the entrance hall and did a twirl, catching sight of her swirling skirts as she pirouetted. Her small waist was whittled to a hand's span by the new corset that Zilla had provided, and the décolletage was not too daring. It was the prettiest gown she had ever possessed, and the iridescent blue-green silk reminded her of a picture she had seen depicting the colourful plumage of a peacock. Gertie had done her hair, showing a surprising talent in creating a coronet of thick coils and glossy ringlets that bobbed flirtatiously with every turn of her head. She came to a sudden halt, staring at the new self who gazed back at her with eyebrows raised.

'You do indeed look quite passable, Mabel.' Zilla's brisk tone shattered the silence.

'The gown is beautiful, Miss Zilla. Thank you.'

'Don't thank me, thank Mr Kettle; he paid for it.'

'Why would he do such a thing? I thought you said...'

'Come along now, girl. You've been here long enough to know that the gentlemen always pay for the services we provide. You didn't think that you would be giving your time for nothing, did you?'

'It didn't occur to me that I'd be beholden to him for my clothes. I really can't accept such a gift.'

'Don't be a fool. Of course you'll take the gown. You're wearing it aren't you? It was made for you and Hubert Kettle paid good money to have a pleasant evening with a beautiful woman. He's waiting for you in the morning room. Come with me and I'll introduce you.' Zilla walked away without waiting for Mirabel's response, leaving her little option but to follow and allow her mentor to usher her into the room. 'Hubert, my dear, this is Mabel, the young lady I told you about.'

He rose from his seat by the fire, which had been lit despite the fact that it was a relatively warm evening. His expression was serious. 'How do you do, Mabel?'

Zilla smiled and inclined her head. 'I'll leave you to get acquainted, Hubert. Mabel will see that you have everything you want.' She backed out of the room, closing the door behind her.

The sound echoed in Mirabel's head, and it might as well have been a prison door closing. She had to curb a sudden urge to escape. 'Good evening, sir,' she murmured, bobbing a curtsey, which seemed appropriate in the circumstances.

'Won't you take a seat, Mabel?'

She hesitated, wondering what sort of man chose to visit a brothel simply for an evening of conversation about flowers. His voice was cultured and she supposed him to be in his late sixties, although he looked older. His skin was prematurely aged, tanned and wrinkled from exposure to the sun in foreign climes. His hair was thick and bushy and snow white, as were his mutton-chop whiskers and moustache. These features, when combined with pale grey eyes the colour of snow melt, gave him a startling appearance, made even more arresting by his alert expression and upright military bearing.

She met his gaze with a steady look. 'It's not

Mabel, sir. My name is Mirabel.'

'I'm sure my hearing is as acute as it ever was. I distinctly heard Zilla call you Mabel.'

'Yes, she did. She chooses to use that name because I'm just a parlourmaid and it keeps me in my place, but that isn't the real me. If you and I are going to get along then I feel we should be honest with each other from the start.'

He sat down suddenly, motioning her to take the seat opposite. 'Well now, you are an unusual young lady. Tell me about yourself, Mirabel.'

'I'm a parlourmaid, sir.'

'I already know that, my dear.' He leaned forward, resting his hands on his knees and his pale eyes bored into hers. 'I'm a very old man, Mirabel. I've travelled the world many times over and I've met people from all walks of life. It doesn't take a genius to see that you are an educated young woman, and that your present position in life is not the one you were brought up to expect. You said you wanted us to be honest with each other, so now you can tell me how and why you came to be living in a house of ill repute.' He reached for his glass and took a sip of wine. 'I'm agog with curiosity. This promises to be a very interesting evening.'

She spoke haltingly at first but Hubert Kettle was a good listener. He sat back in his chair and drank his wine, refraining from comment while she talked of her sheltered upbringing in Cutler's Castle. Although she tried to protect her father's memory it was impossible to relate the true events that had brought her to Tenter Street without mentioning Wiley's involvement, and the hold he had over her father, which she suspected had contributed to his early demise. When it came to his funeral her voice broke on a sob and she struggled to control her emotions.

Hubert filled a glass with wine and handed it to her. 'I suspect that there's a great deal more to your story than you feel able to tell me at present,' he said gently. 'This is an exceptionally good claret. Zilla keeps a supply on hand just for me, so sip it slowly and savour its delights while I tell you about my one great passion in life.'

Resisting the temptation to drink deeply in an attempt to blot out the memory of Wiley with his machinations, threats and downright lies, she treated the wine reverently as her father had shown her. Jacob had developed a liking and deep respect for fine wines, and had taken the time to learn how to appreciate them; something he had attempted to pass on to his daughter.

Hubert watched her with an appreciative smile. 'I can see that we are going to get on very well, Mirabel Cutler. I'll make a connoisseur of you and I'll introduce you to the wonders of the natural world. What do you have to say to that?'

Chapter Seven

Hubert had gone and Zilla was smiling as she pocketed the money he had pressed into her hand. 'You've done well, Mabel. He likes you and there'll be a little extra added to your wages at the end of the month.'

Mirabel had heard the unmistakeable clink of golden sovereigns as they passed from hand to hand, but she knew that her share of this largesse would be minimal. Zilla was undoubtedly a wealthy woman as well as being clever and even ruthless when the need arose. 'Thank you,' she said meekly. There was no point in angering her employer. 'Mr Kettle is a very interesting man. I enjoyed our time together.'

'Even better.' Zilla put her head on one side, watching Mirabel closely. 'I might yet make a courtesan of you, Mabel Cutler.'

Mirabel let this pass. She had no intention of agreeing to any such thing, but she had learned that arguing with Zilla was futile. 'I'll go and change out of my gown. Do you need me again tonight?'

'I think not. You've done well so you may have the rest of the evening to yourself.'

Mirabel acknowledged the compliment with a smile. 'Thank you, Miss Zilla.' She made her way up to the top floor where she had been allocated a small room beneath the eaves.

It was hot in the attic during the day, but at night the temperature fell dramatically at this time of the year. Mirabel suspected that in winter she would find ice on the inside of the window, but that was a small concern when compared to the luxury of privacy. Once again she had a place where she could sit alone and dream. Hubert Kettle had fired her imagination with tales of explorers and plant hunters ranging from Sir Joseph Banks to Baron Alexander von Humboldt and David Douglas, and, more recently, the exploits in China of Robert Fortune. Now she had far-off lands and real-life adventurers to fire her imagination. Hubert had started to tell her a little of his own experiences, but then he had seemed to tire and had brought the evening to an abrupt end. Mirabel had glanced at the ormolu clock on the mantelshelf and could hardly believe her eyes. Three hours had passed in a flash, but she could have sat there all night, listening to Hubert's cultured tones.

She took off her silk gown and laid it over the ladder-back chair, which was the only furniture in the room apart from an iron bedstead and a deal chest of drawers. Her head was slightly muzzy from drinking wine, but after facing an uncertain future where hope had been abandoned in the face of bleak reality, she felt ridiculously optimistic. Hubert had introduced her to another world, and she could not wait to learn more. He might be old enough to be her grandfather, but his enthusiasm and zest for life was infectious and she knew she had found a friend.

Hubert's visits became more frequent and once again Zilla sent for her dressmaker. This time Mirabel was measured for an afternoon gown and a mantle. Zilla had chosen the material from bolts of cloth she kept locked away in the linen cupboard, giving Mirabel no choice in the matter, but the fine woollen cloth in a delicate shade of lavender was what she might have selected had her opinion been asked. When it came to the mantle, however, Zilla shook her head. 'I've changed my mind, Miss Standish. It's an unnecessary expense and I have an old one that could be altered to fit Mabel. I've no longer a use for it.' She swept out of the room.

'You're quite a favourite, Mabel.' Miss Standish jotted down some measurements on a sheet of paper. 'I've worked for Miss Grace these past ten years and this is the first time I've known her to be so generous.'

'How long will it take you to make the gown?'

'Why?' Miss Standish was suddenly alert. 'Do you need it quickly?'

'The days are getting shorter,' Mirabel said casually. 'It would be nice to have something warm to wear before winter sets in.' She did not add that she wanted to look her best for the interesting man who had so unexpectedly come into her life. Gertie had warned her that Emily Standish was a notorious gossip. She had based this titbit of information on a conversation with Lucky Sue and Gentle Jane, two of Miss Zilla's girls, who had learned from bitter experience that the fitting room did not carry similar privileges to the confessional.

Miss Standish folded the sheet of paper and placed it in her reticule. 'Perhaps Miss Grace has plans for you, Mabel. You seem to me to be different from the rest of the women she employs.'

'I don't know what you mean, Miss Standish. But I'm sure the gown will be lovely. Your work is excellent.'

'As I said, you're not the usual type she has working for her, but it's none of my business. Miss Grace probably sees a little of herself in you.' She paused as if waiting for Mirabel to question her further. 'She came from a good family, but I expect she's already told you that.'

'She's been kind to me, that's all I know.'

Miss Standish raised a delicate eyebrow. 'As I said, you are privileged. Miss Grace had to struggle to survive in a world ruled by men. She married against her family's wishes and her father cut her off without a penny.'

'I'm not sure you should be telling me this, Miss Standish. It's really none of my business.'

'Oh, but it is. You need to understand the woman who employs you. To her you are a thing of value, but when your looks fade or should you become indisposed, you will be cast off just as she was.'

Mirabel made a move towards the door. 'I think this conversation is at an end, Miss Standish.'

'I'm just trying to help you, and if you've any sense won't put your trust in Zilla Grace. If she ever had a heart it was torn in two when the man she married deserted her and took up with another woman. She was left penniless and destitute with a small baby to care for.'

'What happened to the child? And who was this man who treated her so badly?' Suspicion clouded Mirabel's mind, and she needed to know if the errant husband was Jack Starke.

'The baby died and Zilla took to the streets. She made her fortune by selling her body to rich men, while respectable women like myself have to struggle to earn a living.'

'It seems to me that she's made the best of things,' Mirabel said icily. 'Why do you associate with her if you dislike her so much?'

'I too have to live.' Miss Standish picked up the bolt of cloth and tucked it under her arm. 'Do you know how much I earn a week? If I'm lucky I take home ten shillings for working all hours of the day and often into the night.'

'I'm sorry, but we all have to make our way as best we can.'

Miss Standish gave her a searching look. 'It's obvious you were brought up with money, and something dire must have happened to bring you so low.'

'I think that's my business, Miss Standish.'

'You won't be so high and mighty when she tires of you and throws you out. You'll learn then what it's like to be a single woman trying to make a living in a world ruled by men.'

'Most women marry for security. Miss Zilla must have been unlucky in her choice of husband.'

'He was a ne'er-do-well, unlike my dear Philip, who was killed in the Crimea. I might have had a home of my own and children if my fiancé hadn't given his life for his country.'

'Who was it who broke Miss Zilla's heart?' Mirabel knew that it was dangerous to pursue the subject but she could not let the matter rest.

'It's none of my business. You made that quite clear, Miss Mabel. Be careful, that's all I have to say to you.' Miss Standish moved to the door. 'As you are still the parlourmaid you must see me out.'

Mirabel obeyed her in silence, uncomfortably aware that she had allowed the conversation to stray onto dangerous ground. No doubt there was an element of truth in Miss Standish's story, and it was a sad tale, but also one of triumph over adversity. Zilla had known tragedy but had survived to become a wealthy woman who commanded respect from all who knew her. For a few painful moments Mirabel had suspected Jack of being the one who had treated Zilla so cruelly; then commonsense reasserted itself, convincing her that the pair would not be on such good terms now had he been the villain of the piece.

Gertie's warning had been timely. Emily Standish was undoubtedly a bitter woman, intent on making mischief and she was adept in gaining the trust of her clients. Confidences exchanged in private might easily be passed on to her other clients, and Mirabel knew from experience that the well-to-do ladies who helped in the soup kitchen liked nothing better than to sit and gossip over a cup of tea when their work was done. Should the tittle-tattle reach Cutler's Castle, Ernestine would take grim pleasure in the knowledge that her stepdaughter was reduced to working in a brothel. Wiley would be jubilant, and if it came to his notice that she was being paid to be a companion to a wealthy, well-respected man, there was no knowing what mischief he might try to make.

On her afternoon off Mirabel decided to visit the soup kitchen. She was, of course, under no obligation to the charity, but she felt that she owed Adela an explanation. She arrived to find her seated at her usual table poring over the neat entries in a ledger. 'Good afternoon, Mrs Hamilton. I've come to apologise for my absence, but I'm now in a position to offer my help.'

Adela looked up and her expression changed subtly. 'We have a full complement today, Miss Cutler. Your assistance is not needed.'

As far as Mirabel could see there were only two women working in the kitchen. 'I'm really sorry that I had to leave without telling you,' she began tentatively.

'We've managed very well, thank you, Mirabel.' Adela averted her gaze, seemingly bent on studying the figures in the ledger.

'I could still come once a week.'

Adela looked up, unsmiling. 'I don't think you are a suitable person to associate with my ladies.'

'You know that I've had to move out of my father's house?'

'I've heard that you're living in Tenter Street. Is it true?'

'Yes, but...'

'Then I'm sorry but I have no further use for you. My ladies would not tolerate working with someone who lives in a house of ill repute.'

'But I'm just a parlourmaid, Mrs Hamilton. Captain Starke introduced me to Miss Grace and I had nowhere else to go.'

'Jack Starke.' Adela threw up her hands. 'I might have guessed that libertine was involved in your downfall.'

'I beg your pardon, ma'am, but I am as respectable a person as I ever was.'

'Nevertheless, you are tainted by association and it won't do.' Adela rose to her feet. 'I'm sorry, Mirabel. I believe you were a victim of circumstance, but you must see that I have a position to keep up. Your services are no longer needed. I can't put it any plainer than that. Good day to you.' She marched into the kitchen, slamming the door behind her.

Shocked and angry, Mirabel stood for a moment staring at the closed door. She was excluded once again, and through no fault of her own.

In the weeks that followed Mirabel did her best to put her old life behind her. She did more than her fair share of the work in Tenter Street, and she looked forward to Hubert's visits. Although she enjoyed the evenings they spent together, she suspected that these pleasant interludes would come to an abrupt end should he discover how her father had won his fortune. Wiley's threats hung over her like the sword of Damocles. It might be impossible for him to prove that Jacob had murdered Cyrus Pendleton, but if he made his knowledge public the damage would have been done. Hubert was an honourable man, she knew that already, and she doubted whether he would want to associate with the daughter of a murderer.

She had tried to forget Adela Hamilton's caustic words, but they came back to haunt her at night when she lay down to sleep, and in rare quiet moments during the day. The house rarely came to life before noon, enabling Mirabel and the chambermaids to do their work unhindered. Zilla rose from her bed midmorning and Mirabel had the task of taking her a pot of strong coffee, which she drank without the addition of milk or sugar. The chore of carrying ewers of hot water from the kitchen to fill the zinc bathtub in Zilla's dressing room was given to Lizzie, but Mirabel often chose to help her. She was on her way downstairs with an empty pitcher one morning when the doorbell rang.

Adjusting her mobcap, Mirabel placed the empty container on a side table and went to open the door to find a scruffy boy standing on the doorstep. 'Can I help you?'

'Are you Miss Grace?'

'No, I'm not. What do you want with her?'

He held out a grubby hand. 'Got a message for her from the gent in Savage Gardens.'

Mirabel was suddenly alert. 'Would that be Mr Kettle?'

The boy sniggered behind his hand. 'What sort of name is that, miss?'

'It's the sort of name that deserves a little respect from a boy like you. If you've got a message give it to me and I'll see that it's passed on to Miss Grace.'

He hesitated. 'Gent said you'd pay me.'

'I'm sure he rewarded you handsomely. Now either give me the note or take it back to Mr Kettle and tell him you wouldn't hand it over without payment.'

'Or I could just throw it in the Thames.'

Mirabel could see that this was going nowhere and she put her hand in her pocket, taking out a penny. 'Take this for your trouble.'

'Ta, miss.' He snatched the coin and thrust a crumpled piece of paper into her hand.

She closed the door before he had the chance to demand more money. There was no envelope and it was a simple matter to unfold the sheet and read the message written in Hubert's copperplate hand.

'What have you there?' Zilla's sharp tone made Mirabel turn with a start to see her employer standing close behind her.

'A ragged boy delivered this, Miss Zilla. It's for you.'

Zilla scanned the note. 'Have you read it?'

'I caught a glimpse of the contents.'

'You're a bad liar, Mabel.' Zilla tucked the paper into her pocket. 'Hubert wants you to visit him at his home this evening. I'm not sure I can allow such a thing.'

Mirabel knew better than to argue. She nodded and was about to walk away when Zilla called her back. 'Don't you want to know why?'

'I suppose you have your reasons, Miss Zilla.'

'Don't put on that meek and mild air, Mabel. It doesn't work with me.'

'What would you have me say? I depend on you for my board and lodging; I have nowhere else to go and you pay me a wage.'

'What a little sea lawyer you are to be sure.' Zilla's stern expression melted into a smile. 'I like you, Mabel, which is why I've given you this chance to better yourself. However, I don't think it's proper to allow you to visit Hubert in his home.'

'You don't seem to think it improper to allow men to pay for your girls' favours under your roof.'

'My girls are protected while they work for me. Any gentleman who forgets himself is shown the door before he can inflict harm of any kind, as you well know. I can't guarantee your safety when

111

you're away from here.'

'Or perhaps he won't pay for my time, is that it too?'

'That does come into it, but I need to know a little more of Hubert's intentions before I agree to such a tryst.'

'It's nothing like that with Mr Kettle. He's an elderly gentleman and past that sort of thing.'

'He's a man, Mabel. They're never past it in their own minds. Leave this with me. I intend to take a carriage ride to Savage Gardens. I'll let you know the outcome of my meeting with Hubert Kettle.'

'Just a moment, Miss Grace.'

'What is it now?'

'I want to know what you intend to say to him.'

'You have a cheek, girl. You work for me and you're mine to do with as I please.'

'Indeed I'm not. You can't sell my favours.'

'This is my business. I make the rules. Now go outside and hail a cab while I fetch my bonnet and shawl.'

That evening, dressed in her newest gown of crimson striped silk, with ruffles adorning the sleeves and an overskirt swept back to form a small train, Mirabel knew that she was looking her best. Lizzie had curled her hair into ringlets using iron tongs heated on the kitchen range, and had pinned them back with two jewelled combs, borrowed from Lucky Sue. 'They're paste, of course,' Sue said, chuckling. 'But the old gent won't know the difference. Anyway, he'll have his eyes fixed elsewhere, if you get my meaning.' She nudged Mirabel in the ribs and winked.

112

'I'm only going to look at his collection of rare orchids,' Mirabel protested.

Lizzie and Sue exchanged amused glances. 'If you believe that you're in for a big surprise.' Sue left the kitchen, chuckling to herself.

'Don't pay no attention to her,' Lizzie said hastily. 'She's just jealous. None of the molls above stairs get invited out, let alone to visit the gents in their homes.'

'It's not like that, Lizzie. Mr Kettle is an old gentleman. He really does want to show me his rare specimens.'

Lizzie doubled up laughing. 'You are a one, Mabel.'

Savage Gardens off Trinity Square was barely a stone's throw from Catherine Court. Terraced four-storey Georgian town houses faced each other across a narrow street with basement areas protected by iron railings. The once prosperous area was now showing signs of age and declining fortunes. Soot-blackened and with peeling paintwork, most of the buildings were now cheap lodging houses, but the few that were still owner-occupied were noticeably well cared for with shiny brass door furniture, clean windows and pristine paintwork.

Mirabel stepped out of the cab that Zilla had insisted on, it being unsafe for any woman to walk out unaccompanied after dark. Having paid the cabby, Mirabel walked up the steps to the front door. She hesitated, suddenly nervous and unsure of herself. Perhaps Lucky Sue had been right and this was a foolhardy venture, but then she remembered how kind Hubert had been, with no hint of anything in his manner towards her which would make her uncomfortable in his presence. She raised the knocker and let it fall. The sharp clatter of metal against metal echoed inside the house and was answered by the sound of swift footsteps. Mirabel had given little thought to Hubert's household and she was agreeably surprised by the plump, homely little woman who opened the door.

'Good evening, miss. We were expecting you. Come in.'

Mirabel stepped over the threshold and found herself in a long, narrow entrance hall lit by a single oil lamp. It was too dark to see much detail but framed watercolours of exotic plants covered the walls with barely an inch to spare between them.

'My name is Mrs Flitton. I'm Mr Kettle's housekeeper and have been for the past twenty-six years.'

'I'm very pleased to make your acquaintance, ma'am.'

Mrs Flitton held a lamp high, taking in every detail of Mirabel's appearance. 'You seem like a nice young lady. I was afraid that he had got into bad company. I never liked the idea of him visiting that place in Tenter Street, although, of course, I understand that a gentleman has needs.'

'Yes, well I'm not like that,' Mirabel said hastily. 'Mr Kettle is my friend.'

'It doesn't matter what I think, but I can see that you're not one of those wanton women. Come this way.' She bustled off along the corridor, stopping to usher Mirabel into a room at the far end. 'Mr Kettle will be with you directly. He's tending his plants, which he does several times a day. It's like having a nursery full of babies who need caring for.'

Mirabel took in her surroundings with a sweeping glance. The furniture was old-fashioned, heavy and ornately carved in dark wood with somewhat faded red-velvet upholstery. The once elegant Georgian mantelshelf was barely visible beneath a welter of bell jars containing colourful stuffed birds, a black marble clock in the shape of a Grecian temple, two spill vases and a collection of strange objects from far-off places. The walls, as in the entrance hall, were covered with botanical paintings, and side tables were littered with books, magazines and more souvenirs brought back from Hubert's extensive travels. The ambience was more like that of a museum than a home, and entirely masculine.

Mrs Flitton waddled over to the fireplace, poked the embers into life and added more coal. 'I'll go and tell him you're here. Make yourself at home.' She turned to Mirabel with a beaming smile. 'It's so good for us to have young company. We were in danger of becoming old and dried up like some of the things he's brought back from foreign lands.' She held her hand out for Mirabel's bonnet and mantle. 'I'll hang these up for you, miss.'

'Thank you.' At a loss for words, Mirabel perched on the edge of a deep armchair by the fire. The steady tick-tock from the marble clock was the only sound in the room apart from the odd crackle from the fire, and she was growing increasingly nervous and on edge. Coming here

115

might be a terrible mistake, she thought, clasping her hands tightly in her lap. It was just possible that Zilla might have lied in order to get her here in the first place, and the real reason for her invitation was to satisfy an old man's carnal desires. The lurid tales in the penny dreadfuls so dear to Flossie's heart sprang to mind, and the sound of approaching footsteps made Mirabel jump to her feet. This had been a terrible mistake. She would make her excuses and leave right away.

The door opened and Hubert strolled into the room clutching a potted plant in his hands. 'Mirabel, my dear, I just had to show you this perfect specimen. Isn't it beautiful?'

'It is indeed.' Forgetting everything other than the need to examine the delicate blooms, Mirabel moved closer. 'I've never seen anything like it.' She touched one of the purple petals with the tip of her finger.

'It's a *Cattleya labiata,* named after a man called William Cattley.' Hubert peered at her over the top of his spectacles, his pale eyes shining with excitement. 'He discovered the species in a shipment of specimens from Brazil earlier this century. It's very rare. When I was younger I went on many plant-hunting expeditions, but I never came across any of these beauties, and now it is too late for me.'

'I don't see why.'

'I'm an old man, Mirabel. Too old to undergo the rigours that such a trip would entail.'

She gazed at the orchid, seeing it through his eyes, and was entranced. Suddenly she understood his passion for finding rare and exquisite blooms. Flowering plants were scarce in the city where even the common dandelion struggled to exist. She looked into his eyes and saw the spirit of a young man fighting to be free from an ageing body. Impulsively she laid her hand on his arm.

'You're not too old, Mr Kettle. I believe that you could do anything you wanted to.'

He put the plant pot down and grasped her hands in his. 'Mirabel, I hadn't meant to spring this upon you, but I have something very important I have to say to you. Something very important indeed, but I hardly know where to begin.'

Chapter Eight

Alarmed, she tried to wrest her hands free but his grip was surprisingly strong for a man of his years. 'Please let me go, Mr Kettle. You're hurting me.'

He released her instantly and spots of colour appeared on his normally pale cheeks. 'I'm so sorry. Please forgive me.'

'Perhaps I'd better leave now.' Mirabel glanced anxiously at the door, willing Mrs Flitton to make an entrance and put an end to what promised to be an embarrassing situation. 'You seem to have mistaken my motives for accepting your invitation tonight, sir. I'm not like the rest of Miss Grace's girls.'

'I know you're not, and I didn't mean to frighten you.' Hubert sank down on the nearest chair. His crestfallen expression might have been comical in different circumstances, but Mirabel was not amused.

'I'm not frightened, but I am disappointed. I thought you were my friend.'

He took off his tortoiseshell spectacles and placed them carefully in his breast pocket. He cleared his throat several times before speaking. 'Mirabel, my dear, I have the greatest respect for you. Won't you take a seat, please?'

Somewhat reluctantly she sat down opposite him. 'I don't know why I'm here, sir.'

'I'm very bad at this sort of thing. I've never been very comfortable with beautiful women, especially when the young lady in question is young enough to be my granddaughter. I want you to realise that I know the enormity of what I am about to propose.'

'Please say it, sir. You're making me very uncomfortable because I don't know what you have in mind.'

'My intentions are honourable, of that I can assure you. In fact, I'm proposing marriage.' He met her startled look with a direct gaze. 'I know this must sound preposterous to a young lady like you, but I've given it a lot of thought. It would be a marriage in name only, but completely legal. You would by my wife, but I would expect nothing of you in the physical sense. You would have the protection of my name, and I would treat you with great respect and sincere affection. Eventually you would inherit everything I own and you would be set up for life.' He hesitated, watching her carefully. 'Do you understand what I'm saying?'

'You're asking me to marry you?' Mirabel stared at him in astonishment. 'You want to marry me?'

A faint smile lit his eyes. 'I know it sounds ridiculous, but as I said, I wouldn't make any physical demands on you. I'm a lonely old man and you are young and vital, which is not a combination that would normally work; but you're beautiful and intelligent, and even more important than that, you have a kindly disposition. You talk to me as an equal and you don't treat me like a doddering fool.'

'You most certainly aren't doddering or a fool, and I'm very flattered, but I don't love you, Mr Kettle.' She turned her head away as the memory of Jack Starke's cynical grin and lazy drawl erased every other thought from her mind. He had left without a word and sailed away to a destination unknown, but he was not an easy man to forget.

'Of course you don't,' Hubert said gently. 'That would be much more than I could ever expect, but perhaps you might feel a little fondness for me? That would make me very happy, and you would have all the material comforts I can provide. I believe I'm a generous man.'

'I don't doubt it, but you don't know everything about me, Mr Kettle.' She was floundering now as she tried to come to terms with his proposal.

He held out his hand. 'My name is Hubert and it would please me greatly if you could bring yourself to use it instead of Mr Kettle.'

'Yes, Hubert,' she murmured.

'And will you at least consider my proposal?'

She thought quickly, closing her mind to the

119

man who haunted her dreams. Hubert was a nice man, if a little eccentric, and he was offering her a home, security and respectability. Living in a brothel and working for a notorious madam like Zilla Grace did not bode well for her future. Her plan to save enough to make herself independent might take years to accomplish, and the secret hopes she had harboured regarding Captain Starke were never likely to become a reality: there were very few choices for a young woman in her position. Hubert's shy and yet eager expression put her in mind of a young boy anticipating a long-awaited birthday gift. The years seemed to have dropped away from him and she saw the person beneath the ageing outer shell. 'I need a little time to think,' she began slowly, but then the need to be honest outweighed every other consideration. 'But there is something you must know first, which might make you change your mind.'

'There can't be anything that would make me think ill of you, my dear.'

'You might feel differently when I tell you that my late father has been accused of making his fortune by murdering his old employer and taking over his business.'

'That's a very serious accusation. Who would say such things about a man who is dead and cannot speak for himself?'

'His name is Septimus Wiley. He was a worker in Mr Pendleton's warehouse where my pa was a clerk. I think he must have been blackmailing my father, and that's why Pa took him on as our butler. Wiley is a hateful creature and he drinks too much.'

'Why would anyone believe such a man? It's obviously a pack of lies, so I don't think you ought to worry too much about him.'

'That's not all, Hubert.' To her surprise his name came more easily to her lips. 'I'm sure that Wiley helped to bring about my father's death in some way, although I can't prove that he was at fault. Then he married my stepmother, which gave him control of Pa's business and all his assets.'

Hubert stared into the fire, frowning. 'He sounds like a despicable creature, but what could he hope to gain by spreading malicious gossip about your father? It doesn't make sense.'

'I don't know.' She clenched her hands into fists. 'He hates me, even though I can't see that I'm a threat to him in any way. Pa left everything to Ernestine, or so I was told. I never saw the will.'

'It should be possible to get a copy.'

'I wouldn't want to do anything to antagonise Wiley. He's a dangerous man and I want to forget I ever knew him. That goes for Ernestine too and her horrid daughters.'

Hubert took her right hand in his, holding it and unclenching her fingers slowly, one by one. He smoothed the angry creases from her palm. 'Don't upset yourself, Mirabel. If you agree to marry me you need never worry about money again. I promise to look after you, and I won't allow anyone to hurt you.'

His touch made her shiver with apprehension and she was tempted to pull free, but she did not want to hurt his feelings. Even so, she had to be ruthlessly honest. 'I do like you, Hubert, but that's all it could ever be. Would you be happy

121

with a woman who married you on such terms?'

'Never mind me, my dear, I'm not important. It's you who would have to put up with an ageing husband.'

She gave his fingers a sympathetic squeeze as she withdrew her hand. 'I don't think I'll ever see it that way, Hubert. You are a kind man and you are young in your heart, which makes all the difference.'

His pale eyes mirrored the flames in the fire, and his thin lips curved in a smile. 'You are the best medicine for me, my dear. Just being in your company makes me feel twenty years younger. You are like one of my precious orchids and I will treasure you as such.'

It was her turn to smile. 'I never saw myself as a flower, but I would be very interested to see your collection.'

'And so you shall. If you agree to marry me I think I might even manage one last trip to find the orchid of my dreams, and we could make the journey together.'

'You would take me on one of your expeditions?' Mirabel asked breathlessly. 'Where would we go and what would we look for?'

'It's long been my ambition to find a ghost orchid. They're very rare and utterly beautiful, although I've never seen one. I've heard that they're to be found in the everglades of Florida.'

'You'd take me with you to America?' She could hardly believe her ears. 'Really?'

'Of course I would. You would be my companion and my helpmate. I believe I could accomplish anything with you by my side.' He rose somewhat unsteadily to his feet. 'I would kneel down, but I'm afraid I might have difficulty in rising.'

Mirabel stood up slowly. She knew that she was about to make a decision that would change her life forever, but she was strangely calm and unafraid.

He took her hand in his, gazing into her eyes which were on a level with his. 'Will you do me the honour of marrying me, Mirabel?'

'Yes, Hubert. I will.'

At first Mirabel was reluctant to have the banns read in All Hallows Church, fearing that news of her upcoming nuptials might reach Ernestine and Wiley, but Hubert insisted that he wanted their marriage to be conducted with due ceremony in the house of God. One of the first things that Mirabel learned about him was that he attended matins and evensong every Sunday, accompanied by the devoted Mrs Flitton. Mirabel had not been to church on a regular basis since her governess had left, and when Hubert proudly introduced her as his fiancée she was afraid that the vicar might remember her father's funeral. Fortunately for her, the reverend gentleman's mind must have been on higher matters when he had conducted that particular service, and he welcomed her as a new member of his flock. It was a relief to know that Wiley's brand of poison had not spread this far. The banns were read and the wedding was arranged for the 21st December.

Zilla was grimly amused by the idea that one of her old friends was to marry her parlourmaid, but Lucky Sue and the rest of Zilla's girls thought it the funniest thing they had heard for a long time. Gentle Jane hooted with laughter and made lewd suggestions as to how Mirabel would cope with her aged husband on their wedding night, and was immediately hushed by Gertie, whose face was suffused with blushes as she hurried Mirabel out of the room. 'Don't take no notice of them, love,' she said in a low voice. 'They're just jealous, that's all.' She dragged Mirabel into the drawing room, which was laid out ready for the evening revelries, and closed the door. 'What do you know about it?'

'It?' Mirabel repeated, puzzled.

'The wedding night.' Gertie's already flushed cheeks deepened in colour. 'I mean what happens when you're alone with your husband in bed at night. Oh, for goodness' sake, Mirabel, you've worked here for months. You must know what goes on between a man and a woman.'

'I've seen more than I wanted to.' It was Mirabel's turn to redden. 'I've heard the grunts and the cries of pain or pleasure, I was never sure which, but I'm not exactly certain what they do.'

Gertie sucked in her cheeks and frowned. 'Well then, it'll be a bit of a shock, but I can tell you it gets easier, although I ain't never done it with a man of his age.' She shot a sideways glance at Mirabel. 'No offence meant, but he's old enough to be your granddad. I ain't even sure he could do what he's supposed to.' She leaned against the door, shaking her head. 'You ain't making this easy, Mirabel Cutler.'

'I know what you're saying, or at least I don't know, but it doesn't matter. Hubert has promised me that we will have separate bedchambers and

124

he will never make demands on me.'

'And you believe him?'

'Of course I do, Gertie. He's a nice man and he goes to church twice a day on Sundays.'

'They're often the worst offenders. Give me a good honest crook any day of the week.'

Despite her embarrassment, Mirabel threw back her head and laughed. 'You are funny, Gertie. But don't worry about me. I'll be quite all right with Hubert.'

'It don't sound very exciting. You'll get fed up with wiping his chin when he starts to dribble.'

'Poor man, he's not so very old. In fact we're going on a plant-hunting expedition together, and I can't wait to see a bit more of the world than Whitechapel and the docks.'

'Well, I wish you luck, Mabel, and should you meet a seaman called Bodger Tinker that'll be my brother. Tell him to come home and rescue his sister from a life of sin. I'm tired of dealing with drunken lechers. I'd like to find a decent man, who'll love me and provide a decent home where we can bring up our children. That's all I want out of life. It ain't much to ask, is it?'

Quashing the doubts that had been growing in her mind about her own future, Mirabel nodded her head. 'Of course not. And if I should happen to meet Bodger I'll be certain to pass on the message.'

Zilla had a more practical approach to Mirabel's upcoming nuptials and she sent for Miss Standish, instructing her to make a wedding dress suitable for the bride of a well-respected gentleman with the means to pay for such luxuries. 'Ivory silk,' she said firmly. 'It should be very simple and virginal. No lace and no frills, Emily.'

Mirabel had not thought of the prim dressmaker as anything other than Miss Standish, and hearing her addressed by her Christian name came as something of a shock. Gertie giggled and received a withering look from Zilla. She bowed her head, but her shoulders shook with silent mirth as she turned away to dust the mantelshelf.

'That sounds lovely,' Mirabel said hastily. 'But I can't afford a new gown.'

'Don't be silly child. Your fiancé will foot the bill.' Zilla turned to Miss Standish. 'The best silk, Emily, and she will need new undergarments too. I suggest Swiss lawn with broderie anglaise trimming for the chemise and a silk taffeta petticoat. Will you be able to cope with such a large order?'

'I have an apprentice now, and I have sewing women I can call upon to help me in cases such as this.' Miss Standish shot a sideways glance at Mirabel. 'Some people have exceptional good luck.'

'I'm aware of that,' Mirabel said quickly. 'Mr Kettle is a fine man.'

'They say it's better to be an old man's darling than a young man's slave,' Miss Standish mused. 'I'm not convinced though. My dear Philip was a young Adonis and so very much in love with me. I carry his likeness close to my heart always.' She indicated the heart-shaped silver locket that hung around her neck.

'I'm sure we have all suffered the loss of someone dear to us in the past.' Zilla moved swiftly to the door. 'The wedding is in just under three weeks. Send the bill to Mr Kettle's residence in Savage Gardens. Mabel will be working here until then.'

Miss Standish dropped her notebook into her oversized carpet bag and left the room without a backward glance. Zilla glanced over her shoulder as she followed her into the entrance hall. 'Back to work, you two. You're not married yet, Mabel. No shirking.'

Gertie pulled a face as the door closed on them. 'Blooming slave driver. You're lucky you'll be out of here before Christmas, Mabel.' She slumped down on the sofa. 'I dunno why we can't use your proper name, but after you're wed we can call you Mirabel again, or will it be Mrs Hubert Kettle?'

Mirabel sank down on the sofa beside her. 'It will always be Mirabel to you, Gertie. When I'm settled with Hubert I'll do my best to get you out of here. Maybe you could come and live with us.'

'That's not likely to happen, love. I don't think Mr Kettle would have someone like me living under his roof.'

'I don't see the difference between you and me,' Mirabel said stoutly. 'Misfortune brought us both to Tenter Street.'

'But you don't pay for your bed and board like I do. If only Bodger hadn't jumped ship I might not have ended up like this.'

Mirabel slipped her arm around Gertie's shoulders. 'How would you like to be my bridesmaid? I haven't any family to stand up for me and I won't have anyone to give me away.'

Gertie's eyes filled with tears. 'Oh, that's so sad. You got no pa, and you're marrying a man three times your age. Poor Mabel.'

'I wish my pa was still alive, but I'm quite content to marry Hubert and I don't mind walking up the aisle on my own.'

'You're very brave, but don't you sometimes wish that things was different?'

'I might have done when I was young and romantic, but I daresay falling in love isn't all it's cracked up to be, and I'll get my wish to travel and see the world.' She closed her eyes as Jack's mocking smile invaded her thoughts. 'I'm not lying,' she added in answer to the unspoken question in his cynical grin.

'I never said you was,' Gertie protested. 'And there's someone at the door, Mabel. You'd best answer it.'

'Yes, of course.' Mirabel let herself out of the parlour and went to open the front door.

The young man who stood on the doorstep looked like any one of the hundreds of seamen who thronged the streets close to the docks. His ditty bag was slung over one shoulder and his clothes were shabby and salt-stained. He tipped his cap and his weathered features broke into a cheerful grin. 'Good morning, miss.'

Despite his open features and candid smile he did not look like the type of client Zilla would welcome. Mirabel knew from experience that her employer was very particular about the men she allowed into her establishment, and anyone who might cause trouble would be refused admittance. This young man looked as though he knew how to handle himself in a fight, and, judging by his broken nose, had probably started a few in his time. 'I think you might have come to the wrong place,' Mirabel said carefully, not wanting to cause offence.

'I ain't come for that,' he said hastily. 'I come looking for information.' He set his bag down on the doormat, making it impossible for Mirabel to close the door.

'What sort of information?'

'I've been all round the houses, miss. I went first to Black Dog Alley where I heard she was living, and found her gone. I was told she was took to a toff's house not far away so I went there and got sent off with a flea in me ear by a cove what looked like he swallowed a poker.'

Mirabel's heart sank. There was only one person that could be. 'Was it a house in Catherine Court? And was the man tall and dark with a sallow complexion and a mean face?'

'All true, miss. So you know what I'm talking about. Have I come to the right place at last?'

'I'm not sure,' Mirabel said cautiously. 'What's your name, mister?'

'Roger Tinker, commonly known as Bodger. I'm looking for me sister Gertie.'

'You'd better come in, but please keep your voice down.' Mirabel ushered him in and closed the door. 'How did you know to come here? The man you spoke of didn't direct you here, did he?'

'I'd say not, miss.' He snatched up his bag and followed her inside. 'I'd have been at a loss but for a young maidservant come running up the area steps as I was leaving. She told me I might find out what I wanted from the women what work in the soup kitchen, so I goes there and speaks to a toffee-nosed old bitch who couldn't wait to get rid of me. She sent me here, and here I am.'

'And you're more than welcome.' Mirabel resisted the temptation to hug him. His sudden appearance seemed like a miracle, or a conjuror's trick which had summoned him from nowhere in answer to Gertie's dearest wish. 'I know someone who'll be overjoyed to see you, Bodger. Come with me.' She led the way to the parlour and opened the door. 'Gertie, I've got a surprise for you.' She stood aside as he lumbered into the room, flinging his ditty bag on the floor and opening his arms wide to receive Gertie as she raced into them.

'Bodger, I knew you'd come for me some day.' Laughing and crying she held him at arm's length. 'You bastard, you didn't half give me a fright. I didn't know where you was or what had happened to you.'

'I was stranded in Rio. Spent too long in a game of poker and got to the dock in time to see the ship sailing into the distance.'

'Captain Jack said you'd jumped ship.'

'Not true. It weren't intentional. I'd lost all me money and I had to find another vessel to bring me back home.'

Mirabel could hear voices at the end of the corridor. 'I suggest you find somewhere else to talk,' she whispered. 'I think Zilla is coming this way, and she doesn't encourage us to entertain gentlemen friends or even relations.'

'Not unless they're very rich,' Gertie said, chuckling. 'I don't care what she says. I got me brother back. I can leave here now and we can get a place to live together, can't we, Bodger?'

His smile faded. 'The trouble is I got no money, my duck.'

Gertie faced him like an angry hen who was about to peck him to death. 'You got home didn't you? You must have worked your passage because you ain't got no wings, so you didn't fly like a bird.'

He bent his head, avoiding her gaze. 'I'm sorry, love. I did find a ship, but I didn't get no pay for me labours.'

Gertie flew at him, beating her small fists against his broad chest. 'You fool. Your bloody gambling has ruined us. Where's Captain Jack? He'll take you on again, I know he will.'

Bodger caught her by both wrists, holding her away from him. 'Stop it, Gertie. You'll do yourself a mischief. As to the Cap'n, I'm afraid it's bad news. It's all round the docks that the *Lady Grace* went down in a storm off Havana.'

Chapter Nine

Mirabel escaped from the room. The dire news had literally taken her breath away and she gasped for air as if winded by a sudden fall. From inside she could hear the sound of brother and sister arguing fiercely. What seemed to concern them most was not the loss of the ship and its crew, but the fact that Bodger would have difficulty in convincing another master to take him on.

131

Perhaps it was merely a rumour, or a terrible mistake, Mirabel thought miserably. Jack Starke was a survivor, of that she was certain, and he would not endanger his vessel and the lives of his men by taking foolish risks.

'Mabel.' Zilla's harsh tone brought Mirabel back to the present with a start.

'Yes, Miss Zilla.'

Zilla came towards her clutching a rolled-up newspaper in her hand. 'Don't loiter around as if you have nothing to do. Get on with your work.'

Mirabel was quick to note the pallor of Zilla's cheeks, and unless she was very much mistaken, her hard-bitten employer had been crying. 'Is anything wrong, Miss Zilla?'

'Mind your own business. I want you to tidy my parlour. I can't trust those stupid women to do it without breaking something, or prying into my private affairs. I'm going to lie down for an hour or two.' She thrust the newspaper into Mirabel's hand. 'Use this to light the fire.' She headed for the stairs.

Even though her days in Tenter Street were numbered, Mirabel knew better than to disobey Zilla. She did not open the newspaper until she reached the privacy of the parlour, where she laid it out on the desk and found it to be a copy of *Lloyd's List*, with the loss of the *Lady Grace* featured on the front page. She sat down suddenly as her legs seemed to turn to jelly beneath her, but a hysterical laugh bubbled up in her throat at the thought of how amused Jack would be if he knew that two women were grieving for him. He had come into her life and had left without realising that she was halfway to falling in love with him. How could he have known, when she had barely understood her own feelings? She tore off the offending page and screwed it into a ball, tossing it into the grate. The time for girlish dreams was past, and now she must face the reality of a loveless marriage to a man many years her senior. But Hubert was no ordinary man; he was kind and considerate and expected little in return for taking her from a life of servitude. She made a silent vow to be loyal and to do her best to look after him in his declining years.

It was midmorning but the city was suffused in gloom, and cast-iron clouds were bulging with the threat of snow. As Mirabel left Zilla's house the cold air enveloped her like a shroud, biting through the fine silk of her wedding dress and snapping at her heels like a bad-tempered terrier.

Oblivious to the weather and bubbling with excitement, bridesmaid Gertie did her best to keep the train from trailing in the mud while Bodger helped Mirabel into the waiting hackney carriage. Having seen her settled he turned to his sister. 'In you go, Gertie,' he said, picking her up and tossing her onto the seat opposite Mirabel. 'I'll ride on the box with the cabby. Can't stand being cooped up in small spaces.' He slammed the door.

Gertie rearranged the skirts of her new gown, which had been run up by Miss Standish at the last moment. 'I ain't never had such a lovely frock,' she said happily. 'I feel like a bride meself, although who would want to marry me?'

'Don't be silly,' Mirabel said automatically.

'You'll make someone a wonderful wife one day,' she added hastily, when she realised she had spoken harshly. Even so, she could not help wishing that she could share Gertie's excitement. She had spent a sleepless night and was filled with doubt. What if this was a terrible mistake? Everyone, from Lucky Sue to Lizzie the scullery maid, had warned her not to expect too much from a husband who was old enough to be her grandfather, but Lizzie was a bit simple and Lucky Sue was openly envious, so perhaps they were not the most reliable counsellors. Zilla said little, but she had been tight-lipped and irritable since the loss of the *Lady Grace* became public knowledge. The slightest misdemeanour by any of her girls or the servants was enough to send her into a rage. In the end it was Gertie's enthusiasm for the coming nuptials that eclipsed the doubters, and gave Mirabel the encouragement she needed. She had been touched by Bodger's offer to give her away, and although her initial reaction had been to refuse tactfully, Gertie's eager expression had made such an ungracious act unthinkable. She accepted with as much good grace as she could muster, and Gertie had been ecstatic. Bodger had merely grunted and pointed out that he had nothing suitable to wear. A quick trip round the second-hand clothes shops had procured a black tailcoat, more suitable for an undertaker than a best man, and a pair of pinstripe trousers, which when teamed with a slightly yellowed white shirt made him look like a butler, but he seemed pleased with the result.

'Are you all right, Mabel?' Gertie asked anxiously. 'You're very pale. You ain't going to puke, are you?'

'No, I'm quite all right.'

'I expects you're nervous. I know I would be if I was getting wed today.' Gertie settled back against the worn leather squabs. 'I ain't half looking forward to the wedding breakfast. Your Mr Kettle is a toff to treat us all to a slap-up dinner. He's a lovely man even if he is old.'

'Yes,' Mirabel said slowly. 'He is a lovely man, and I'm very lucky.'

Gertie smiled and lapsed into silence for the rest of the short journey, for which Mirabel was truly grateful.

It was snowing gently when Bodger handed Mirabel out of the cab, with Gertie fussing around her. Inside the church Zilla's girls were huddled together on the pews like a colourful collection of exotic birds. Their garish feathered hats were matched by the lurid hues of their satin gowns, lavishly trimmed with braid, frogging and frills. In complete contrast, Miss Standish sat alone, dressed entirely in black with a veiled bonnet more suitable for a funeral than a wedding.

Zilla occupied the front pew, resplendent in a fur-trimmed purple mantle with a matching hat designed to look like a hussar's shako. Her expression was sombre and she did not smile when she turned her head to give Mirabel an appraising glance.

Hubert stepped forward and through the white mist of her veil she saw him as a grey ghost. His normally pallid face was ashen and his white hair even whiter in the cold light. His eyes were dark pools and she could not read the expression in them even though his lips were fixed in a tentative smile. She shivered, and was tempted to turn and run and keep on running until she was too exhausted to go a step further.

The vicar was saying something, but he might as well have been speaking in a foreign tongue for all the sense she could make of his words. Then Hubert took her hand in his and she was comforted by the warmth of his touch. She found herself making her responses even though she barely understood what she was saying, and then he slipped the ring on her finger. He lifted the veil and kissed her briefly on the lips. She had to steel herself not to recoil at the strong odour of lavender cologne mixed with Macassar oil and the unfamiliar, sour smell of his breath. It was the first time he had made so bold, and it dawned upon her that she was now his to do with as he pleased. It was a sobering thought, but it was too late to change her mind. She recoiled instinctively, but at that moment the heavy church door was flung open, and the creaking, grinding sound echoed throughout the building. Everyone turned to see who had burst into the ceremony uninvited, and Mirabel's hand flew to her mouth when she saw Wiley striding up the aisle.

'Stop,' he cried, waving his arms. With his coat tails flying out behind him, he resembled a crow about to launch itself into flight, and it seemed to Mirabel that he was a bird of ill omen. 'Stop, I say.'

The vicar stepped forward. 'What is the meaning of this, sir? Kindly cease this vulgar display and leave.'

'Vulgar display is it?' Wiley moved closer to Hubert. 'Don't marry this woman. She's tainted by the sins of her father. He was a murderer.' Wiley paused, turning to glare at Zilla's girls, who were chattering amongst themselves. Silenced by a single glance, they stared back at him, eyebrows raised. 'You may look startled, ladies,' he continued. 'This woman has kept the truth from you all. She is the daughter of a man who killed his employer, stole his business and went on to make a fortune from his illgotten gains.'

'Sounds like the ideal plan. Tell us how to do it, mister.' Gentle Jane's mocking laughter echoed off the vaulted ceiling. 'No disrespect meant, Miss Zilla, but the thought has crossed many of our minds afore now.'

Someone tittered and Lucky Sue clapped her hands. Zilla remained unmoved. 'I'm sure the feeling is mutual, Jane,' she said sharply.

'So what are you going to do about it, mate?' Wiley demanded, turning his back on them and leaning towards Hubert with a malicious smile twisting his features.

'Nothing at all, sir. You are talking about my wife's father, who is no longer with us and has gone on to the final judgement. I'll thank you to show a little respect.'

'I'm too late then?' Wiley scowled at Mirabel. 'I haven't done with you yet.' He uttered a strangled cough as Bodger caught him round the throat. 'L-let me g-go.'

'I've a good mind to throttle you here and now,' Bodger muttered through clenched teeth.

137

'I'll have no violence in the house of our Lord,' the vicar said firmly. 'If you intend to carry out your threat I suggest you take this man outside.'

Bodger released Wiley, giving him a shove that sent him sprawling onto the tiled floor. 'You heard the reverend gent. Get out and don't come back, or do you want me to persuade you with me fists?' He shot a sideways glance at the vicar. 'No offence meant, your worship.'

'None taken, my good man, but I'd be grateful if you would remove this fellow. He's frightening the ladies.'

A titter rippled amongst the assembled women and Zilla stood up. 'We'll follow Mr and Mrs Kettle quietly. Remember where you are, ladies.'

'Ladies,' Lucky Sue murmured in a stage whisper. 'That's the first time she's called us that.'

Bodger lifted Wiley by the seat of his trousers and frogmarched him down the aisle. Gertie clapped her hands but subsided beneath a scorching look from Zilla. 'Sorry, miss. I forgot meself.'

Wiley struggled free as they reached the outer door. Turning his head he shook his fist at Mirabel. 'If you try to contest the will you're a goner. I'll have your liver and lights and the old man won't be able to protect you.'

Hubert slipped Mirabel's hand through the crook of his arm. 'Come, my dear, let's leave this wretch to consider his own folly. You are my wife now and you'll be treated with the respect you deserve, or I'll want to know the reason why.'

Outside the snow was falling in earnest. Large feathery flakes swirled and spun like tiny ballerinas in the still air, falling gracefully to the ground and blanketing the pavements in pristine whiteness. Bodger was sent to find cabs to take them to Leadenhall Street, where Hubert had booked a private room at the Ship and Turtle. 'A bowl of their excellent soup will bring the roses back to your cheeks, Mirabel,' he said softly as he handed her into a hackney carriage. He climbed in beside her and sat down, but when the door closed and they were alone together as man and wife she experienced a panicky feeling in her stomach.

She managed a tight little smile. 'That sounds lovely, Hubert.'

He patted her clasped hands, held tightly on her lap. 'You mustn't worry about anything, my dear. From now on it's my duty to look after you and keep you safe from men like Wiley.'

The Ship and Turtle in Leadenhall Street was famous for its turtle soup and fixings. Hubert was obviously well known there and they were welcomed in person by the landlord, Adolphus Painter. Mirabel soon realised that it was Hubert's open-handed generosity that endeared him to the staff as well as his pleasant manner. The food was delicious and with each bottle of wine consumed the pitch of the conversation rose another octave. Bodger munched his way through several helpings of each dish, washing the meal down with several pints of ale, but Gertie was a giggling heap after two glasses of claret and fell asleep over her pudding. Mirabel sat next to Hubert but she had little appetite and only took small sips of wine. If her husband noticed, he was too polite to comment and he chatted easily to Zilla and her girls, taking their teasing with a good-humoured smile even when their advice for the wedding night became too lewd even for Zilla, who silenced them with a frown.

When the last crumb was eaten Hubert rose from his seat, holding up his glass. 'I'd like to propose a toast to my bride, who is more beautiful than the most precious orchid in my collection.' He turned to Mirabel with a tender smile. 'Mirabel.'

Somewhat tipsily the rest of the party stood up and raised their glasses. 'Mirabel.'

'Mrs Kettle,' Zilla said with a wry smile.

Gertie opened her eyes, blinking in the candlelight like a small owl. 'What have I missed?'

Bodger sat down heavily. 'Nothing, my duck. Go back to sleep.'

Hubert remained standing, fixing his gaze on Zilla. 'With your permission, I'd like to take Gertie home with us. I think my wife ought to have a lady's maid and Gertie would seem to be the ideal person.'

Bodger gazed at him bleary-eyed. 'Hold on, mister. I'm her brother and her only relative so you should ask me first.'

Hubert remained unruffled by the interruption. 'And what do you say?'

'I say yes, of course. Anything is better than earning her living flat on her back.' Bodger's flushed face turned a deeper shade of red. 'Begging your pardon, ladies. No offence meant.'

'None taken, dearie,' Gentle Jane said, leaning across the table to expose a deep cleavage. 'It takes a special type of woman to be in our profession.

You're welcome to the little scrap, Mr Kettle sir. She's a bit of an amateur when it comes to knowing what tickles a gent's fancy.'

'Do you really mean it, Hubert?' Mirabel asked anxiously. She had watched her husband drinking glass after glass of claret, although he did not appear to be drunk. It would be too bad to take Gertie away from Tenter Street only to have him change his mind when completely sober.

He held out his hand. 'Of course I do. Mrs Flitton has enough on her hands without extra duties being thrust upon her. She'll enjoy having a young person to boss around.'

Gertie raised her head. 'I don't feel too well, Mabel.'

Mirabel leapt to her feet and with Bodger's help lifted Gertie from the chair. They managed to get her outside into the back yard before she vomited. Bodger wiped his sister's lips on a grubby hanky. 'That'll learn you, Gertrude Tinker. Wine ain't no good for girls your age.' He lifted her in his arms. 'I'll take her outside and hail a cab, Miss – I mean Mrs Kettle. You will look after her for me, won't you? I got to find another ship as quick as possible because I'm broke.'

'Of course, I'll take care of her,' Mirabel said firmly. 'She's my friend.'

Any awkwardness Mirabel might have felt on entering her new home was quickly dispelled by the urgent need to find a bed where Gertie could sleep off the excesses of the wedding feast.

Mrs Flitton pursed her lips and folded her arms across her chest, but when she realised that Gertie

141

was not at all well she turned her disapproving face to her employer. 'What possessed you to allow this child to drink alcohol, Mr Kettle?'

Hubert bowed his head like a schoolboy caught out in a naughty deed by a stern governess. 'I didn't realise that she had imbibed so much wine, Mrs Flitton.'

'Don't worry,' Mirabel said hastily. 'I'll see to her.'

Mrs Flitton raised an eyebrow. 'She's staying here?'

'It's all right, Mrs Flitton.' Hubert gave her an encouraging smile. 'This won't mean more work for you. I've taken the girl on as my wife's maid, and she'll relieve you of some of your more onerous duties.'

'Are you saying that I'm getting too old to run this house, Mr Kettle?'

'No, of course not. You know I didn't mean anything of the sort.'

Mirabel could see that this argument was going to escalate and Gertie was no light weight. She hooked the semiconscious girl's arm around her shoulders. 'Gertie will need your help, Mrs Flitton,' she said tactfully. 'She hasn't had the benefit of training, but she's willing and eager to please. I'm sure she will respond to someone like yourself who is experienced in such matters.'

Mary Flitton puffed out her chest. 'Indeed, ma'am. I have trained such girls in the past, although I'm a little out of practice. There's a small room next to mine. I'll make up the bed, but in the meantime I suggest you put her in the parlour. The sofa is quite comfortable and I can keep an eye on her until she's recovered enough to climb the stairs.'

'An excellent suggestion, Mrs Flitton. I know I can rely on you for a commonsense solution to every problem.' Hubert's relief was palpable as he slipped Gertie's limp hand through the crook of his arm. 'The sofa will do nicely, as Mrs Flitton so wisely says.'

'Thank you, sir.' Mrs Flitton walked towards the staircase with her head held high.

Hubert winked at Mirabel. 'Well done, my dear,' he whispered. 'Mary is a good sort, but get on her wrong side and you're in trouble.'

'I think I've passed the test,' Mirabel said cautiously. She had won a small victory and she hoped that it boded well for the future.

When Gertie was settled comfortably in the parlour Hubert closed the door, facing Mirabel with a satisfied smile. 'She'll be in good hands. Mary will look after her.'

'I'm sure she will.' Mirabel looked round the sombre wainscoted entrance hall with the sudden realisation that this was her new home, and she was overwhelmed by a feeling of being trapped and unable to break free. She clenched her hands beneath the silken folds of her wedding gown, fighting for each breath like a drowning woman. The excitement of the wedding preparations was over and now she must face the reality of living with a man she barely knew. She was no longer a girl; she was a married woman with all that entailed.

Seemingly oblivious to her state of near panic, Hubert laid his hand on her arm. 'I have something to show you, Mirabel.'

'Really?' To her surprise and relief her voice sounded quite normal. 'What is it?'

'Come with me.' He led her towards the baize door at the rear of the entrance hall. 'I'll go first in case you fall. Perhaps I should have allowed you to change into something more suitable, but I can't wait to show you my treasures.' Holding her hand, he led the way to the basement kitchen.

'I hope you don't expect me to cook for you, Hubert,' she said with an attempt at levity. 'It's not one of my accomplishments.'

'Of course not, my dear.' He sounded genuinely horrified and his pale cheeks flushed with embarrassment.

'I was joking,' she said hastily. 'What is it you want me to see?'

He avoided her amused gaze, staring at a point somewhere above her head. 'I'm not very good at seeing the humour in jokes. It was always a cross I had to bear at boarding school, and did little to endear me to my fellow students.'

She slipped her hand through the crook of his arm. 'I'm sorry, Hubert. You must have had a difficult time.'

'I was always a little out of step with the other chaps. Wearing spectacles puts a boy at a disadvantage, especially when sport is an important part of the curriculum, and I'm afraid I was what they called a swot. The fact that I was passionate about botany and collecting wild flowers set me apart from the others. It was not a happy period in my life.' He took a deep breath, forcing his lips into a smile. 'But you will see the result of my

144

lifelong studies now. It's a secret I've been keeping for this moment.' He guided her through the kitchen and the scullery, stepping outside into the small back garden, most of which had been given over to a large conservatory. He opened the door and ushered her inside. The heat and humidity almost took her breath away as did the heady scent emanating from the delicate blooms. The rows of staging were packed with clay pots overflowing with orchids of every shape, size and colour.

'This is where I spend the majority of my time,' Hubert said proudly. 'Each plant has its own special requirements, and I treat them all as individuals. You might say that they are my children, and I love each and every one of them.'

Mirabel hesitated, gazing at him with new insight. 'You haven't been married before, have you, Hubert? We've never discussed such matters and I didn't think to ask.'

'No, my dear. I've rarely met a woman who mattered to me as much as you do. I suppose it might have been nice to have had children, but as I said, my orchids fulfilled my need to nurture and care for living things.'

She moved along the rows, inhaling the fragrance of each individual bloom as she examined them closely. 'They are incredibly beautiful,' she said softly. 'I've never seen anything like it.'

'Really?' His voice shook with emotion. 'Do you mean it, or are you just saying that to please me?'

She looked up in surprise. 'I wouldn't lie about something that you care for so deeply, and I can see now why you are so enthusiastic about these lovely flowers.'

'Flowers,' he repeated, frowning. 'Roses are flowers, daisies and daffodils are flowers; these delicate blooms are far and away superior. You should see them growing in the wild, Mirabel. They inhabit the most inhospitable places and their beauty shines out, taking one's breath away. If it's the last thing I do I want you to see the miracle for yourself.'

'I would love to see them in their natural state,' Mirabel said enthusiastically. 'I've always dreamed of travelling abroad.'

'Men have died in their search for rare specimens, and some have committed murder to further their ends, while others have plundered an area and then destroyed what was left so that their rivals would gain nothing. It seems that the world has gone mad with orchid fever.'

Mirabel gazed at him in surprise. The passion in his voice was matched by the fire in his pale eyes, and his face was flushed, with beads of sweat standing out on his brow. 'Are you all right, Hubert? It is very hot in here. Perhaps we ought to go outside and get some air.'

He shivered as if feeling a sudden cold draught, and the wild look in his eyes faded. 'Of course, my dear. You are unused to these temperatures. We will go indoors.'

'I'm quite all right,' she protested. 'I would like to hear more about your collection.'

'Later, perhaps.' Like a man exhausted by an overwhelming burst of emotion, he moved slowly to the door and opened it. 'Hurry, my dear. We mustn't allow a sudden drop in temperature.'

She stepped outside, taking deep breaths of the

146

icy air. It had stopped snowing and darkness was already overtaking the city. Pinpricks of starlight pierced the indigo sky and frost particles sparkled on the surface of the fallen snow. Mirabel felt the cold strike up through her satin slippers and she wrapped her arms around her body in an attempt to keep warm as she hurried into the house. Hubert followed more slowly, having taken time to check the fire in the boiler house which heated the conservatory.

Mrs Flitton looked up when Mirabel entered the kitchen. 'I thought he wouldn't be able to keep his little darlings a secret much longer,' she said, smiling. 'You'll get used to it, ma'am.' She slapped a pastry lid onto the pie dish. 'Those plants come first above everything else.'

'I'd better check on Gertie.' Mirabel headed for the staircase. 'And I need to change out of my gown.' She hesitated, conscious that she was blushing. 'I – I don't know which room is mine.'

Mrs Flitton wiped her floury hands on her apron with a barely suppressed sigh. 'I'll show you the way, ma'am.'

'It's all right, Mary.' Hubert strolled into the kitchen. 'I'll show my wife to our room.' He crossed the floor swiftly and led the way up the narrow staircase.

Their tacit agreement that she would have her own room seemed to have been forgotten. Mirabel picked up her skirts, following him as fast as her long train would allow. 'Wait a minute,' she said breathlessly when they reached the main staircase. 'I thought I was to have my own room, Hubert.'

With one foot on the bottom step he turned his head slowly. 'Did you really? Come along, my dear, you'll need to change for dinner.'

Chapter Ten

Mirabel hurried after him. She was angry now, and anxious. She was not afraid of Hubert, but she knew that as a married woman she was bound to obey her husband in everything, including the rites of the marriage bed. He had promised, she told herself as she negotiated the steep stairs; he had said that he would not expect anything of her in the physical sense, and now he seemed to have gone back on his word. She caught up with him as he opened the door of a room on the second floor, directly above the drawing room.

'Come in, my dear.' He stood aside. 'This is our bedchamber.'

'You promised, Hubert. You gave me your word that you did not expect anything other than companionship and mutual respect from this liaison.'

'Won't you take a look?' A grim smile curved his lips, but there was no spark of humour in his eyes.

She peered over his shoulder. The room, lit by a brass oil lamp with a cranberry glass shade, was uncompromisingly masculine, with cumbersome mahogany furniture, a four-poster bed with a tapestry tester and curtains in sombre autumnal colours which might once have been vibrant but were now faded to almost nothing. The polished floorboards gleamed with a rich chestnut sheen and the occasional Persian rug provided islands of subdued colour, but it was a man's room with no hint of femininity. 'You promised me,' she repeated dully. 'I thought you were a man of honour.'

'I was teasing you,' he said, raising a smile and puffing out his chest. 'It's a joke, Mirabel.'

'A joke?' She stared at him incredulously. 'You call this a joke?'

'It's the sort of joke they played on a fellow at school, only then it had nothing to do with the marriage bed, I need hardly add.' His expression darkened. 'I thought you would find it funny. I wanted to prove that I have a lighter side to my nature and that I understand humour.'

Relief gave way to anger and she realised that she was shaking from head to foot. 'You don't understand anything, Hubert. This is not the least bit funny, and now Mrs Flitton thinks that you will be sharing your bed with a woman young enough to be your granddaughter.'

'That's unkind, my dear.'

'No, Hubert, it's the truth.'

'I know, but it hurts my pride.'

'I'm sorry, but we had an agreement.'

He hung his head. 'You're right, of course, and I doubt if I could honour my duties as a husband even if I felt so inclined. I thought if I could make you laugh you might feel more at home. I know this is a big change for you.'

'It is, but I promise I'll do my best to be a good wife to you in every other way.'

149

'Thank you, my dear. I know you will.' His shoulders sagged and he stared down at his feet, as if inspecting the polish on his shiny shoes.

'And I love the orchids,' she added in an attempt to raise his spirits. 'I want to learn everything I can about them.'

He looked up, meeting her gaze with an eager smile. 'Do you mean it? You're not just saying that?'

'I'm fascinated by everything I've seen, and if you should decide to make a trip abroad to find more I'll gladly go with you.'

'Thank you, Mirabel.'

There was no doubting his sincerity and she felt ashamed of thinking ill of him, but she was cold and a draught was whistling up the stairs like an angry spirit out to cause havoc amongst the living. 'Now, do you think I could see my room?' she said, hugging her arms around her body. 'I'm freezing to death in this thin gown.'

'You are my prize orchid, Mirabel,' he said earnestly. 'I'll take good care of you and I promise never to try to be funny again.'

Touched by his desire to please her, she laid her hand on his arm. 'You don't have to prove anything to me.'

Picking up the lamp, he moved quickly to open the door to the room a little further along the landing. 'Your room is next to mine. Mrs Flitton made it ready for you. She understands our arrangement so you have no need to feel embarrassed. I hope this meets with your approval.'

Mirabel entered the candlelit room, her breath catching on a gasp of surprise and delight. In complete contrast to her husband's bedchamber hers was as feminine as she could have wished. Despite the fact that the curtains had been drawn and a fire blazed in the grate, it was like walking into eternal summertime. The wallpaper was patterned with a tracery of rosebuds, pinks and cornflowers garlanded and adorned with blue ribbons. The theme was repeated in the curtain material, the cushions on a velvet-covered chaise longue and the coverlet on the rococo eighteenth-century French bed. The dressing table and clothes press were of the same period, and vases spilling over with hothouse flowers filled the warm air with their sweet scent. Her feet sank into the thick Aubusson carpet and she turned to Hubert with a bemused smile. 'I – I don't know what to say.'

'Do you like it, Mirabel?' he asked eagerly. 'I've had expert advice on furnishing a room fit for a lady, but if it's not to your taste...?'

'Oh, it is. It's perfect and I love everything in it. I'm not used to this sort of luxury.'

He frowned. 'Your father was a rich man and you were his only child.'

'I didn't want for anything, if that's what you mean, Hubert. But Pa didn't believe in spoiling anyone, at least not until he married that awful woman. She saw to it that I was put firmly in my place.'

'Well, this is your place now, my dear. You are my wife and will be treated as such by all and sundry. Our private arrangements are nobody's business but ours.' He backed towards his own room. 'I'll see you at dinner, Mrs Kettle.'

That night, after a tasty meal served by Mrs Flitton, and a pleasant evening sitting by the fire listening to Hubert's accounts of his travels, Mirabel slept in state feeling like a queen. She awoke next morning to the sound of someone raking the ashes in the grate. For a moment she thought she was back in the small attic room in Tenter Street, but the softness of the feather mattress and the crispness of the Egyptian cotton sheets reminded her that she was now a married woman, lying in her own bed in a room more luxurious than she could ever have imagined. She raised herself on her elbow, peering into the semi-darkness. 'Who's there?'

A small figure scrambled to her feet, adjusting the mobcap which had fallen over one eye as she worked. 'Good morning, ma'am. I'm sorry I never meant to wake you.'

'What time is it?'

'Gone six o'clock, ma'am. I'm a bit late starting but I'll get the fire going in a minute and then I'll bring you your hot water and a nice cup of tea.' The girl, who could not have been more than ten or eleven, wiped her nose on the back of her hand. Even in the poor light Mirabel could see the smudge of soot on the child's cheek. She sat up and swung her legs over the side of the bed. 'What's your name?'

'Tilda, ma'am. I comes in every morning to do the fires and put out the slops for the night soil collector.'

'But you don't live in?'

'No, ma'am. I lives in Black Raven Court with me Pa. Ma died last year and now there's ten of us living in one room, so I gets work when and wherever I can.'

'And your pa? Does he work too?'

Tilda squared her small shoulders. 'He works on the docks, but he's got the rheumatics something chronic and it's worse in winter, so all of us what's old enough to earn a penny or two has to help out.'

'I see.' Mirabel reached for her wrap. 'So you've eight brothers and sisters, is that right?'

'That's right.' Tilda shifted from one foot to the other. 'There was ten of us until last month when baby Joe was took.'

'He was taken from you?'

'Died from whooping cough, ma'am. Went to heaven to join Ma.' Tilda went down on her knees and proceeded to light the fire.

Despite the relative warmth of the room Mirabel felt a cold shiver run down her spine. 'I'm so sorry.'

'Pa said it's one less mouth to feed.' Tilda glanced up at her with a wry grin. 'But he didn't mean it. Pa does his best to make us feel better, but I seen him crying at night when he thinks we're all asleep.' She leaned over to blow on the flames and soon had them licking round the kindling.

Mirabel put on her wrap, watching Tilda as she worked. Life was unfair, she had learned that long ago, but this poor child with her scrawny arms and legs and the face of an old woman was a victim of poverty and ignorance. 'The fire has caught well,' she said, tying the satin sash around her trim waist. 'I'll come downstairs with you, Tilda.'

'Why, ma'am? Are you going to tell her in the kitchen that I was spouting off about me family? Please don't. I'll get a clip round the lughole and she won't want me no more.'

'Nobody is going to harm you in any way. This is my house and Mrs Flitton will do as I ask.' Mirabel stuffed her feet into the slippers that Zilla had handed down to her. She knew what it was like to be poor, but she had never suffered such abject poverty as the frail girl standing before her now.

'But Mrs Kettle, the child is too small and puny to do a full day's work,' Mrs Flitton protested, glowering at Tilda who was seated at the kitchen table making short work of a bowl of porridge.

'All she needs is good food and some warm clothing,' Mirabel said calmly. 'She's barefoot and it's snowing again.'

'That's how the poor live, madam.' Mrs Flitton lowered her voice to a whisper. 'I pay her a penny a day to come in and see to the fires and do other jobs that I don't have time for.'

'I know what she does, but a penny a day is not nearly enough. Do you know what her home conditions are like?'

Mrs Flitton drew herself up to her full height. 'It's none of my business, Mrs Kettle. The girl came to me on the recommendation of the verger who had recently made arrangements for the latest Coker infant to be interred.'

Mirabel thought for a moment, staring at Tilda's bent head as she shovelled food into her mouth. 'What time does Mr Kettle take break-fast, Mrs Flitton?' Even as the words left her lips she realised that it must seem like an odd question, but then she was a newly wed wife and unlikely to have acquired such knowledge. She met Mrs Flitton's blank stare with a steady look.

'Nine o'clock sharp, madam. The master likes to have his meals punctual to the stroke of the hour, and that goes for luncheon at one o'clock and dinner at eight. Will you be making any changes?'

'No. That sounds quite satisfactory.' Mirabel glanced at the clock on the mantelshelf. 'It's only half past six so I'll have plenty of time. I want you to pack a basket with as much food as you can spare.'

Mrs Flitton's eyes opened wide and her raised eyebrows disappeared beneath the goffered frill of her white mobcap. 'A basket, madam? For a picnic, in this weather?'

'Certainly not. I intend to take it to Black Raven Court. Tilda may finish her breakfast and then I want her to show me the way.'

'But she hasn't completed all her tasks yet, Mrs Kettle. She has to riddle the ashes and fetch water for the boiler, and I don't know what else, but I'll think of something.'

'All for a penny a day.' Mirabel shook her head. 'I don't think that's a fair wage. I'll be putting it up to threepence a day, and her breakfast will be included, as well as her midday meal if she needs to stay on longer.'

Tilda raised her head, swallowing a mouthful of porridge. 'Are you talking about me, missis?'

'Eat up. I'm taking you home. Will your pa be there at this time of day?'

'I daresay he will. It all depends if there's work

155

for him or not.'

'I have a pair of boots that might do for you. They'll probably be too big, but anything is better than going barefoot in the snow. Wait here, Tilda. I'm going to get dressed.' She moved towards the stairs, pausing to look over her shoulder. 'Don't worry, Mrs Flitton. I'll be back in time to take breakfast with my husband.'

Mirabel approached the building in Black Raven Court with some trepidation. Even with the softening effect of the newly fallen snow, it was a sinister place; narrow, dark and dirty. Barefoot boys pelted each other with snowballs and the prostrate body of a ragged beggar blocked a pub doorway. Whether he was dead or dead drunk was a matter of concern for the landlord, and Mirabel walked by, following Tilda who skipped ahead in her newly acquired boots. They were at least two sizes too large for her but Mirabel had found an old pair of woollen stockings, which she had insisted that Tilda must have, and with the addition of some carefully folded newspaper in place of insoles, the boots were now a reasonable fit. Tilda stopped, waiting for Mirabel to catch up with her. She pointed to the basement area. 'We got a room down there, but the steps is a bit rotten so you have to tread careful like.'

'Lead on,' Mirabel said with more confidence than she was feeling. A bitter wind had risen from the east, whipping the soft snow into eddies and causing small avalanches to slide off roofs. She trod carefully, holding up her long skirts and making sure she kept to the inside of the steps where the wood was less worn. Tilda jumped the last few, landing catlike on the snow. She opened the door, allowing a gust of putrid air to billow out in a suffocating cloud. Mirabel's hand flew to cover her mouth and nose. She had grown up with the stench from the river at low tide and overflowing sewers, but there was a sickly odour of death and decay, like gangrenous flesh, emanating from the basement. Tilda marched in, seemingly inured to the terrible smell and the lack of light below street level. Mirabel hesitated in the doorway, fighting down a feeling of nausea, but Tilda was calling to her and she stepped inside, holding her nose and breathing through her mouth in an attempt to escape the worst of the foul smell.

The room occupied by Tilda's family was small, dank and airless. Mirabel could feel the cold striking up through the flagstone floor, and although there was a small fireplace there was no fire to warm the hapless occupants. Small children leapt to their feet and threw themselves at Tilda, clinging to her like burrs on a dog's coat, and in the light of a single candle Mirabel could see the shape of a man, lying on a pallet. He peered at them through the gloom. 'Is that you, Tilda?'

Disentangling herself from her siblings, Tilda moved swiftly to his side. 'Yes, Pa.'

He raised himself on his elbow, peering at Mirabel. 'Who's that with you?'

'It's Mrs Kettle, Pa. She's been ever so kind to me, and she's brought food for you and the little 'uns.'

He sat up. 'What does she want here?'

'I can speak for myself, Mr Coker.' Mirabel set

the basket down on the table, which seemed to be the only piece of furniture in the room, apart from a couple of rickety-looking chairs.

He rose unsteadily to his feet. 'I don't want charity from the likes of you, missis. You can take your basket and toss it in the Thames for all I care. I can provide for my family.'

Mirabel could see shades of her father's stubborn pride in this ungainly man, whose sinewy arms hung limp at his sides; his hollow eyes and sunken cheeks a testament to his suffering. 'I didn't mean to offend you,' she said softly. 'You could say that this is in lieu of the wages Tilda should have received for her hard work. Things will be different from now on.'

He glared at her, as if studying every line and contour of her face. 'You're the young wife then? Married him for his money, did you?'

'You can insult me all you like, but I'll put it down to the pain you must be enduring.' She glanced at the children who were huddled together, the younger ones clinging to Tilda and sucking their thumbs.

Tilda put her arms around them, gathering them up like a small mother hen protecting her chicks. 'The nippers are starving, Pa. It's a sin to waste good food.'

Mirabel saw a flicker of doubt in Coker's eyes and she held out her hand. 'I'm Mirabel,' she said softly. 'Tilda will be paid a proper wage in future. That's a promise.'

Reluctantly he shook her hand. 'Alf Coker.'

She smiled. 'I really didn't mean to offend you, Alf.'

'I'm a proud man, missis. I used to earn a good wage on the docks until the rheumatics caused me to lose work. But we ain't paupers. My boys are mudlarks and they're out now, even in this weather.'

'It ain't easy for them if the mud is frozen.' Tilda looked up from unpacking the basket. 'I'll save some of this for them.' She eyed the younger children who had gathered around, watching eagerly. 'No grabbing, d'you hear me? This has got to go round everyone.'

'I ain't hungry,' Alf said hastily. 'Never mind me.'

'You'll have some anyway,' Tilda told him firmly. 'You got to keep your strength up.'

Mirabel could see that Tilda had her father and the children well in hand, and she hid a smile. What Tilda lacked in size and age she made up for with determination and courage. 'I'll leave now, but if there's anything I can do to help, please don't be afraid to ask.'

'You mean well, missis. But you don't belong here and it ain't safe for the likes of you to wander round on your own.'

'I grew up round here and I know how to take care of myself.' Mirabel made for the door, pausing as she lifted the latch. 'If I hear of any jobs that might suit and were not as rigorous as working outside on the docks, would you be interested?'

'You mean well, no doubt, but I can manage on me own, missis.'

'He'd be very interested, ma'am,' Tilda said firmly.

'I'll see you tomorrow morning, Tilda. Good day to you, Alf.' With a smile encompassing the smaller

159

children, who were busy munching bread and scrape, Mirabel made her escape from the dire surroundings, holding her breath until she was outside in the alley. She set off for home, quickening her pace as she marched through a crowd of slatternly women standing on the street corner. One of them spat at her.

'You're no better than the rest of us, ducky.'

Mirabel walked on, head held high. They were right, of course. Not so long ago she herself had been destitute, and if Zilla had not taken her in she might well have ended up selling her body to pay for a night's lodging in a flea-ridden doss.

She arrived home just in time to join her husband for breakfast.

Hubert was already seated at the table and he rose politely when she entered the room. 'Mary tells me that you took the little skivvy home.' He frowned. 'I don't like the thought of you wandering around the back streets unaccompanied, my dear.'

His unconscious repetition of Alf Coker's words made her want to laugh, but she kept a straight face. 'Thank you, Hubert, but I'm quite capable of looking after myself.' She took her seat at the place laid for her at the foot of the table, although it would have been easier and more comfortable to sit beside Hubert. She filled a dainty bone-china cup with coffee from the silver pot. 'I hope you don't mind that I took some food for the family. I saw for myself that they are only just surviving in dire conditions.'

'We employ the child. We cannot be responsible for the whole family.'

'She was getting a penny a day for doing heavy work which should be done by someone older and stronger. I told Mrs Flitton to give her threepence a day, and I'm not sure that's enough.'

'I'd say it's more than generous, but if that's what you want then the child will be paid threepence a day.' He glanced at Mirabel's empty plate. 'Now you must eat. I can recommend the kedgeree; it's one of my favourites. They served it in the officers' mess when I was in India.'

'You've led such an interesting life, Hubert.' Mirabel rose from her place and went to serve herself from one of the silver entrée dishes on the sideboard. She lifted the lid of a breakfast warmer containing bacon, kidneys and mushrooms. Buttered eggs were in another and in the third was spicy kedgeree. She had been brought up to live well, but this array of food for two people seemed gluttonous and downright wrong. A vision of the Coker children eating bread and scrape and thinking it a luxury robbed her of her appetite. She sat down to eat, toying with the delicious dish of rice, haddock, soft-boiled eggs and spices, but her stomach rebelled and she had to force herself to swallow.

Hubert looked up from reading his copy of *The Times* and frown lines puckered his brow. 'Don't you like it?'

'It's delicious, but I keep thinking of those poor hungry children. Their father is a stevedore, but he's not well enough to work.'

Hubert lowered the newspaper, peering at her over the top of his tortoiseshell spectacles. 'I'm sure he could find something if he tried hard enough. You mustn't believe everything these people tell you, my dear. They can spot a soft-hearted person and will use all their wiles to extract monies, which will probably be spent on drink or in an opium den.'

She could see that it was useless to argue and she did her best to finish her breakfast, hiding the last mound of rice beneath her fish eaters. She sipped her coffee, but her thoughts were still with the unfortunate family in their unheated basement room. She looked up as the door opened and Mrs Flitton entered with Gertie following close behind.

'This young person has an apology to make, Mr Kettle.' Mrs Flitton stood arms akimbo, staring hard at Gertie who was blushing furiously. 'Go on, girl. Speak up.'

Gertie bobbed a curtsey. 'I apologise for my behaviour yesterday, sir and madam. I hope you will forgive me, but I ain't used to drinking.'

'Is this really necessary, Mrs Flitton?' Mirabel protested angrily. 'Gertie was hardly to blame and it was a special celebration.'

'A servant has to know how to behave, ma'am.'

Hubert folded his newspaper slowly and carefully. 'I think we can overlook her behaviour this once, Mary. You will teach by example, and I'm sure that Gertie could have no better tutor than you.'

'Well, sir, that's very kind of you to say so. Back to the kitchen, my girl.'

Mirabel rose swiftly to her feet. 'I'm sure she will benefit greatly from your experience, Mrs Flitton, but as she will be my personal maid I would like to

162

spend some time showing her what I require.'

'Of course, ma'am.' Mrs Flitton nodded her head and marched out of the room.

Gertie's bottom lip trembled ominously. 'Th-thank you, ma'am.'

'If you'll excuse me, Hubert?' Mirabel moved to Gertie's side, the Coker family momentarily forgotten.

'Of course, my dear. I thought that we could spend time together later. There is so much more that I would like to show you regarding my collection.'

'That would be lovely.' Mirabel hurried Gertie out of the room.

'What do you want me to do, ma'am?' Gertie asked nervously.

'You can stop calling me ma'am when we're on our own. I prefer Mabel if that makes you feel more comfortable.'

'Oh, you are a one,' Gertie said, chuckling. 'What would his nibs say if he could hear you talking like that?'

'Never mind. We'll go to my room and you can help me sort out my things, although heaven knows I haven't got much. I think Miss Standish is needed because I must have something more comfortable to wear if I'm going to be working with my husband's plants. Silks and satins don't go with watering cans and the like.'

They hurried upstairs, giggling like a pair of naughty schoolgirls. Mirabel threw open the door of her room and ushered Gertie in. 'What do you think of this?'

Gertie's eyes widened and her mouth dropped

163

open. 'Blimey, you ain't half done well for yourself, Mabel. He's treating you like a queen.'

Mirabel pulled a face. 'I know, and I really appreciate it, but I took the little skivvy home today and saw the terrible poverty she has to suffer. It doesn't seem fair.'

Gertie slipped her arm around Mirabel's shoulders and gave her a hug. 'I suppose I shouldn't do this now you're a toff's wife, but you got a big heart. I was poor like that and you saved me, but you can't save the world, Mabel. No one can.'

'I suppose not, but you'll meet Tilda tomorrow and you'll feel the same as I do.' Mirabel moved to where the carpet bag containing her clothes had been left. 'I was too tired to unpack last night.'

Gertie rushed to her side. 'That's my job, my lady. Sit down and look beautiful while I do what I'm supposed to. I learned a lot from the girls in Tenter Street.' She shot a mischievous look in Mirabel's direction. 'And not what you think. They taught me how to keep clothes nice and how to get stains out of silk and all sorts. I bet I could teach old Flitton a thing or two.'

Mirabel sat down at the dressing table and watched while Gertie busied herself with the unpacking. She had just about done when someone knocked on the door.

'Come in.' Mirabel turned her head to see Mrs Flitton standing in the doorway.

'You have a visitor, Mrs Kettle. A lady called Mrs Hamilton is waiting in the morning parlour.'

Chapter Eleven

Adela Hamilton had her back to the door and was examining a framed daguerreotype she had taken from a drum table by the window.

'Good morning, Mrs Hamilton.'

Adela turned with a start but recovered quickly. 'Good morning, Mrs Kettle.' She replaced the photograph and advanced on Mirabel with a fixed smile. 'I came to offer my felicitations on your recent marriage.'

Mirabel remembered their last encounter only too well. 'How kind of you, ma'am. I know how busy you are.'

'Indeed I am, and that's partly why I'm here.'

'Won't you take a seat, Mrs Hamilton? May I offer you some refreshment?'

Adela moved gracefully to the sofa and sat down, spreading her skirts around her. 'No, thank you. I won't take up too much of your valuable time and I'll come straight to the point, my dear. Your husband is a well-known benefactor of many charities, and we would consider it an honour if you would spare some time to help out in the soup kitchen.'

'I seem to recall that when I last offered my services I was rejected out of hand.'

'That was a dreadful error on my part, for which I fully apologise.' Adela's momentary look of discomfort was replaced by a confident smile. 'I can assure you that your presence would be more than welcome.'

'But I'm still the same person I was then,' Mirabel insisted. 'The only difference is that I'm married to a wealthy man.'

'You are now a respectable married woman. You must realise that we have to be very careful whom we select to work for our charity.' Adela's small eyes narrowed and a muscle in her jaw twitched.

'I don't think the unfortunates who are starving on the streets care who fills their bowls with soup.'

'Then you'll join us?'

'No. Thank you for your offer, but I'm afraid it's come too late.'

Adela's jaw dropped and she rose to her feet in a flurry of silk petticoats. 'There's no need to take that tone with me, Mrs Kettle.'

'There was no need for you to refuse my help in such an insulting manner just because I was down on my luck. However, I will ask my husband to make a donation to your fund, and you can find someone else to peel potatoes and carrots.'

A whole range of emotions flitted across Adela Hamilton's face. 'I'll take my leave then.' She made a move towards the door, stopping to turn her head with a spiteful sneer. 'And I wish you joy of a marriage to an elderly gentleman. If I were not a lady I would say that you are little better than an adventuress.' She wrenched the door open and swept out of the room.

Forgetting that she was a lady, Mirabel poked her tongue out, and was instantly ashamed of the childish gesture more suited to Charity or Prudence Mutton than to Mrs Hubert Kettle. She went over to the table and picked up the daguerreotype which had caught Adela's eye, and found herself staring down at the faded sepia image of a beautiful young Indian woman. It seemed odd that she had not noticed it before, but Adela had been quick to spot the exotic beauty, and was more than likely to have assumed the worst. She would undoubtedly take great pleasure in entertaining her society friends with the story of Hubert Kettle's involvement with a native woman. The large doe-eyes stared back at Mirabel from behind the glass, and she found herself consumed with curiosity. Slipping the frame into her pocket, she went in search of her husband.

She found him, as she had expected, in the conservatory. He was intent on his task and appeared to be painting the exquisite face of an orchid. 'What are you doing, Hubert?'

He turned his head to give her a brief smile. 'I'm pollinating,' he said calmly. 'There are no insects to do this for me at this time of year. It's a trick I learned from my friend Frederick Sander. You've heard of him, no doubt?'

'No, I'm afraid not.'

'He's an orchidologist and nurseryman with premises in St Albans and I've been dealing with him for many years. I've purchased most of my best specimens from him.'

'That's very interesting, Hubert.' She hesitated, taking the daguerreotype from her pocket. Why, she wondered, had he never mentioned the young woman? She must have meant a great deal to him or he would not have treasured her portrait. 'I've

167

just had a visit from Adela Hamilton,' she said tentatively.

'Really?' He did not sound particularly interested. He went back to his task with an intense look of concentration, biting his lip as he performed the delicate operation.

She tried again. 'Mrs Hamilton wanted me to return to the soup kitchen to help them.'

'Did she, my dear?'

'I said no, because I...' She faltered. It seemed childish to say that she refused out of pique. 'Anyway, I thought I'd be too busy helping you, but I said you might give them a donation.'

'Of course. It's a good cause.'

'And she was studying this portrait when I found her in the parlour.' She held it in front of his nose. 'Who is she?'

He stopped what he was doing to take the frame from her. 'Anjuli,' he murmured, gazing down at the faded image. 'I'm sorry, Mirabel. I should have packed this away with the rest of the mementoes of my time in India.'

'Who is she?' Mirabel repeated, sensing a romance, which she found oddly touching.

'She was a high-born lady.' He hesitated as if struggling to find the right words to describe something that obviously meant a great deal to him. 'It was a long time ago.'

'She's beautiful. How did you come to know her?'

'I was stationed in Delhi. We met at a ball in the British Consulate and we fell in love. It was as simple as that.'

Mirabel put her head on one side, eyeing him

curiously. 'It's never as simple as that, Hubert.'

'No,' he said slowly. 'It was an unlikely match. She was just twenty and I was forty-four: a confirmed bachelor, or so I thought. But the moment I saw her I knew I was lost, and for some reason I've never been able to understand, she felt the same.'

'That's very romantic. What happened?'

'The mutiny,' he said simply. 'We all knew that trouble was brewing, but the suddenness of the violence still took us by surprise.'

'So your love affair ended?'

'Her father forbade her to have anything to do with me, and I can't say I blame him. But Anjuli had a mind of her own.' A smile softened his expression and his eyes misted with tears. 'I only discovered afterwards, from her ayah, that Anjuli had defied her father and had slipped out of the palace one night to warn me of impending danger. She was caught up in a skirmish between sepoys and British soldiers and killed by a single shot.' He took a handkerchief from his breast pocket and wiped his eyes. 'I'm sorry, my dear. I should have told you all this before, but it was so long ago. I thought I had buried the past in my heart, but it still hurts.'

She laid her hand on his arm. 'Don't apologise, Hubert. I understand, and I'm so sorry. She must have been a wonderful woman.'

He nodded his head. 'You reminded me of her from the first moment I saw you in Tenter Street.'

'I'm flattered, but I'm not Anjuli.'

'Of course not, and I respect you for who you are, Mirabel. I count myself very fortunate to have persuaded you to be the companion of my declining years, but I owe you an apology for not telling you the whole truth.'

'There's no need. We had an agreement and I'm prepared to honour it. You've given me a home and the protection of your good name, although according to Mrs Hamilton I'm an adventuress who married you for your money.'

'We both know that's untrue.'

'It's what everyone will think, and I'm afraid I've made an enemy of Mrs Hamilton by refusing to help in the soup kitchen.'

'Don't worry, my dear girl. I'll silence her with a generous donation to her cause.'

'I don't care what anyone says, I'm determined to make you a good wife.'

'You're a very special young woman, and I will do everything in my power to make you happy.' Hubert slipped the daguerreotype into his jacket pocket. 'I'll put this away where it belongs.'

'No, don't do that.' She shook her head. 'Let it remain where you can still see it. I'm not jealous of a ghost.' She picked up the paintbrush. 'Will you teach me how to pollinate these beautiful blooms?'

Hubert's eyes shone with enthusiasm. 'Do you mean it?'

'Of course I do.'

'It's very delicate work, but if you're really interested I'd be more than happy to teach you everything I know.' He stared at her as if seeing her for the first time. 'I never expected anything like this from you, Mirabel. It's very exciting.' He frowned, peering at a thermometer set on small marble obelisk. 'The temperature is dropping. I must stoke the fire in the boiler house.'

'How often do you have to do that?' Mirabel asked as a sudden thought occurred to her. 'It must entail a lot of effort.'

'It does, I'm afraid.' Hubert reached for his jacket and shrugged it on. 'Particularly in this freezing weather, but I can't allow the temperature to fall too low or my precious orchids will die.'

'Why don't you employ a man to do the work for you, Hubert?'

He frowned. 'I suppose I could. I've never considered it before because my whole life has centred around my collection. It would have to be someone trustworthy and completely reliable.'

'I think I might know the ideal person,' Mirabel said, smiling.

Alf Coker was sitting at the table holding his head in his hands. 'Shut the bloody door, Tilda,' he snapped without looking up. 'It's cold enough in here without you letting in the draught.'

'Pa, I ain't alone.' Tilda glanced anxiously at Mirabel who was standing in the doorway. 'He's not always like this, missis.'

'You call her Mrs Kettle or ma'am,' Gertie hissed, giving Tilda a shove so that she stumbled, almost tripping over her youngest sister who was sitting on the floor gnawing a bone more suitable for a dog than a toddler.

Alf rose to his feet. 'Why did you bring her here again, Tilda? Ain't it bad enough we has to live like rats in a sewer without being the object of pity, dependent on the charity of others?'

Mirabel had come empty handed. Her first instinct had been to bring food for the children, but she remembered Alf Coker's previous reaction and she realised that he was a proud man. She faced him with a steady look. 'Good morning, Mr Coker. I'm sorry to intrude, but I was wondering if you could help me.'

'Me? Help you?'

'Yes, that's what I said. I find myself in a difficult position and you would seem to be the ideal person to assist me.'

He dusted off the chair with a scrap of soiled towelling. 'Won't you take a seat, missis?'

'Thank you.' She was about to sit down when the child on the floor started to choke.

'Oh Lord, she's got a bit of bone stuck in her throat,' Tilda wailed.

Mirabel scooped the little one up in her arms and put her finger into the toddler's mouth, feeling for the object that was causing her to turn blue in the face. She hooked out a large piece of gristle and the choking stopped, but was replaced by a loud howl. Mirabel sat down, holding the baby close and rocking her in her arms. 'There, there. It's all right.'

Alf wiped beads of sweat from his forehead with a swipe of his hand. 'I thought she was a goner.'

Tilda snatched up the bone. 'She shouldn't have had this, Pa. It's only fit for the glue factory, not for a little 'un like Kitty.'

'She's teething,' Alf protested. 'What am I supposed to do?'

Mirabel handed the sobbing child to Tilda. 'Mr Coker, I have a proposition to put to you.'

His anxious gaze was fixed on his youngest

child, but he flicked a curious glance in Mirabel's direction. 'What would the likes of you want with the likes of me?'

'My husband grows exotic orchids. He needs help to stoke the boiler and keep the glasshouse at the right temperature.'

'Why me, missis? You ain't short of a bob or two, I can see that. I got rheumatics something chronic and there's a limit to what I can do.'

'It's time-consuming but it's not like the heavy work you must have done on the docks. My husband is not a young man. He would pay you a fair wage.'

'Take it, Pa,' Tilda urged. 'Mr Kettle is all right, and he's very old.' She shot an apologetic look at Mirabel. 'Begging your pardon, ma'am, but it's true. His hair is as white as the snow afore it gets trod underfoot.'

'I ain't one to take charity,' Alf said stubbornly.

Mirabel stood up. 'I'm not offering you the work out of pity, Mr Coker. Take it or leave it, but I suggest you think it over carefully. If you want the job come tomorrow morning with Tilda and you'll be shown what to do.'

Tilda nodded her head. 'Jane can look after the little 'uns until I get home, Pa.' She handed the baby to her sister, who had been listening wide-eyed to the conversation.

'I can do it, Pa,' Jane said, nodding fiercely. 'Maybe the lady will bring us a basket of food again. I'm hungry.'

'Me too.' The two younger girls took their thumbs from their mouths to add their voices, and immediately plugged them in again.

'All right,' Alf said grudgingly. 'But I don't expect something for nothing. I'll do a day's labour for a day's wage.'

'I'm sure you will.' Mirabel opened her reticule and took out her purse. She placed a florin on the table. 'An advance on your wages, Mr Coker.' She made a move towards the doorway but Gertie was already there and had opened it wide. 'Good day to you,' Mirabel added, smiling. 'I'll see you and Tilda tomorrow.'

Outside in the street, Gertie turned to Mirabel with a frown. 'Are you sure you're doing the right thing? He looks like a rough type to me.'

'Everyone deserves a chance, and he's got all those small children to bring up. I'm sure Hubert will agree that he should be helped.'

Next morning Mirabel rose early, dressed and went down to the conservatory. It was still dark but light from several paraffin lamps spilled out of the windows and she could see Hubert already hard at work. She let herself in, closing the door quickly to keep the warm air in. 'Hubert, I didn't realise you were up so early.'

'I don't seem to need sleep much these days.' He straightened up, gazing at her with a puzzled frown. 'Is anything the matter?'

'No, not at all. In fact I think I may have the solution to your problem with stoking the boiler and the other heavy jobs that need doing.'

'Really, Mirabel, you mustn't interfere. I've managed my own affairs for more years than I care to remember. I don't imagine you can do better.'

Hurt by his dismissive tone, she tossed her

head. 'I'm not trying to tell you how to do things, I just thought you could use some help.'

He put down the watering can. 'I'm sorry, my dear. I didn't mean to snap, but it is very early in the morning and I'm used to being on my own. I do things in my own way.'

'And I'm not trying to interfere, as you put it. I just think you could use some help with the more mundane tasks, which would give you more time to do the important work.'

'What do you suggest?' He did not sound convinced.

The sound of footsteps outside made Mirabel turn her head. 'Tilda's father suffers from rheumatics and he can't find work on the docks. He's a widower with nine children to support, and some of them are little more than babies. Tilda is the eldest girl and you've seen how hard she works. They exist in dreadful conditions.'

Hubert glanced out of the window. 'He's probably lazy and not worth his hire. I've met his sort before.'

'You don't know that. Just give him a chance, that's all I ask.' She reached out to grasp the door handle. 'Shall I let him in?'

'I suppose so, but I'm not promising anything.'

Mirabel opened the door. 'Come in and meet my husband, Mr Coker.'

Tilda mouthed her thanks and scuttled back along the path to the house, and Alf stepped inside. He stood to attention, staring straight ahead.

'Are you a military man by any chance, Coker?' Hubert moved closer, peering at him with sudden interest.

'I was, sir.'

'What regiment?'

'The 56th (West Essex) Regiment of Foot, sir.'

'Where did you serve?'

'Bombay, until '68, sir. I'd done my ten years and I left the army because the missis wanted to settle down. It's a hard life for a regimental wife, sir.'

'I'm told you're willing to work hard, Coker.'

'Indeed I am, sir.'

'Come outside. I'll show you the boiler room and explain what needs to be done. When can you start?'

'Right away, sir. I was afraid we might end up having our Christmas dinner in the workhouse.'

Mirabel uttered a sigh of relief as she watched them step outside into the cold. They disappeared into the brick outhouse, but Alf's words had reminded her that Christmas was almost upon them, and she had done nothing to prepare for the festivities. Her wedding and the beginning of a new life with Hubert had put all such thoughts out of her mind. She had relied heavily on Mrs Flitton, but it was time she asserted herself as mistress of the house. She slipped out of the conservatory and hurried to the kitchen, hugging her shawl around her.

Tilda was stoking the fire in the range and Mrs Flitton was at the kitchen table breaking eggs into a bowl. She looked up in surprise. 'I didn't expect to see you so early in the morning, ma'am.'

'I've just realised that it's Christmas Eve, Mrs Flitton,' Mirabel said excitedly. 'What do you normally do at this time of year?'

Mrs Flitton stared at her blankly. 'What do I do, ma'am?' She shook her head, puzzled. 'The same as every other day, I suppose. I hadn't given it much thought.'

The memory of Christmas in the past, before her father had come under the thrall of Ernestine Mutton, flashed into Mirabel's mind, together with the rich aroma of roasting turkey, the spiciness of the pudding bubbling away in the copper, and the pine-scented tree laden with candles, glass baubles and tinsel. Pa had been kinder in those days and more generous. At home he had shown a nicer side to his nature than that which he presented to the outside world. They had been happy then, and she had had her dreaming place where she could sit and look up at the stars twinkling in the night sky, and allow her imagination full rein.

'Did you want anything special, ma'am?' Mrs Flitton's sharp tone broke into her reverie.

'No. I mean, yes. Of course we must celebrate Christmas properly. I daresay my husband had no taste for such celebrations in the past, but things will be different from now on.'

'The master always attends church on Christmas Day,' Mrs Flitton said, bristling. 'Dinner consists of roast goose followed by apple pie, and I have the bird on order at the butcher's.'

'Then cancel it,' Mirabel said recklessly. 'Order a large turkey, Mrs Flitton. We'll have stuffing and gravy and everything that goes with it, followed by Christmas pudding.' She came to a halt, frowning. 'Have you made a pudding this year?'

Mrs Flitton stiffened visibly. 'I haven't been required to do so, ma'am. The master likes simple food.'

'Fortnum and Mason,' Mirabel said eagerly. 'Where's Gertie? She should be up by now. We'll take a hansom cab to Fortnum's and buy whatever you haven't got in store, Mrs Flitton.'

Tilda looked from one to the other, shaking her head. 'We'll be lucky to have bread and dripping at home.'

'Who asked you, girl?' Mrs Flitton snapped. She sat down heavily, fanning herself. 'Really, Mrs Kettle, this is very short notice. We were a quiet household...'

'Things change,' Mirabel said airily. 'And we need a tree. I'll send Alf out to the market to see if he can get one.' She frowned. 'We need decorations too. I'm sure I can find some somewhere. This is so exciting.'

Mrs Flitton's frown deepened into a scowl. 'Such goings on, ma'am. The master won't like it a bit; I'll tell you that for nothing.'

Mirabel ignored this outburst. 'I'll have a bowl of porridge when it's ready, Mrs Flitton, and then I'm taking Gertie with me to buy what we need.' She did not stop to argue, hurrying outside instead to seek out her husband.

'I need some money, please,' she said, holding out her hand. 'I'd almost forgotten about Christmas with everything that's happened recently, but Alf reminded me.'

Hubert stared at her, eyebrows raised. 'What do you need money for, my dear?'

'To buy certain things, Hubert. I'm not telling you because it's to be a surprise.'

He smiled. 'You are so young, Mirabel. I'd quite forgotten what it's like to have the enthusiasm of youth.'

'Nonsense. I won't allow that. You're extremely enthusiastic about your plants.' She wiggled her fingers. 'I do need some money, though. If it weren't for Ernestine I would have been a wealthy woman in my own right.'

He put his hand in his pocket and took out a leather purse. He counted out a handful of silver, adding two golden sovereigns. 'I think we ought to apply for a copy of your father's will so that we know exactly how you stand,' he said calmly. 'But what I have is yours, Mirabel. I'm not a mean man, and I want you to be happy.'

Out of the corner of her eye she saw Alf heading for the boiler house, carrying a bucket of coal in each hand. She smiled. 'I'm very happy, Hubert.' She reached up to brush his cheek with a kiss. 'Thank you.'

She left him staring after her with a bemused expression on his face. Outside a bitter wind slapped her cheeks as she made her way to the boiler house to give Alf the money to purchase a tree. 'A nice big one,' she said firmly. 'And I want you to bring the children here for dinner tomorrow.' She saw that he was about to refuse and held up her hand. 'You can't deny me this pleasure, Alf. It's an army tradition, you know that. Officers serve the men their dinner on Christmas Day. I read about it in the newspapers so it must be true.'

'But missis, I've only just started here today. Captain Kettle won't like it.'

'Captain?' She smiled, trying to imagine Hubert

179

as a dashing young officer and failing miserably. 'Captain Kettle will be delighted to entertain you and your family and so will I.'

'You never told him that, did you?' Gertie stared at her incredulously as they sat side by side in the hansom cab on their way to Piccadilly.

'I most certainly did.' Mirabel stared straight ahead, noting for the first time the festive atmosphere that pervaded the streets away from the gloom of the East End. The snow might have turned to slush but holly and mistletoe were draped around lamp posts and naphtha flares illuminated the costermongers' barrows, breaking through the gloom of the early morning fog. It was not quite a peasouper, but Mirabel knew that when darkness fell smoke and fumes from manufactories and domestic chimneys would engulf the city in a dense, choking yellow mass that clogged lungs and brought traffic to a standstill.

'What was you thinking of, Mabel?'

'Those children deserve better. I'll never have a baby of my own, so the least I can do is to help others when I see them in dire need.'

Gertie eyed her doubtfully. 'Are you sure you know what you're doing, Mabel? You might end up back in Tenter Street if you go on at this rate.'

Chapter Twelve

The horse plodded along slowly, edging its way through the traffic, which was gradually coming to a halt as the suffocating pea-green fog descended on the city, blanketing everything and muting sound. Mirabel and Gertie sat inside the hackney carriage, holding their handkerchiefs over their mouths and noses to keep out the noxious smell of sulphur and soot. The floor of the carriage and the opposite seat were piled high with the result of a day's shopping, and Mirabel was tired but content. She had purchased two large plum puddings, a box of glace fruits and a jar of brandy butter from Fortnum's, and a foray into a street market had found glass baubles and tinsel for the tree, and a box of candles with metal holders to clip onto the branches. She had visited a tobacconist and bought a box of Hubert's favourite Havana cigars, and, at Gertie's suggestion, she had purchased an ounce of tobacco for Alf. They had spent an hour in William Hamley's newly opened toy shop in Regent Street where she found presents for all the Coker children, with the exception of Tilda. A short walk away she and Gertie had visited Dickins, Sons and Stevens department store, where Mirabel bought a brightly coloured scarf and hat for Tilda. A silver bar brooch caught her eye and she had a feeling it would be just the thing for Mrs Flitton, but there was still Gertie to buy for. Having distracted her maid's attention by sending her to look for buttons of a certain shape and colour, Mirabel selected a cashmere shawl and asked the shop assistant to wrap it quickly before Gertie returned.

Such a shopping expedition was enjoyable but exhausting, and Mirabel sat back against the stale-smelling leather squabs, closing her eyes. This would be the best Christmas ever. She might not be leading the life she had dreamed of as a young girl, but there were compensations. She had a home of her own and a kind husband. Hubert was a good man and deserved a little happiness. The faded portrait of his lost love had haunted Mirabel's thoughts, and it was not hard to imagine how the young army officer had felt on learning of his beloved's death. Perhaps her senses had been made more acute by her own feelings for Jack Starke, although she doubted if he had given her a second thought, and now he was gone she would never know.

The cab drew to a halt and Gertie scrambled to pick up the larger parcels. She climbed down and disappeared into the gloom, leaving Mirabel to cope with the smaller packages and pay the fare. The thickening fog was made even more oppressive by the gathering darkness, and as the vehicle lumbered off Mirabel found herself alone in the eerie silence. She was disorientated, and could see neither the kerb nor the railings outside her house.

'Mirabel Cutler.'

Her heart thudded against her ribs at the sound of her maiden name and she spun round, but she could see no one. For a moment she thought it must have been her imagination but then it came again, deep and sonorous as if the man had disguised his voice in an attempt to hide his identity. 'Who's there?' she demanded. 'What do you want?' The blood was pounding in her ears as she peered into the murk. Her instinct was to hurry indoors, but she had lost all sense of direction and in the dense fog she might as well have been blindfolded. The ensuing silence was more frightening than the sound of a strange voice, and she blundered towards what she hoped was the railings, only to bump into something solid. She dropped her packages, and the scream that left her lips was instantly muffled by a gloved hand.

'You should have listened to me, you stupid little fool.'

She knew that voice, and she recognised the odour of stale alcohol and tobacco that followed Wiley wherever he went.

'I'll take me hand away, but if you scream I'll break your neck.' He shifted his grasp to encompass her slender throat.

'Let me go. They'll come looking for me when I don't go into the house.'

'My understanding is that your old man is planning to get a copy of old Cutler's will.'

'How do you know that?'

'I knew he wasn't the sort to let matters lie. I have my informants and pay for information.'

'So Pa did leave something to me.'

'That you'll never know. Tell your old man to stop interfering in my business or it'll be the worse for you. I've gone this far to get what I want and a slip of a girl ain't going to stop me now. You're the only thing that stands between me and a fortune, so you'll tell him to leave well alone if he wants to enjoy his child bride.' He gave her a violent shove that sent her cannoning into the railings, and then he was gone, his footsteps muffled by the fog.

'Mirabel. Where are you?' Hubert's anxious voice was just a few steps away.

'I've dropped something,' Mirabel called out. 'Can you bring a lantern?'

'What happened?' Hubert demanded as he ushered her into the house. 'You're white as a sheet and you're trembling. What frightened you out there? And don't say it was because you dropped your packages and couldn't find them in the fog because I don't believe it.'

She took off her bonnet and mantle, handing them to Gertie who was staring at her with a worried frown. 'You was ages, ma'am,' she whispered. 'I thought something bad had happened to you.'

'Come into the parlour, Mirabel,' Hubert said firmly. 'Gertie will see to your purchases, although heaven knows what you've been buying.' A flicker of amusement lit his pale eyes. 'Is there anything left in the department stores?'

Mirabel made her way into the parlour and sank down on a chair by the fire, warming her chilled hands. 'I didn't want to say anything in front of Gertie, but Wiley was waiting outside. Heaven knows how long he must have been lurking there, or if it was just by chance that he was passing the house when I arrived.'

Hubert stood with his back to the fire, eyeing her anxiously. 'Did he hurt you? If he did I'll...'

184

'No,' Mirabel said hastily. 'He grabbed me and I couldn't get away, but he didn't harm me. His intention was to scare me. He knows that you mean to apply for a copy of my father's will, and it was his way of warning you not to continue with your searches.'

'How in hell's name did he find that out?'

'He said he'd paid someone to keep him informed. I don't know any more than that.'

He moved swiftly to a side table and picked up a decanter, pouring a tot into two glasses. He handed one to her. 'Sip this. It will help to calm you.'

The smell of the brandy made her stomach churn and she put the glass down. 'I can't. It reminds me of Wiley. He used to drink my father's best cognac and he reeked of it. I can't bear the smell.'

Hubert took a swig of his drink. 'I'll go to the police. He can't be allowed to get away with behaviour like this.'

'What could they do?' Mirabel asked tiredly. 'He's only made threats. They can hardly arrest him for that.'

'Well I won't stand by and see you tyrannised by a man like him. I'll think of something, so you mustn't worry.'

She could see that he was sincere even though she doubted his ability to prevent a man like Wiley from doing exactly as he pleased. She rose to her feet. 'It's Christmas Eve. I've got presents to wrap and a tree to decorate.' She moved to his side and took his hand, raising it to her cheek. 'Thank you for being so understanding, and for allowing the

185

Coker family to come to dinner tomorrow.'

His cheeks flushed and he lowered his gaze. 'I've lived a selfish life, my dear. I think it's high time I did something for someone other than myself.' He downed the last drop of brandy. 'And I must thank you for suggesting Coker. He's been a tremendous help today. He's a good man who's fallen on hard times.'

'I'm so glad you found him useful.'

'He bought the most enormous tree. I think it was left unsold because it was too large for most people's taste.'

She pushed her encounter with Wiley to the back of her mind. 'Really? Where is it?'

'Come upstairs to the drawing room and you'll see it.'

'I can't wait,' Mirabel hesitated. 'But first I think I'd better go and make my peace with Mrs Flitton.'

'Why is that?'

'Don't pretend you aren't aware that I've rather coerced her into cooking a huge meal when she's used to catering for you only. The poor woman had no choice and I feel rather guilty about that.'

'She is a servant after all, my dear.'

'She's more than that, Hubert. She's served you faithfully for many years and she's fiercely loyal to you.'

'I hope she hasn't been treating you with disrespect, Mirabel. I won't stand for it.'

'No, on the contrary, she's doing her best to accommodate to a situation she can hardly have imagined. I've bought her a small present to put under the tree and she must join us at dinner

186

tomorrow. I insist.'

In the kitchen Mrs Flitton was preparing the evening meal. Her face was red and strands of grey hair had escaped from her mobcap. From the scullery came sounds of splashing and the plop of vegetables being dropped into pans of cold water. Mirabel could see Tilda standing on a box as she worked at the large stone sink. She held up her hands in a gesture of submission. 'Before you say anything, Mrs Flitton, I've come to apologise for putting you to so much trouble, and to thank you for agreeing to cook for so many on Christmas Day.'

Mrs Flitton's lips pursed into a prune-like expression of disapproval. 'I do what's required of me, ma'am.'

'And much more,' Mirabel said gently. 'Gertie and Tilda will help you tomorrow and I want you to join us at table for the festive meal.'

'What? No, ma'am – I wouldn't think of it.'

'It's an order, Mrs Flitton,' Mirabel said, tempering her words with a smile. 'Mr Kettle is carrying on the army tradition where the officers serve their men on Christmas Day. We will wait on you for a change, and we'll all eat together in the true spirit of Christmas.'

'I don't know what to say, ma'am.'

'Not all change is for the worse, Mrs Flitton.' Mirabel glanced at the clock on the mantelshelf. 'I didn't realise it was so late. There's so much left to do, but now I'm going to take a look at the magnificent tree that Coker found for us.'

Hubert retired to his room soon after dinner that

187

evening, leaving Mirabel free to decorate the tree with Gertie's help. The result was stunning, even before the candles were lit, and Mirabel stood back to admire their work. 'I can imagine the children's faces when they see this tomorrow,' she said happily.

'It is tomorrow already.' Gertie stifled a yawn. 'Merry Christmas, Mabel.'

Mirabel gave her a hug. 'Merry Christmas, Gertie, and thank you for all your help.'

Gertie put her head on one side, eyeing Mirabel curiously. 'What happened when you stopped to pay off the cabby? You wasn't in a state because you'd dropped a few parcels, was you?'

'No, it was Wiley. He scared me, but he didn't hurt me.'

'You want to watch out for that one. I see'd him at the church and I didn't like the cut of his jib.'

'He's all talk, Gertie. There's very little he can do apart from trying to frighten me. I don't think he'd harm me physically because he's got too much to lose.'

'Bodger would sort him out for you.'

Mirabel smiled and shook her head. 'I wouldn't want him to waste his time on a man like Wiley. He's married to Ernestine and that will probably be punishment enough.' She leaned over to kiss Gertie on the cheek. 'Go to bed, dear. You've earned a good night's sleep.'

'What about you? Don't you want me to help you?'

'I can put myself to bed, and I've got a few things to wrap and put under the tree. Good night, Gertie.' Mirabel waited until Gertie had left the room before embarking on opening the packages, sorting the presents and wrapping them in brown paper tied with coloured ribbon she had bought for the purpose. When the last one was labelled and placed under the tree she stood back with a contented sigh. It would be a Christmas to remember, she thought, but her happiness was tinged with sorrow. There was someone missing and a secret longing in her heart that could never be fulfilled. She made her way through the silent house to her room.

Ragged, but freshly scrubbed and very subdued, the Coker children filed into the house after their father. Alf took off his cap, clutching it nervously in both hands. 'This is more than kind of you, sir.'

Hubert smiled, although Mirabel could see that he was not entirely comfortable in the presence of the young family. 'You're very welcome, Coker,' he said hastily. 'Will you come into the parlour and share a glass of punch with me? My wife will look after the children.'

Alf turned to the children, addressing himself mainly to the boys. 'I wants you to be on your best behaviour. D'you hear me?'

A murmured chorus of assent was accompanied by nods. Tilda held Kitty by the hand and Nora clung to her skirts, but Jane and Maisie hung back, largely due to the fact that the four older boys had pushed forward and were taking in their surroundings open-mouthed.

Mirabel encompassed them all with a genuine smile of delight. Suddenly the staid old house seemed to burst into life, and she was touched to see the effort that must have gone into making the children presentable. 'Merry Christmas to you all. Come upstairs with me and see what I've got for you.'

'It's a bit early to go to bed, ain't it?' Daniel, the eldest boy, who Mirabel judged to be thirteen or fourteen, received a clout round the ear from his father that wiped the cheeky grin off his face. He reddened, clutching the side of his head, and his eyes watered as he struggled to hold back tears.

'It's all right, Alf,' Mirabel said hastily. 'Don't worry about them. I'll see that they behave.'

'Me too, Pa,' Tilda added fiercely. 'I'll keep 'em in order.'

'You and whose army,' Daniel muttered rebelliously.

Mirabel chose not to hear. 'Come on then,' she said cheerfully. 'Follow me.'

In the drawing room the tree, ablaze with lighted candles, was an instant hit, causing the children to exclaim loudly and even the boys clapped their hands in delight, with Daniel apparently forgetting that he was almost a man and a breadwinner in his own right. Mirabel could not help noticing that the smell of the river still clung to all four boys, and despite their efforts to scrub themselves clean the mud of the foreshore was ingrained in their hands and under their nails. She moved swiftly to the octagonal table in the window where she had, with Gertie's help, laid out a selection of small cakes and two jugs of lemonade. The children needed no second bidding to help themselves to the food. They sat round the tree, gazing at it and munching happily. Mirabel was pleased to see that the older boys and girls looked after the little ones, and she caught Tilda's eye, smiling at her in approval.

'What's them little parcels under the tree, miss?' eight-year-old Jim demanded, pointing a sticky finger.

'Shh, Jim,' Tilda said sternly. 'It ain't polite to ask questions.'

'It doesn't matter,' Mirabel said, smiling. 'It's Christmas and they're presents. There's one for each of you.'

They looked at her blankly. 'What's a present, miss?' Ned asked curiously.

Tilda scrambled to her feet. 'A present is what rich people give to their family and people they like, Ned. It's like what the Wise Men brought for baby Jesus. They taught us that in the ragged school.' She gave Mirabel an apologetic smile. 'He don't remember much, missis. He's a bit slow,' she added in a whisper.

'Well you'll find out what a present is after we've had dinner, Ned.' Mirabel patted him on the head. 'I think you'll like yours.'

'Weren't that dinner?' Daniel asked, rubbing his belly. 'We never has cake at home.'

'No, Daniel, that wasn't dinner. There's more to come.'

Despite Alf's efforts to maintain discipline, the festive meal was noisy and chaotic. The sight of so much food caused the boys to forget their manners, and when twelve-year-old Pip speared a potato on the point of his knife and was about to put it in his mouth he received a sharp rebuke from Hubert.

Tilda scowled at her brother. 'You ain't fit to eat with the pigs, Pip.'

Pip hung his head and his cheeks reddened. 'Shut up,' he muttered angrily.

'Such manners,' Mrs Flitton said, shaking her head. 'I suppose such behaviour is only to be expected from motherless children.'

'I done me best, missis.' Alf turned on Ned, who was giggling nervously. 'That's enough of that, boy.' He pointed his knife at each of the children in turn. 'You'll treat this meal with respect or we'll leave now and let these good people enjoy their Christmas dinner in peace. What do you say?'

Kitty started to whimper and the other girls joined in, except for Tilda who rose to her feet, glaring at her brothers. 'We're all very sorry, ain't we, boys?' She focused on each of them in turn, waiting until they murmured an apology. 'That's better.' She sat down again and picked up her knife and fork. 'We ain't savages,' she added sternly. 'Ma taught us how to eat proper, and proper is how we'll behave from now on.'

'Well said, Tilda.' Mirabel moved swiftly round the table with a plate of roast potatoes and another piled high with turkey. 'Who wants more?'

This time there was no grabbing and more orderly behaviour. Alf nodded his approval, and Mrs Flitton relaxed sufficiently to smile when Hubert complimented her on the meal. 'There's more to come, sir,' she said, blushing like a girl. 'But I have to confess I didn't make the pudding, although I can take credit for the trifle, which I think you'll find every bit as good.'

'We'll clear the table and fetch the dessert, Mrs Flitton.' Mirabel was already on her feet.

'Of course. Stay there, Mary. That's an order.' Hubert rose from his chair to join his wife. 'Best keep the boys off the sherry trifle,' he whispered, grinning. 'Heaven knows what will happen if they get drunk.'

She glanced over her shoulder at the youngsters who were sitting bolt upright, doing their best to be patient as they waited for the next course to be served. 'Best go easy on the brandy to flame the pudding too,' she murmured, giggling.

Gertie jumped up from her seat. 'I'll finish up here, ma'am. Then I'll give you a hand in the kitchen.'

The puddings surrounded by a blue halo of flaming alcohol, were greeted with cheers and applause. Plates swimming in warm custard or crowned with a generous helping of thick cream were passed round the table, and when every last morsel had been eaten Mirabel fetched the trifle. The younger children refused reluctantly, complaining that their bellies ached, but the boys held out their bowls, eager to try the sweet confection. Mrs Flitton positively glowed with the praise heaped upon her. 'It is one of my most tried and tested recipes,' she said modestly.

'It's a culinary triumph, Mary.' Hubert raised his glass to her. 'I propose a toast to the cook.'

The toast was drunk and Mirabel could see that Kitty was already half asleep, as was four-year-old Nora. She stood up, pushing back her chair. 'I think perhaps this is a good time to go upstairs and give out the presents.'

Alf was on his feet before anyone else. A frown puckered his brow. 'Really, ma'am. We weren't expecting anything, and we've nothing to give in return.'

Hubert rose from his seat. 'We've had the pleasure of entertaining you and your family, Coker.'

Alf shook his head. 'No, sir. I mean, thank you, Captain, but we got to do something in return. Me and the nippers will wash the dishes and clear up the kitchen.'

It was Mrs Flitton's turn to rise to her feet. 'No, indeed you will not. I don't want my best china smashed to smithereens, thank you very much. I will supervise and Gertie and Tilda will help.' She stared at seven-year-old Jane, who was licking custard off her top lip. 'And that one can give a hand, but the others are too small.'

Alf opened his mouth as if to argue but Hubert held up his hand. 'We'll decide that after we've given out the gifts.' He headed for the doorway, beckoning Mrs Flitton to follow him. 'You too, Mary. I believe my wife has a surprise for everyone.'

Outside it was dark but the drawing room was filled with warmth and light. A fire crackled merrily in the grate and the air was redolent with the mingled scents of hot candle wax and pine needles. Mirabel ushered the children in and for once they were silent as they gazed at the lit tree in awe. She motioned them to sit and they sank down on the Chinese carpet, cross-legged and open-mouthed.

Hubert led Mrs Flitton to a comfortable chair by the fire and Alf stood to attention, as if awaiting orders. 'Take a seat, Coker,' Hubert said with a vague wave of his hand. 'No need to stand on ceremony.'

'Thank you, Captain.' Alf perched on an upright chair near the door, as if ready to make a quick escape.

Mirabel gave him an encouraging smile. 'The children are a credit to you, Alf.'

'Thank you, ma'am. It's kind of you to say so.'

'I hope things will get easier for you from now on,' she added in a low voice. 'You might even be able to find somewhere better to live.'

'That would be my aim, ma'am.'

'I'm sure it is.' She turned to Gertie who was standing at her side. 'I think now is the time to give out the presents.'

Mirabel stood at Hubert's side as they saw their guests off. Each of the children, with the exception of Kitty, who had not yet mastered the art of speech, thanked their hosts politely for the food and the presents. Alf and Tilda were last to leave.

'I can't thank you enough, Captain,' Alf said humbly. 'I'd forgotten what Christmas meant until you was kind enough to take me on. I promise to serve you faithfully.'

Hubert shook his hand. 'I know you will, Coker, and it was a pleasure to entertain your children.'

'I'll be here first thing in the morning with my pa,' Tilda said as she stepped outside. She twirled her scarf around her neck and adjusted her woollen hat. 'I could walk miles in the snow I'm so warm and cosy now. Ta ever so, missis.'

Mirabel blew her a kiss. 'You're very welcome,

Tilda.' She watched the family troop out into the starlit night. 'I hate to think of them going home to that awful place, Hubert.'

He slipped his arm around her shoulders. 'Fond as I am of you, Mrs Kettle, I am not adopting Coker's family or inviting them to live here.'

'I wouldn't dream of suggesting it,' she said, chuckling at the thought. 'But we might be able to find them somewhere more suitable. You haven't seen their home, but I can assure you it's truly awful.'

He closed the front door and stood staring down at her with a thoughtful expression. 'Finding Coker has made it possible for me to plan ahead in the knowledge that I have someone I can rely on to keep the boiler going and tend to the plants in my absence.'

She looked up at him in alarm. 'You're going away, Hubert?'

He smiled. 'I haven't given you your present yet, my dear. Can you guess what it is?'

Chapter Thirteen

Hubert's smile lit up his normally serious face, and his eyes shone with enthusiasm. 'I plan to take you on a plant-hunting trip to Florida.'

Mirabel stared at him in astonishment. 'You're going to take me to America?'

'I am indeed. It's long been my ambition to find a ghost orchid and we'll do it together, Mirabel.'

The thought of travelling to such an exotic place seemed too good to be true. 'The ghost orchid,' she repeated, mesmerised by the image the name conjured up in her mind.

'It was first discovered by Jean Jules Linden in Cuba about forty years ago, but it was found more recently growing in the Fakahatchee swamp in Florida, which as I believe I've already told you, is one of the most inhospitable places on earth.' He grasped her hands in his. 'Ever since I heard of their existence it's been my dearest wish to see them in their native habitat, and bring specimens home. I never imagined I could do it, until I met you, Mirabel. You've given me hope for the future.'

Looking into his eyes, Mirabel caught a glimpse of the young man who had loved so ardently and lost so tragically, and she was humbled by his trust in her. 'That's the best Christmas present anyone could have, Hubert,' she said softly. 'When do we leave?'

He released her, turning his head away as if overcome by emotion. 'The orchids flower from May onwards. The trip will take a lot of planning and preparation, but I hope to book a passage to America in late March or early April.'

Mirabel could hardly contain her excitement. 'How wonderful. I can't believe this is really happening.'

He shot her a sideways glance, taking off his misted spectacles and polishing them on a spotless white handkerchief. 'I'm so pleased you feel this way, my dear. But there is a lot to do, and you will need suitable clothing for such an expedition.'

'I suppose I'll have to call on Miss Standish,'

Mirabel said thoughtfully. Somehow she did not relish the idea of inviting the dressmaker into her home, where no doubt the embittered woman's sharp eyes would be on the lookout for telltale signs of cracks in what she obviously considered to be a doomed relationship.

'No, that's not what I had in mind.' Hubert shook his head. 'There are outfitters who specialise in providing pith helmets and garments suitable for tropical climes. It will be rough going, Mirabel, and it will be dangerous.'

'Really?' She clasped her hands, her pulses racing. 'What sort of danger?'

'Wild creatures,' Hubert said vaguely. 'Alligators and venomous snakes, and that's just for a start. Then, of course, there's the risk of disease.'

'I'm not afraid. It will be the most wonderful adventure, just like the ones I dreamed of as a child.'

He moved to a side table and filled a glass with port, holding it up to the gasoliers and studying the ruby glow. 'Will you join me in a toast to our expedition, my dear?'

She held out her hand. 'How could I refuse?'

The next few weeks were filled with preparations for the voyage to America. Hubert made many visits to Thomas Cook's head office in Ludgate Circus, discussing itineraries for the trip and the various routes by which they might reach their destination. Mirabel's time was taken up with domestic matters and pleasurable visits to various department stores, including Gamages in Holborn, the Civil Service Store in the Strand and Harrods, where she purchased the list of items that Hubert had made out for her. Back in the privacy of her own room she had a dress rehearsal, donning the divided skirt which was daringly short and only just covered the tops of her boots, a safari jacket and lastly, the crowning glory, a pith helmet. Gertie was suitably impressed and asked if she might try them on.

'No, you may not,' Mirabel said, keeping a straight face although she wanted desperately to giggle.

'Oh!' Gertie's cheeks flamed and she cast her eyes down. 'I'm sorry. I shouldn't have been so bold.'

Mirabel relented immediately. 'You may not try these on, but you may try on your own outfit.' She reached under the bed and pulled out a cardboard box which she laid on the coverlet. 'There you are. Open it, silly. You didn't think I'd leave you out, did you?'

Gertie stared at her open-mouthed. 'For me?'

'Yes, of course. Hubert insists that I have a maid to accompany me, which is fortunate because I would have refused to go without you.'

'I dunno what to say.' Gertie stared at the box as if expecting the lid to pop open of its own accord.

'Go on. It won't bite.'

Gertie opened the box and examined the contents, exclaiming in delight at what she found. She held the jacket up against her, studying her reflection in the cheval mirror. 'I never expected nothing like this. Am I really to go with you and the master?'

'Yes, indeed you are. Hubert has booked our passage on the *Servia,* the newest Cunard liner.

We sail from Liverpool at the beginning of April.'

Gertie slumped down on the bed, clutching the safari jacket to her bosom. 'Well, I never did. I'm at a loss for words, Mabel. What will Bodger say when he finds out?'

Mirabel smiled, shaking her head. 'I haven't the faintest idea.' She unbuttoned her top, frowning thoughtfully. 'There's just one thing I must do before we go. I promised Alf I'd find them somewhere better to live, but so far I've been unsuccessful.'

'It ain't easy to find somewhere cheap and decent.' Gertie stood up and began packing her outfit back in its box. 'It's even harder for a large family.'

'I know.' Mirabel stepped out of her travel garments and slipped her merino gown over her head. 'I've had an idea, but I need to speak to Hubert before I do anything.' She glanced at the discarded clothes lying in a heap on the floor. 'Will you put these away for me, Gertie? I'll go and find him now.'

'Yes, ma'am,' Gertie said meekly.

Mirabel shot her a curious glance. 'Why so formal all of a sudden?'

'Just practising, ma'am. If we're going to travel with the toffs I can't go on calling you Mabel. It wouldn't do at all.'

'You're right, of course,' Mirabel said, laughing. 'But when we get to the Fakahatchee swamp you can call me what you like. There'll only be alligators and the like to hear you.' She left Gertie to tidy up and hurried downstairs to look for Hubert.

She found him in his study poring over a map.

'Might I have a word with you?'

He turned his head, peering at her as if dragging himself back to the present with difficulty. 'Yes, of course, my dear. What is it?'

She pulled up a chair and sat down beside him. 'I've been thinking about Alf and his family. They can't go on living in that hovel, and I rather rashly promised to find them somewhere else to live.'

He sat back in his chair, eyeing her thoughtfully. 'What had you in mind?'

'You'll be leaving him in sole charge of your precious collection, won't you?'

'Yes, indeed.' He frowned. 'It's a big risk but one I'm prepared to take, and Coker is a good man. I think I can trust him.'

'Then why not let them stay here while we're away? You'll know that your plants are being cared for and there's plenty of room.'

'I can't have all those children rampaging around my home. They'll smash everything and drive poor Mrs Flitton to distraction.'

'We could let them have the attics, Hubert. They're unused at present and Alf would have to make sure that the children didn't wander into our private rooms. Tilda would see to that too. She's very conscientious.'

'But Mrs Flitton might object.'

'I'm sure she would prefer to have Alf living in the house to protect the property, and I've seen her filling baskets with food for Tilda to take home for her brothers and sisters. Mary isn't as hard-hearted as she likes to make out, and she might enjoy the company.'

Hubert held up his hands in submission. 'My

201

dear, if you can persuade Mary Flitton to share the house with Alf and his family it will be a miracle.'

'But you have no objections, Hubert?'

'None at all. On consideration I think it might be the sensible thing to do, but what do we do on our return? I don't want to share my home with the Coker family forever.'

'That won't happen. Alf will be able to save some of his wages while he isn't paying rent, and he can look round for somewhere better to live in the meantime.'

'I can't argue with the logic of that, Mirabel. If Mrs Flitton is willing, I am too.'

Mary Flitton folded her arms, her brows furrowed and her lips pursed. She shook her head slowly. 'I don't know, ma'am. It's not for me to say, of course, but has the master thought it through?' She paused, taking a deep breath. 'I mean, all those youngsters living here. Just think of the cost of feeding them, let alone anything else.'

'The boys work and they'll contribute to the housekeeping,' Mirabel said hastily. 'And Mr Coker will have his wages too. I'll tell him that he and Tilda must see to their meals so that you aren't bothered.'

'I don't want people interfering in my kitchen, ma'am. I don't mind cooking for them, just as long as they don't take advantage of my good nature.'

'That's very kind of you, and I'm sure they would be very grateful.'

'I draw the line at doing their laundry. Where

would they all sleep?'

'You have your quarters on the ground floor, so I thought that the disused attic rooms would be more than suitable.'

'I daresay they would,' Mrs Flitton said doubtfully. 'But my rheumaticky knees won't cope with all those stairs.'

'You won't have to do a thing. The cleaning women will do anything that's necessary and Alf can do the rest.'

'Then I suppose it will be all right, ma'am. To tell the truth, I'd feel safer with a man about the house than if I were left on my own.'

'Exactly,' Mirabel said, trying not to sound too relieved. 'Now all I have to do is convince Alf that it's a good idea.'

It was more difficult to persuade Alf than Mirabel had expected. He was a proud man, and although she had tried to convince him that she was not offering charity, his initial reaction was to refuse. She was not going to accept defeat so easily and she enlisted Hubert's help, hovering outside the study door while the two men discussed the matter in private. She was never to know what passed between them, but Alf emerged from Hubert's study with a grim smile on his craggy features.

'Is it settled?' Mirabel asked anxiously. 'Will you stay here and look after things, Alf?'

'Yes, ma'am. Captain Kettle values them plants above everything. They need tending to as if they was little babies and I'll see to it that they come to no harm.'

'You'd best go upstairs and inspect the attics.

You'll need beds and bedding, but just let me know your requirements and I'll see that they're met.'

'Thank you, ma'am.'

'And you must move in as soon as the rooms are habitable. I hate to think of the children spending the rest of the winter in that damp cellar.' She headed for the stairs, beckoning him to follow. 'I'll come up with you and see for myself what's needed.'

Mirabel pushed ahead with arrangements for the Coker family to move their few belongings into their new home. She was, as she had told Alf, concerned for their welfare during the worst of the winter weather, but in truth she was eager to see them settled in case Hubert or Mrs Flitton might undergo a change of heart.

The cleaning women were duly sent up to the top floor and the contents of the attics, which consisted mainly of cabin trunks and assorted items of luggage, was removed and stored in a box room on the floor below. Then there was the more pleasurable activity of purchasing everything that the family needed to make them comfortable. With Gertie at her side Mirabel visited a warehouse in Wapping, where she purchased beds and enough furniture to make the space habitable. Another warehouse provided bedding and towels and yet another supplied drugget matting to cover the bare boards. Having suffered at the hands of her stepmother Mirabel was determined to make the Coker family feel welcome in their new home, even if it proved to be only temporary. If she were to be honest, the prospect of having children in the house fulfilled a need that she could not easily explain. She thought she had come to terms with the fact that she'd never bear a child of her own, but Christmas spent with the young family had made her realise what she was missing. Such thoughts were disturbing and must be pushed to the back of her mind. Hubert had given her a home and status and she vowed never to let him see the secret yearning for a life that she could never have, or the constant and painful grief she felt for a dead man. She had tried to convince herself that to have such feelings for a man she hardly knew was ridiculous, but in her heart she knew she had been lost from the first moment she had set eyes on him.

Not that she had much time to think about herself. The next few months were filled with preparations for the trip to America, as well as the initial chaos of moving the Coker family into their new home. There were a couple of incidents while the older boys were getting used to the rules as set down by Mrs Flitton, the most notable being the day when they returned home, having spent hours on the foreshore, and had trailed the stinking Thames river mud throughout the house. This thoughtless act incurred Mrs Flitton's wrath, as well as a taste of leather from their father's buckled belt. After that, Danny, Pip and Ned had to suffer the indignity of washing in ice-cold water in the outhouse, leaving their soiled clothes in the copper before making their way upstairs barefoot and wrapped in towels. Tilda was put in charge of washing their garments, which were then hung up to dry in the boiler house, ready for work next day.

The two older girls, Jane and Maisie, looked after four-year-old Nora and two-year-old Kitty, but sometimes the sound of the little one sobbing was too much for Mirabel and she hurried upstairs to see what was the matter. More often than not the toddler had fallen over and bumped her head, quickly resolved with a kiss and a cuddle. At other times it was a quarrel between Jane and Maisie which involved hair-pulling and an exchange of insults, which had made both Nora and Kitty cry. Mirabel dealt out summary justice, followed by a trip to the kitchen where Mrs Flitton dispensed biscuits and cups of milk; a sure and certain cure-all.

On one such occasion, Mirabel sat in the rocking chair by the range with Kitty on her knee while Jane, Maisie and Nora finished their snacks. Tilda looked on with a worried frown. 'You are very naughty fighting like alley cats,' she said, glaring at her sisters. 'You won't get spoilt like this when we leave here.'

Maisie's eyes welled with tears. 'We'll be good from now on.' She turned to Mirabel with a pleading look. 'Don't send us away, missis.'

'You'll be staying here for quite a while yet,' Mirabel said hastily. 'But you must behave yourselves, girls. That means no fighting. You must look after the little ones and do as Tilda tells you.'

Mrs Flitton looked up from slicing meat for the pot. 'And if you don't I'll tell your pa. He'll sort you out.'

Jane paled visibly. 'We'll be good, Mrs Flitton.

Maisie and I didn't mean to get into a scrap; it just happened.' She reached out and ruffled Nora's curls. 'We'll look after the little 'uns.'

'Well, you've been warned,' Mirabel said, trying hard to keep a straight face. She kissed Kitty's chubby cheek. 'You must look after baby. She's only little.'

'And I can't keep an eye on you all the time,' Tilda added, shaking her head. 'I was sent out to work at your age, Jane. I was washing bottles in the brewery from early morning until late at night, so think yourself lucky that all you have to do is to look after the young ones.'

Kitty began to struggle and reluctantly Mirabel placed her on the floor where she toddled over to Tilda, who scooped her up in her arms. 'I'll take you upstairs,' she said sternly. 'And you three come as well. Some of us have work to do and that don't include feeding you biscuits and milk whenever you feel hungry. You wait your turn for dinner, and I don't want to hear another peep out of any of you.' She held her hand out to Nora, who obeyed instantly and hurried to her side. Mirabel watched them troop out of the kitchen with a barely disguised sigh.

'I don't want to speak out of turn, ma'am,' Mrs Flitton said quietly, 'but you mustn't get too fond of the nippers. They'll have to leave as soon as you and the master return from your travels.'

Mirabel turned to look at her and saw sympathy and understanding in the older woman's eyes. 'I realise that, Mrs Flitton.'

'I never had children, but there are compensations.'

'I'm sure you're right.' Mirabel rose to her feet. 'It's not long until we leave for Liverpool, and I've got things to do.'

'I don't envy you, ma'am,' Mrs Flitton said, sniffing. 'Foreign parts are nasty dirty places.'

Mirabel escaped to the privacy of her bedroom. She had sent Gertie out to purchase the medicaments that Hubert considered necessary for the journey, including everything from Carter's Little Liver Pills to Lamplough's Pyretic Saline, which claimed to relieve or cure everything from typhus to prickly heat and smallpox. Hubert had unearthed the brassbound medicine chest that had accompanied him during his army service, and he spent hours in his study making lists of everything they would need for their travels. Mirabel was left with little to do other than see to her own wardrobe and make sure that Gertie was also suitably kitted out.

She went to sit by the window, looking down on the street below with unseeing eyes. Their departure date was growing closer but her initial excitement was dimmed by the nagging ache in her heart that simply refused to go away. Again and again she told herself that she should be happy and grateful to Hubert for plucking her from a life of servitude, which of course she was, but it was tempered by the feeling of loss, not only of the man she loved, but of the children she would never bear. No matter how many times she tried to convince herself that her feelings for the louche, world-weary sea captain would have been tempered by a closer acquaintance, she could not banish him from her mind or her heart. She dashed

208

away a tear, rising from the window seat at the sound of footsteps outside her door. Busying herself at her dressing table she turned her head to smile at Gertie as she burst into the room with only a cursory knock. 'Well? Did you get everything?'

Pink-cheeked and breathless, Gertie set her basket down on an occasional table. 'I got the lot, Mabel. We got cures for everything from headaches to gout and snake bite.'

'In two weeks' time we'll be setting off for Liverpool,' Mirabel said dreamily. 'We'll be on our way across the Atlantic Ocean to America.'

'It would be just perfect if Bodger was in the crew. I want him to see me travelling like a proper lady.' Gertie shrugged off her cape.

'You'll be able to tell him all about it next time you see him.' Mirabel picked up the basket. 'I'll take this to Hubert so that he can check it against his list.' She hurried from the room. Hubert had left earlier for a final fitting at his tailor in Savile Row, but she needed to be alone, which was difficult in a house crowded with servants and children. Leaving London for a trip that might take many months was like saying a final farewell to those she'd lost and the life she'd previously led. It was going to be a new beginning, or so she hoped.

Finally, at the end of April, they sailed from Liverpool on the new Cunard steamship, the *SS Servia*, which boasted a total of one hundred and six first class state rooms, a smoking room and a luxuriously fitted ladies' drawing room, as well as a music room and a library. Hubert had booked two state rooms on the main deck, and Gertie was to share a cabin with another lady's maid on the lower deck. Mirabel exclaimed in delight when she found a large bouquet of hothouse flowers awaiting her, together with a basket of fruit.

'Welcome on board, my dear,' Hubert said, smiling. 'I want only the best for my beautiful young wife.'

She reached up and kissed his whiskery cheek. 'Thank you. It's all wonderful.'

He took a rectangular shagreen case from his breast pocket and handed it to her. 'I should have given you this on our wedding day, my dear. But to tell the truth I'd forgotten that I had it until I opened one of my travelling cases.'

She lifted the lid, uttering a gasp of surprise at the sight of the sapphire and diamond necklace and earrings. 'For me, Hubert?'

'They belonged to my mother and I kept them to give to the woman I would marry. So now they belong to you, Mirabel.'

She shook her head. 'I don't know. I mean, I don't think I should have them.' She tried to give them back but he closed her hand over the case.

'Of course you should have them, and I want to see you wearing them this evening. I'll see you at dinner.' He prepared to leave the room but she caught him by the sleeve.

'Thank you, Hubert.' She hesitated, feeling suddenly shy. 'Would you like to explore the ship with me?'

He smiled ruefully. 'I've been on many such voyages, Mirabel. You'll have to forgive me if I don't seem to be as excited as you are.'

She exchanged glances with Gertie, who was busy unpacking one of the large cabin trunks. 'Yes, of course. I'll see you at dinner then.' She was disappointed but she managed a tight little smile as he left the room.

'The master's getting on a bit,' Gertie said pointedly. 'He ain't as young as he once was, Mabel.'

'I know, but I forget sometimes,' Mirabel said, sighing. 'I suppose I should be more understanding.' She took off her fur-trimmed mantle and flung it on the bed. 'I'm dying to go up on deck and look round, but perhaps I'd better wait until we're under way.'

'That might be best.' Gertie shook the folds out of a blue-silk gown. 'Will you wear this down to dinner, Mabel? I mean ma'am?'

Mirabel giggled and the tense feeling she had been experiencing since coming on board dissipated like morning mist. 'I think you may still call me Mabel when we're alone. As soon as they weigh anchor we'll go out on deck together. That can't be considered the wrong thing to do.'

On deck the throb of the engines seemed to echo the beating of Mirabel's heart as the liner slid away from the quay wall. The people on shore were waving and blowing kisses to their loved ones who were at the start of their voyage to America. That there was no one to wave her off seemed to emphasise the fact that Hubert was the only family she had, and would ever have. Mirabel wrapped her shawl around her shoulders as a cool breeze tugged at her bonnet and slapped playfully at her cheeks. Taking a deep breath of salt-laden air she leaned against the railings, watching the dock gradually disappear from view. 'A penny for 'em.'

Gertie's voice broke into her thoughts and Mirabel turned with a start. 'I was just thinking how wonderful this is. I've never seen the sea let alone travelled on a beautiful ship like the *Servia*.'

'It is grand, isn't it?' Gertie glanced round at the huge twin funnels and the masts with the sails still tightly furled. 'I never been on a ship before, but Bodger told me about his travels. He said that some folks get seasick, but not him.'

'I hope I don't,' Mirabel said anxiously. 'I don't want to miss a moment of this experience. Let's explore a bit, shall we?'

Gertie looked round nervously. 'I ain't sure if I should walk beside you, Mabel. The toffs don't seem too friendly with their maids.'

Mirabel linked her hand through Gertie's arm. 'You're my friend. I don't think of you as a servant.'

Gertie did not look convinced, but she did not raise any objections as they promenaded slowly round the deck, taking in all the new and exciting sights and sounds. The smell of hot engine oil and smoke mingled with the scent of Macassar oil and expensive perfume as they walked past the few first class passengers who had braved the sharp salty breeze and the spray from the bow waves as the great vessel picked up speed. A sudden shower sent everyone looking for shelter and Mirabel headed for the ladies' drawing room, but a stern-looking man wearing a tailcoat, whose starched shirt collar threatened to behead him every time he nodded, prevented them from entering. 'Ladies only, ma'am,' he said, staring pointedly at Gertie. 'Servants are not allowed in the drawing room.'

Mirabel was about to protest when a young woman who had been seated at a table nearby rose to her feet and came towards them, holding out her hand. 'Forgive me for introducing myself, but I saw you on deck earlier. May I be of assistance?' Her disarming smile encompassed them all.

The steward had the grace to look bashful. 'It's nothing, Miss D'Angelo.'

'Nonsense, Grimwood. Of course it's something or this young lady would not look so perturbed.' She turned her lambent gaze on Mirabel. 'I'm Jerusha D'Angelo. How do you do?'

'Mirabel Kettle,' Mirabel said dazedly. 'And this is my maid, Miss Tinker.'

'Well, Miss Tinker, I'm very pleased to make your acquaintance,' Jerusha said in her charming Southern drawl. 'But might I suggest that you abide by the company's rules? Even if they are somewhat archaic.'

Mirabel was about to argue but she could see by the implacable look on the steward's face that he was not going to be moved. She nodded to Gertie. 'I'll not stay long.'

Gertie bobbed a curtsey and backed away, shooting a defiant look at Grimwood before turning on her heel and marching off with her head held high. Mirabel was tempted to follow her but Jerusha caught her by the sleeve. 'Won't you join me for a cup of tea? I've grown quite accustomed to your English habits.' Without giving Mirabel a chance to respond she turned to the

213

steward. 'We'll have a fresh pot of tea, please, Grimwood, and some more of those darling little pastries.' She led the way to her table and sat down, spreading her magenta silk skirts around her like the petals of an exotic flower. Her slanting green eyes were alight with interest as she studied Mirabel's face. 'Do sit down, honey, and tell me all about yourself. I think I saw you with your father earlier. He looks like a military gentleman.'

Mirabel perched on the tapestry-covered seat of the chair opposite her inquisitor and her heart sank. This was exactly what she had feared. People would almost certainly jump to the wrong conclusion. 'He's not my father,' she said in a low voice, sensing that Grimwood was hovering in the background. A waiter had appeared seemingly from nowhere at the single ring of a bell and had gone off to fetch their order. She leaned forward, fixing Jerusha with a steady gaze. 'Hubert is my husband.'

For a split second Jerusha D'Angelo appeared to be lost for words. Her eyes widened and her cheeks flushed a delicate shade of pink. 'I'm so sorry. I had no idea.'

'It's an easy mistake to make,' Mirabel said hastily. 'Hubert is a great deal older than I, but we are very happy together.'

'I'm sure you are.' Jerusha's eyes danced and her lips curved into a mischievous smile. 'But I'm afraid you'll have to get used to others making the same assumption, honey. You'll be the talk of the first class dining room.'

'I daresay, but it doesn't matter to me. Hubert is a fine man.'

'I admire your spirit, Mirabel. I like you already, and I can see we're going to be great friends. You must sit next to me at dinner so that we can talk.'

Mirabel managed a smile, although she found Jerusha's ebullience and direct manner slightly overwhelming. 'Thank you. I'd like that.'

'What will you do in New York?' Jerusha continued, seemingly unaware of the effect she was having on her new friend. 'Will you be staying there?'

'Not for long. We're going to Florida in search of rare orchids.'

'My goodness, how exciting. How do you plan to get there, honey? It's a long way from New York.'

'I can't remember the itinerary exactly, but I know we're travelling by train and then by sea.'

Jerusha seized both of Mirabel's hands. 'Then you must come and visit with us. We have a tobacco plantation near Richmond, West Virginia. Papa took it over after the war, when I was just a baby. He bought up most of the surrounding land so that we're one of the biggest growers in the whole state.'

Coming from anyone else this might have sounded like bragging, but Jerusha spoke with such naïve enthusiasm that her words were merely a statement of fact. Mirabel smiled and nodded. 'Thank you, that's very kind and I'd love to, but I would have to check with Hubert first. I know he's very eager to get to Florida.'

'You must introduce me to him, Mirabel. I'll talk him round, you'll see. If I set my heart on anything I always get my way.' She raised her hand to beckon to the waiter as he entered the drawing room carrying a laden cake stand. 'You must try the macaroons, they melt in the mouth. I know because I've already had one or maybe two. Papa says I'll be as fat as butter if I keep on eating as I do, but I don't care. I adore food, especially sweet things.'

Speechless and fascinated by her new friend, Mirabel sipped the tea poured by a disapproving Grimwood. She nibbled on an éclair while Jerusha devoured macaroons at an alarming rate, somehow managing to give a detailed account of her travels in Europe in between mouthfuls. Having apparently tired of that particular subject she went on to talk about her home and her father's rise from poverty to riches. Mirabel was feeling quite dizzy with trying to keep up with Jerusha's butterfly mind.

'So you see,' Jerusha said, dabbing her lips on a crested linen napkin, 'Papa was what they used to call a carpetbagger.'

'Really?' Mirabel said, mystified. 'What is a carpetbagger?'

'Pa is a Yankee from the north. He was all but destitute when the war ended, but he won a fistful of money in a card game, moved south and bought the plantation at a fire-sale price. He worked hard and made a fortune, which the old families resent. They prefer to live in genteel poverty rather than deal with the likes of us.' Jerusha tossed her head and her fiery auburn tresses caught the last rays of the sun as it fought its way through heavy cumulus clouds. She rose to her feet. 'I think it's time we went to change for dinner, honey. I know I take hours to complete my toilette.' She smiled down at

Mirabel. 'You will sit with us in the dining room, won't you? I want to hear all about you and your husband.' She lowered her voice. 'I can't wait to see the older wives' faces when they realise you aren't his daughter.'

Chapter Fourteen

As she entered the dining room on her husband's arm Mirabel was comforted by the fact that she was as fashionably turned out as any woman present, but there was a sudden lull in the conversation as heads turned to stare at them, and she felt the blood rush to her cheeks. Hubert patted her hand. 'You've caused quite a sensation, my dear,' he said softly.

She knew that was true, but not for the right reasons. The temptation to turn and run was almost overpowering, but she held her head high as they made their way towards one of the long tables. The room was crowded with passengers in evening dress. The dark dinner suits of the men complemented the elegant silks and satins worn by their wives. Diamonds blazed beneath the electric lighting, which was the most modern of all features on the ship, and the air was redolent with expensive perfume and cologne. A tall gentleman boasting an unmistakeably military moustache and an air of command stepped forward to slap Hubert on the shoulder. 'Hubert Kettle. I haven't seen you for years.'

'Brigadier Fortescue-Brown.' Hubert shook his hand. 'It's been a long time since Delhi.'

'Indeed it has. We're both civilians now, of course.' The brigadier turned to the tall, angular woman who stood at his side. 'My dear, you must remember Captain Kettle.'

Mrs Fortescue-Brown raised a silver lorgnette, staring through it at Hubert as if he were a specimen in a glass case, Mirabel thought, eyeing the lady warily. She could feel a set-down coming and she was not disappointed.

'Yes, of course I do.' She turned to Mirabel with a patronising smile. 'And you must be his daughter.' A frown creased her brow. 'I didn't know you were married, Hubert. I thought after that episode with—' She broke off, biting her lip.

'Mrs Fortescue-Brown, Brigadier, may I introduce my wife, Mirabel?' Hubert said stiffly.

The brigadier was first to recover. He bowed gallantly over Mirabel's hand. 'How do you do, Mrs Kettle? It's a pleasure to make your acquaintance.'

'How do you do, sir?' Mirabel inclined her head, conscious of the fact that the brigadier's wife was staring at her, eyebrows raised.

'Prudence?' Brigadier Fortescue-Brown gave his wife a meaningful look, but she turned away.

'I thought better of you, Hubert,' she said icily. 'The girl is young enough to be your granddaughter. Thank heaven you've left the regiment. That's all I can say.' She stalked off to take her seat at the table.

'You'll have to excuse my wife,' Fortescue-Brown said in an undertone. 'Dashed high standards and all that, Hubert. She'll come round.'

Hubert slipped his arm around Mirabel's slender waist. 'I'm sorry if our relationship offends your good lady, sir. But I won't allow anyone to insult my wife.'

'It's all right, Hubert,' Mirabel whispered.

'No. It's far from all right. Perhaps we should dine in your state room.' Hubert guided her firmly towards the door, but their way was barred by a stranger. 'Excuse me, sir,' Hubert said politely. 'We're just leaving.'

'Indeed you are not, sir.' The gentleman extended his hand. 'Vincent D'Angelo. It's a pleasure to make your acquaintance, Mr Kettle. Won't you join us at our table?'

Mirabel realised at once that this must be Jerusha's father, and although there was barely a passing physical resemblance between him and his daughter they shared a similar outgoing nature that made it impossible to ignore their friendly overtures. She was quick to note the heavy gold signet ring on Vincent's right little finger, and the diamond-encrusted cufflinks which flashed gaudily with even the slightest movement of his arms. Unlike his daughter, whose complexion was milk and honey, Vincent D'Angelo was olive-skinned and his mop of dark hair had been tamed by the use of strong-smelling pomade. In fact he exuded an aura of mixed scents that made him smell like a barber's shop, taking Mirabel back to the days of her childhood when she was allowed to sit on a stool watching the barber expertly shave her pa. She realised that she was staring at Vincent and she turned to her husband. 'Hubert, this is Jerusha's father. I told you about the young American lady I met earlier.'

'How do you do, sir?' Hubert allowed Vincent a brief handshake. 'If you'll excuse us, please?'

Vincent leaned closer. 'I saw what happened just now, my dear sir. Might I suggest this is not the best time to retreat? I recognise an army man when I see one. I myself served with the Union army many years ago.'

Mirabel could see Jerusha beckoning frantically and she made a move towards the table. 'Mr D'Angelo is right, Hubert. I don't want to hide away.'

'That's the spirit, ma'am,' Vincent said with an approving smile. He hooked his arm around Hubert's shoulders. 'And after dinner perhaps you would like to join me in the smoking room. I have some particularly fine cigars you might like to try.' Without giving Hubert a chance to argue, he led him to a seat at the table.

Mirabel gave him an encouraging smile as she joined Jerusha. Mrs Fortescue-Brown's reaction might have been expected but it had been humiliating, and very public. Mirabel had been prepared for such a reception, but she could see that it had come as a shock to Hubert.

'Are you all right, honey?' Jerusha asked anxiously. 'I saw the way that woman treated you and I'd like to slap her silly face.'

'It's not worth worrying about,' Mirabel said firmly. 'Tell me more about your plantation. I grew up in London so it's hard to imagine what it must be like to live in the country.'

'As I said before you must visit with us and then I can show you in person.' Jerusha leaned across the table, catching her father's eye. 'Pa, you must make Mr Kettle break his journey and stay awhile with us.'

Vincent smiled indulgently. 'Of course, kitten. Anything you say.' He turned to Hubert. 'I guess I'll have to do my darndest to persuade you, sir, or I'll never hear the last of it.'

Hubert inclined his head with a wry grin. 'I imagine kittens have claws, Mr D'Angelo.'

'I sure do,' Jerusha said, laughing. 'Oh, here's the soup.' She looked up expectantly as the waiter served them. 'I'm starving.'

Between them Vincent and Jerusha kept the conversation going throughout the meal, but Mirabel was relieved when it was over. It had been difficult to ignore the covert looks from the other diners. The women were frankly disapproving and the knowing gleam in their husbands' eyes made her feel distinctly uncomfortable. She left on Hubert's arm, holding herself erect and staring straight ahead. Outside in the cool of the late evening, with the moonlight creating a silver pathway across the inky sea, Jerusha caught up with them. 'Pay them no heed, Mirabel honey. The old crows are just jealous.'

Vincent advanced on them, taking long strides. 'I'm heading for the smoking room, Hubert. Now can I tempt you to a fine Havana cigar?'

Mirabel felt her husband hesitate and she quickly withdrew her hand from his arm. 'Don't refuse on my account.'

'Will you be all right, my dear?' His face was even paler than usual in the moonlight and the lines on his face were deepened by worry.

'Of course I will. I have Jerusha to keep me company and Gertie will be waiting in my state room. Please go.'

'If you're sure I'll say good night. I'll see you at breakfast.' Hubert strolled off with Vincent, heading for the smoking room.

'He's a great guy,' Jerusha said softly. 'I'd marry him myself if he wasn't already spoken for.' She walked to the railings and leaned on them, gazing out to sea. 'I just love the ocean. I think I could live quite happily on board an ocean liner.' She turned her head to give Mirabel a quizzical look. 'Wouldn't that be just fine, honey?'

A sharp pain knifed through Mirabel's heart as she thought of a seafaring man who had lost his life to the angry ocean, and she nodded dully. 'Yes, it sounds wonderful.'

Jerusha stretched her arms above her head and sighed. 'I could just die for something sweet and a cup of hot chocolate. Come to my state room, Belle, and I'll ring for the steward.' She linked her hand through Mirabel's arm. 'You don't mind if I call you Belle, do you, honey?'

A storm in the night created great waves that sent the ship plunging into the troughs and rising again only to drop with a stomach-churning thud that made the steel hull judder and shriek like a soul in torment. To her intense relief, Mirabel discovered that she was a good sailor, as was Gertie, but Hubert suffered terribly and was confined to his bed. Mirabel tended to his needs but he preferred to be alone with his mal de mer, and she found herself more and more in Jerusha's sparkling company. Vincent was unperturbed by the rough seas, but the dining room was almost deserted at meal-times, and it was too dangerous to promenade around the deck.

After nine days of continuous rain and gales Grimwood told them that this was the worst crossing he had experienced in a long time as he served their afternoon tea. Even the waiter looked a little green around the gills, but Jerusha's hearty appetite had not deserted her and she worked her way steadily through a second plate of cream cakes. Mirabel watched her in awe, sipping her tea and taking care not to spill the hot liquid on her afternoon gown as the vessel pitched and tossed on the turbulent waters.

Back in her state room early that evening she sat at the dressing table while Gertie worked quickly and neatly, brushing, combing and twisting her dark hair into a coronet and ringlets. 'At least the bad weather keeps the old frights from looking down their snooty noses at you, Mabel,' she said cheerfully. 'Serve 'em right if they're sick as dogs until the ship docks in New York.'

'Seasickness is a horrible thing,' Mirabel said, thinking of Hubert. 'I wouldn't wish it on any-body.'

'At least the master is on the mend. Will he venture down to dinner this evening?'

'I think he might.' Mirabel stood up to inspect her reflection in the cheval mirror. Her gown of cream satin, enriched with waterfalls of Brussels lace, its skirt draped and drawn back into a fash-ionable bustle, emphasised her tiny waist and flattered her gentle curves. Her fingers strayed to the sapphire and diamond necklace, which she had worn every evening, together with the matching earrings. Hubert was a kind and generous man, who didn't deserve censure or ridicule for marrying her. If anyone had the nerve to say anything on this, their last evening at sea, she would tell them exactly what she thought of them.

'Shall I go and see if the master is ready to go down to dinner?' Gertie asked, busying herself tidying away Mirabel's discarded garments.

'Thank you, but I'll do it myself. I've spent most of the day with Miss D'Angelo, and I'm afraid I've rather neglected him.'

Hubert was fully dressed, but he lay on his bed looking frail and drained. Mirabel hurried to his side. 'Are you unwell again? I thought you were recovering.'

He managed a weak smile. 'I'm much better than I was, but I'm rather tired.'

She perched on the edge of the bed. 'Would you rather dine in here, Hubert? I could order food for both of us.'

'It's your last chance to be with your new friend,' he said weakly. 'Go and enjoy yourself, my dear. I'll ring for service if I feel hungry.'

She stared down at him, frowning. 'We're due to make landfall tomorrow, Hubert. Perhaps you'll feel better when you're ashore.'

'I'm sure I will.'

'But you're obviously not in a fit state to travel on. What will we do?'

'We'll find a small, quiet hotel where I can rest for a few days.' He laid his hand on hers and closed his eyes. 'Now leave me, my dear. I just need to sleep.'

In the dining room she found Jerusha and her father talking to a group of people. Jerusha broke away and came towards her with a beaming smile. 'There you are, honey. I was beginning to think you weren't going to join us.' She glanced over Mirabel's shoulder. 'Where's Hubert? I thought he was improving.'

'I'm worried about him, Jerusha. He seems very weak.'

'It's hardly surprising after what he's been through. I know how I feel if I get an attack of the collywobbles.'

'I know, but I'm not sure what we'll do when we leave the ship tomorrow.'

'That's easy, honey. You'll come with us. Pa will see to everything. He always does, so you mustn't worry. Now let's sit down and enjoy our last dinner on the *Servia*, and tomorrow will take care of itself.'

Jerusha's faith in her father was completely justified. Mirabel discovered that she need not have worried about anything as Vincent seemed to have a magic touch, or perhaps it was the generous tips that she had seen him hand out that helped their smooth transition from ship to shore. Carriages appeared at the flick of a porter's fingers and they were transported through the teeming city streets to the grand Fifth Avenue Hotel on 23rd Street, where rooms had been booked by a messenger sent on ahead. Their luggage was waiting for them in their suite of rooms on the fourth floor and they had their own bathroom, a luxury virtually un-heard of in England. Hubert moved like a sleep-walker, barely able to put one foot in front of the other, but the hotel boasted an elevator powered by a stationary steam engine, which enabled him to reach the fourth floor without too much difficulty.

Mirabel was grateful to Vincent but she was worried about the cost. Finances were something that Hubert refused to discuss with her, and she had no idea how much he had set aside for ex-penses along the way. When she saw the luxurious interior of the hotel and the small army of staff who were waiting to serve them she turned to Vincent, demanding to know how much it would cost. He smiled, kissed her hand and told her not to worry. They were his guests, he said, and it was an honour to entertain them and show them what New York had to offer. Mirabel thanked him, but she was certain that Hubert would have some-thing to say when he recovered sufficiently to take control of the situation. In the meantime she abandoned herself to the excitement of the thriving metropolis with its polyglot population who went about their business with such verve and enthusiasm.

On the first afternoon Jerusha took her shop-ping, and that evening they saw a vaudeville show on Broadway, with supper afterwards in a noisy, colourful Italian restaurant. Hubert declined the invitation and retired early, but next morning he was up and about before Mirabel, and insisted on taking breakfast in the dining room.

Jerusha, as usual, was already at their table and

Vincent rose to his feet, pulling up a chair for Hubert. 'Good morning. I'm mighty glad you feel well enough to join us.'

Jerusha put down her knife and fork, wiping her lips on her napkin. 'Are you feeling better, sir? You had us quite worried, you know.'

Hubert sat down, smiling gently. 'I'm quite recovered now, thank you, Jerusha.' He turned to Vincent and his smile faded. 'I have to thank you for all this, and I want you to know I'm truly grateful, but you cannot be expected to foot the bill for relative strangers.'

'Call it Yankee hospitality Hubert,' Vincent said casually. 'I've no doubt you'd do the same for us if we were in similar circumstances.'

'We're only here for two days,' Jerusha added earnestly. 'Papa has to get back home to make sure that everything is running as it should, but I'm hoping you'll accompany us. It would be so good to have you visit with us for a while.'

'It would indeed.' Vincent signalled to a waiter. 'More coffee, and a pot of tea for my English friends.'

Mirabel sat down next to Jerusha. 'May we, Hubert?' she asked eagerly. 'Perhaps a few days in the country'd help to restore you to full health.'

He looked from one to the other and a slow smile spread across his thin features. 'I can see that I'm outnumbered.'

Vincent resumed his seat, tucking his napkin into the top of his plum-coloured waistcoat. 'I'll take great pleasure in showing you round my plantation and the curing barns. If it's all right by you, Hubert, I'll book us tickets on the Peninsula

227

railroad tomorrow. It's over three hundred miles to Richmond, and then a carriage ride from the railroad station to Loblolly Grove.'

Mirabel's lips twitched. 'Loblolly? What's that?'

'It's a species of pine tree,' Vincent explained without giving his daughter a chance to respond. 'The early settlers had to clear acres of it before they could use the land. It's a common tree in the south-eastern states.'

'Well, I think it's a lovely name,' Mirabel said, laughing. 'I love the place already.'

'You'll love it even more when you're there.' Jerusha reached out to take a bread roll. 'What shall we do this morning? Do you fancy a carriage ride to see the sights? Or shall we explore Ladies' Mile and see what the department stores have to offer?'

Vincent smiled indulgently. 'I can see this is going to be an expensive outing, Hubert.'

Next day they left for the D'Angelo plantation, travelling by train. It was late afternoon when the carriage that had picked them up at the station drove through the gates into a tree-lined allée, which led to a white house built in the Greek revival style. Bathed in golden sunshine, the wide veranda with its colonnaded portico seemed to welcome them with a smile.

Jerusha was bubbling with excitement as the carriage drew to a halt. 'I love travelling, but it's so good to be home.' She was the first to alight with the help of a servant who had rushed forward to open the door. Mirabel followed more slowly, and finally Vincent who had stopped to assist Hubert to the ground.

'Are you all right, Hubert?' Mirabel asked anxiously. His haggard appearance was alarming, and he was visibly unsteady on his feet, but his smile was undimmed.

'I'm fine, thank you, my dear.'

Vincent took him by the arm. 'A mint julep will set you to rights, my friend.'

'Come along, Belle,' Jerusha said eagerly. 'I want to show you your room.'

Mirabel glanced at Gertie, who had opted to travel on the driver's seat with Caleb, the coachman: a striking young man with a skin like ebony and a wide grin that revealed startlingly white teeth. 'Come along, Gertie.'

Gertie shot Caleb a sideways glance, fluttering her lashes. 'Ta, cully.'

He winked and flicked the whip over the horses' ears, driving off in the direction of a stable block.

Mirabel followed Jerusha up the steps onto the shady veranda and through double doors which led into a spacious entrance hall. The scent of lilies filled the air and the white-painted walls seemed to have trapped the last remnants of sunlight. The parquet flooring gleamed like the skin of a conker newly plucked from its spiny case, and a hint of lavender polish emanated from the reception rooms on either side of the hall. Mirabel caught a glimpse of the understated elegance of the furnishings as she followed Jerusha upstairs, with Gertie tagging along behind.

Jerusha led the way to a room at the back of the house which overlooked a wide sweep of lawns surrounded by oaks and stately magnolias which were just coming into bud. 'The fields are over yonder,' she said, pointing vaguely. 'The servants' quarters are behind the curing barns.'

Mirabel peered out of the window. 'You don't have slaves to work the fields, do you?'

'Heavens, no. What gave you that idea, honey? Pa fought to abolish that practice many years ago, and he's employed freed slaves ever since he took over the plantation. Some of them have been with us for as long as I can remember.' Jerusha turned away from the window. 'Can you ride a horse, Belle?'

Taken by surprise, Mirabel stared at her. 'I – I don't know. I never tried.'

'I've got just the mount for you, honey. She's a sweet little mare with a darling nature. Sitting on her is like being in a big old armchair. Tomorrow we'll go for a ride around the plantation and I'll show you how it all works.'

'Better you than me,' Gertie whispered. 'Shall I start unpacking, ma'am?'

Jerusha grabbed Mirabel by the hand. 'Come on, Belle. Leave her to sort out a gown for dinner tonight and I'll show you my room. It's just along the landing.' She turned to Gertie with a smile. 'My maid, Zenobia, will show you your quarters, Gertie. She'll look after you.'

Carried along in the wake of Jerusha's enthusiasm, Mirabel followed her friend to her room, which was a mixture of boudoir and nursery. The frilled lace curtains and tester on the four-poster bed, similar to the one in Mirabel's room, were complemented by the patchwork quilt made from tiny hexagons of pastel-coloured silk. A solemn row of dolls sat propped up on the pillow shams, their painted faces staring straight ahead and their ornate gowns neatly arranged by loving hands. A white wooden rocking horse stood in front of one of the tall windows, its grey mane tied with ribbon and a matching pink bow on its tail. The dressing table with its triple mirror was, in contrast, very much the domain of a grown-up lady with its array of silver-backed combs, brushes and mirror and cut-glass pots filled with all manner of creams and lotions.

Jerusha stripped off her travelling clothes, stepping out of them as they fell to the floor. She stood very still while her maid slipped a clean gown over her head and fastened the tiny buttons on the back of the bodice.

'All done, Miss Jerusha.' Zenobia stepped away, folding her hands on her spotless white apron.

'I'll be back directly to change for dinner. Have the emerald green satin ready, Zenobia.' Jerusha spun round to face Mirabel. 'Come with me, Belle. There's someone I want you to meet.' She headed for the doorway.

Once again Mirabel followed in her wake, wondering why her friend had chosen to change into an afternoon gown when it was almost time to dress for dinner. 'Where are we going now?'

'You'll see.'

Mirabel was tired and conscious of her travel-stained garments. She would have liked to return to her own room, but Jerusha marched on ahead. 'Here we are,' she said, ushering Mirabel into a bedroom shaded from the sunlight by the overhang of the portico. White net curtains fluttered at

231

the open windows and a cool breeze circulated, but the sickly sweet smell of illness pervaded the atmosphere.

Jerusha moved slowly towards the bed where a woman lay propped up on a mountain of lace-trimmed pillows, staring blankly into space. She might, Mirabel thought, have been a life-sized doll similar to the ones in Jerusha's room, but for the rise and fall of her chest beneath a white cotton-lawn nightgown. Jerusha leaned over the sick woman. 'Mama, I've brought someone to see you.'

A movement in the corner of the room caught Mirabel's eye and she turned to see a young and extremely beautiful black woman standing by a side table, holding a medicine bottle in one hand and a spoon in the other. 'It's time for Miss Betsy's medication.'

'Thank you, Kezia.' Jerusha made way for her, watching while the maid spooned medicine into the invalid's mouth.

Kezia wiped the excess from Betsy D'Angelo's chin with the corner of a towel she had tucked into her apron. 'Don't tire her, Miss Jerusha.'

'Has she missed us, Kezia? Do you think she realised we weren't here? I changed my gown so that she didn't see me in my outdoor clothes.'

'I can't say whether she did or did not, Miss Jerusha. We got along just fine, considering.'

'I'm glad,' Jerusha said, sighing. 'I was worried about her. She was never far from my thoughts.' She beckoned to Mirabel. 'Come closer so that she can see you. I believe she understands what we say even if she cannot respond.' She dropped a kiss on her mother's forehead. 'Mirabel has come all the way from England, Mama.'

'I'm very pleased to make your acquaintance, ma'am,' Mirabel said softly. For a brief moment she thought she saw a flicker of interest in Betsy's green eyes, but it was gone almost instantly.

'I have so much to tell you, Mama,' Jerusha said eagerly. 'But I can see by the way Kezia is glaring at me that this is not the right time. I'll come in the morning when you're rested.' She raised her mother's limp hand to her lips, holding it to her cheek briefly before laying it back on the coverlet. Blinking away tears, she turned to Mirabel. 'We'd best get changed for dinner, Belle. I declare I'm quite faint from lack of nourishment.'

Outside the sick room, Mirabel patted Jerusha on the shoulder. 'I'm so sorry. I had no idea that your mother was an invalid.'

'Pa never mentions her to anyone outside the family,' Jerusha said, sniffing. 'She's been like this for three years or more, since the riding accident, but she used to be so full of life and so beautiful. We had big parties in those days, with lanterns in the trees and dancing on the lawn. She used to love music and she could sing like an angel, but that's all gone now. Pa has taken her to the best doctors but none of them can do anything for her. They say she might improve with time, so we keep on hoping.'

'I'm truly sorry,' Mirabel said earnestly. 'I never really knew my mother; she died when I was very young.'

'I'm sorry to hear that, I truly am.' With a palpable effort Jerusha managed a wobbly smile. 'At least my mother is still with us, and I believe she understands more than she lets on.' She walked on. 'It's time we got changed and joined the gentlemen, or they'll be wondering what's happened to us. I do hope Cook has done something special for dinner.'

The meal in the elegant dining room had been a lively affair with Jerusha at her best, and Vincent regaled them with stories of his struggles to rebuild the plantation after the war. Hubert had eaten well and Mirabel was reassured by his improved appearance, although he retired to bed early, leaving Vincent to sit and smoke his cigar alone on the veranda. Jerusha was seemingly tireless but Mirabel had begun to wilt. After coffee accompanied by crystallised fruits, which Jerusha tucked into even though she had just enjoyed a substantial meal, Mirabel was forced to admit defeat and go to her room.

That night she was lulled to sleep by the hypnotic sounds of the cicadas and katydids and the haunting call of the whip-poor-will. A breeze rustled the leaves of the mighty oaks, but in her dreams the sighing of the wind became the sound of the sea. She was once again on a ship, but this time it was not the *Servia,* but a three-masted schooner buffeted by a great storm. She was on deck, calling out to the man who struggled to control the ship's wheel as it fought to escape his grasp. Even before a sudden flash of lightning illuminated his face she knew who it was. She awoke to the sound of thunder, her heart was racing, and for some inexplicable reason she was convinced that he had survived.

Chapter Fifteen

The certainty that Jack was still alive, however ill-founded, made the world a more colourful place and infinitely more interesting. The next morning Mirabel joined in with everything Jerusha suggested with an enthusiasm she had not felt for a long time. She put her fears aside and allowed the D'Angelos' groom to help her onto the grey mare, riding side-saddle around the plantation with Jerusha, who was an accomplished horsewoman. In the afternoon she sat in Mrs D'Angelo's bedroom while Jerusha read several passages from *Daisy Miller*, a novella by Henry James. Whether or not the story registered with Betsy was questionable, but the sound of her daughter's voice seemed to soothe her and she drifted off to sleep. Jerusha closed the book with a sigh. 'I keep hoping that one day she'll come back to us.'

'Miss Betsy's doing just fine,' Kezia said, moving silently from her chair to the bedside. 'She understands more than you think, she just don't have much to say. When the time comes she'll open her mouth and speak.'

The sound of horse's hooves broke the ensuing silence. Jerusha leapt to her feet and ran to the window. 'It's Ethan, and about time too. I declare I'm going to give him a piece of my mind.' Picking up her skirts, she raced from the room.

Mirabel sent a questioning glance to Kezia, who

shrugged her shoulders. 'Ethan Munroe. His family own the neighbouring plantation.' She turned her attention to Betsy, plumping her pillows and smoothing the sheets.

'I – I'll leave you to do your work,' Mirabel said lamely. She hurried from the room and made her way slowly down the wide staircase.

In the entrance hall Jerusha was berating a tall young man, whose fair hair flopped over one eye as he raised her hand to his lips. 'I came as soon as I heard you'd come home,' he protested.

'I might just forgive you,' Jerusha said, smiling. 'But only if you promise to stay for dinner.'

'I'd love to, honey, but I have a business meeting in Richmond.' He bowed from the waist, clicking his heels together. 'I regret that I cannot accept your kind invitation, Miss D'Angelo.'

She slapped his wrist. 'If you mock me, Ethan Munroe, you can just get back on your old horse and ride on to your boring old meeting.'

He grinned and gave her a hug. 'I've missed you more than you'll ever know.'

'Oh, well, since you put it that way, I guess I'm pleased to see you too.'

Mirabel cleared her throat to announce her presence and Jerusha spun round, her eyes shining and her cheeks flushed. 'Mirabel honey, may I introduce my old friend, Ethan Munroe.' She turned to Ethan, adding proudly, 'Mirabel is from London, England.'

Mirabel met his curious gaze with a smile. 'How do you do, sir?'

He acknowledged her with a courtly bow. 'How do you do, Miss Mirabel? I must say it's a pleasure to meet an English lady.'

Jerusha slipped her hand through the crook of his arm. 'We'll take tea on the veranda, Amos,' she called to the servant who was standing to attention awaiting instructions. 'I'm dying to tell you about the things we saw in Europe, Ethan.' She turned to Mirabel with an eager smile. 'Will you join us, Belle?'

Mirabel nodded. 'I'll come in a minute.' She had just spotted Hubert sitting in the parlour reading a newspaper, and she realised with a pang of conscience that she had not seen him since breakfast. She entered the room, pausing in the doorway to give him a searching glance. To her intense relief she noted that his colour had improved and he looked more like his old self. 'Hubert.' She crossed the floor and pulled up a stool to sit by his side. 'I'm so sorry. I'm afraid I've been neglecting you.'

He looked up, peering at her over the top of his spectacles. A slow smile spread across his thin features. 'Nonsense, my dear. You have every right to relax and enjoy yourself.'

'But you are feeling better, aren't you?'

He folded the newspaper and set it aside. 'I'm completely recovered and looking forward to continuing our travels.'

Somehow the thought of moving on had lost some of its appeal. Their unplanned detour had been a delight, and Mirabel knew that she would be sorry to leave: she would miss the plantation and the generous hospitality of their hosts. 'I think we should stay here a while longer, Hubert. You need to get your strength back.'

'It was a passing sickness. No doubt I'll suffer it

again when we embark on the next part of our journey, but we must get to Florida in time to see the ghost orchids in bloom.'

'Of course, but wouldn't it be better to travel overland instead of by sea?'

He shook his head. 'I went into all the possibilities in London, and I think I can safely say I have the best itinerary possible. I've discussed it with Vincent and he also agrees that the best route would be by rail to Newport News and from there by sea.'

'But you were so ill on the *Servia*, Hubert.'

'I hope to find my sea legs, as they say.' His eyes glowed with enthusiasm and he grasped her hands in his. 'This is my last chance to find a ghost orchid to add to my collection. Any amount of physical suffering will be worth it in the end.'

She withdrew her hands and stood up. 'All right, Hubert. If you're sure.'

'I am absolutely certain. We'll do it together, my dear. I can't fail if you're at my side.' He picked up the newspaper and opened it. 'Now go outside and join your young friends. Make the most of your time here, my dear girl.'

'I will.' She knew that there was no use arguing with her husband once he had made up his mind, and for herself she was undaunted by the prospect of a long sea voyage. She left him reading his paper and went outside to join Jerusha and her beau, for it was obvious that Ethan Munroe was not a casual acquaintance. Mirabel suspected that her friend was more interested in the young man than she was prepared to admit.

Ethan stayed for an hour or so before taking his

leave, promising to return next day to take them on a picnic on the banks of the James River. Jerusha jumped to her feet and gave him a hug. 'You darling man, I just knew you'd think of something particularly nice to do for Belle. Sadly she's leaving us the day after tomorrow.'

Ethan hesitated as he was about to step down from the veranda. 'That's too bad, Miss Belle. We could have shown you all the sights had you been able to stay a while longer.'

'That would have been lovely,' Mirabel said with feeling.

'I hope there'll be a cherry pie in the picnic basket.' Jerusha followed Ethan down the steps to where Caleb stood holding his spirited mount. 'And fried chicken.'

He leapt into the saddle. 'Our cook most probably has a list of the things you love to eat. I'll be here at noon tomorrow. Good day, ladies.' He rode off along the allée, waving his hat as his horse broke into a canter and then a gallop.

'That boy just loves showing off,' Jerusha said with a satisfied smile. 'I only encourage him because the Munroes' cook is the best in the county, and I just die for her cherry pie.' Twin dimples played on either side of her lips and her eyes twinkled mischievously. 'I might just have to marry him so that I can have cherry pie every day of my life.'

'You don't mean that, Jerusha.'

'Why not?' Jerusha put her head on one side. 'It wasn't a love match between you and Hubert was it?'

Mirabel felt the blood rush to her cheeks and

239

she looked away. 'No, I told you the reason why I accepted his offer, but I am very fond of him.'

'Of course you are, honey. I didn't mean to imply that you married the man for his money. I understand, I really do.' She angled her head, frowning thoughtfully. 'Now what can we do for the rest of the day? We must make the most of our time together.'

The picnic on the banks of the mighty James River ended a day of sightseeing organised by Ethan. Mirabel was totally in love with everything she saw, and the way of life at the plantation seemed idyllic compared to the harsh realities of London, but she also knew that nothing was perfect. There was poverty and hardship in communities outside the plantations and in the city itself, just as there was at home in England. Beneath Jerusha's carefree smiles there was the tragedy of her mother's crippling accident, which had struck her down in the prime of life. It was, Mirabel thought, as they drove back to Loblolly Grove in the dying rays of a fiery sunset, the way of the world.

'It's such a shame you have to leave tomorrow,' Jerusha said, breaking into Mirabel's reverie and bringing her back to the present with a start.

'I know, but I've had a wonderful time,' Mirabel said wholeheartedly. 'I can't thank you and your father enough.' She smiled at Ethan, who was seated next to Jerusha, holding her hand. 'And today has been lovely. I'll remember it forever.'

His tanned cheeks flushed and he smiled. 'Why thank you, Mirabel. It's been a pleasure showing you around. I just wish I could accompany you on your voyage south.'

'I suppose we'll be able to book passage on a ship bound for Florida,' Mirabel said, frowning. 'Hubert had our journey all worked out in London, but he couldn't have foreseen our detour. Although,' she added hastily, 'I've never enjoyed myself so much as I have the last few days.'

Jerusha exchanged meaningful glances with Ethan. 'Maybe you could persuade your husband to stay on a little longer, honey. I mean to say, the old ghost orchids aren't going anywhere.'

A vision of orchids flying off like huge butterflies made Mirabel chuckle. 'I don't think Hubert sees it that way. It's his long-held ambition to find them growing in the wild and take specimens home. I don't think anything or anyone could stop him now.'

'Well, I'll accompany you to Newport News tomorrow,' Ethan said easily. 'I have a shipment of tobacco, last year's crop, ready to send to England, and I like to be there to make sure everything goes to plan.'

'I wish I could go too,' Jerusha said, sighing. 'But Papa would never allow it.'

'If we were married you could go anywhere with me.' Ethan lifted her hand to his lips, and although he was smiling there was a question in his blue eyes.

Mirabel could see that he was serious, and she held her breath.

'Why Ethan Munroe,' Jerusha said, staring at him wide-eyed. 'That surely sounds like a proposal of marriage.'

'Will you marry me, Jerusha? I had intended to

241

ask you with moonlight and magnolias, but the question is still the same.'

She blushed rosily, attempting to pull her hand free, but he tightened his grasp, curling his fingers around hers. 'Hush now, Ethan. We've got company.'

He glanced at the straight back of the coachman, who seemed to be affecting deafness, and turned his gaze on Mirabel, who could feel her own cheeks reddening. 'I'm sorry, Mirabel. I didn't plan it this way, but it just seemed to be the moment.'

'Don't mind me,' Mirabel said hastily. 'I think it's wonderful.'

'You do?' Jerusha stared at her, raising a delicate eyebrow. 'And you're so English.'

Mirabel tried to keep a straight face and failed. 'We're not as prim and proper as you seem to imagine. Do give him an answer, Jerusha. Make us both happy.'

'Well, I can see that I'm outnumbered.' Jerusha tossed her head, but her eyes were sparkling and her lips curved in a delighted smile. 'I suppose I'll have to agree then, or I'll never hear the last of it.'

Ethan released her hand, wrapping his arms around her. 'You're saying yes?'

'I guess I am. Yes, Ethan Munroe, I will marry you.' Her last word was muffled by his kiss. She pushed him away, but only after returning the kiss with equal enthusiasm. 'You're very forward, sir,' she said, laughing. 'You should have asked Pa first.'

'But I don't want to marry him.'

She slapped his hand. 'You know very well what

I mean.' She turned to Mirabel, her eyes glowing and dimples dancing. 'I'll leave Ethan to deal with Pa, but I want you to come with me when I tell Mama. It might be the very thing that will bring her back to us.'

Betsy D'Angelo's room was lit with the soft glow of candlelight, although it was not quite dark outside. Kezia hovered in the background, ever watchful. Mirabel stood back as Jerusha went to kneel at her mother's bedside. 'How are you today, Mama? I hope you're feeling stronger because I have some news that I know will make you smile.' Jerusha clutched her mother's thin hand as it lay on the coverlet like a broken butterfly. 'I'm to be married, Mama. Ethan has proposed at last and I said yes.'

Mirabel took a step forward as Betsy's eyelids flickered and she turned her head almost imperceptibly, and for a brief moment she thought the sick woman's lips moved, but the mask-like expression returned so quickly that it seemed she had imagined any change. Jerusha stroked her mother's hand, gazing intently into the glassy eyes. 'I know you can hear me, Mama. Squeeze my fingers if you can.' She stiffened, holding her breath and exhaling with a sigh. 'She did, Belle. It was the slightest pressure, but I felt it.' She laid Betsy's hand down on the counterpane, rising to her feet with a triumphant smile. 'She knows and she's happy for me. I can feel it.'

Mirabel could not look away. She was certain that Betsy's eyes were staring directly at her, although she could not imagine why. Then, quite suddenly, Betsy's lips moved. 'Be happy.' The words were faint, just a breath of a whisper, but Mirabel heard them clearly.

'What did she say?' Jerusha leaned over the bed, peering into her mother's face. 'You spoke, Mama. What did you say?'

Kezia moved swiftly. 'She's coming back to us, Miss Jerusha. Leave her to do it in her own good time. Don't tire her.'

Tears ran freely down Jerusha's cheeks. 'But she spoke to me. I couldn't hear what she said.'

'Never you mind,' Kezia said firmly. 'She will speak again when it suits her. Now let her rest.'

Mirabel moved to Jerusha's side, slipping her arm around her shoulders. 'She said "be happy". She meant it for you.' Even as she uttered the words Mirabel knew that they were untrue. Betsy D'Angelo had been looking directly at her. For some unknown reason Jerusha's mother had spoken her first words for years to someone who was almost a complete stranger.

'She approves,' Jerusha sobbed. 'I knew she would. She always liked Ethan and the news brought her back from that awful place where no one could reach her. It's a miracle, Belle. I must go and find Pa and tell him.'

Mirabel glanced over Jerusha's shoulder and her eyes met Kezia's. She understands, Mirabel thought with a shiver. The handsome woman had an understanding far deeper than she would have thought possible. Kezia knew that the two words uttered on a sigh had not been meant for her mistress's daughter. It was inexplicable and Mirabel did not try to understand, but deep down she felt that a burden had been lifted from her, and it was with a lighter step that she accompanied Jerusha downstairs to pass on the news, and the hope it raised of a partial or even a full recovery from the accident that had laid Betsy D'Angelo so low.

'I don't know how you did it,' Jerusha said next morning as Mirabel and Hubert were about to leave. 'But somehow I think your being here made everything change for the better.'

Mirabel smiled, shaking her head. 'It's kind of you to say so, but it's just not true.'

'Oh, but it is, honey. Ethan and I might have gone on for years in the same old way, and then you were there and he proposed. I'm sure it was that news which brought Mama out of the dark place, and this morning, would you believe, she whispered my name.' She hugged Mirabel, kissing her on both cheeks. 'You all must come to the wedding. It wouldn't be the same without you.' She clung to Mirabel's arm as they descended the veranda steps, making their way to where Ethan and Hubert were waiting for them. Gertie was already seated beside Caleb on the driver's seat of the D'Angelos' carriage, which was being used to transport the bulk of the Kettles' luggage to the railway station.

'You'd better leave now, Caleb,' Vincent said with a wave of his hand. 'Come straight back, you hear? No loitering in town.'

'Yes, Cap'n.' Caleb grinned and saluted, flicked the reins and encouraged the matched pair of bays to walk on.

'You must take good care of my friends on the

journey to Newport News, Ethan,' Jerusha said sternly. 'I've told Belle that they must return for our wedding.' She released Mirabel to clutch Hubert's hand. 'You will bring her, won't you? I'll be devastated if you don't come.'

He smiled, squeezing her fingers. 'I'll do my very best.'

'Not good enough, sir,' Jerusha said, pouting prettily. 'I want a solemn promise.'

'Then you have my word.' Hubert helped Mirabel into the Munroe carriage and climbed in after her.

'Make sure they get berths on a ship with a reliable captain and crew,' Jerusha said tearfully. 'Hubert suffers dreadfully from seasickness.'

Ethan kissed her briefly on the lips, keeping a wary eye on Vincent, who was standing aside having already said his goodbyes. 'Don't fret, honey. I'll take good care of them, and I'll be home tomorrow to plan our engagement ball. Mother has already made out the guest list, and my sisters spent last evening discussing what they would wear.' He leapt into the carriage and took his seat. 'This is the beginning of your great adventure, Mirabel.'

The great adventure did not seem quite so exciting by the time they arrived in Newport News and were greeted by an intense thunderstorm. The darkening sky was illuminated by jagged forks of lightning, and ear-splitting claps of thunder reverberated off the land like cannon fire. Gertie was clearly disturbed by the storm, although she made an obvious effort to stop herself screaming every time the thunder roared like an angry bull. Mirabel was sympathetic at first, but even she began to lose patience when Gertie continued to utter muffled shrieks, covering her face with her hands at the slightest sound.

Hubert's lips were set in a thin line but he said little during the carriage ride from the station to the hotel. Ethan booked them in, explaining that this was the best that the town could offer. It had been built only recently to cope with travellers on the newly completed railway line, which linked what had been little more than a fishing village to Richmond. 'You might have difficulty in finding a vessel to take you south,' he said as he was about to leave for his business meeting. 'But I have a good friend who owns a pungy and might just be able to be of assistance.'

'What is a pungy?' Mirabel asked eagerly. Everything here was new and different. There was what she imagined to be a pioneering atmosphere in the small town, and the smell of the sea was in the air. Her stomach was filled with what felt like a million fluttering butterflies, and she could not wait for the adventure to begin again in earnest.

'It's a schooner used for trading along the coast,' Ethan said in answer to her question. 'I have to go now, but I'll be staying here tonight, so I might have some good news for you.' He tipped his top hat and left them standing in the lobby. A flash of lightning was followed by a rumble of thunder that made the glass shades on the oil lamps clatter like chattering teeth. Gertie clutched Mirabel's arm. 'I'm scared. Is it going to be like this all the time?'

'No, of course not, silly. It's just a storm.' Mira-

247

bel glanced anxiously at Hubert, noting his pallor and the dark circles beneath his eyes. She turned to the desk clerk. 'Might we have our room keys?'

He emerged from behind the desk. 'I'll show you to your rooms, folks,' he said cheerfully. 'I'll send the boy up with the rest of your luggage when he gets back from running an errand.' He stared meaningfully at the cabin trunks and portmanteaux. 'I guess you all must be going a distance.' Without waiting for an answer he plodded across the bare boards to the wooden staircase.

'Are you sure you're all right, Hubert?' Mirabel laid her hand on his arm. 'You look a bit pale.'

He smiled valiantly. 'A short rest and I'll be absolutely fine. We're on our way again and that's all that matters.'

Mirabel was not convinced; she would have liked to send for the doctor, assuming that there was one nearby, but Gertie was hurrying after the clerk and Mirabel had little choice but to follow them. The clerk stopped on the first floor landing and opened the door to the nearest room, standing aside to usher her in. 'This is one of our best rooms, miss. There's a bed in the dressing room for your maid, and your father is next door. You'll find the bathroom at the end of the corridor. We have hot and cold running water,' he added proudly.

'Thank you.' Mirabel did not bother to correct him as to the relationship between herself and Hubert. It was easier to allow people to assume that they were father and daughter, although the clerk would get a shock if he bothered to read their entry in the hotel register.

She closed the door and placed her small valise on the bed, taking in her surroundings with a sweeping glance. They were basic compared to the luxury of the *Servia* and the D'Angelos' beautiful home, but the room was clean and the bed sheets were starched to a glazed crispness that would have gladdened Mrs Flitton's heart. She went to the window and looked out across the small town to Hampton Roads. The worst of the storm seemed to be over, and with any luck Ethan would find them a ship to take them on the rest of the long journey to the Fakahatchee swamp.

Gertie came out of the dressing room, shaking her head. 'You can't swing a cat in there. It's a cupboard, or a closet as they call it over here. I learned that from Zenobia.' She glanced out of the window and shuddered. 'The sky still looks a bit black. I hope it ain't going to thunder all night because I shan't sleep a wink, and the mattress in there is lumpy.'

'Don't grumble,' Mirabel said wearily. 'I think this will seem like luxury when we travel on.'

Gertie sniffed. 'I'll unpack your night things, Mabel. I don't suppose they change for dinner in this establishment.'

Dinner that evening was simple but delicious. Hubert toyed with his lump crab soup but Mirabel ate her broiled lobster with relish. Gertie sat apart from them at the far end of the dining room, sharing her table with a plump young woman who appeared to be travelling on her own. Hubert said little during the meal and Mirabel was relieved when it came to an end, and they went to sit in the public lounge, awaiting Ethan's return. Gertie remained in the dining room, having struck up an unlikely friendship with the plump woman, and seemed likely to remain there for some time. Mirabel sat in a chair by the fire and ordered coffee, having to shout to make herself heard above the sound of male voices interspersed with bursts of laughter. The air was thick with tobacco smoke, and she was the only woman present. Hubert sat opposite her and picked up a newspaper, and was soon engrossed in its contents. The waiter brought a tray of coffee and hurried off, summoned by one of the gentlemen demanding more drinks. She filled a cup and sat sipping the coffee for what seemed like an eternity.

Ethan arrived shortly before eight o'clock, shrugging off his coat and handing it to the waiter. Mirabel stood up to attract his attention, and he came towards them, smiling broadly. 'I think I've found you a ship. My friend the captain was otherwise engaged this evening, but the mate has accompanied me and you can sort out the details with him.' He turned to the man who had followed him into the lounge. 'Come and meet these good folks.'

Mirabel stared at the tall figure wearing sailors' slops, hardly able to believe her eyes.

Chapter Sixteen

'Bodger!' His name escaped her lips on a gasp of surprise. 'What are you doing here?'

He moved towards her, grinning broadly. 'Well, missis, I might ask you the same.' He tipped his cap, slanting a wary glance in Hubert's direction. 'Begging your pardon for being so forward, guv.'

Hubert peered at him over the top of his newspaper. 'Bodger Tinker?'

'Aye, sir. That's me all right.' Bodger pulled off his cap and tucked it under his arm. 'This here gent says you're looking for a passage south.'

Ethan looked from one to the other, eyebrows raised. 'You know each other? But then I guess England's a small country.'

Mirabel laughed outright. 'Compared to America it's very small, but this is pure coincidence. Bodger is Gertie's brother.'

'That is a coincidence indeed.' Ethan glanced at the clock on the mantelshelf. 'If you'll excuse me, I'll leave you to sort out the details while I have my dinner.'

'Of course,' Mirabel said quickly. 'And thank you for going to so much trouble on our behalf.'

He inclined his head, smiling. 'No trouble, I assure you.'

Bodger watched him walk away, standing awkwardly like a child caught out in a naughty deed.

'So how do you come to be in Newport News?'

251

Mirabel asked, breaking the ensuing silence.

'I seem to have a habit of missing my ship,' Bodger confessed, hanging his head.

Hubert put his paper down. 'And now you're mate. That's a big leap, isn't it?'

'I know what you're thinking, guv.' Bodger's face flushed beneath his weathered tan. 'But I can do the job all right. I been at sea man and boy and there ain't much I don't know about ship handling.'

'Well good luck to you, that's all I can say.' Mirabel sent a warning look to her husband. How Bodger managed to convince an American sea captain that he was capable of acting as mate was no one's business but his own, and there were more important things to discuss. 'Where is your ship bound, Bodger?'

'Charleston, ma'am.'

'Is that far from where we hope to go, Hubert?'

'A little less than half way I should think, my dear.' Hubert focused his attention on Bodger. 'When does your ship set sail?'

'On the morning tide, sir.'

'Then we'll be ready.' Hubert's eyes gleamed with enthusiasm. 'Tell your captain that he has three passengers bound for Charleston. We should, with luck, be able to find another ship that will take us the rest of the way to Florida.'

'Just one thing, sir.' Bodger shifted from one foot to the other. 'It ain't no liner. It's a working ship, not meant for taking passengers in comfort. Cap'n Butler is only doing this as a favour to Mr Munroe.'

'And I'm very much obliged to the captain.'

Hubert headed for the door. 'I'm going to get a good night's sleep and I suggest you do the same, Mirabel.'

She had not seen him so filled with enthusiasm since they left Liverpool and she turned to Bodger with a grateful smile. 'Thank you, Bodger. You don't know how much this means to me.'

'Glad to be of service, ma'am.'

'You'll want to see Gertie, of course.'

'She's here? I was hoping it was me sister who come with you.'

'She was in the dining room chatting to a lady when I last saw her. Wait here and I'll see if I can find her.'

Bodger glanced down at his salt-encrusted trousers and shabby shoes. 'I'd best wait in the lobby, ma'am. I ain't exactly dressed for polite company.'

'I'll send her to you. She'll be so happy to see you.'

Next morning in a pearly dawn Mirabel, Hubert and Gertie boarded the two-masted gaff-rigged schooner, its green and pale pink paintwork making it stand out amongst the other Chesapeake Bay workboats. Captain Butler greeted them with a cursory nod and a curt welcome before returning to the business of weighing anchor and setting sail. It was a shock to realise that this was indeed a working vessel and there were only three cabins; one for the captain and the mate, another for the crew and one that all three of them must share for the duration of the voyage. Mirabel laid her hand on Hubert's arm. 'Are you sure about this? I mean, we could perhaps wait for a more

253

suitable ship. This isn't going to be comfortable and you know how ill you were on the *Servia*.'

He patted her hand. 'It's a small inconvenience, my dear. I think we will face even more hardships when we eventually get to Florida. From what I've read about the Fakahatchee swamp it's primeval to say the least, but I'm prepared to suffer almost anything to achieve my dream of finding ghost orchids in their native habitat. I just hope I'm not exposing you to too much danger.'

She staggered sideways, lurching against him as the schooner's sails filled and they entered the choppier waters of Hampton Roads. 'We've come this far, Hubert. I'm not one for giving up.'

'Bodger will look after us,' Gertie said stoutly. 'He's the mate, just as he should be. I'm proud of him.'

Mirabel righted herself, moving away quickly from physical contact with her husband. 'I'm sure you are. Let's hope he manages to stay on board until we get to our destination.'

Bodger proved himself to be an excellent seaman during their four day journey, but when they landed in Charleston he announced that he intended to leave the ship and accompany them to Florida. 'I ain't going to let my little sister go to that godforsaken place without me to protect her,' he said stubbornly.

Mirabel did not challenge his decision. Hubert had survived the voyage largely due to the fact that the winds had been fair and the seas slight, but he looked tired and she worried about his health. It would, she reasoned, be useful to have a man to help them with their luggage and to assist Hubert should he fall ill again, but they were now a party of four and that meant more expenditure. She knew that her husband had paid Captain Butler a considerable sum for the privilege of being transported swiftly, even with little or no creature comforts, but Hubert was close-lipped when it came to discussing their finances.

Ashore in Charleston they found another small hotel and Hubert booked four rooms at, Mirabel suspected, considerable expense. He did not seem unduly worried and immediately retired to his room to rest. Mirabel and Gertie were left to explore the town while Bodger made it his business to find them berths on a ship that would take them on the last lap of their journey to Florida. He was gone a long time and Mirabel was beginning to think that something had happened to him, but Gertie remained calmly confident in her brother's ability to take care of himself.

He returned late that evening, wearing a silly grin on his face and reeking of rum. 'I've found a steamship bound for Havana and stopping off at Key West,' he said proudly.

'Where is Key West?' Mirabel asked suspiciously. It did not sound like any of the ports on Hubert's neatly written itinerary.

'At the tip of Florida, so I was told.' Bodger hiccuped and covered his mouth with his hand. 'Begging your pardon, ladies.'

'Bodger Tinker, you're drunk,' Gertie snapped angrily. 'Are you sure you know what you're talking about?'

His pained expression might have made Mirabel laugh if she had not suddenly been seized with doubts. What if this whole venture was a wild goose chase? She met Bodger's tipsy smile with a withering look. 'You'd better sleep it off. We'll talk again in the morning.'

Bodger shook his head, wagging his finger at her. 'Too late then, missis. Ship's sailing in two hours' time. Best hurry if you want to be on it.'

'But we don't even know if there are berths for the four of us,' Mirabel protested.

Gertie slapped her brother on the arm. 'Sober up and tell us what you've arranged, if anything.'

'Go down to the quay,' Bodger said, pulling himself together with a visible effort. 'I'll get the boss up and ready to go.' He tottered off towards the stairs, his rolling gait exaggerated by his drunken state.

'Do you believe him?' Mirabel asked anxiously.

'I dunno, Mabel.' Gertie scratched her head. 'But can we afford to lose this chance? It might be our last for days, if not weeks.'

'You're right. After all, it's not far to the docks, and if it should prove to be a wild goose chase we can still return here and get a good night's sleep.' Mirabel sighed. 'I was so looking forward to lying in a proper bed.'

The *Angelina* was a tramp steamer of reasonable proportions and Bodger, despite his inebriated state, had managed to secure their passage as far as Key West where, he said, they might pick up another ship which was headed around the cape. Hubert was not himself. He had no better suggestion to offer, appearing dazed and still half asleep as they boarded the vessel, which by moonlight looked large and impressive, emanating power as smoke belched out of its twin funnels. The smell of burning coal and hot engine oil was oddly comforting as Mirabel stood on the throbbing deck. It was obviously a working boat and as unlike the *Servia* as the pungy, but she felt at last that they might be nearing their destination.

The crew were getting ready to cast off and Hubert was as white as one of his ghost lilies. He looked frail and unsteady on his feet, but he managed a brave smile as a seaman led them below deck to their cabins, and he raised no objection to sharing with Bodger. Mirabel and Gertie were also to share, and they set about making themselves as comfortable as was possible in a small space with narrow wooden bunk beds and a single chair. 'It's not exactly the state room on the *Servia*,' Mirabel said cheerfully. 'But it will have to do.'

Gertie plumped up the pillow on her bunk and examined the sheets in the light of a paraffin lamp. 'I don't think these were washed after the last person slept in them,' she said crossly.

'I don't care,' Mirabel sighed. 'I'm so tired I could sleep on a bed of nails.'

The *Angelina*, as Hubert wryly remarked next morning, was a little rusty. In daylight Mirabel could see its flaws, and certainly cleanliness was not one of its redeeming features, but the captain and crew were hearty and cheerful enough, with one or two notable exceptions. One seaman in particular seemed to have taken a dislike to Bodger, who threatened to punch his lights out and caused quite a stir in the dining saloon.

257

Hubert stepped in and smoothed things over, but Mirabel could see that both men were going to harbour grudges for the rest of the voyage. It did not bode well.

There was little to keep them occupied on board. Hubert spent most of his time in his cabin, a victim once again of seasickness as the steamer ploughed through the waves regardless of the weather. Gertie spent most of her time cleaning their cabin and she even managed to obtain clean sheets. Mirabel did not enquire how she procured them, but she was grateful all the same. She herself spent most of her waking hours on deck, leaning on the ship's rail, watching the sea in all its moods from silky turquoise calm to angry dark waters that roiled and slapped at the ship's hull and threw spray into her face. This was the world that Jack had loved and the ocean that had claimed his life. She still harboured a glimmer of hope that he had somehow survived, but it was fading fast.

They were in limbo for the whole of the journey, with brief and tantalising glimpses of the distant coastline. Mirabel hoped that they would make landfall soon, although when she asked the captain how long it would take to get to Key West he was evasive, shrugging his shoulders as if to say that it was in the hands of the gods of wind and weather.

It seemed that the fair spell they had enjoyed on the pungy was over, and on the fifth night at sea the foghorn wailed like a soul in torment. It was obvious to Mirabel that the crew were on edge as the *Angelina* moved slowly over the inky water, cutting into the thick fog like a knife through butter with visibility almost nil. Wrapped in her cloak against the cold and damp, Mirabel went up on deck, but was told in no uncertain terms to return to her cabin and remain there. Frustrated and restless, she went to check on Hubert and found him sleeping, exhausted after several days of sickness, and shockingly gaunt; she was beginning to wonder if he would survive another long journey. Closing the cabin door softly she went to look for Bodger and found him in the saloon with Gertie. She took a seat at their table. 'Does this sort of weather occur regularly on this coast?'

'Only at this time of year as far as I know, missis. It will clear by dawn, that's if we don't run aground on one of them little islands along the coast.'

'Ta, love,' Gertie said with a sarcastic smile. 'You know how to make a girl feel better.'

'I'm only speaking the truth. The sea bed must be littered with wrecks.'

'I wish I hadn't asked,' Mirabel said, sighing. 'It's going to be a long night.'

'Aye, missis. It's a good thing the guv is sleeping.'

She nodded. 'It is, but I'm worried about him. He was so determined to make this journey but it's not doing him any good. Is there any chance that we could do the rest of the trip overland?'

'I dunno, missis. I've done this run many times in the past but we was on the way to Havana, so we never put in to port along this part of the coast.'

'And when you do go ashore you spend all your time in pubs and bars or bawdy houses,' Gertie said, wagging her finger at him. 'You've jumped

259

ship so many times I'm surprised that anyone takes you on.'

Bodger's reply was lost as the vessel lurched and bucked like a wild stallion, followed by the terrible grinding sound. They were thrown off their seats, landing on the deck in a tangled heap of arms and legs. Stunned by the fall and winded, Mirabel lay there gasping for breath until Bodger pulled her to her feet. He bent down and picked up his sister, dumping her unceremoniously on the nearest chair. 'Stay here,' he commanded. 'I'm going to find out how bad it is.'

Mirabel bent double, trying to regulate her breathing. 'Must go to Hubert,' she gasped.

'Let me.' Gertie jumped to her feet. 'I ain't hurt. I'll go.'

She had left the saloon before Mirabel had a chance to stop her. She sat down heavily, holding her bruised ribs until at last she could breathe easily. Rising shakily to her feet she realised that the deck was sloping at a strange angle and the furniture which was not screwed down was sliding towards the starboard bulkhead. With a supreme effort she managed to reach the door and staggered along the companionway towards their accommodation. Bodger appeared in the doorway of Hubert's cabin. 'I got the guv back onto his bunk. I don't think he's broken any bones but he's a bit shaken.'

Mirabel pushed past him. 'Find out what's happened, Bodger. I'll stay with my husband.'

Gertie emerged from their cabin next door. 'We're going to die. I know it.'

Bodger grunted and lurched off towards the

stairs which led up to the deck. Mirabel glanced at Hubert's inert body. 'Don't panic, Gertie. We don't know how bad it is.' She went to sit on the edge of Hubert's bunk, noting with a sigh of relief that his eyes were open and focused. 'Are you hurt?'

He shook his head. 'I was asleep and then suddenly I was on the floor in a tangle of bedding. It must have saved me from injury.' He reached out to hold her hand. 'I'm so sorry, my dear. I brought you to this because of my insane desire to find a ghost orchid. Can you ever forgive me?'

She squeezed his fingers, biting back tears. 'Don't talk like that, Hubert. You've given me everything and I was as eager as you for this adventure. We're in it together no matter what happens.'

'You're a brave woman, and you deserve a better husband than I.'

'Stop it,' she said firmly. 'We're not finished yet. Bodger has gone up on deck to find out exactly what's happened. You mustn't give up. I won't let you.'

Even as she spoke Bodger burst into the cabin. 'We struck a reef and we're aground.'

Gertie flew at him, pummelling him with her small fists. 'What does that mean? Are we going to drown?'

Bodger caught both her hands in his big fists. 'Not unless you jump overboard. Cap'n says it's safer to wait until the fog lifts so that we know exactly where we are. We ain't sinking yet.'

'Yet?' Gertie sank down to her knees, covering her face with her hands. 'We're doomed.'

'Nonsense,' Mirabel said sharply. 'The captain knows what he's doing. If we're not in imminent danger of sinking it seems more sensible to wait for daylight.'

Hubert patted her hand. 'Bravely said, my dear.' He turned his head to look up at Bodger. 'Look after your sister. I'm all right here. My wife will take care of me.'

Mirabel nodded to Bodger. 'Do as he says, but come and tell me if there's the slightest chance we have to abandon ship.' She leaned back against the bulkhead, holding Hubert's hand until his grip slackened and he slept. She closed her eyes.

Someone was shaking her by the shoulder. She opened her eyes and found herself looking up into Gertie's pale face. 'What is it? What's happened?'

'It's getting light, Mabel. Bodger says we're stuck on the reef in sight of the Fowey Rocks lighthouse. We're to be taken to shore in the jolly boat, but you must come now.'

'Pack a few things in one of the smallest valises,' Mirabel said, instantly alert. Rising to her feet, she stretched her cramped limbs. 'Where's Bodger? We'll need him to carry my husband.'

Hubert raised himself on his elbow. 'I'm not a cripple, Mirabel. I walked on this vessel and I'll walk off it.'

The sun was struggling through the fog, which hung a thin mist over the mainland, hiding its face like a bride's veil. The *Angelina* sloped at a precarious angle, part of her hull impaled on a submerged reef. The crew were prepared to launch the jolly boat with a seaman ready to man the oars and another to help the passengers into the small craft, but Hubert refused to climb in until the captain promised to ensure the safety of their luggage, although it was obvious that this was the lowest in his list of priorities. 'I hope to refloat the old girl at high tide,' Captain Butler said ruefully. 'The carpenter will try to patch up the hull so that we can continue to Havana for a more thorough repair.'

'I must have the rest of our luggage,' Hubert insisted. 'This is a very important scientific venture, sir. I cannot continue without my equipment.'

'I fully understand your problem, Mr Kettle. But I have a cargo to deliver and a considerable sum of money to lose if I cannot do so.'

'Then we understand each other, Captain. I will pay extra if necessary, although if you leave us in this wild place you will not have fulfilled your part of our agreement, which was to take us to Key West.'

Polite and professional to the last, the captain agreed to send their baggage ashore as soon possible, and he assisted Hubert into the boat. 'You'll land at a small settlement called Coconut Grove. I could take you to Havana if we can refloat my vessel, but I wouldn't want to risk making landfall at Key West.'

'Thank you, but I'm sure we'll find another ship to take us on to our final destination.' Hubert sank down beside Mirabel and turned his face resolutely towards the shore.

Mirabel was watching the captain's expression when he gave the order to lower the jolly boat into the water, and it was not encouraging. As they approached land she could see that this was not a busy harbour where they might easily find another ship to take them on the rest of their journey. The heat was suffocating and the light intense, creating the illusion that the pale yellow sand was flecked with gold, and the background of lush vegetation was in a palette of colours ranging from lime green to the deepest viridian. It might look like a tropical paradise but there were only a few buildings and most of them little more than wooden shanties.

Bodger was the first ashore and he offered to carry Hubert through the shallows to the beach. Hubert refused politely, but accepted his help to climb out of the boat and then waded through the shallows unaided. Mirabel did not fancy having soggy petticoats and a wet skirt clinging to her legs and she allowed Bodger to carry her ashore, as did Gertie. He retrieved their cases and the crewmen rowed back to the ship, leaving them stranded like shipwrecked mariners on a coral atoll.

'What now?' Gertie asked, shielding her eyes from the sun, which was beating down relentlessly.

'We should seek shade,' Hubert said with a determined lift of his chin. 'There seems to be some sort of habitation close by. I'll go and see if there's an inn or a boarding house that will put us up until the next ship arrives.'

Mirabel and Bodger exchanged worried glances. 'But Hubert,' Mirabel said, choosing her words with care, 'this isn't exactly a busy port. How do we know that ships will put in here?'

'We will find out shortly, my dear. If not I'm sure we can find transport to take us to where we will find some other means by which to travel.'

'Don't see no railway station,' Gertie grumbled. 'No roads neither.'

'Those who live here arrived by some route or other,' Hubert said cheerfully. 'It's good to be on terra firma. I feel better already.' He left his case for Bodger to carry and marched off across the sand towards a collection of small huts.

Gertie shoved her small valise into her brother's hand, pointing to Mirabel's, which was considerably larger. 'Best make yourself useful, and you can go first in case there are cannibals and the like hiding in the trees.'

Bodger shrugged his broad shoulders. 'You don't half talk nonsense, Gertie Tinker.' Laden with all their baggage he trudged off after Hubert with Mirabel and Gertie following close behind.

'I'm thirsty,' Gertie complained as they neared the first shanty, which was built of wood with a stoop shaded by a canopy of woven palm fronds. A man of indeterminate age was sprawled on a chair, his grubby linen shirt open to the waist exposing a hairy chest, and his loose cotton trousers rolled up to his knees. He was barefoot and his chin boasted several days' stubble. He raised a tin mug to his lips and drank thirstily, staring at them with a suspicious look on his face.

Hubert took off his top hat, wiping the sweat from his brow with a silk hanky. 'Excuse me, sir. Where might I find accommodation for myself and my party?'

The man drained his cup and dropped it on the floor where it bounced on the wooden planks, ending up on the bottom step. 'Who's asking?'

'Forgive me,' Hubert said politely. 'I should

265

introduce myself. I'm Captain Hubert Kettle and this is my wife, her maidservant and my man, Bodger Tinker.'

'You don't say.' The man seemed unimpressed. He reached for a bottle which had been concealed beneath his chair, taking the cork out with his teeth and spitting it so that it landed at Hubert's feet. He took a swig and wiped his mouth on the back of his hand. 'You want bed and board? You come to the wrong place.'

'Then can you tell me where I could find the information I need?'

'You ain't from round here, mister. Where are you from?'

Mirabel could feel trickles of sweat running down between her breasts and her shoulder blades. The sun was beating down on her head, striking through her straw bonnet and burning her scalp. She was hot, thirsty and hungry. They had snatched a bread roll and a cup of water from the dining saloon, but that was all she had eaten that day and it was, she guessed by the position of the sun, high noon.

'We came from England,' Hubert said patiently. 'We're trying to get to the Fakahatchee swamp.'

'One of them orchid hunters, are you?'

'You know about orchids?'

'Not me, mister. But occasionally one or two of them might land up here, thinking they can get a passage home.' He uttered a bark of laughter. 'Some of us have been here for years.'

Mirabel stepped forward. 'We came from the ship that ran aground in the fog last night. There must be others that call in here?'

He turned his gaze on her, looking her up and down with a lascivious grin. 'You can warm my bed any night, little lady.'

Bodger dropped the cases and lurched towards the man, taking the steps in one stride and grabbing him by the throat. 'Show a bit of respect to a lady, you drunken sot. Is there anywhere we can put up until we can get away from this wilderness?'

The man's face was turning blue beneath the pressure of Bodger's fingers.

'Let him answer,' Mirabel said hastily. 'He can't breathe.'

Reluctantly Bodger released his hold and the man clutched his throat, making croaking noises. His gaze slid to the doorway as another man emerged from the gloomy interior.

Mirabel felt his presence, turning slowly to stare as if seeing a ghost. She could neither move nor speak as she gazed at him in disbelief. The figure leaned against the wooden doorpost as he took in the scene with a sweeping glance. He did not speak – he had no need to. She would have known him anywhere.

Chapter Seventeen

'Jack.' His name escaped her lips on a breath that was little more than a whisper. 'It is you.'

'Mirabel!' The look of surprise and delight that lit his blue eyes made her dizzy with relief, but as her hands flew to her burning cheeks the diamonds on her engagement ring flashed in the sunlight, and it would have been impossible for him to ignore her golden wedding band. Jack's glance flickered to Hubert and his expression hardened. 'I see that you're married, Mirabel. I take it that this is your husband.' His smile froze.

The sudden stomach-churning joy she had felt on seeing him was replaced by anger and disbelief. He was supposed to be dead and yet he was here, facing her like a judge about to sentence a miscreant for her wicked deeds. It was unjust and it was unfair. She turned to Hubert like an automaton, drawing on the lessons in etiquette that Miss Barton had drilled into her. 'Hubert, may I introduce an old acquaintance of mine, Captain Jack Starke?' She took a deep breath. 'Captain Starke, this is my husband, Hubert Kettle.'

Hubert stared from one to the other. 'This is an amazing coincidence indeed.' He turned to Jack, holding out his hand. 'How do you do, sir? I believe we might have met some time in the past. Your face looks familiar.'

Now seemingly in complete control of his emotions, Jack stepped forward to shake Hubert's hand. 'I think we might have a friend in common, sir. Miss Zilla entertains many gentlemen in her establishment. I believe we met there on a couple of occasions.'

Without giving Hubert a chance to respond Bodger pushed past them all to fling his arms around Jack. 'Cap'n! You're alive! We was told you was drownded. It was in the papers.'

'As you can see, it wasn't true.' Jack patted him

on the back, easing him away gently. 'How come you're here?' He glanced over Bodger's shoulder. 'And there's Gertie too. It's quite a family reunion.'

She bobbed a curtsey. 'It is, sir. I'm delighted to see you alive and kicking, so to speak. We was all upset when we heard your ship went down.'

Hubert cleared his throat. 'This all sounds very interesting and I'm sure we'll hear all the details later, but could I trouble you for a glass of water, Mr Starke?'

'It's Captain Starke,' Mirabel reminded him gently. 'My husband has been ill, Captain. We need somewhere to stay while we sort out some kind of transport to take us on the rest of our journey.'

'What happened to the vessel you arrived on?' Jack demanded, eyeing her with a touch of his old humour. 'Did you lose it in the fog?'

'Us hit the reef, Cap'n,' Bodger said, grinning. 'I didn't jump ship this time; it jumped us so to speak. It's out there stuck on the rocks until high tide when they'll refloat it, providing the carpenter can shore up the hole in the hull.'

'We could continue to Key West, but I rather think we'll try to make the rest of the journey overland,' Hubert said thoughtfully.

'So where are you headed?' Jack asked curiously. 'What on earth would bring you to this desolate spot?'

'Orchids, sir.' Hubert's tone was not encouraging. 'We are making for the Fakahatchee swamp, where I hope to find a particular rare orchid.'

'It's not the sort of place to take a woman, but

269

you're here now so you'd better step inside. It's no cooler but at least you'll be in the shade.' Jack ushered them into the shack and for the first time Mirabel noticed that there was no door, and the only window was simply a glassless hole in the wall. It was dark and the floor was packed earth, or it might be sand, it was hard to tell. A table in one corner was littered with bottles and a couple of wooden kegs, some tin cups and a wicker basket filled with oranges. Jack indicated a roughly made wooden chair. 'Take a seat, Mr Kettle. This heat takes some getting used to, but I've grown accustomed to it.' He poured large tots of rum into two mugs, handing one to Hubert and the other to Bodger. He glanced at Mirabel, eyebrows raised. 'Do you partake of strong liquor, Mrs Kettle?'

The acid in his tone cut her like a razor. 'I'll take a tot with some water.' She met his gaze with a toss of her head. She had no liking for spirits but she was not going to give him the satisfaction of seeing her at a loss. It was obvious that he considered their expedition foolhardy to say the least, and her initial delight on seeing him alive and well had given way to bitter disappointment. What right had he to criticise Hubert for bringing her on the voyage of a lifetime when he himself had allowed everyone who cared about him to think he was dead?

Jack poured a drink, added a generous amount of water and handed it to her, but his attention had turned to Gertie and he relaxed visibly. 'And a tot for you, Gertie?'

'I wouldn't say no,' she said demurely. 'Ta, Cap'n.'

Hubert sank down on a stool by the makeshift bar and drank thirstily. 'So how did you come to be here, Captain Starke? Did your ship also come to grief on the reef?'

'We lost a mast in a storm off Havana. The ship was crippled, but we got as far as Key West before another more vicious storm put an end to the poor old girl. Some of us managed to get ashore, but the *Lady Grace* went down in less than half an hour.'

'That's terrible,' Mirabel said, remembering the shock she had felt and the utter dismay when she had read about the sinking of his ship in *Lloyd's List*. 'So how did you get here?'

His expression was guarded. 'We bought a disused long boat, intending to sail as far north as possible in order to reach a large seaport and get a passage home. Unfortunately the timbers were rotten and we were lucky to get this far.'

'So you decided to turn native, Captain Starke.' Hubert's voice was tinged with sarcasm, so unusual for him that Mirabel caught her breath. She shot him a wary glance, afraid that he might have sensed that there had been something between herself and Jack, even if it had been one-sided.

Jack raised his glass, seemingly unperturbed. 'I always take the easy way out, Mr Kettle. Here's to you and your lovely young bride.'

Hubert tossed back the remainder of his drink and rose to his feet. 'I'd be obliged if you would point us in the direction of a guest house or an inn where we might stay.'

'There's a hotel being built but it's not finished yet.' Jack's tone was not encouraging.

271

'We need to stay somewhere,' Mirabel said softly. 'My husband has been unwell.'

'I'm perfectly all right, and ready to continue our journey to the Fakahatchee swamp. There must be somewhere we can stay.' Hubert loosened his collar, swaying on his feet.

Mirabel rushed forward but Bodger was there first and he pressed Hubert down on the stool. 'Don't worry, guv. Cap'n Starke will find us a berth for a night or two.' He turned to Jack, frowning. 'The guv needs to rest awhile.'

'I can see that.' Jack tossed back his drink and abandoned the glass to the chaotic jumble on the table. 'I think I know the ideal place. If you'll wait here, Mr Kettle, I'll take the ladies with me and they can make the decision. Bodger, stay with him. We won't be long.'

Mirabel followed Jack outside onto the stoop, where the drunken man had fallen asleep with his head lolling to one side. She moved closer to Jack, lowering her voice. 'I ought to stay and look after Hubert. Gertie could go with you.'

'I don't want to go wandering round the jungle, Mabel.' Gertie hesitated in the doorway, wringing her hands. 'I'm scared of spiders and things and if I saw a snake I swear I'd die of fright.'

'All right.' Mirabel held up her hand. 'Stay here and help Bodger to look after Mr Kettle. I'll go with Captain Starke.' She was in control of her emotions now, or so she hoped. She braced her shoulders, determined that he would not see the effect he had on her. 'Lead on.'

Jack walked ahead, leading the way along a dirt road that wound its way through dense vegetation and swaying palms, the like of which Mirabel had never seen. The air was filled with strange sounds, the whirring of insects and the calls of animals that were also foreign to her. She kept close to Jack, walking in silence until she could bear it no longer. 'Why didn't you send word home?' she demanded, coming to a sudden halt. 'Why did you let us believe that you were lost at sea?'

He stopped, turning slowly to look at her. 'Why would you care, Mrs Kettle? You seem to have done pretty well for yourself.'

'That was uncalled for.' Shocked by the implied criticism and stung by its unfairness, she tossed her head. 'You don't know anything about my circumstances.'

'Aren't you forgetting something?' He fixed her with a hard stare. 'I introduced you to Zilla because I knew she'd look after you. She's a tough businesswoman but I knew she would see something more in you than just another of her girls.'

'No, you didn't.' Mirabel countered angrily. 'You left me there to fend for myself and that's exactly what I did. Think what you like but I married a good, kind man and it wasn't for his money.'

He curled his lip. 'So it was a love match, was it? You married a man in his dotage because you'd fallen madly in love with him.'

'No, of course not.' Mirabel knew she was blushing furiously and she turned her head away, staring into the dense liquid greenness of the forest. 'I – I like and respect Hubert. It was a marriage of convenience for both of us, and...'

'Yes, I can see that.' He shrugged and walked on.

She hurried after him. 'No, you don't. You're the same as everyone else, making a judgement simply because it doesn't suit your way of thinking. I'm happy with Hubert, very happy.'

'If you say so, Mrs Kettle.' He quickened his pace, leaving her little alternative but to follow.

Inwardly fuming she did her best to keep up with him, although her long skirts hampered her movements and her tight stays made it difficult to catch her breath. The searing heat and the strangeness of their surroundings only added to the maelstrom of emotions that she thought she had well in hand, but which kept returning to choke her with unshed tears. She was furious with Jack for not caring and furious with herself for caring too much.

After a while she was too hot and tired to think of anything other than her own discomfort. In his cotton shirt with his sleeves rolled up, exposing muscular forearms, and his long legs encased in loose-fitting trousers, Jack was better dressed for the climate, and he strode on without looking back. She kept up with him out of pride as well as necessity, but eventually the road widened as they reached a small settlement of single-storey wooden houses. Wood smoke curled into the air and the scent of roasting meat made her mouth water. Jack walked up to one of the clapboard buildings, rapped on the door and waited. Moments later it was opened by a smiling black woman, her large frame enveloped in a cotton-print gown and her hair tied up in a colourful turban. They exchanged a few words and Jack turned his head, beckoning to Mirabel. 'Come and meet the kind lady who has agreed to take you in.' He made it sound like a huge favour and this irritated Mirabel even more. She walked slowly towards them.

'Mama Lou, this is Mrs Kettle.'

Mama Lou beamed at Mirabel, inclining her head. 'It's a pleasure to meet you.'

'And you, Mama Lou.' Mirabel shook her hand. 'Did Captain Starke explain that my husband is not in the best of health?'

'Indeed he did, honey. I have a cabin out back where he can rest undisturbed.'

'It's only a short stay,' Mirabel said hastily. 'We'll be travelling on as soon as we can arrange transport to take us to the Fakahatchee swamp.'

Mama Lou threw back her head and laughed. 'Then I guess you'll still be here when the Bay View House Hotel finally opens. You might be its first guests, although I can tell you you'll get the best food here. I'm famous for my conch fritters and johnnycake.'

'I can vouch for that.' Jack's lazy smile embraced Mirabel for a brief moment before he turned away, addressing himself to Mama Lou. 'I'll bring them here now, if that's all right with you?'

'Sure, Jack.' Mama Lou held her hand out to Mirabel. 'Come in, honey, and rest yourself. You shouldn't be out walking in the heat of noon. It ain't the thing for no one, least of all a fair-skinned lady like you.'

Mirabel had been about to follow Jack but she opted to stay. The thought of trudging back to the shore in the blistering heat outweighed her feelings of responsibility for Hubert; after all, he had Bodger and Gertie to take care of him. She stepped into the relative cool of Mama Lou's house.

Their accommodation turned out to be two cabins at the rear of the property. In the shade of a huge avocado tree skinny hens pecked at the dry soil and goats munched on the sparse vegetation. Each cabin contained two beds draped with mosquito netting, and a washstand. It was not the height of luxury but the bedding was clean and the floors were swept daily by one of Mama Lou's daughters, who volunteered to do their laundry for a small price: a service that was invaluable as sweat-soaked garments smelled unpleasant and were uncomfortable to wear.

Mirabel and Gertie shared one of the cabins, while Hubert and Bodger took the other. Jack, it seemed, had accommodation elsewhere, and having settled them in he had made himself scarce. Mirabel was at a loss to understand his attitude towards her. He seemed indifferent, but if he cared so little for her why would he have taken her marriage to Hubert so much to heart? She could not explain it and she did not choose to confide in Gertie, who was notoriously tactless and bad at keeping secrets. Besides which, Hubert was giving her cause for concern. He had recovered from the sickness that laid him low during their sea voyages, but he had developed a fever and spent most of his time lying on his wooden bunk, his needs cared for by Bodger. Mirabel found herself barred from the cabin at Hubert's command in case what he had was contagious, but Bodger declared himself to be immune to all foreign diseases.

During the next few days Mama Lou kept them amused with her constant stream of chatter and fed them delicious meals, eaten outside on a wooden bench in the shade of the tree. In the evenings lanterns hung from its branches, and large colourful moths fluttered around them attracted by their flickering light. The air was filled with the aroma of roasting goat meat and exotic spices, and the workers from the Bahamas who had come to build the hotel could be heard singing as they cooked their supper over wood fires. Bodger joined Mirabel and Gertie for meals and when he was not tending to Hubert he went off on his own, returning late in the evening. Gertie shrugged her thin shoulders and said it was none of her business what her brother did in his own time, but Mirabel suspected that he joined Jack and the other men in the beach shack to smoke and drink rum.

After several days of enforced idleness Mirabel had had enough. First thing in the morning, before the heat struck the land like a flaming torch, she set off in search of Jack. She found him on the stoop of the shack, talking to a scruffy-looking individual whose shaggy grey beard and tow-coloured hair made him look like Robinson Crusoe. They stopped talking as she approached and the man stared at her, looking her up and down as if he had not seen a woman for a very long time.

'You didn't tell me you had a lady here, Jack.'

'Mrs Kettle, may I introduce Bill Bundy?' Jack stepped down to stand beside Mirabel, placing himself squarely between them. 'Bill is a plant collector. He would have something in common with your husband.'

Bill Bundy seized Mirabel's hand and raised it to his lips. 'Madam, it's an honour to meet you.'

Mirabel snatched her hand free. The look in his eyes seemed to strip her down to her chemise, sending a shiver down her spine. 'How do you do, Mr Bundy?' She moved a little closer to Jack.

'All the better for seeing a pretty young woman. Your husband is a damned lucky man to have a wife willing to accompany him on such a journey.'

'He is indeed,' Jack said casually. 'You'll excuse us, Bundy, but we have business to discuss.'

'I bet you have.' Bundy gazed fixedly at Mirabel's breasts as he backed into the shack. 'I hope to see you again, Mrs Kettle.'

'How did he get here?' Mirabel demanded. 'Where did he come from?'

'I don't know. I didn't bother to ask him, but I do know that Bundy has made it his life's work to explore places where he knows he can find rare plant specimens. He ships them back to England and makes a small fortune, although I doubt if he is ever at home long enough to spend it.'

She glanced out to sea, realising with a sudden feeling of panic that the *Angelina* had sailed. 'So he must have travelled overland,' she said thoughtfully. 'We might do the same if he would be willing to act as our guide. Hubert could get his ghost orchid after all.'

'That's important to you, isn't it, Mirabel?'

'It's why we came here,' she said simply.

'What the hell possessed Kettle to bring you on

such a wild goose chase?'

She met his angry gaze with a frown. 'What is it to you anyway? And why are you still here? Do you intend to spend the rest of your life living like this?' She encompassed their surroundings with a wave of her hands.

'Why would Mrs Hubert Kettle worry about someone like me?'

'I think that you can't forgive me for rising above the misfortunes that beset me at home. You were happy to leave me in a house of ill repute, regardless of what might happen to me after you'd gone back to sea.'

He grasped her by the wrist, locking his fingers together as if he would never let her go. 'You were able to take care of yourself as far as I can see. You did well to trap an old man into marrying you.'

She wrenched her hand free. 'How dare you talk to me like that? You've no idea what I went through.'

'Ahem.' Bill Bundy emerged from the shack. 'Excuse me for interrupting this domestic spat, but it's getting boring. However, I believe I heard the young lady mention ghost orchids?'

Jack's lips curved in a rueful smile. 'My apologies, Mrs Kettle. I seem to have spoken out of turn.'

'Never mind that, mate,' Bundy said, chuckling. 'I don't care if your fancy runs to married women, but I sense a bit of business coming my way and I need some money to get me back to England.' He advanced on them purposefully. 'You and me need to have a talk, little lady.'

Jack stepped in between them. 'Don't trust this

chap, Mirabel. He'll take your money and disappear with it.'

'That ain't fair, Jack.' Bundy screwed up his face. 'Sticks and stones, mate.' He turned to Mirabel with a gap-toothed grin. 'Take me to your husband, ma'am. If he's so intent on finding the ghost orchid, I'm his man. I could find me way across the wilderness blindfold, and I can take you there in three days, four at the most. Of course we'd have to talk money.'

The news that they might have found a guide to take them to the Fakahatchee swamp acted on Hubert like a miracle cure. He spent hours closeted with Bill Bundy making plans for their venture into the wilderness. Mirabel was excited but also nervous, and Gertie was simply terrified. Bodger remained unmoved but to Mirabel's surprise Jack took an active interest in their expedition. She was even more astonished when he turned up on the morning of their departure and announced that he intended to accompany them. 'Why?' she demanded incredulously. 'Have you an interest in finding rare orchids?'

'No, not at all, but I don't think you understand the risks you're taking or the dangers you'll face. You could stay here in safety with Mama Lou.'

'I could,' she said evenly. 'But I don't choose to.'

'Then you need someone to look after you.' He held up his hand, a smile creeping into his eyes. 'There's no need to defend your husband, but he's neither young nor fit, and Bundy is a law unto himself. He's as likely to wander off after some wild species that will make him money as to

280

honour his agreement with your husband.'

'I trust Hubert's judgement,' Mirabel said, avoiding Jack's intense gaze. He had a way of looking at her that was disturbing and exciting. She did not want to admit it, even to herself, but it would be a huge relief to have him with them on their expedition.

'Anyway,' he said casually. 'I have little else to do. It will be a new experience.'

Bundy arrived with a rifle slung over his shoulder, a machete tucked into his leather belt and a sheathed bowie knife hanging from his waist. Hubert stared at him in a mixture of surprise and amusement. 'My dear fellow, you look like a frontiersman. Is all that weaponry really necessary?'

Bundy grinned. 'You'll find out soon enough, boss. When you're face to face with a 'gator you don't stop to ask him the time of day. Same goes for a black bear. Cussed critters, you don't want to get on the wrong side of one of them. And don't forget the panthers and the wild hogs.'

'It sounds very dangerous,' Mirabel said, frowning.

'It's fine if you know what you're doing.' Bundy jerked his head in the direction of the men who had accompanied him. 'They're from the Bahamas, like Mama Lou. They're strong fellows, used to working hard constructing the hotel, but the building is all but complete. They didn't take much persuading to earn a bit of extra money to take home when the time comes for them to leave. You'll be safe with us, ma'am.'

Mirabel was not entirely convinced but she did

her best to reassure Gertie, who had been given the option of staying with Mama Lou, but had insisted on accompanying them albeit with the air of a martyr faced with burning at the stake. Bodger on the other hand was eager and willing, promising to carry Hubert on his back if that was what it would take to grant him his dearest wish to see the ghost orchid in bloom.

'Why couldn't we use mules to carry our equipment?' Mirabel asked Jack as he fell into step beside her. They had been walking for several hours with minimal stops to take sips of water from leather flasks, but already Mirabel could feel blisters on her heels and thirst seemed to be a constant companion. The sun beat down relentlessly on the treeless prairie, where the baked-brown grass stretched like an endless sea of crushed velvet. She stopped to mop her brow, but her whole body was moist with sweat, and her bodice was stained with damp patches. 'Why can't we ride? The land is flat and hard. I thought there would be swamps and jungle.'

Jack threw back his head and laughed. 'Wait a while and you'll find yourself knee deep in water and duckweed. I've listened to Bundy's tales of his excursions into the swamp and this will seem like paradise in comparison.' He took off his necktie and handed it to her. 'I don't possess anything as gentlemanly as a handkerchief. Try this, it's reasonably clean.'

She took off her pith helmet and used the cloth to wipe away the trickles of perspiration that ran like tears down her cheeks. The material smelled of him, bringing back memories of their brief time together in London. It was a scent that had stayed in her memory long after he had gone. She handed it back, resisting the temptation to tuck it into her pocket. 'Thank you, but you haven't answered my question. Why didn't we use mules? I saw plenty of them back at the settlement.'

'Mules need water and plenty of it in this heat.' He shielded his eyes against the sunlight, staring at the vast expanse of openness. 'The black bears and panthers would be attracted by their smell, and even if we reached the swamp without mishap mules would flounder in the mud and be fair game for alligators and cottonmouth snakes.'

'Snakes?' Gertie had taken the opportunity to stop, and she stared at him open-mouthed.

'Watch out for rattlers,' he said, grinning. 'The diamondback is deadly if you disturb it, but at least it gives a warning.'

Gertie uttered a shriek of horror, covering her face with her hands.

'Stop it, Jack.' Mirabel stifled a giggle. 'You're scaring her.'

'Just look where you're going, Gertie,' Jack said cheerfully. 'You'll be fine. The snakes are more scared of you than you are of them.' He strolled off to join Bodger and Bill Bundy who had come to a halt just ahead of them.

'I want to go home to England,' Gertie sobbed. 'I hate this place, Mabel.'

Mirabel patted her on the shoulder. 'If you cry then I will too, and they'll think that we're weak women. Chin up and we'll show them that we're just as tough as they are.'

'I am a weak woman,' Gertie whispered. 'I'm scared.'

'So am I, but I'll die before I let them see it.'

Gertie wiped her eyes on her sleeve. She slanted a sideways look at Mirabel. 'You won't get the better of Captain Jack, but be careful, Mabel.'

'I don't know what you mean,' Mirabel said, turning away.

'You like him and he likes you.'

'We get along tolerably well, I suppose.'

'The girls back at Zilla's told me that she and he was together for a long time, if you know what I mean.'

Mirabel had forgotten, or perhaps she had deliberately put it out of her mind, but she knew very well that Jack and Zilla had been lovers. 'That's his business,' she said with a careless shrug. 'It has nothing to do with me. Come along now, you can do this, Gertie. Best foot forward.'

'I just don't want you to get hurt,' Gertie said softly.

'You needn't worry about me,' Mirabel said with an attempt to sound casual. 'I have Jack Starke's measure.'

Arm in arm they walked on.

After another couple of hours, just when Mirabel was beginning to feel she could not go another step, and Gertie was so exhausted that she had stopped grumbling, they saw what appeared to be a forest of giant cypress trees and palms that had burst forth from the flat prairie in an eruption of tall trunks supporting a canopy of green leaves and palm fronds. The thought of shade and coolness was exhilarating and without any need to be told they picked up their pace.

Bundy stopped, surveying the area with a critical eye. 'We'll stop here for the night.'

An audible sigh of relief was followed by a flurry of activity as the porters dropped their loads and began to unpack and set up camp. Hubert looked exhausted but his dogged cheerfulness was undimmed, and he was deep in conversation with Bundy, leaving Mirabel with nothing to do other than wait for their meal to be prepared. Gertie had flopped down on the ground, looking round nervously as if expecting to be attacked by wildlife from every quarter. Bodger was making himself useful building a fire with brushwood and dried grass and Jack was frowning over the crudely drawn map that Bundy had been using as a guide.

Mirabel felt oddly detached from everything that was going on around her. She was hot and tired and the stand of trees loomed dark and mysterious; its cool depths seemed like an oasis in the middle of the parched prairie. Although close to exhaustion, she felt drawn there as if an unseen hand was beckoning to her. No one seemed to notice as she walked slowly, hypnotised by the siren song of exotic birds as she entered a strange and alien world. She was looking up into the branches of a great cypress, not paying attention to where she put her feet, when she trod on something that moved. A creature slithered from beneath a ragged bush and she froze. The telltale rattle made the blood run cold in her veins and a scream of sheer terror escaped her lips.

Chapter Eighteen

'Don't move. Stand very still.'

Her first instinct was to turn and run to Jack, but she dared not take her eyes off the snake as it reared up in front of her. Her limbs felt like lead and her heart was thudding wildly against her ribcage, making it difficult to breathe. The rattlesnake drew back its head as if to strike and she closed her eyes. This was how she was going to die. She steeled herself for the pain when the fangs pierced her skin, but the sudden crack of a rifle fired from close range reverberated off the tree trunks, sending birds flapping into the leafy canopy. She opened her eyes and saw the severed head of the snake lying on the dried palm fronds beneath the trees. The body twitched eerily and then was still.

'What the hell d'you think you were doing?' Jack demanded angrily, breaking the rifle and discarding it to take her by the shoulders. He shook her and then held her to him in a crushing embrace. 'A bite from that snake would have killed you within hours, and it would have been a slow and painful death.'

Speechless and trembling she could feel his heart pounding against hers through the thin cotton of his shirt. The warmth of his body enveloped her in a haven of safety and the scent of him, so familiar now, was charged with particles of fear. He released her suddenly, turning away. 'Go back to your husband, Mrs Kettle, and don't wander off again.' He picked up his rifle and stood very still, staring straight ahead, waiting until she gathered enough strength to walk away.

She was met by Gertie and Bodger with Hubert close behind. Gertie flung her arms around her. 'What happened? We heard the shot. Are you hurt?'

'No. I'm all right, really.'

'What were you doing wandering off on your own?' Hubert demanded breathlessly. 'You should know better than that, Mirabel.'

She hung her head, feeling like a child being scolded for disobeying a strict parent. 'I – I'm sorry, Hubert. I just wanted to be in the shade.'

'You're all right now, missis,' Bodger said, proffering his arm to her. 'No harm done, guv.'

Jack strolled out of the trees, his gun crooked over his arm. 'It was a rattler,' he said casually. 'It's dead.' He walked off towards the camp.

That night the fire was kept going and Jack took the first watch while the others slept. Mirabel was still shaken by her narrow escape and angry with herself for stepping so carelessly into danger. She should have known better, as Hubert had told her repeatedly while they waited for their supper to be cooked over the smoky campfire, and again afterwards as they settled down for the night, making themselves as comfortable as was possible when sleeping on the sun-baked ground.

The sound of gentle breathing was interspersed by loud snores, but Mirabel could not sleep. She could see Jack silhouetted against the flames as he sat cross-legged with Bundy's rifle at the ready. He had not spoken a word to her since the incident with the rattlesnake, which had been retrieved by one of their Bahamian porters, skinned and cooked. Bundy and his men had eaten the flesh with relish but no one else had the stomach for it, not even Jack. Mirabel had managed to eat some of Mama Lou's stale johnnycake, but she had little appetite. She stared at Jack's profile, willing him to turn his head, and even though he refused to obey her mute command she sensed that he was as aware of her as she of him. She closed her eyes in a futile attempt to shut him out of her mind. She could still feel the pressure of his arms around her and the warmth of his body as he held her close. It was a moment that would live with her forever, but it was a moment that must never be repeated. She was a married woman and her loyalty must be to Hubert. She turned her head so that when she opened her eyes she would see her sleeping husband just yards away, but when she awakened at first light it was Jack she saw. He was kneeling by the fire, stoking it with brushwood, and he looked up as if he had heard her call out to him. For a few heart-aching seconds their eyes met and then he turned away. This, she thought miserably, was how it must be from now until their mission was over. Their proximity promised to be both heaven and hell.

According to Bundy's calculations it was over eighty miles to their destination and on the first day they had travelled less than twenty. The next

288

day they made slightly better time and to Mirabel's surprise Hubert appeared to be growing stronger, or perhaps it was simply his determination to reach his goal that kept him going. The days seemed to merge into each other in a cloud of dust and searing heat that left them parched no matter how much they drank. Mirabel suffered from aching muscles and painful blisters which burst and became open sores, but the physical pain was nothing compared to her emotional turmoil. It was agonising to be close to Jack and yet miles apart. She barely spoke to him and as if by mutual consent he said little to her. No one, least of all Hubert, seemed to notice that an atmosphere existed between them, and Gertie was too wrapped up in her own misery to worry about anyone else. She complained endlessly of aches in every part of her body from her head to her toes.

Life on the march was far from easy and their supply of fresh food had run out after the second day. They existed on a diet of boiled rice and beans, which even with the addition of spices was monotonous in the extreme. Water was also in short supply and personal cleanliness was impossible to maintain.

On the fifth day the landscape began to change and clusters of trees were interspersed with sinkholes linked by channels of clear water. They camped that night on the banks of a lake at the edge of what Bundy proudly announced was the Fakahatchee swamp. 'We're almost there,' he said with his mouth full of omelette made from blue heron eggs that one of their porters had risked life and limb to collect. To everyone's amazement he had shinned up a tree and taken them from the nest, but the hot meal was a welcome change and there was ample water for both drinking and washing, although Bundy warned them to be ever watchful for the deadly cottonmouth snakes, snapping turtles and alligators. 'Tomorrow we will head into the depths of the swamp, although maybe the ladies might want to remain in camp.' He sent a meaningful look at Mirabel's divided skirt, which had seemed eminently suitable when she tried it on in London. 'We will be wading through water for much of the time.'

'We'll leave Abraham and Isaac here to look after you,' Hubert said firmly. 'I insist, Mirabel. You'll do as I say and remain with Gertie where I know you'll both be safe.'

Mirabel said nothing, but she had not travelled this far to be put off simply because her clothing was considered to be unsuitable. She shot a sideways glance at Jack and found him looking at her with a knowing smile. Irritated beyond measure, she turned her head away. He knew her only too well, but she had earned her right to see the ghost orchid for herself and nothing was going to stop her now.

Later, when everyone apart from the man on watch had lain down to sleep, Mirabel raised herself on her elbow, watching the moonlight playing on the silver ripples of the lake. She could see vague shapes on the far bank as animals came to the water's edge to drink, and yellow eyes winked at her from the depths of the cutgrass and cattails. The odd call of the barred owls sounded like weird laughter and the heady scent of the night orchids filled the air, together with the saw-like chorus of the tree frogs. A sudden sound, barely more than a sigh, made her look up and in a shaft of moonlight she saw Jack standing further along the bank, staring into the dark water. Then, as if she had spoken his name out loud, he turned round, and although she could not see his features clearly she knew that he had felt her presence. Oddly comforted even though their situation had not changed one iota, she lay down and closed her eyes, drifting off into the world of dreams she had inhabited as a child.

'I will go with you, Hubert.' Mirabel faced her husband angrily next morning as he prepared to leave. 'I've come this far and I refuse to stay here on my own.'

'My dear, you won't be alone,' Hubert said mildly. 'Abraham and Isaac are staying to protect our camp and Gertie has no desire to venture into the swamp.' He looked to Gertie for confirmation and she nodded vigorously.

'I'm staying here, sir. Wild horses wouldn't drag me into that place.'

'You must do as you please.' Mirabel tossed her head. 'I came all this way to see the ghost orchid growing in the wild and that's what I intend to do. You promised, Hubert. This was supposed to be my Christmas present.'

He sighed. 'All right, if you insist, but I strongly advise against it.'

'I'm a grown woman. I'm perfectly capable of making my own decisions.' Relenting slightly, she patted his hand. 'I will be careful.'

Hunching his shoulders Hubert walked off to join Bundy, who was making preparations for their trek into the swamp.

'You've upset him now,' Gertie said in an undertone. 'Perhaps you should have listened to him, Mabel. Cap'n Jack agrees with him, I can see that by the way he's staring at you.'

'Men are all the same,' Mirabel said lightly. 'They think they're the lords of creation and we are weak little creatures who need to be protected.'

'I got no problem with that.'

'Well I have. I'm not returning home without seeing the wretched ghost orchid in its natural surroundings.'

They had been walking for more than an hour, although most of the time they had been wading through the hot and airless swamp. The foliage was slicked with moisture and the tree trunks appeared to be sweating as profusely as the human intruders in their primeval midst. Mirabel had hitched her skirts up to her knees but at times the water reached her thighs and she was weighted down by her sodden garments. She bunched them up, wishing she had the freedom of wearing breeches like the men, but saying nothing. She would not give them the satisfaction of knowing they were right, and she did her best to keep up with their long strides. Her feet sank into the mud making each step twice as difficult as the last, and they were all plagued by flying insects.

Bundy led the way, using a long pole to test the ground for sinkholes, warning them yet again to keep an eye out for alligators and snakes. Moses and Ephraim had accompanied them and Hubert, with Bodger at his side, walked between them. Mirabel suspected that Bundy had planned it this way in case Hubert should stumble or be overcome by heat and exhaustion. Both Bahamians were big men who could easily carry a lightweight like Hubert should the need arise, although she could not imagine Bodger relinquishing his duty to men whom he considered foreigners and therefore not to be trusted. It never failed to surprise her that someone who had spent most of his life sailing the seven seas was so insular in his outlook, but Bodger was devoted to Hubert and that, in Mirabel's opinion, was all that mattered. She was acutely aware of Jack's presence as he brought up the rear and it was a comfort to know that he was there, even though they only spoke to warn each other of fallen branches or roots hidden beneath the surface of the water.

As the day wore on Mirabel forgot her own discomfort in her growing concern for her husband. Hubert was obviously tiring, and although he had been excited by the variety of the plant life they came across, including many beautiful and rare specimens, they had not found the elusive ghost orchid. When they stopped to rest and take some refreshment she took Bundy aside. 'My husband is not a young man, Mr Bundy. He's close to exhaustion, anyone can see that. Are you certain this is where we find the ghost orchid?'

He took a swig from his flask. 'The ghost orchids favour the trunks of pop ash, pond apple and maple. I've never seen one myself, but I had it first hand from the man who discovered them growing hereabouts.'

'And this is how you make your living? Is there much money to be made out of exotic plants?'

'There is, ma'am, and feathers too,' he said, patting the sheathed bowie knife. 'Ladies love their feathers and I've provided bushels of them. You'll see them being paraded in the fashionable salons in London, Paris and Rome, but I'm not averse to bringing back the odd plant specimen if the price is right.' He glanced up into the tree canopy where spiky plants with bright red and green leaves roosted on the branches like flocks of colourful parakeets. 'They call those bromeliads. Ugly things in my opinion, but there are collectors back home who'll pay well for specimens.'

'I suppose so,' Mirabel said vaguely. Her attention had wandered and was now fixed on Hubert, who had slumped down on the ground regardless of the moving carpet of giant lubber grasshoppers. Bodger was at his side, flapping a bundle of twigs in an attempt to keep the lumbering insects away from him.

'It won't be long before the damn crazy plant hunters come here in their hordes,' Bundy said, warming to his theme. 'You wouldn't believe the lengths they go to in the hunt for rare plants, especially orchids. They'll slit each other's throats without a second thought because there's money in it for them. I prefer to hunt birds.'

'I had no idea it was like that, but surely this place is safe. It's so inaccessible.'

Bundy gave her a pitying smile. 'We're here, aren't we?' He strolled off to speak to Jack.

Mirabel was hot, plagued by biting insects, and

her wet skirts clung to her legs, hampering her movements. She had never felt so uncomfortable in her whole life. When they stopped at noon she ate the corn pone that Abraham had made that morning. The outside was charred and smoky and the inside soft, salty and doughy, but it was food and she would need all the energy she could muster to keep up with the men.

There was a momentary lull, for which Mirabel was grateful. She was tired but she was not about to give in and prove herself to be a weak female. Men had it all ways, she thought wearily: they dressed appropriately and they had the advantage of height. Bundy was comparatively short, but he was stocky and seemed to have boundless energy. Ephraim and Moses were young, probably in their late twenties or early thirties, and used to hard labour in the sweltering heat. Bodger had been toughened up by years of sailing before the mast, and Jack appeared to be indestructible, she thought with a frisson of pride. He had survived shipwreck and she knew for a fact that since the start of their journey he had slept very little, keeping a constant watch in the long hours of darkness. He was tireless and did not seem troubled by the physical discomforts suffered by everyone else. She had come to realise that beneath the cynical, world-weary attitude lurked a man to be reckoned with; a man to be trusted. She glanced at her husband and saw an elderly man, frail and exhausted, but she could tell by the gleam in his eyes that he was not about to give up. He had the fanaticism of a collector determined to achieve his goal, no matter what the personal cost. She felt a sneaking admiration for him, tempered with concern for his well-being.

'We'll move on,' Bundy said, hitching his rifle across his shoulders as he prepared to step into the dark, tannin-stained water. 'Keep your eyes peeled for 'gators and snapping turtles. This is where we're most likely to run across the bastards – begging your pardon, ma'am,' he added as an afterthought. 'Women,' he muttered to himself, although his deep voice carried on the still air. 'Bloody women, shouldn't be allowed.'

Mirabel stepped into the water. She was already soaked but it did not seem to matter. Her only aim now was to find the orchid and escape from this awful place. Surely hell must be like this, she thought miserably, but as they advanced slowly she could not help being impressed by the un-tamed beauty of her surroundings. She drifted along in a dreamlike state, ignoring the discomfort and focusing her eyes on the water, ever watchful for the slithery shape of a cottonmouth gliding towards them. Sometimes she stopped, paralysed with fear, thinking something was a poisonous snake only to find it was a dead palm frond, but she was not prepared for the sudden cry of 'Alligator!' She came to a halt, peering through the leaves on an overhanging pop ash branch.

Ephraim and Moses were suddenly alert and Bodger stepped in front of Hubert, shielding him with his body. Bundy raised his rifle. The resonat-ing percussive sound of the shot echoed off the tropical hardwood hammock, reverberating so that it felt as if they were under fire from an army of marksmen. Mirabel stiffened, watching in horror as the huge reptile thrashed about in its death throes. She could not move. Her feet seemed to be sinking into the mud and her limbs were turned to stone. The horrific scene was about to be repeated as Bundy raised his rifle again, this time aiming it at another of the creatures that had emerged from the mangrove. She barely heard the shot as strong arms scooped her from the water, and despite her protests she was slung over Jack's shoulder as he waded towards what passed for dry land.

He set her down on her feet. 'There were more,' he said tersely.

'We can't just leave the others to fight off the alligators.' Mirabel faced him for the first time in days, looking him in the eye.

'Are you all right?' he demanded anxiously. 'You should have stayed in camp. If you were my wife I wouldn't have brought you to this.'

'If I were your wife I wouldn't have wanted to come with you,' Mirabel snapped, her over-wrought nerves getting the better of her even though she knew it was a lie.

'You made your feelings for me very clear.'

'And you've hardly spoken a word to me since the first day.'

'You almost got yourself killed.'

'I suppose you blame me for the alligators too.'

They faced each other, glaring like gladiators about to fight to the death. This was not how it should be, Mirabel thought dazedly. They were on the same side, or so she had thought. She turned away, unable to bear the harsh lines of his set expression or the angry look in his eyes. Perhaps she had imagined that he had feelings for her. She shook out her skirts. 'I'll never be able to dry my clothes in this steamy heat.'

'For God's sake, Mirabel.' Jack seized her by the shoulders, twisting her round to face him. 'Is that all you can think about? You might have died back there.'

'So might you,' she said softly. 'We're not safe even now...' Her last words were lost as he drew her into his arms and devoured her mouth in a kiss that was savage in its intensity. Her response was instant, and without thought for anything or anyone she abandoned herself to the desperate need she had tried so hard to ignore. It was the first time she had been held in a passionate embrace and the first time she had been kissed in such a way other than in her dreams, but this was infinitely more exciting. She responded with fervour, sliding her arms around his neck so that their bodies were intertwined, fitting together in what felt like a perfect match. The rest of the world ceased to exist: they were the only two people on the planet and at that moment in time. They were two souls who had become as one and she would have given herself to him gladly.

He released her on a sigh and she opened her eyes, drowning in the depths of his gaze, hardly able to breathe. Then the world came crashing in on them as a wild boar emerged from the under-growth and charged. Jack thrust her behind him, taking the revolver from his belt and firing. The animal dropped to the ground and Moses ap-peared, wading through the swamp with a grin on his face. 'Roast pork for dinner, mister.' He was followed by Ephraim, with Bundy and Hubert, who was being supported by Bodger, close behind.

Shaken more by the startling shift in her relationship with Jack than the slaughter of the wild beast, Mirabel said nothing. She shot a sideways glance at Jack and his lazy smile embraced her in a silent caress.

'Are you all right, my dear?' Hubert demanded anxiously. 'We heard the shot.'

Bundy stepped forward, prodding the inert body with the toe of his boot. 'We'll eat well tonight. Let's be done here and make our way back to camp.'

'But the ghost orchid,' Hubert protested.

'There's always tomorrow,' Bundy said carelessly.

Back at camp Gertie greeted them as if they had been gone for a week. 'I thought something had happened to you, Mabel,' she said, holding a blanket up to shield her mistress from prying eyes as she changed out of her soiled and still damp garments. 'I thought you'd all been eaten by 'gators.'

'I'm hot and sticky and I must smell like the swamp,' Mirabel said, chuckling. 'I'm going to run out of clothes at this rate.'

Peering at her over the top of the blanket, Gertie gave her a searching look. 'Why are you so cheerful? You look like you've been dragged through a hedge backwards, and you got scratches on your face that will fester if you're not careful.'

'I survived,' Mirabel said, turning her head away. Gertie knew her only too well and she would know instinctively that something had changed. She glanced at Jack, but he had set himself apart from the rest of the men and was standing at the water's edge, smoking a cigarillo. The faint scent of it mingled with the wood-smoke from the campfire and the rich aroma of the hog meat as Moses roasted it on an improvised spit. 'We'll eat well tonight,' she added casually.

'I dunno if I can stomach eating a wild pig,' Gertie said warily. 'You never know where it's been.'

'It's better than alligator. Now that would be hard to swallow, but if you're hungry enough you'll eat almost anything.' Mirabel slipped a cotton-print gown over her head. 'I'm semi-decent. Will you do me up, please?'

Gertie folded the blanket and proceeded to fasten the tiny buttons at the back of Mirabel's bodice. 'Something's changed. What happened out there?'

'I don't know what you're talking about,' Mirabel said, shrugging. 'You've been alone too much and you're imagining things. Anyway, it's just as well you didn't accompany us today. You wouldn't believe what it was like in there.' She shivered, but it was the memory of Jack's embrace that sent a tremor running down her spine. The dangers and discomfort of the Fakahatchee swamp were forgotten, but the memory of that passionate embrace would last a lifetime.

'And you've got to go back there tomorrow, I suppose,' Gertie said, sighing. 'Better you than me, that's all I can say.' She fastened the last button, patting Mirabel on the shoulder. 'All done, and you're right about the hog. I don't suppose it'll be as good as Mrs Flitton's roast pork and all the trimmings, but I'm starving so I won't be too fussy.'

'Quite right.' Mirabel nodded in agreement, although she had barely heard a word that Gertie said. Her thoughts were for Jack only and she knew that it was foolish, dangerous even, but she had to be near him. She needed to speak to him and reassure herself that what had happened in the swamp had not been merely a spur of the moment reaction to the dangers they had faced. 'I want to ask the captain something,' she said vaguely. 'I'll only be a minute.' She walked away, heading towards the lake, but she had only taken a few steps when Hubert called out to her. He was lying on his bedroll with a blanket covering his legs, although it was still uncomfortably hot.

'Come and sit with me, my dear. I've hardly had time to speak to you since we returned.'

Mirabel glanced anxiously at Jack, who was still standing staring out across the water. Soon it would be dark and they would eat their evening meal before turning in for the night. She needed him but she knew that what she wanted was impossible. When this was over they would go their separate ways and she might never see him again. She moved to Hubert's side. 'You should be resting.'

He patted the ground. 'Sit with me for a while, Mirabel. You must have had a terrible fright today, and I wanted to apologise for placing you in such dire peril.'

She went down on her knees in the dust. 'I'm all right, Hubert. Really, you mustn't worry about me.'

301

'But I do, my dear girl. It was my selfish desire to find the ghost orchid which brought us here. I should have been looking after you.'

'I wanted to come and I wouldn't have missed the experience for the world.' She scrambled to her feet. 'Would you like some tea? I know that Bundy will have a kettle on the boil.'

He nodded wearily. 'You're too good to me, but yes, I would love a cup of tea, with perhaps a drop or two of brandy.'

'Of course.' She walked over to where Bodger was sitting with his knees drawn up to his chest. 'My husband would like some tea, but I don't like to disturb the men at the campfire.'

'Of course, missis.' Bodger unravelled his long legs and leapt to his feet. 'I know just how the boss likes it.' He winked and tapped a silver flask tucked in his shirt pocket. 'Leave it to me.'

Mirabel smiled and thanked him. She hesitated, turning, her head to look at Jack. She desperately wanted to be at his side, to inhale the musky scent of him that made her sense spin out of control, but she was painfully aware that every move she made would be observed by someone in the camp, especially Hubert. She was about to abandon her plan to join him on the pretext of watching the sunset when he turned his head and their eyes met. She knew she was lost and she moved slowly towards him, like a sleepwalker drawn to him by a silken cord that could never be broken. She could feel him smiling even though his face was in shadow, and then the atmosphere changed. She felt the air crackle with danger even before he shouted a warning. He was running towards her.

302

'Get back,' he shouted hoarsely. 'Run.'

Behind him she saw the sleek silhouette of a panther moving so fast it was like a streak of golden silky fur and it was heading straight for Jack.

Chapter Nineteen

Frozen to the spot, Mirabel could only stand and stare in horror as the animal raced towards Jack. She heard Bundy shout and the sound of a rifle being cocked but Jack had drawn the pistol from its holster and he fired into the air. The panther came to a skidding halt, and in one graceful movement it turned and fled into the stand of cypress trees bordering the lake. Moses raced past Mirabel brandishing a flaming branch he'd plucked from the fire, but the panther had disappeared into the undergrowth. Jack slipped his gun back into its holster. 'We'll double the watch tonight.' He laid his hand on Mirabel's arm. 'Are you all right?'

She nodded slowly. The nightmare vision of what might have been flashed before her eyes. 'You could have been killed.'

'But I wasn't.' He glanced over her shoulder, frowning. 'Your husband looks upset, and so he should for putting you in danger in the first place.'

She drew away from him, fear turning to anger. 'I chose to come here. I'm not a child, Jack. I knew it would be dangerous.' The desire to hold him and be held was almost overpowering, but somehow she managed to cling on to her wavering self-control. For the second time that day they had faced danger together: all her senses were alert and her emotions raw with the need for him and him alone. She could hear her husband calling her name and she forced herself to walk away, each step hurting as if she were walking on shards of broken glass.

Hubert had risen shakily to his feet and he tottered towards her, arms outstretched. Their relationship had never entailed more than a chaste peck on the cheek and the mere thought of being embraced by him made her recoil in horror. She clutched his hands, giving them a comforting squeeze, and by doing so managed to avoid any closer contact. 'Are you hurt?' he demanded querulously. 'I couldn't quite see what happened. It was all so sudden.'

'It was a panther,' she said, leading him back to where he had been sitting. 'It came from nowhere.'

'And Starke shot it?'

'No, Hubert, he fired into the air and it ran away.'

'It will return. It must have smelled the meat. We must be on our guard.' He sank down on his bedroll with a sigh. 'I've brought you into terrible danger, Mirabel. I'm so sorry, my dear.'

'Nonsense,' she said briskly. 'Let's not go over it again. I'm here because I chose to be.'

He looked up at her, his eyes moist. 'You've given me so much, and I've given you so little in return.'

'That's silly,' she said, patting his shoulder. 'You've given me everything I could possibly want.'

'I'd be lost without you. You've made my life worthwhile.' His voice shook with emotion. 'I know that I'm a selfish old man, but I want you to know that I love and respect you, and all I want now is for you to be happy too.'

She sketched a smile, struggling with feelings of guilt and frustration. She was trapped and there was no escape. Hubert deserved better than to be cuckolded by an unfaithful wife. 'I am happy,' she murmured, avoiding his anxious gaze. 'And I'll be even happier when we've found the ghost orchid.' She withdrew her hand gently. 'Maybe we'll come across one tomorrow.'

Hubert nodded, reaching for his none too clean handkerchief and mopping his brow. 'I hope so, my dear.' He looked up as Bodger approached them carrying a tin plate laden with roast meat and corn pone.

'Here you are, guv,' he said cheerfully. 'Eat this and you'll be fit as a fiddle by morning.'

Hubert accepted the food, staring at it doubtfully. 'I'm not very hungry.'

'You must try to eat,' Mirabel said, frowning. 'Bodger's right; you need to keep your strength up if we're to find the ghost orchid.'

'I'll do my best.' Hubert met her worried glance with a smile. 'Go and enjoy your meal, my dear, and thank Captain Starke for his quick action, which probably saved your life. I'm deeply indebted to him.'

Mirabel left him, although she doubted whether he would eat much. Thinking back she realised that he rarely ate a big meal, even those prepared by a good cook like Mrs Flitton, and large chunks of hog meat burnt at the edge and pink in the middle were hardly likely to tempt a delicate appetite. She fetched her own plate and went to sit beside Jack. 'I'm sorry,' she said softly.

'What for?' He regarded her with the slow smile that had the power to send her senses reeling and her pulses racing.

'I behaved very badly in the swamp, but it was fright that made me act as I did.'

'I kissed you.'

'And I kissed you back, but it was a mistake. It can't happen again.'

He seized her free hand, holding it in a firm grasp. 'I love you,' he said in a low voice.

She stared down at their clasped hands. 'You can't and I can't. I'm married.'

'To a man who's old enough to be your grandfather? That's not exactly a union of souls.'

'Shh. Someone might hear.' She glanced around anxiously, but the others were intent on enjoying their supper and Hubert had lain down, closing his eyes. 'This has got to end now, Jack.'

'But you love me. Don't deny it. I know you do.'

She bowed her head. 'Don't make it worse than it is. I can't bear it.'

'Leave him. Come away with me. I'll find another ship and we'll sail the world together.'

'In a dream, maybe.' She looked up and met his intense gaze with a smile. 'It's a lovely dream, but that's all it is. Hubert rescued me from Zilla's and he's treated me like a queen. I can't break his heart. He doesn't deserve such treatment.'

'I would have come back for you. I thought I

could forget you as I had the other women in my life, but it wasn't so. I'm not giving up now.' Jack rose to his feet, tossing the contents of his tin plate into the fire where the fat exploded into flames and the meat sizzled and curled, burning to ash in seconds.

Mirabel had lost her appetite. She sat for a while, not wanting to attract attention to herself, and then she rose quietly, giving her untouched food to Bodger as she made her way to where Gertie had laid out their bedrolls. No matter what Jack said, it was over before it had begun. She would not betray Hubert: her marriage vows had not been taken lightly. Her heart might be breaking, but she would have to be strong.

Gertie was curled up on her bedding with an empty plate at her side. She stared at Mirabel, her brow ridged in a frown. 'What was all that about, Mabel?'

'I don't know what you mean.' Mirabel sat down, preparing to sleep. 'I'll be glad to get back to Mama Lou's so that I can have a proper wash and clothes that aren't crawling with insects.'

'I saw you two with your heads together. I keep warning you about Captain Jack, but you don't seem to listen.'

'I'm worn out and all I want to do is sleep. I suggest you do the same.' Mirabel had not meant to speak so sharply, but she knew from past experience that once Gertie got an idea in her head it was almost impossible to convince her otherwise.

Gertie subsided with a sigh. 'He's trouble and always was.'

'Goodnight, Gertie.' Mirabel lay down and closed her eyes, although it was a long time before she drifted off to sleep.

The search for the elusive ghost orchid continued next day. Mirabel had toyed with the idea of remaining in camp with Gertie, but the stubborn streak in her nature would not allow her to give up so easily. She kept as far apart from Jack as possible and was careful not to catch his eye, although she sensed when he was looking at her, which was often as the day progressed. Each part of the swamp looked the same to her as they waded through water and clouds of biting insects. She had almost given up hope when a sudden cry from Hubert brought about a sudden halt. Jack was close behind her and she could feel the heat of his body. The temptation to lean back and rest her head against his shoulder was so great that she had to dig her fingernails into her palms to bring herself back to the real world.

'There it is,' Hubert shouted, his voice breaking in his excitement. 'The ghost orchid, and there are several beautiful specimens.'

Mirabel moved forward slowly. She was already up to her waist in water and Abraham, who had accompanied them that day, had stepped into a sinkhole earlier and disappeared beneath the surface. It had taken the combined efforts of Jack and Moses to get him out. She peered up at the trunk of the custard apple tree and saw the startlingly white ghost orchids. Unreal and ethereal, they seemed to be floating in midair, their long fluttery tails moving gently in the light breeze. It seemed unimaginable that anything so delicate could live in such a hostile environment. 'They're so beautiful,' she breathed softly.

'Let me get nearer, Bundy,' Hubert said, his voice trembling with emotion. 'Give me your knife so that I can ease the roots free. I want to take home living specimens.'

Jack moved closer to Mirabel. 'This might take some time. Let's get you onto dry land.'

She was about to refuse, but Bodger was pushing so that he could get closer to Hubert and there was a scramble of bodies churning up the water, to the obvious annoyance of a couple of snapping turtles that had been lazing just below the surface. 'I'll follow you,' she said reluctantly. The dark water felt like treacle as she waded slowly towards dry ground, and her sodden skirts hampered her movements. The mud sucked at her feet, and fronds of resurrection fern growing on overhanging tree branches slapped at her face. Jack reached out to help her onto firm ground.

'Thank you.' She withdrew her hand, wrapping her arms around her body as she turned to watch Hubert's efforts to prise the orchid roots from the tree trunk.

'You can't avoid me forever,' Jack said softly. 'And you can't deny that you have feelings for me.'

'No, I can't deny it, but it's no good, Jack. You can see how things are.'

'I see a beautiful young woman tied to an elderly man by a promise she made when she was under duress.'

'That's not true. I wasn't forced into anything.'

'He took advantage of your situation.'

'Don't do this. I meant what I said yesterday.' She turned away resolutely. 'There can never be anything between us, Jack.'

'Never is a very long time.'

Hubert was like a new father, nurturing his ghost orchids as if they were his own flesh and blood. They were packed individually and carried as tenderly as newborn infants, each one receiving his full attention. He seemed to have forgotten his aches and pains and his eyes shone with enthusiasm as they packed up camp next day and made ready for the trek back to Coconut Grove.

Mirabel was everything a solicitous wife should be during the long days that followed. She kept close to her husband, making sure that in his desire to protect his precious orchids he did not neglect himself. It was the only way she could demonstrate to Jack that she meant what she had said. She was Hubert's wife and there it must end. It was only at night, when she lay beneath the stars listening to the steady breathing of those around her punctuated by Abraham's loud snores, that she allowed herself to grieve for the love she must deny. In the velvety darkness she was painfully aware that Jack was wide awake even when it was not his watch. The telltale scent of his cigarillo wafted in the night air, and the desire to join him, if only to talk and take comfort from his presence, was almost unbearable. She resisted somehow but wanting to be with him was a nagging ache that would not go away.

They had endured the steamy heat of the Fakahatchee swamp and survived the scorching sun on the prairie, and on the fifth day they finally reached their destination. Hubert's first concern was for his plants and he rushed them into the cabin at Mama Lou's, leaving Mirabel to her own devices. Bundy had been paid and he announced that he was going to the beach hut to get drunk, inviting Jack to join him. The Bahamian porters said their goodbyes and marched off to the hotel. Gertie was left to unpack on her own as Bodger had mumbled an excuse and followed in Bundy's wake.

Mirabel found herself alone with Jack for the first time in almost a week. 'I suppose this is goodbye,' she said lamely.

'If that's what you want.'

'It's what must be, you know that.' She could not bring herself to look him in the eye.

He seized her by the hand. 'You can't do this, Mirabel. Leave him and come away with me.'

'Don't.' The word came out on a sob as she snatched her hand free. 'I can't.'

He fixed her with a hard stare. 'You're prepared to destroy both our lives for the sake of a selfish old man who loves orchids more than he does you.'

'That's not fair and it's not true.'

'You're condemning yourself to a loveless marriage with no hope of having children of your own.'

It was true and she knew it, but she was trapped both by her own conscience and the vows she had made in church. Miss Barton had quite literally instilled the fear of God in her at an early age, and although Mirabel was in no way superstitious, she still believed in eternal hell. It was a place with which she had become familiar during the journey back to Coconut Grove. Her mouth was dry and she was overcome by exhaustion. 'I'm sorry,' she whispered. 'I can't do this any more.' She was about to walk away when Bodger suddenly re-appeared, waving his arms as he ran towards them. 'A ship,' he cried joyfully. 'There's a ship at anchor and a jolly boat heading for shore.'

Events moved so quickly that Mirabel was swept along like a leaf caught up in a fast current. The ship had come from Nassau, stopping off to take on fresh water before setting sail for Newport News with a cargo of fresh fruit, vegetables and rum. Hubert had been revitalised by the prospect of taking his prizes home and had hurried off with Bodger intent on speaking to the captain. They returned two hours later, tipsy from imbibing a quantity of rum, but triumphant, having secured berths for them all as far as Newport News.

'You must tell Captain Starke, Bodger,' Mirabel said urgently. The thought of leaving Jack without a word was too much for her to bear. 'He should know what we're planning.'

Bodger grinned drunkenly. 'He must come with us. I shall tell him so.' He wagged his finger at Mirabel and tottered off into the undergrowth.

That night they slept in their cabins at Mama Lou's and the next night they slept on board the *Virago*, having said their goodbyes to everyone except Jack, who was nowhere to be seen. Mirabel had watched and waited, hoping that he would at least come to say a final farewell even at the last minute, but there was no sign of him and she knew she had only herself to blame. She boarded the *Virago* feeling as though she had left a vital part of herself on shore.

It was only when she awakened next morning to the sound of the waves lapping the wooden hull of the ship and the captain shouting commands to his crew that she realised they were really on their way home. London with its teeming streets and terrible poverty existing cheek by jowl with extreme wealth had seemed like another world. Now they were on their return journey to a life that she had come to question, but which nothing could alter. She had chosen her path and she must bear the consequences of that decision.

Hubert did not put in an appearance for breakfast in the cramped saloon where the crew took their meals. Mirabel made a show of eating but she was not hungry. She made her excuses and went to Hubert's cabin, expecting to find him prostrate from sickness, but he was sitting on his bunk holding one of the orchids in his cupped hands. 'Isn't it perfect?' he said, smiling. 'They've survived this far, although I doubt if we'll get them to London in this state, but I hope they will set seed. I can't be sure if they've been pollinated but it would be such a coup to be able to propagate them myself.'

'I thought you might be unwell,' Mirabel said, staring at the delicate bloom with a rush of near hatred. It was something tangible to blame for her heartache. But for the wretched ghost orchid she would never have gone to Florida, and if she had remained in ignorance of Jack's survival she might have lived a reasonably contented life. Knowing that he was alive and well and that he loved her was going to torture her as long as she lived, and it was all the fault of the peerless little flower that had captured her husband's heart and soul.

'I am quite well, as you see,' Hubert said happily. 'Perhaps I have conquered mal de mer after all.' His smile faded. 'If I should fall ill I want you to promise me that you'll look after the orchids. You mustn't allow them to die.'

A sudden desire to snatch the plant from him and toss it overboard was quickly crushed and she managed a faint smile. 'Of course, Hubert. Just tell me what to do.'

They were two days out when a sudden tropical storm hit them in the middle of the night. The ship bucked and tossed on the giant waves, hurled about like a child's toy. Mirabel climbed out of her bunk and was thrown against the bulkhead with such force that she was momentarily winded.

'What are you doing?' Gertie shrieked, holding on to the rails of her bunk. 'Are you mad?'

'I've got to make sure that Hubert is all right.'

'Don't go out there. You'll be killed.'

Mirabel lurched towards the door and wrenched it open. The ship ploughed into the trough of a wave and she slithered along the deck towards Hubert's cabin. Despite the fact that Bodger would be there to look after him she had a terrible feeling that all was not well. Seawater came crashing down the companionway but she struggled on, slipping and sliding, her nightgown already soaked and clinging to her like a cold compress. The

314

vessel peaked momentarily on the crest of a huge wave and she was able to grab the door handle. She burst into the tiny cabin expecting to see Bodger but Hubert was on his own, slumped against the bulkhead with the ghost orchids clutched in the crook of his right arm.

'Are you all right?' Mirabel demanded anxiously. In the pale light of the paraffin lamp swinging precariously from its hook in the masthead, she could see that something was wrong. 'Hubert, speak to me.' She peered closer and was horrified to see his mouth hanging slack with a dribble of saliva running down his chin. His facial features were distorted and his left arm hung limply at his side. 'What's wrong?' She tried to prise the orchids from his grasp but a low moan escaped his lips and he recoiled from her. 'All right,' she said hastily. 'I won't take them.' She took a step backwards, eyeing him warily. 'Where's Bodger? He should be here taking care of you.'

Hubert remained motionless, but he was in little danger of falling from his bunk as he seemed to have wedged himself against the bulkhead. There was nothing she could do other than to sit with him and pray that the ship would weather the storm, although it felt as if hell had been let loose and the Atlantic Ocean was about to swallow them in one great greedy gulp.

Someone was shaking her by the shoulder and she opened her eyes, staring blearily into Bodger's anxious face. 'What's up with the guv, missis? I can't get a word out of him.'

In her dreams she had been with Jack, sailing on

a calm sea towards eternal happiness, but Bodger's bedraggled appearance brought her back to reality. 'Is he worse?' She rose to her feet, leaning over the bunk. Hubert had not moved and the orchids were still clutched to his chest. She prised them gently from his grasp. 'I'll take great care of them, my dear. Bodger has come and he'll make you more comfortable.' She turned to Bodger, lowering her voice, although it did not seem as though Hubert was aware of his surroundings. 'How far are we from port?'

'The captain reckons we'll make landfall this afternoon, in spite of the bashing we had from the storm. It was one of the worst I've seen on this coast that wasn't one of them tornadoes. Our cabin trunks were washed overboard even though I lashed them down.'

Mirabel was too concerned for her husband's state of health to care about the loss of personal items. They had not been in a position to bargain when the captain refused to stow their belongings below decks as the hold was filled with cargo. There were, she thought grimly, more important matters to discuss and Hubert must be her main concern. 'We're heading for Newport News?'

'Aye, missis.'

'Will we be able to get a ship to take us back to England from there? Or will we have to return to New York? I know so little about these things.'

'We might find a tramp steamer to take us home if we wait long enough, but if you want to travel quickly and in luxury we'll have to get to New York, and it'll cost you money.'

She dismissed this with a wave of her hands.

'That won't be a problem. My husband has made ample provision for our travelling expenses. The most important thing now is to make him comfortable. If you could lift him I'll fold back the coverlet and we can get him into bed properly, but he's in desperate need of a doctor.'

'What's up with him?' Bodger lifted Hubert, holding him while Mirabel rearranged the bedding. 'There you are, guv,' he said, laying him down gently. 'That's the ticket.'

Mirabel drew him aside. 'I don't know, but I think it might be apoplexy. I seem to remember one of the men who used the soup kitchen collapsing with something similar. He died.'

Bodger laid his hand on her shoulder. 'Don't worry, missis. We'll get him to a sawbones on shore.'

Battered and with ragged sails, the *Virago* limped into Newport News in the early afternoon as the captain had promised. An hour later they had booked into the hotel where they had stayed on their way to Florida. It was, Mirabel realised, only a few weeks ago, but it felt like a lifetime. She sent Bodger to find a doctor while she sat with her sick husband, but she did not need a physician to tell her that Hubert was mortally ill. He was quiet most of the time but only as long as he could see his beloved orchids, and they had been placed on a table at the foot of his bed. The papery white flowers were drooping sadly, the delicate petals turning brown at the edges. Mirabel knew in her heart that they would not survive the journey home, but she dare not think too far ahead. The main thing was for Hubert to believe that they would live and produce seed so that he could fulfil his ambition to propagate the species. The flowers might be dying, but she suspected that in Hubert's eyes they were as fresh as the day they were hacked from the trunk of the custard apple tree.

She jumped to her feet as someone tapped on the door. It was, as she had hoped, Bodger returning with a doctor.

Mirabel went down to dinner that evening accompanied by Gertie. She had not wanted to leave Hubert, but Bodger had insisted on remaining at his employer's bedside, and Gertie had persuaded her that she must eat in order to keep up her strength. The doctor had not been hopeful. His words echoed in Mirabel's head, and they were not encouraging. 'Your husband is a very sick man, Mrs Kettle. I don't wish to alarm you, but I would not recommend a long sea voyage in his condition which might deteriorate quite suddenly, although I sympathise with your desire to return home. The decision must be yours, ma'am.'

A black-coated waiter hovered anxiously at their table as Mirabel studied the menu with unseeing eyes. Her mind had gone completely blank, and for once she was at a loss as to what to do next. She looked up at him dazedly. 'I'm sorry, what did you say?'

'He said that the clam chowder is good,' Gertie said without giving him a chance to respond. She waved her hand to attract his attention. 'Yes, mate. Two of them, please.' Waiting until he was out of earshot she leaned across the table, lowering her voice. 'Are you all right, Mabel? You're whiter than the tablecloth.'

'I'm just tired. I didn't get much sleep last night.' Mirabel picked up the starched white table napkin but it slipped through her fingers, and as she bent down to retrieve it she spotted someone she thought she recognised. 'That man sitting by the window, Gertie,' she said urgently. 'He's not looking this way, but I'm sure I know him.'

Chapter Twenty

Gertie spun round, craning her neck to follow Mirabel's gaze. The setting sun shone on the young man's fair hair, creating a golden halo around his well-shaped head. 'I think you're right,' Gertie said, chuckling. 'What a coincidence.'

'Not really.' Mirabel studied him carefully, taking in the details of his expensive well-cut jacket, and immaculate trousers with knife-edge creases. She rose to her feet and made her way between the tables where businessmen and commercial travellers were taking their meals. There was a brief lull in the conversation as they turned to stare at her but she ignored them, holding her head high as she approached the table by the window. She cleared her throat to attract his attention and he looked round with a slow smile of recognition. Ethan Munroe stood up, holding out his hand. 'Mirabel, upon my honour, this is a pleasant

319

surprise. I thought you were deep in the Florida everglades.'

She breathed a sigh of relief. It was wonderful to see a familiar face. 'It's a long story, Ethan.'

'I'd be delighted to have you join me for dinner.' He glanced over her shoulder. 'Where's that husband of yours? Are you dining alone?'

'Gertie is with me, but Hubert is extremely unwell. I really need some advice because I have to get him home to England before...' Her voice broke on a suppressed sob. 'I'm sorry. It's been a long day and we sailed through a storm last night. I'm just tired.'

He pulled up a chair and pressed her down on the seat. 'I'm happy to be of service in any way I can.' He beckoned to Gertie. 'You must both join me. You'll feel better when you've eaten.'

Gertie needed no second bidding. She took her seat opposite Ethan, interposing frequently when Mirabel faltered over her account of their travels and the difficulties they had encountered during Hubert's quest for the ghost orchid. The waiter brought their food and Ethan ordered a bottle of wine, listening attentively as he filled their glasses. Mirabel faltered when it came to repeating the doctor's grim prognosis. 'But he may be wrong,' she added defensively. 'Doctors don't always get things right, do they?'

'Indeed they don't,' Ethan said earnestly. 'Take Mrs D'Angelo, for instance. She started to speak again while you were visiting, and now she seems to be well on the road to recovery. Jerusha says it's a miracle but I just think the time was right. Betsy waited until she was good and ready and then she came back to us. Maybe it will be the same with Mr Kettle.'

Gertie dipped her bread in the creamy chowder, keeping her head down over her food, saying nothing, but Mirabel was not convinced by Ethan's optimism. 'I do hope so,' she said vaguely.

'In any event, I must insist on taking you back to Loblolly Grove.' He refilled his own glass. 'I know it's what Jerusha and her pa would want me to do.' He reached across the table to cover Mirabel's hand with his, and his eyes brimmed with sympathy. 'You are tuckered out, Mrs Kettle. It's plain for all to see, and if you should fall sick there'll be no one to look after your husband. I suggest that you accompany me back to Richmond tomorrow morning, and that you postpone your journey home until Mr Kettle is well enough to travel. What do you say to that?'

Ethan had sent word ahead, and when his carriage drew up outside the mansion Jerusha and her father were waiting for them on the veranda. Jerusha rushed down the steps to fling her arms around Mirabel. 'I declare I was so excited when the messenger brought the news this morning. I've been running to the window every few minutes to look out to see if you were coming, and here you are.'

Ethan and Bodger lifted Hubert to the ground, placing him in a chair that Amos had had the forethought to bring from the house. Vincent D'Angelo descended the steps more slowly, greeting Mirabel with equal enthusiasm. He leaned down to speak to Hubert, who lolled helplessly against the back of the chair. 'It's good to see you again, sir. We'll make you as comfortable as possible.' He straightened up, moving closer to Mirabel and lowering his voice. 'I've sent for my doctor. He's looked after Betsy since the accident that almost took her from us. You must stay as long as it takes to get Hubert back on his feet.'

Mirabel was about to thank him when Hubert began to make inarticulate noises, waving his good arm in a frantic attempt to attract her attention. She moved to his side. 'What's the matter? Are you in pain?'

He pointed to Gertie who was perched on the driver's seat next to Caleb with the ghost lilies clutched in her arms. 'Can somebody take these blooming plants?' She leaned forward, holding out the bundle. Mirabel stepped forward to relieve Gertie of her burden, but the delicate blossoms were brown and shrivelled and it was obvious that they were dying. She hesitated before handing them to her husband. If he saw the parlous state of his beloved orchids it might make his condition worse, but he was holding out his hand, fixing her with a pitiful gaze and she had not the heart to deny him. Placing the orchids on his lap she held her breath, waiting for his reaction, and to her relief Hubert's paralysed muscles twisted into the parody of a smile.

'He sees them as they were,' Vincent said softly.

'The bloody things are dead as a door post. Best throw them out, missis.' Bodger made as if to take the bundle from Hubert, but he hugged them to his chest, mumbling words Mirabel could not catch, although his meaning was clear.

'No,' she said firmly. 'Let him keep them. They might have set seed and we'll be able to grow them on when we get home.' She spoke with more conviction than she was feeling.

Vincent beckoned to Amos, who was hovering in the background. 'Help Mr Kettle's man carry the chair into the house.'

'I had the blue room made up for Mr Kettle,' Jerusha said, linking arms with Mirabel. 'And Zenobia is getting yours ready, Belle. Come inside and take some refreshment, and then I want to hear every last detail of your travels. I can't tell you how happy I am that you're here. I truly thought we'd never see each other again.'

'I must make Hubert comfortable first,' Mirabel protested, watching anxiously as Bodger and Amos lifted the chair.

'Steady, man.' Bodger scowled at Amos. 'This is a person, not a sack of spuds.'

Amos stared at him, a puzzled frown furrowing his brow. 'Spuds?'

'Potatoes,' Bodger said impatiently. 'Don't you speak English?'

Gertie had clambered down from the carriage and she faced up to Bodger. 'Mind your manners, you big oaf.'

Hubert was comfortably settled on a chaise longue in front of the open windows in his room. Kezia had been assigned to look after him, which she did with quiet expertise and gentle understanding of an invalid's needs. Mirabel was able to relax at last and enjoy a glass of iced tea on the veranda as she listened to Jerusha's excited

323

account of the ball that had been held at the Munroe plantation to celebrate her engagement to Ethan. 'It's such a pity you missed it, Belle. It was wonderful and we danced the night through.'

Mirabel smiled. 'I'm so glad for you. Ethan is a fine man and I know you'll be very happy.'

Jerusha gave her a searching look. 'Something has changed, but I can't say what it is. You have me puzzled.'

'I'm just tired. It wasn't an easy journey, and now Hubert must be my main concern.'

'I don't claim to have Mama's gift of second sight, but I am a woman and I know very well there's something you aren't telling me.' Jerusha angled her head, smiling. 'What really happened in the Florida swamp?'

Mirabel had vowed never to tell a soul, but it was a relief to unburden her emotional turmoil on someone as kind and sympathetic as Jerusha, who sat in silence listening intently until Mirabel faltered to a halt, fumbling for her handkerchief. Jerusha produced one from her pocket and handed it to her. 'I'm sorry, honey. I feel for you, I really do.'

Mirabel sniffed and blew her nose. 'I've never told anyone about Jack, not even Gertie.'

'I guess you did the right thing as far as the world is concerned, but what about you?'

'Me?' Mirabel stared at her, frowning. 'There's nothing I can do. I don't know why fate chose to throw us together again. I thought he was dead and then suddenly he was there, very much alive.'

'It must have been such a shock. I just don't know what I'd do in the circumstances.'

'It was. I couldn't believe my eyes when I saw him in that shack on the beach. At first I thought I was imagining things, and then I felt as though I would shout for joy,' she hesitated, biting her lip. 'And then I was angry to think of the pain he had put me through. Why hadn't he returned to England as any normal man would after losing his ship? Why had he allowed me to suffer so badly? And then I realised that he didn't know how I felt about him, and he probably didn't care.'

'What did you say to him?'

'I can't really remember. It's all a blur – I just remember the confusion I felt. I didn't know whether to laugh or cry, but then he was so cold and distant that I froze.'

'I guess he must have realised that you were a married woman.'

'Yes,' Mirabel said slowly. 'It was obvious what he was thinking when he found out that Hubert was my husband. I wouldn't say this to anyone else, Jerusha, but I would not have married him if I'd known that Jack was alive, even though I had no idea then that Jack had feelings for me.'

Jerusha threw back her head and laughed. 'No wonder you've gotten yourself in such a tangle, honey. You can't even admit that he loves you and you love him. What's so terrible about that?'

'I'm married,' Mirabel said dully. 'You wouldn't betray Ethan, would you?'

'Ethan isn't an old man.' Jerusha was suddenly serious. 'I don't mean to be cruel, but I guess it wouldn't have hurt to give Jack some hope. After all...' She left the sentence hovering in the air between them.

Mirabel was in no doubt as to her meaning, but she rejected the idea that Hubert might die soon and release her from her vows. She screwed the hanky into a tight ball. 'I'll give this to Gertie to wash and iron.'

'Now I've offended you.' Jerusha's bottom lip trembled ominously. 'I'm sorry, honey. I was just telling it like it is.'

'I know, and I expect everyone thinks the same as you, but I was happy with Hubert. When we were at home in London everything seemed normal and easy. It was just a huge coincidence that Jack had made his way as far as Florida.'

'You go on thinking that if it comforts you, but I say it was fate.'

Mirabel rose slowly from her chair. Her limbs were bruised and aching after being thrown about during the storm at sea, but her first concern must always be Hubert. 'I'd better go and check on my husband,' she said, putting the stress on the last word.

'Kezia will see that he's looked after. Why don't we go and visit Mama? She'll be pleased to see you; after all, she spoke her first words when you were here last. Maybe you'll be good for each other.'

Betsy D'Angelo was sitting in a chair gazing out of the window into the glossy greenery of a huge magnolia. The waxy white flowers, the size of tea plates, exuded a scent of citrus and jasmine, filling the room with their fragrance. Betsy turned her head as they entered the room and smiled, holding out her hand. 'You've returned,' she said softly. 'I knew you would.'

Jerusha gave Mirabel a gentle push towards the window. 'You remember her, Mama? That's wonderful.'

Mirabel held Betsy's thin hand in a firm grasp. 'It's good to see you looking so well, Mrs D'Angelo.'

'You've suffered.' Betsy gave her a penetrating look. 'All will be well.'

Mirabel shivered even though it was stiflingly hot in the room. 'I'm sure it will, Mrs D'Angelo.'

'What are you saying, Mama?' Jerusha knelt at her mother's side. 'What can you see?' She turned her head to meet Mirabel's anxious glance with a smile. 'I told you that Mama has the gift of seeing into the future.'

'Didn't see branch,' Betsy said with a touch of humour.

'The branch?' Mirabel looked to Jerusha for an explanation.

'It was how she came off her horse,' Jerusha said in a low voice. 'She remembers some things and not others, but her speech is improving daily.'

'Not deaf,' Betsy said drily.

'No, Mama.' Jerusha gave her a hug. 'And the doctor says that one day you might be able to walk again.' She kissed her mother's cheek. 'Rest now. I'll come back later.'

Betsy looked up at Mirabel and her eyes clouded as if a veil had covered her face. 'Danger,' she said softly. 'I see danger.'

'What did she mean?' Mirabel whispered as Jerusha ushered her out of the pleasant room.

'Don't pay no mind to her, honey,' Jerusha said

a little too quickly for Mirabel's liking. 'She muddles her words from time to time.'

'But you said she had second sight.'

'I was joking, of course. Anyway, it's time to change for dinner.'

Mirabel hesitated. 'I'm afraid I haven't anything suitable to wear. We lost most of our luggage in the storm.'

'I'm sure I have something that will fit you. Let's go see.' She led the way to her room where Zenobia was setting out the dress Jerusha had chosen to wear that evening. It lay on the four-poster bed a shimmering mass of silk and lace, the gown cut à la polonaise with a cutaway basque, and a draped and swagged overskirt revealing a frilled petticoat. Mirabel had seen such fashionable garments in London but had never aspired to owning one herself. 'It's beautiful,' she said, fingering the material. 'You'll look wonderful in this, Jerusha.'

'I surely will.' Jerusha's dimples deepened and her eyes sparkled. 'Now, my lady, we have to find a gown for you. Zenobia, what do you think?'

'I'd suggest the magenta satin, Miss Jerusha.' Zenobia opened a large cedar chest and took out another equally fashionable gown. Its rich colour caught the last rays of the setting sun as she held it up against her.

'I love it,' Jerusha said, clapping her hands. 'I had it made especially for my engagement ball but Papa took against it, and Mama shook her head, so it's never been worn. Try it on, Belle, and if you like it you may keep it, because I doubt if I'll ever wear it myself.'

Gertie was in raptures as she helped Mirabel dress. 'It's the most beautiful thing I've ever seen. It could have been made for you, Mabel.'

Mirabel gazed at her reflection in the tall cheval mirror. 'It is lovely. I feel very grand, but I didn't realise how much the sun had tanned my skin. I make Jerusha look as pale as the ghost orchid itself.' She came back to earth with a jolt. 'I'd quite forgotten poor Hubert. How awful of me. I must see him before I go down to dinner.'

'He's well cared for. I never met such kindly toffs. They've even made Bodger and me feel like part of the family. I think I could live here forever.'

Mirabel smiled as she pulled on her long white gloves. 'I doubt if Bodger feels the same. I think he wants to get another ship, despite the dangers and discomforts of living and working on board a merchantman.'

'You're right. He's got the sea in his blood and there ain't nothing no one can do about that.' Gertie sighed as she fastened the last of the tiny buttons down the back of the bodice. 'There you are, Mabel. You look a treat. A proper lady, you are.'

'I don't know what I'd do without you, Gertie.' Mirabel picked up the fan that Jerusha had loaned her and made for the door. 'We mustn't get too used to this way of living, lovely and leisured though it might be. We have to leave as soon as Hubert is well enough.'

Gertie shrugged her thin shoulders. 'I love it here, but I do miss London. If Bodger has salt water in his veins then I've got the muddy old

Thames in mine.'

Mirabel was still chuckling as she made her way to the room on the ground floor where Hubert had been made comfortable. She opened the door and went inside. 'Hubert, look at me...' Her voice tailed away and she uttered a cry of alarm. He was prostrate on the floor in front of his chair, as if he had attempted to stand but had collapsed. Her first thought was to summon help and she tugged at the bell pull before hurrying to his side. She threw herself down on her knees, lifting his head so that it rested on her lap. 'Hubert, speak to me.' She patted his sunken cheek, willing him to open his eyes. For a terrible moment she thought that he was dead, but then she realised that he was still breathing. 'Hubert, I'm here. You'll be all right.' She looked round frantically, hoping that someone would answer the urgent jangling of the bell, and after what seemed like an age the door opened and Amos entered, followed by Bodger. 'Help me, please,' Mirabel cried. 'We must get my husband into bed and send for the doctor.'

In a combined effort Amos and Bodger managed to lift him onto the bed. Mirabel perched on the edge, chafing his hands. 'Hubert, can you hear me?'

'You heard the missis, Amos mate,' Bodger said gruffly. 'Fetch the doctor.'

Amos retreated, muttering beneath his breath, but Mirabel was too anxious to take any notice of his mumbling. She looked up at Bodger, her eyes filling with tears. 'I shouldn't have left him. Someone ought to have been with him.'

'I was having me supper,' Bodger said apologetically. 'Sorry, missis.'

She relented, shaking her head. 'It wasn't your fault, Bodger. I should have been at his side, but I was dressing for dinner and thinking only of myself.'

Bodger laid his large hand on her shoulder. 'These things happen, missis, but he'll be all right. The guy is tougher than he looks.'

Mirabel brushed a lock of snow white hair back from Hubert's forehead. 'I do hope so.'

Almost as if her touch had vitalised him, Hubert opened his eyes. He focused them on Mirabel's face. 'Anjuli,' he whispered. 'Anjuli.' His eyelids fluttered and closed on a sigh and his hand went limp in Mirabel's grasp. She stared at him in disbelief.

'He's gone, missis,' Bodger said gently. 'He ain't breathing.'

'No, he can't be dead. He just spoke.' Mirabel raised Hubert's hand to her cheek, but even in her denial she knew that Bodger was right. Hubert had died with the name of the Indian lady who had given her life in her attempt to save him on his lips. He had loved her to the last. Tears fell from Mirabel's eyes as she released his lifeless hand and laid it on his chest. 'You're with her now,' she whispered. 'You've found her again, Hubert, my dear.'

Bodger helped her to her feet. 'You can't do nothing for him, missis. Leave it to the doctor when he comes. I'll take you to your room, shall I?'

Mirabel shook her head. 'I must stay with Hubert. I don't want to leave him on his own.' She was about to sit down again when the door opened and Vincent strode into the room.

331

'I came as soon as Amos told me.' He grasped Mirabel's hands in his. 'I am so sorry. Everything will be taken care of, I promise you.'

Hubert's remains, together with what little was left of his precious ghost orchids, were interred in the D'Angelo family plot in a simple ceremony attended by master and servants alike. Mirabel had at first insisted that she wanted to take her husband's body back to London for burial, but the logistics of such a journey outweighed everything and Vincent urged her to think again. Bodger, surprisingly, was on his side, as was Gertie, and Mirabel had to admit that they were right. After all, she could not think of a more beautiful place for him to find eternal rest than the neatly kept graveyard shaded by tall trees. Vincent promised that the grave would be honoured and tended as if Hubert had been a relative, and there was little that Mirabel could do other than allow the interment to take place. Despite the illness that had struck him down so suddenly Hubert's passing had come as a shock. She could not pretend to be a grief stricken widow, but she grieved for the loss of a dear friend. Their relationship might have seemed strange to the outside world, but she had been genuinely fond of Hubert and she knew she would miss his unfailing kindness and understanding.

Jerusha and her father were sympathetic, although Mirabel suspected that they had not really understood the relationship between her and her elderly husband. The only person who seemed to know instinctively what was in Mirabel's heart was Betsy. She said little, but Mirabel felt comfortable and at ease in her company. In the days that followed, while she planned her journey home, she spent more time with Betsy than before. In the late afternoon, when they waited for Jerusha and Ethan to return from visiting his family, Mirabel and Betsy sat in the shade of the magnolias, sipping iced tea in companionable silence. The rustle of the breeze in the stiff green leaves above their heads was as hypnotic as the lapping of waves on the shore. Mirabel tried hard to keep her thoughts from straying to the white sands of Florida and the man she loved with all her heart and would never see again, but she could feel Jack's presence as if he was sitting beside her. If she closed her eyes she could feel the pressure of his lips on hers and the hardness of his body when he held her in his arms. No matter the distance between them, he would always have a place in her heart.

'What will be, will be, honey.'

The touch of a hand on hers was like the flutter of a moth's wing and Mirabel opened her eyes to find Betsy leaning over her with a gentle smile. 'Thank you,' she said in a whisper. 'You understand.'

Betsy clutched her hands to her heart, nodding. 'I do indeed.'

Despite Jerusha's pleas for her to stay until the wedding, Mirabel felt that she could not impose much longer on the D'Angelos' hospitality. She chose a quiet moment one afternoon and was seated in the parlour, going through the papers that her husband had kept with him on their travels, when she discovered the true extent of their finances. Hubert had always said that money was no object, but she discovered to her horror that there was very little left of the funds he had allocated for their travels. They might, she thought, have enough left for the train journey to New York, but there was no question of travelling first class on the *Servia;* they would have to cross the Atlantic steerage. She was mulling this over when Bodger erupted into the room. 'I got to tell you something, missis. I couldn't leave it no longer.'

'What is it, Bodger? Has something awful happened?'

'Mr Munroe has bought a ship.'

Mirabel stared at him, frowning. 'Has he? That's good news but I don't see how it affects us.'

Bodger shifted from one foot to the other, eyeing her warily. 'I know it's my duty to see you and Gertie safely back to England, but he's offered me a job and it's something I can't pass over.'

'But why is it so urgent? Surely you could find a vessel in London?'

'Mr Munroe has plans to run a fleet of ships carrying cargoes of tobacco from Newport News to London and Bristol. If I'm in at the beginning who knows where I might end up in a few years' time? I might even make captain one day.'

'Yes, I understand that, but why now? Couldn't it wait for a while?'

'It's a one-off voyage, but the ship sails tomorrow bound for Havana, stopping off with supplies for the new hotel at Coconut Grove.'

Mirabel's heart did a funny little flip inside her chest. 'Why do you want to go back there?'

'I got loyalties, missis. Jack Starke is a mate and

334

I don't want him to end up a drunken rummy. He's worth more than that.'

'He didn't want to leave Florida. He chose to stay.'

'Begging your pardon, missis, but I know different.' Bodger hesitated, fixing her with a straight look. 'If you say you can't manage without me then I'll forget it and I'll see that you get home, but if you're the woman I think you are you'll let me go. If I don't do something the cap'n will likely drink his self to death or die of fever, or be killed by an alligator or a poisonous serpent. You got the final say.'

Chapter Twenty-one

After the golden sunshine of Virginia and the vivid colours of Florida, London seemed uniformly grey and drab. It was raining when the hackney carriage drew to a halt outside the house in Savage Gardens, and a thick blanket of impenetrable cloud hung over the rooftops. Mirabel paid the cabby with the last few coppers in her purse before helping Gertie to heft their luggage onto the pavement. It had been a long and tortuous journey from New York. Travelling steerage was an experience she would not wish to repeat and would rather forget. Vincent had offered to pay for a second class cabin but Mirabel had her pride and she could not impose on his generosity any further. The D'Angelo family had been more than

335

kind and her parting from them had been accompanied by tears and promises to keep in touch, but Mirabel knew that from now on her life was about to change, and not for the better. As the wife of a rich and respected man she had enjoyed the protection of her husband's name, but as a young widow things would be different. Her financial situation seemed to be precarious and she would not know how she stood until she returned to London.

She hesitated, looking up at the house which seemed small and shabby when compared to the mansion at Loblolly Grove. Raindrops coursed down the windowpanes like tears, as if the house itself was in mourning for its dead master. She had still to break the news to Mrs Flitton.

'Come on, Mabel. What d'you think you're doing standing in the pouring rain?'

Gertie's brisk tone broke through the confused thoughts that were flitting like bad dreams through Mirabel's brain. She took a deep breath, picked up her valise and climbed the steps to the front door. Having rapped on the knocker she waited, listening for the sound of footsteps. The door opened and she was enveloped in a wild embrace with Tilda clinging to her like a burr.

'Let us in, you silly goose,' Gertie said impatiently. 'It's raining cats and dogs.'

Mirabel wriggled free from Tilda's clinging arms. 'It's good to be home.' As she stepped over the threshold she realised that she meant what she said. The smell of lavender and beeswax mingled with the aroma of cooking emanating from the kitchen below stairs. She dropped her valise on the floor, noting with a wry smile the puddle of water seeping onto the polished boards. Mrs Flitton would have something to say about that.

Gertie bustled in behind her, slamming the door with a sigh of relief. 'Home at last. I never want to do that journey again. I could do with a cup of split pea. Where's Ma Flitton?'

'Is that you, Gertie Tinker?' Mrs Flitton's mob-cap appeared first as she negotiated the steep stairs, followed by the rest of her plump body. She waddled along the hallway holding out her hands. 'Mrs Kettle, you're home.' There was a note of disapproval in her voice. 'Why didn't you let us know you were coming, ma'am? We're quite un-prepared.'

Gertie dumped her suitcase at the foot of the stairs. 'I'll take the bags up later, if you don't mind. I hope the kettle is on, Mrs F. I'm parched.' She grabbed Tilda by the hand. 'Come with me, miss. You can make yourself useful in the kitchen.'

Mirabel smiled as she took off her cape and bonnet. 'I'm afraid it wasn't possible to send a telegram when we arrived at Liverpool. I'd run rather short of funds.'

Mrs Flitton hurried to the front door and opened it, peering out into the rain. 'Where's the master?' She closed it again, turning to fix Mira-bel with a suspicious stare. 'What's happened? Why isn't he with you?'

Mirabel led her into the study, closing the door behind them. 'Sit down, Mrs Flitton. I'm afraid I have some bad news.'

'The master?' Mrs Flitton sank down on the nearest chair.

'I'm afraid the expedition was too much for him. He was taken ill on board ship. We managed to get him to the home of friends we'd made on board the *Servia,* but he had another attack which proved fatal. I'm sorry to be the bearer of such sad tidings; I know how fond you were of him, and he of you.'

Mrs Flitton stared at her blankly for a few seconds, but her expression changed subtly and she rose to her feet. 'You killed him as sure as if you'd put a gun to the poor man's head. If he hadn't taken up with a woman young enough to be his granddaughter he wouldn't have gone gallivanting halfway around the world and the poor man would be alive now.'

Shocked and startled by her housekeeper's reaction, Mirabel was momentarily at a loss for words. 'I know you're upset, but really it wasn't like that.'

'You encouraged him to hunt for rare orchids. He was quite happy here at home, tending the plants he had. He'd never have thought of such a stupid venture if it hadn't been for you.' The venom in her voice echoed round the room, and her eyes were filled with hatred. 'It was a bad day for us when he met you.'

'That's enough.' Mirabel faced her angrily. 'I understand that you're upset but if that's how you feel I don't think we can continue to live under the same roof.'

'Wiley said you were a hellcat, and he was right.'

'What has Wiley to do with this?'

Mrs Flitton recoiled, her eyes widening. 'Nothing. Forget I said it.'

338

'No. You can't take it back now it's out in the open. What's been going on in my absence?' Mirabel spun round as someone rapped on the study door. 'Not now.'

Despite her angry tone the door opened and Alf Coker marched into the room. 'Tilda told me you was home, ma'am. I knew there'd be trouble and I could hear her screeching at you from outside in the hall.'

'Go away, you wretched man.' Mrs Flitton subsided onto the chair, covering her face with her hands. 'Don't believe a word he says. He's a liar.'

'I'm not the one who's been consorting with Wiley.' Alf closed the door and leaned against it. 'I've heard them plotting together, ma'am. That man's got his feet well and truly under the kitchen table.'

'Mrs Flitton?' Mirabel folded her arms across her chest, struggling to control the feeling of panic roiling in her stomach. Wherever Wiley went there was sure to be trouble. 'What's all this?'

'Wiley is a good man. He wants to marry me.'

'He's already married.'

'She's a mad woman. He was forced to have her admitted to Colney Hatch.'

'The lunatic asylum?' Mirabel sat down suddenly as her knees gave way beneath her. She looked to Alf for an explanation. 'I don't understand.'

'I dunno, missis. I suppose he had his reasons, but what he wants with this one is anyone's guess.' He nodded towards Mrs Flitton, who was sobbing quietly.

'I'm a respectable widow,' she said, mopping

her eyes on her apron. 'Mr Wiley is an honourable man. He came to me for advice and comfort. You don't know what he's suffered at the hands of that crazy person.'

'My stepmother is a mean woman, but she's not insane.' Mirabel stared at her housekeeper, shocked by the sudden turn of events. 'But I always thought Wiley married Ernestine to get his hands on the house and gain control of my father's money.'

'Perhaps he found out he'd been misled,' Alf said thoughtfully. 'Maybe everything was left to you after all, ma'am.'

'That might explain why he wants to rid himself of Ernestine and her troublesome daughters, but what purpose would it serve for him to wheedle his way into this house?'

'The master promised to make sure I was taken care of when he passed away, but I daresay you persuaded him to cut me out of his will so that you could take everything.' Mrs Flitton raised herself to her feet, holding her head high. 'I gave the master the best years of my life, but I won't stay where I'm not wanted. Mr Wiley has asked me to marry him.' She ripped off her apron and dropped it on the floor at Mirabel's feet. 'I'm going to Septimus. He'll take care of me.'

Alf barred the doorway, folding his arms across his chest. 'You'll regret it, woman.'

'Let me out, Alf Coker. I'll not stay here another minute.'

'Let her go,' Mirabel said tiredly. 'I'm afraid she'll have to learn the hard way.'

'I'll collect my wages at the end of the month,'

Mrs Flitton said as she wrenched the door open. 'And I don't need a character. I won't have to work again: Septimus said so.' She stormed out of the room, leaving Mirabel and Alf staring at each other in disbelief.

'She was always so nice and obliging when my husband was alive,' Mirabel said sadly. 'I blame Wiley for the change in her. Goodness knows how he did it, but he's turned her head, and for what purpose I can't imagine.'

'I dunno, ma'am. But I wouldn't trust him any further than I could throw him.' Alf hesitated in the doorway, his craggy features creased with concern. 'I was sorry to hear about the master. I was in the kitchen when Gertie and Tilda came rushing down the stairs. I guessed that you might need some help.'

'Thank you, Alf.' Mirabel leaned her elbows on the desk, resting her head in her hands. 'I don't know what's going to happen now. I'm not even sure if I can afford to keep this house on.'

'I've been looking for accommodation ever since you left. I ain't left a stone unturned, but it's hard when you've got so many nippers to care for.'

'You can stay here as long as I can afford the upkeep of this house. That's all I can promise at the moment. It's going to take me a while to sort out my affairs.'

A gentle tap on the door was followed by Gertie entering with a tray of tea which she placed on the desk. 'I thought you could both do with some refreshment.'

'That's what I've missed since we've been away,' Mirabel said, halfway between laughter and tears. 'A proper cup of tea.'

'I'm afraid there's no cake,' Gertie said apologetically. 'And I don't think there'll be any supper. Mrs F come flying down the stairs, grabbed the saucepan off the range and tipped the stew down the drain outside. The rats'll get a good supper tonight, but not us.'

Mirabel had a sudden vision of the hog meat roasting on a spit over the campfire, and Jack standing at the water's edge, gazing out across the ink-black lake. She pulled herself together, realising that Gertie and Alf were staring at her. 'I have the key to the safe. If there's money in it we'll have pie and mash or a fish dinner.' She reached for her reticule and took out a bunch of keys that she had found in Hubert's dressing case.

It took a while and a considerable amount of patience to try all the keys on the ring, but eventually she managed to open the small safe and found a cash box which contained a crisp five pound note, three golden sovereigns, some silver coins and a handful of copper. 'It's a fish supper then,' she said, sighing with relief. 'Tomorrow I'll go to the bank and find out exactly what my position is.' She turned to Alf with a worried frown. 'I'd be grateful if you could see Mrs Flitton off the premises. I don't trust Wiley and she seems to be in his thrall, so I wouldn't be surprised at anything she does from now on.'

He nodded. 'Gladly, missis. And the master's orchids are all doing well. I nursed them like babies while you was away.'

'I suppose I could sell the collection,' Mirabel said thoughtfully. 'Hubert spoke of a man called

Frederick Sander who has a nursery in St Albans. Maybe he'd take the plants. Hubert would have wanted them to go to someone who loved and appreciated them as he did.'

'Yes'm, whatever you say. I was just about to check the temperature in the greenhouse when you arrived.'

'That can wait. Here's a sovereign. I don't feel like going out, but that should buy us all a decent meal. It's been a long hard day and tomorrow I want to be up early. There's so much to do.'

'Yes'm.' Alf pocketed the coin. 'I'll be as quick as I can.'

The study seemed oddly silent when Alf had gone, with nothing but the barely audible tick-tock of the clock on the mantelshelf to disturb Mirabel's thoughts. She moved to sit in Hubert's chair at the desk where everything was as he had left it, neat and tidy as the man himself. She leaned her elbows on the polished mahogany rim that surrounded the tooled leather, staring absently at the rows of books on the shelves, lined up in strict alphabetical and subject order. It was as if Hubert had simply left the room to check on his beloved orchids and might return at any moment to report on a new bud or a flower about to open. It was going to be difficult to convince herself that he was gone forever: she missed his gentle humour and even the fussy little ways he had developed during his years of bachelorhood. Theirs had been a marriage of convenience on both sides, but she had felt a genuine affection for him and deep respect. Tonight she would mourn his passing, but tomorrow she would have to take her affairs in hand and visit Hubert's solicitor and the bank.

She left the solicitor's office in Lincoln's Inn with Hubert's will clutched in her hand and hailed a cab to take her to his bank in the City. It had been painful to relate the events surrounding her husband's sudden death in a foreign country, but Mr Yardley was sympathetic and advised her to take the document to the bank and reveal its contents to the manager, who might be persuaded to allow her to draw funds until such time as probate was granted. A hansom cab drew up at the kerb. 'Threadneedle Street, please, cabby.'

After a short wait she was ushered into the bank manager's office where she had to go through it all again, ending with an emotional break in her voice and genuine tears in her eyes. The manager consulted his records, nodding his head as he ran his fingertip down the entries logged under Hubert's name. He looked up, a frown knotting his lined brow. 'I'm afraid your late husband made some investments that have proved ill-judged.'

Mirabel's breath hitched in her throat. 'What does that mean exactly?'

'It means, my dear lady, that the late Mr Kettle suffered considerable losses.'

'How much is there in the account, Mr Browning? I really need to know.'

He stared at the figures, his lips moving silently, and Mirabel waited, clasping her hands tightly in her lap.

After what seemed like an eternity he looked up. 'When probate is granted you will have an approximate income of one hundred pounds a year from the remaining investments, and there is fifty pounds ten shillings and ninepence halfpenny available in the account as it stands now. Mr Kettle drew heavily on his funds for the expedition to Florida.'

'And that's all I have to live on?'

'There is another matter, but I would need to see your husband's death certificate before I can discuss it.'

Mirabel delved into her reticule and produced the document. 'I have it here.' She placed it on the desk in front of him.

Browning studied it carefully and a slow smile curved his lips. 'Then I believe I have good news for you, Mrs Kettle.' He laid the paper on his desk, smoothing it with his hands. 'Your late husband was a member of a tontine, which he entered many years ago when he was quite a young man. Have you heard of such a scheme?'

Mirabel shook her head. 'No, sir.'

'It's an arrangement between interested parties who subscribe to a scheme of investments from which they each draw an annuity. When a member dies his share is devolved to the other participants, and this continues until the last surviving person inherits the capital sum. I will have to check this, but it would seem from the date on the death certificate that Mr Kettle was that person.'

'I still don't understand. Does it come to me?'

Browning scanned through the will. 'It does. I haven't got the figures to hand but I imagine the final sum will be more than sufficient for your needs.'

'And I'll have it to invest as I think fit, once

probate is granted, of course.'

'I think perhaps you should leave that to the experts, Mrs Kettle.'

His tone was patronising and his indulgent smile made her feel like a child. 'It seems that the experts did not give my late husband very good advice.' Mirabel reached for the will, folded it and placed it in her reticule. 'I'll see that this goes to the right quarter and I'll leave you to investigate the tontine, Mr Browning. I hope to hear from you before too long.'

He opened his eyes wide like a startled owl. 'Of course, but I hope you will consult me before you make any investments.'

She rose to her feet. 'I'll consider it, but I need money to be going on with.'

'My head clerk will furnish you with sufficient funds to keep you going. The bank is always at your service, Mrs Kettle.' He hurried around the desk to open the door for her. 'Hindle,' he called, beckoning to a bald-headed, bespectacled clerk. 'Give Mrs Kettle what she requires.'

Mirabel left the bank with enough money in her purse to keep them in modest comfort until probate was granted and the first instalment of her annuity was due. The inheritance from the tontine had yet to be confirmed, but anything would be better than nothing. The time for dreaming was past; she must be practical and face the future with a clear mind. She was determined never to be dependent on anyone ever again, and, should there be a considerable sum of money due to her, she would not entrust it to men who gambled on the stock exchange. Hubert had made that mistake and she was not going to repeat his error.

She had intended to walk home, but her footsteps had taken her towards Lower Thames Street and the river, where she had always found solace as a child. The jingling of the stays against the wooden masts and the toot of the steamboats was a sound as familiar as the chirping of sparrows or the mournful mewing of seagulls swooping overhead. The metallic clanking of the umbrella cranes and the rumble of barrels being rolled into warehouses was accompanied by the constant babel of voices and the shouts of the stevedores. The smell of fresh fish mingled with the tarry odour from the fishing smacks, hot engine oil and belching smoke, and the ever present stench of horse dung that carpeted the streets. It was all familiar territory to someone raised in Shad Thames and St Catherine's Court. She only realised now how much she had missed her native London, despite the luxury she had enjoyed on board the *Servia* and in the plantation mansion at Loblolly Grove. She chose not to remember the Fakahatchee swamp and the burning prairie; those memories were woven around the intimate moments with Jack and were too poignant to think about without pain and tears.

She found herself standing on Custom House Quay, staring into the tea-coloured water of the River Thames. Watching the busy river traffic was oddly soothing, and there was the ever present element of mystery and excitement attached to the ocean-going vessels. The smaller coasters unloading their cargoes at the wharves on either side of the river still had the power to capture her imagination, and the lighters and other small craft criss-crossed the water as they went about their daily business. She realised suddenly that the sun had disappeared behind an ominous bank of clouds and the oily smooth surface was suddenly pockmarked with drizzle, which evolved rapidly into a downpour. Mirabel wrapped her cape around her shoulders and headed home, but she had drawn strength from the familiar surroundings and the river which was the heart's blood of the capital. She put her head down and hurried towards Great Tower Hill.

She arrived home and found the house in an uproar. Tilda's cheeks were streaked with tears as she let her in, but before she could control her sobs enough to speak Gertie appeared at the top of the basement stairs, red in the face and furious. 'Thank God you've come home. You'll never guess what's happened.' She grabbed Mirabel by the hand and dragged her along the hallway without giving her time to take off her sodden bonnet and cape.

'What's going on?' Mirabel demanded breathlessly.

'You wait until you see what that evil person has done.' Gertie released her hand, leading the way downstairs and out through the kitchen into the back yard. She came to a halt by the greenhouse. 'Look.' Her finger shook as she pointed towards the shattered windows, and the shards of glass sticking out of the wet ground below like icicles thrown by the hand of a vengeful Norse god.

Mirabel's hand flew to cover her mouth as she gazed in horror at the carnage within. Pots were strewn on the floor, the precious orchids bruised and damaged beyond help. Alf was standing in their midst, a look of horror etched on his face and tears running down his cheeks. 'Who did this?' Mirabel demanded breathlessly. 'Who would do such a terrible thing?'

Alf looked round slowly, wiping his eyes on his sleeve. 'Can't you guess? It's Ma Flitton's way of getting her own back on you, missis.'

'I can't believe she'd do such a thing,' Mirabel said slowly. 'She knew how much my husband loved the orchids. They were his life.'

'And he's dead.' Gertie's shrill voice reverberated off the tall brick walls surrounding the yard. 'She blames you for that, Mabel. I don't think the old bitch would have the guts to do this herself, but I know who would and he's not a million miles away from here.'

'Wiley,' Alf said angrily. 'She had a key to the back gate and it's missing from its hook. That was the first thing I checked when I come out here this morning. She must have given it to him and told him to do his worst. It don't take a 'tec to work that one out. I'm going round there now to give him what for.'

'No.' Mirabel stepped over the fragments of broken glass, and made her way into the wrecked greenhouse. 'It's probably what he wants and I refuse to play his game.'

'I'll go and find a copper,' Gertie said eagerly. 'Let them deal with it.'

Mirabel shook her head. 'We can't prove anything and who'd believe that a nice old lady like Mrs Flitton would suddenly turn into an evil witch? Wiley can be very convincing too, if he puts his mind to it. I'll deal with this in my own way.'

'I dunno how, missis.' Alf pushed his cap to the back of his head, staring round at the ruined plant collection. 'This lot must have been worth a small fortune. He should be made to pay.'

'He will. Just give it time.' Mirabel picked up a crushed flower, holding it to her cheek. 'I'm just glad that Hubert didn't live to see his beautiful orchids crushed and dying.'

Alf signalled to Tilda, who had been hovering anxiously outside the door. 'Put the kettle on, girl. The missis looks as though she needs a cup of tea with a good splash of brandy. I'll have one too; plenty of sugar, if we can afford it.' He laid his hand on Mirabel's shoulder. 'Chin up, missis. I'll get me boys to help and we'll have this lot cleared up in a jiffy.'

'Yes,' Mirabel said dazedly. 'Thank you, Alf.' She made an attempt at a smile. 'At least we'll save money on coal.' She stepped outside, turning her back on the vandalised greenhouse. It was the end of an era as far as Hubert's orchid collection was concerned, but someone would pay for it, and that someone would be the man who had tried to destroy her and take what rightfully was hers.

Leaving Alf and his sons to sort out the green-house and clear up the mess, Mirabel braved the rain and paid another visit to the solicitor. Yardley himself was in court and likely to be there for some time, according to his clerk. It seemed that the day was going to be one of frustration and disaster, but Mirabel was not about to give up. She left Hubert's will with the clerk, instructing him to send it for probate on her behalf, and asked him to get a copy of her father's will. Hubert had promised to do so, but he had been busy arranging the expedition to Florida and must have forgotten.

She left the office feeling that at least she had done something constructive, and was even more determined not to be beaten by Wiley. At least the rain had stopped and a pale sun was edging its way through the clouds. She was halfway across the lawn in Lincoln's Inn Fields when she saw a fashionably dressed woman walking towards her. There was no mistaking her identity. 'Zilla.' Mirabel quickened her pace, realising that Zilla Grace was about to walk past. 'Zilla, it's me.'

Zilla came to a halt, looking her up and down. A slow smile animated her painted face. 'Why, it's Mabel. You look so fine I didn't recognise you. How is Hubert?'

Chapter Twenty-two

'Dead?' For once Zilla seemed at a loss for words. She tucked Mirabel's hand in the crook of her arm. 'Walk with me, Mabel.'

Zilla had never been one to show emotion, but Mirabel sensed that she was genuinely upset at the news of Hubert's demise. 'It was quite sudden.'

'I suppose he was getting on in years,' Zilla said slowly. 'If it was anyone but you I'd suspect foul play.'

Mirabel withdrew her hand, coming to a halt.

351

'That's a terrible thing to say.'

'It's what many people would think, although I know better. How did it happen?'

'The doctor said it was an apoplectic fit.' Mirabel was in no mood for lengthy explanations and she set off, walking briskly in the direction of Carey Street.

Zilla hurried after her. 'I would have liked to pay my respects at his funeral, and I'm sure my girls would have too. Why didn't you let me know?'

'Hubert was taken ill and died in America. He's buried there.'

'It might have proved expensive to travel so far for a funeral.' Zilla quickened her pace to keep up with Mirabel. 'I'm teasing you, Mabel. I know it was in poor taste but I'm agog with curiosity, and I won't be satisfied until you tell me the whole story.'

'I have to be somewhere, Zilla. I really can't stop.'

'Now I know there's something you're not telling me.' They had reached Serle Street, where a cab had just drawn up in order to drop off its passenger. Zilla hailed the cabby. 'Tenter Street.' She seized Mirabel's hand. 'Hubert was my friend and I'm truly sorry to hear that he's gone to his maker. You can spare me a few minutes of your time – you owe me that, Mrs Kettle.'

It seemed like years since Mirabel had set foot in Zilla's establishment, although nothing had changed. Florrie acknowledged her with a curt nod of her head as she let them in, and Gentle Jane gave her a hearty slap on the back as she

352

passed them wearing nothing but a skimpy robe, with her hair wrapped in a towel. 'Left the old bloke and come back to join us, have you?' she chortled. 'Welcome home, Mabel.' She clattered off towards the stairs, her slippers making wet slapping sounds on the floorboards.

'Never mind her,' Zilla said impatiently. 'Come to my parlour and we'll talk.' She glanced over her shoulder at Florrie, who was loitering by the front door. 'Don't stand there looking like an idiot, girl. Bring us coffee and cake. No, make that my best Madeira and cake.' She marched off along the narrow hallway towards her parlour.

Mirabel followed her more slowly. The house with its familiar furnishings and the stuffy atmosphere heavy with the smell of stale cigar smoke, wine and cheap perfume had once been a welcome refuge, but the memories it held were bittersweet. It was not her husband's ghost haunting the corridors; it was the memory of Jack, whose lazy, lopsided smile was etched forever in her memory. Resolutely closing her mind to his presence she entered Zilla's parlour. 'What were you doing in Lincoln's Inn?' she demanded without giving her hostess the chance to speak. Perhaps, she thought, if she could deflect the conversation away from herself she might get away with a brief explanation as to why Hubert had died on foreign soil.

Zilla pulled a long and vicious-looking hatpin from her wide-brimmed hat, which was embellished with ostrich feathers dyed an unbelievable shade of purple. She laid it on the rosewood table next to a bowl of bronze chrysanthemums. 'Oh, the usual,' she said casually. 'The police raid us on a regular basis. My solicitor attends court in my absence and I pay a fine. That's an end to it until the next time.' She slipped off her mantle and tossed it on a chair before taking a seat. 'Now then, Mabel. What is it you're not telling me?' She reached for a silver box, took out a small black cigarillo, struck a match and lit it, inhaling with obvious enjoyment. 'Go on, I'm listening.'

It was impossible to keep anything from Zilla. The scent of the tobacco and the relaxing effects of the fine Madeira, which Florrie had delivered with her customary lack of finesse, made it easier to mention Jack's name when it came to that particular part of her narrative. Mirabel kept her eyes focused on Zilla's face, searching for a change in her expression when his name cropped up, but she merely nodded her head and tapped the ash from the cigarillo into the grate. 'He has a habit of turning up unexpectedly. I suppose you're in love with him.'

'Of course not,' Mirabel said hastily. 'I hardly know him.'

'When did that ever stop a female heart from fluttering, especially when the man in question is an attractive devil like Jack Starke?' Zilla downed the last of her wine. 'So you left him in Florida.'

'He chose to stay. There's nothing between us, Zilla. You can have him back for all I care.'

'My dear child, I wouldn't take him back if he crawled from Liverpool to London on bended knees. I like my freedom and I treat men in the same way they treat us. I take what I want and then I move on.' Zilla put the cigarillo to her lips and inhaled, exhaling slowly and thoughtfully.

'So what were you doing in Lincoln's Inn? You must be a wealthy woman now.'

'Not exactly. Hubert spent a great deal of money on the expedition and the bank manager told me that he'd made some ill-judged investments.'

'So you're broke – I can give you a job here?' Zilla's lips twitched and she tossed the butt of her cigarillo into the fire. 'Maybe I could find you another elderly suitor?'

'Thank you, no. I expect to inherit a considerable some from a tontine that Hubert had belonged to, and I intend to invest the money myself. I don't trust banks.'

Zilla eyed her thoughtfully. 'What sort of investment were you thinking of?'

'I don't know exactly. I want something to do, Zilla. I can't see myself as a woman who occupies her time with domestic matters and good works. I'm never going to have children of my own and I need something that will occupy my mind. I'd like to have my own business; I just don't know how to go about it.'

'I might just have an idea, but I'd need to look into it further.' Zilla rose to her feet and tugged at an embroidered bell pull. 'Florrie will find you a cab. I'm sure you have things to do at home. I'll let you know whether or not I think my idea will be of benefit to you.'

Mirabel stood up, swaying slightly as the Madeira wine took its full effect. 'Thank you, Zilla. I know you're a good businesswoman and I'd appreciate your help, but I'd like to hear more before you go to any trouble on my behalf.'

Zilla resumed her seat, reaching again for the

silver box. 'One of my clients is a seafaring man.' She selected a cigarillo and struck a match. 'Don't look so worried, my dear. He's nothing like Jack. He's a serious sort of fellow but he enjoys the comforts my girls provide when he spends a night ashore.'

'I don't know anything about ships,' Mirabel said hastily. 'I was thinking of a shop, perhaps, or setting up a lending library.'

'Poppycock. You'd be bored to death within weeks. My client is master and owner of the ship but a poor businessman. He needs a partner who would be prepared to invest and run the business side of things. If he doesn't find someone soon I'm afraid he'll go bankrupt and lose everything, which would be a shame because he's a decent man.'

'I'm not looking for a husband,' Mirabel said warily. 'I hope you don't think you're acting as a marriage broker.'

Zilla threw back her head and laughed. 'Edric Hamilton has a wife and five children, as well as a stuck-up sister-in-law and a brother who won't have anything to do with him.'

'The name sounds familiar,' Mirabel said thoughtfully. 'He wouldn't be related to Adela Hamilton, would he?'

'Do you know her?'

'She runs the soup kitchen where I used to help. Anyone related to her has my sympathy.'

'Does that mean you'll consider the idea?'

'If you can arrange a meeting with Mr Hamilton I'll be happy to hear what he has to say.'

At first sight Edric Hamilton was not a prepossessing figure. He stood on the quay wall, a towering figure over six feet in height. His fiery red hair stood out around his head in a mass of tight curls, matched by a beard and moustache that masked the whole of his lower face. His eyes, rimmed with sandy lashes, were the intense blue of a summer sky and a livid scar on the left side of his face showed up white against his tanned skin. 'Mrs Kettle.' He advanced towards her holding out a huge hand at the end of a muscular forearm exposed by his rolled up shirt sleeve. 'How good of you to come.' His voice was surprisingly cultured and at odds with his appearance. 'Would you care to come aboard and see for yourself?'

Mirabel shook hands, trying hard not to wince as strong fingers crushed her bones together in a firm grip. 'Yes, Captain Hamilton. I think I would.'

He descended the wooden ladder placed precariously on the deck of his vessel and propped against the wooden stanchions of the quay wall. Standing at the bottom he held out his arms. 'I'll catch you if you fall.'

'Thank you, that won't be necessary, Captain.' Mirabel put one foot on the top rung, holding on for dear life as she climbed down the ladder. The vessel was a paddle steamer with one funnel amidships and its deck lined with wooden benches. 'What exactly do you carry, Captain Hamilton?' She gazed in horror at the disarray on the deck, which was covered in a film of black oil, and the benches were splattered with bird droppings.

'Passengers, ma'am. I used to carry sightseers in summer, although to be truthful not too many want to step on board these days.'

Looking round Mirabel could understand why. She tried to be positive. 'What about cargo?'

'Sometimes I get a charter, but I don't have time to go looking for work. I'm a seafaring man, used to sailing bigger craft than this, but needs must.'

'I'm afraid I don't understand. Why do you continue with this type of work if it doesn't pay?'

'I have little choice, Mrs Kettle.' He stared at her, his sandy brows lowered in a frown. 'I have a family to keep, and taking sightseers downriver used to pay well, but when the *Princess Alice* went down four years ago with such a terrible loss of life my business suffered too.'

'Perhaps what you offer isn't quite enough these days,' Mirabel suggested tactfully. 'Maybe a clean-up and a coat of paint would attract more custom.'

Edric threw up his hands. 'Ma'am, do I look as though I can afford to pay for such things?'

'You can afford Zilla's prices. I would have thought this would be your priority as it's your way of earning a living. What does your wife have to say about all this?'

'She says it was a bad day when I split with my old partner. He bought me out five years ago. I sold the brig and bought this, thinking I could run the business by myself.'

'What happened to your partner? Wouldn't he be the one to go to for advice?'

'The poor fellow's ship was lost off the coast of Havana with all hands.'

'What was his name?' Mirabel's breath hitched in her throat and her heart pounded against her ribcage, and she already knew the answer.

'Jack Starke. He was a good mate, God rest his soul. It was through Zilla that we met.'

'He didn't drown. Last time I saw him he was alive and well.'

The corners of Edric's eyes crinkled into a smile. 'You don't say so. Well I never did. Where is the old devil?'

'Florida. At least that's where he was a few weeks ago.'

'Zilla told me you're well travelled, but I'd no idea you knew my mate Jack. How is he?'

'He's enjoying life as far as I know.' It was painful to talk about Jack in such a casual way, but knowing that he had been this man's friend had made her think differently about helping Edric. Suddenly his needs and her own seemed to be inextricably interwoven, and dragging him from a pit of despair was a challenge she could not ignore. 'But this isn't about Jack Starke; this is about your business, Captain Hamilton.'

He ran his hand through his untidy mass of hair. 'Do you mean you'll help me?'

'I'd like to talk it over with you, but I might be interested.'

'Why would a lady like you want to take on something like this?'

'My father was a businessman, Captain. Perhaps I've inherited some of the instincts that made him a success.'

'With all due respect, I'm not sure about working with a woman, ma'am.'

'I haven't agreed to anything yet, but as I see it you haven't got much choice. What does your wife think about all this?' She encompassed the vessel with a wave of her hand.

'She threw me out, Mrs Kettle. I've been living below deck for the past six months.'

'I need to see the whole of the ship, Captain. And a report from a surveyor would be helpful. There's no point putting money into the boat if it's about to sink to the bottom of the river.'

Mirabel's first mission, having inspected the vessel and arranged for a survey to be done, was to visit Edric's wife. The family home was in Limehouse, close to the river, and the dwelling was, like the boat, in a state of disrepair. Tiles were missing from the roof and several of the windows were boarded up. Fronting directly onto the street, the house was sandwiched between a pawnbroker and a pub. It was not the most salubrious area even in broad daylight. She rapped on the knocker and somewhere inside a dog barked and a baby began to cry. The door was opened by a thin woman whose pale face was lined with fatigue, but vestiges of her youthful prettiness still lingered. She stared at Mirabel, looking her up and down without saying a word.

'Mrs Hamilton, may I come in for a moment?'

'Who are you?'

'My name is Mirabel Kettle.'

'If you're from the school board I don't know where Jimmy is.'

'I'm not from the school board. I'm here because I might be able to help your husband with his business, but I wanted to speak to you first.'

'You'd better come in, then.'

360

Mirabel followed her into the dingy parlour where a baby lay in a wooden crib by the window while a toddler crawled round the floor, trying to pick up a cockroach. The walls were covered in faded prints of ships, and every available surface was littered with strange objects presumably brought back from foreign parts. The only furniture was a square pine table, several wooden stools and a rocking chair by the fire. The grate was empty and the air was thick with the smell of soot, rising damp and the odours creeping in from the river. 'My husband's sister-in-law didn't send you, did she?'

Mirabel had a sudden vision of fastidious Adela Hamilton standing in her place, looking round with her nose in the air. 'No, she didn't. May I sit down?'

'Tell me what you want. I have a baby to feed and a meal to cook for my boys. They're down at the water's edge, scavenging for anything that will fetch a copper or two. Why have you come here?'

'I'm thinking of investing in your husband's business, but he can't go on living on board the *Beatrice*.'

'He named the boat after me, but that was in better times. I don't want him back, Mrs Kettle. He squanders any money he gets on women and drink.'

'I won't part with a penny until I'm certain he'll change his ways. Would you be prepared to give him another chance if he promises to behave?'

A wry smile lit Beatrice's eyes for a brief moment. 'He's not a schoolboy, Mrs Kettle. I can see that you mean well but you've obviously led a sheltered life. You wouldn't know what women like me have to put up with.'

'Did he beat you?'

'Never!'

Mirabel glanced at the baby in the crib. 'But he obviously loves you.'

'Men will have their way and love doesn't always come into it. You're a married woman, Mrs Kettle. You know the way it is.'

Mirabel felt the blood rush to her cheeks and she turned her head away. 'Of course, but do you love your husband?'

'I did once, but he was different then. We aren't the same people now.'

'I doubt that, Beatrice.' Mirabel tried another tack. 'You weren't born to this sort of life, I can tell that. You deserve better.'

'You can work miracles, can you, Mrs Kettle?'

'It's Mirabel, and no, of course I can't, but I've had a long talk with your husband, and I think I can judge character. I believe he is sincere in wanting to mend his ways.'

'He's made more promises than I care to re-member, but they always come to nothing. We're better off without him.'

Mirabel looked round the room, suppressing a shudder. 'Are you sure about that? If your hus-band's business improves you could move some-where more suited to your needs.'

'It wasn't always like this.' Beatrice leaned over to pick up the baby. 'Hush now, Charlotte.' She cradled the infant in her arms. 'When Eddie was in business with Jack we had a good living, but they went their separate ways, and now poor Jack is dead.'

'I know Captain Starke and I believe he was a good friend to you and Captain Hamilton. I'm happy to say that he's alive and well.'

'Jack is alive?'

'He survived the shipwreck, along with most of his crew. I met him by chance a few weeks ago in Florida.'

Beatrice sank down on the rocking chair. 'Well I never did!'

'I think Jack would want me to help you out of your present difficulties,' Mirabel said, pressing home her advantage.

'What is he to you, if you don't mind me asking?' Beatrice unbuttoned her bodice and put the baby to her breast.

'It's a long story.'

A slow smile lit Beatrice's eyes. 'I'm not going anywhere for a while.' She beckoned to the toddler, who had abandoned her efforts to catch the elusive insect. 'Come and sit with me, Lily. The lady has a tale to tell.'

'I'd make you a cup of tea, but I'd need to light the fire first,' Beatrice said when Mirabel came to the end of her narrative. 'Thank you for being so frank with me. I had you down for one of those rich women like Adela, who patronise the poor because it makes them feel better about themselves, but now I know different.'

'I would like to help you and your husband, but I would be doing it for my benefit as well. I intend to make money, which of course we would share. I can't spend the rest of my life feeling sorry for myself.'

'What about that nasty man Wiley? My Eddie would sort him out in two seconds flat.'

'I hope it won't come to that, but I'll deal with Wiley. His threats don't bother me, and he can't hurt poor Hubert now.' Mirabel rose to her feet. 'Don't worry about the tea, Beatrice.'

'Have you decided whether or not to go into business with Eddie?' Beatrice hitched the baby over her shoulder. 'He has his weaknesses but he's an honest man.'

'I'm sure he is, and if the surveyor's report is favourable, then I just have to find out exactly how much I'm due to collect from the tontine, and I'll make Edric an offer.'

'Jack was a fool to let you go,' Beatrice said, holding out her hand. 'I'll tell him so in no uncertain terms when I see him again.'

The surveyor's report was favourable. The Beatrice was sound, but in need of a considerable amount of hard work to make it an attractive proposition as a passenger craft. The money from the tontine was paid into Mirabel's bank account, and although it was not enough to keep her in comfort for the rest of her life, there was sufficient to allow her to enter into a business contract with Edric Hamilton. It was an easy decision to make, and although Jack seemed unlikely to return to London, working with his ex-partner made her feel that he was not altogether lost to her. As a married woman she had made the heartbreaking decision to walk away from him in Florida, and there was no going back now.

He had probably moved on, or else he was content to live out his life on the beach with rum as his constant companion. She set her sights on building up a business with Edric and taking care of her surrogate family.

With autumn upon them and winter snapping at its heels, she set up an office in what had been Hubert's study, and employed Alf to start work on the *Beatrice*, helping Edric to clean, paint and generally tidy up the vessel, while she put all her efforts into renewing the licence to trade and finding suitable work. It was a chance remark from Alf that led her to visit the Anglers' Association in Clerkenwell Road, where she was met by the supercilious secretary, who seemed to think that she was trespassing in a purely masculine domain. She had been prepared for this, however, and sat listening patiently while he expounded on the difference between men and women. 'Wives,' he concluded pompously, 'are the angels of the house. They should leave all other matters to their husbands, who are far better suited to deal with the outside world.'

Seizing on the fact that he had run out of bluster, Mirabel put her proposition to him as simply as she could, allowing for the fact that he was so entrenched in his opinions that it would take a team of navvies to dig him free.

'There it is, sir,' she said finally. 'Our company can offer anglers safe and comfortable trips to any part of the river they choose, within the bounds of the law, of course, at a very reasonable price. Parties or single gentlemen are catered for, and refreshments provided.'

'The railway companies offer anglers' tickets at reasonable rates, ma'am.'

'With which we can compete, and give better value for money. I've counted over one hundred and fifty angling clubs in the greater London area. There must be scores of your members who would jump at the chance of a day out on the river, away from the cares of home and hearth.' She could see by the flicker of uncertainty in his eyes that she had won. She took a bundle of leaflets from the document case that had once belonged to her husband and laid them on the desk. 'Well, sir? What do you say?'

Chapter Twenty-three

Trade with the anglers was brisk while the weather held, and Mirabel put all her energies into securing small contracts with a range of industries, transporting their goods from factories to ports downriver. She could have done even better had they had a larger vessel with a bigger hold, and she realised that to make money they had to expand the business. Edric was not so sure. 'We'll have to employ another master and crew if we're to do that,' he said, scratching his head. 'We're doing quite well with the anglers, and next spring we'll have the day trippers back.'

'We will, but we can do even better. Will you trust me on this?'

He grinned. 'Beatrice would kill me if I didn't

listen to you. She thinks you're the cleverest woman she's ever met.'

'And she's happy in your new home?'

'It's not quite up to my brother's residence in Spital Square, but we're on our way up, thanks to you.' He gave her a searching look. 'Jack was a fool to let you go. I agree with my wife on that.'

She turned away, busying herself with the pile of papers on her desk. 'It wasn't to be, Eddie.' Despite her attempt to sound positive she could not prevent a sigh escaping from her lips.

'I still say he was an idiot, and if I ever see him again I'll tell him so.' He picked up the manifest for the cargo he was about to take to Deptford. 'Perhaps you're right, Mirabel. We could make a bigger profit with another vessel. There's plenty of work out there for a small company, as you've proved without a doubt.'

Mirabel looked up at the sound of someone knocking on the study door. 'Come in.'

Tilda put her head round the door. 'It's Danny, missis. A copper's brought him home, says he's been brawling and wants to see Pa, but he's not here.'

'Do you want me to deal with this?' Edric asked, grinning.

'It's not funny,' Mirabel said, trying not to laugh. 'The boy needs work other than sifting through the Thames mud.' She met his amused gaze with a speculative look. 'You could take him on as a deck hand and train him for when we get another boat.'

'Do I have a choice?'

She shrugged her shoulders. 'Far be it from me

to tell you how to run your vessel, Captain Hamilton.'

'Really?' Tilda looked from one to the other. 'Will you really take him on, mister? He's a good worker and strong like Pa.'

Mirabel made for the door. 'Let me sort out the policeman and then you can discuss it with Danny.'

To her surprise and annoyance not only were Danny and the constable standing on the doorstep but Wiley was on the pavement, exhorting the policeman to arrest the boy immediately.

'What's the matter, constable?' Mirabel asked, ignoring Wiley who was complaining bitterly.

The constable turned to him. 'Will you keep your comments to yourself, sir? I can't hear myself think, let alone speak to the lady without raising my voice.'

'I done nothing wrong,' Danny protested, wriggling and grimacing as the constable tightened his grip on his ear. 'Let me go.'

'Not until this matter is cleared up, sonny. Does this boy live here, ma'am?'

'Of course he does,' Wiley said crossly. 'This is a den of thieves.'

'I'll thank you to keep quiet, sir.' The policeman released Danny. 'Don't try to scarper, son. You'll only make matters worse.'

Mirabel laid a protective hand on Danny's shoulder. 'What has he done?'

'According to this gent, he caught the lad stealing.'

'That's a lie,' Danny exclaimed angrily. 'I've been working the river bank all morning.'

'Look in his sack, constable.' Wiley pushed forward, snatching the canvas bag from the policeman and tipping the contents over the threshold onto the polished floorboards. 'Look, a silver teaspoon and a lady's watch.'

'And there's a shard of pottery, two pennies and a broken chain,' Mirabel said calmly. 'Everything is covered in mud.'

'It's where he hid the things he stole from my house,' Wiley said, floundering.

'Nonsense.' Mirabel picked up a rusty horseshoe, covered in mud. 'Daniel is a mudlark, and I'd be prepared to stand up in court and swear to that, if necessary.'

'Of course she'd say that. She's the daughter of a murderer and a thief.' Wiley stood back, folding his arms across his chest. 'They're all in it together, if you ask me.'

'This man is a known troublemaker, constable. I'm sure you've met many men like him in the course of duty.' Mirabel met the young policeman's worried glance with a smile, and his cheeks heightened in colour.

'It looks as though you were mistaken, sir,' he said, turning to Wiley. 'There's no case to answer here.' He tipped his helmet to Mirabel and descended to the pavement. He ignored Wiley's protests and walked off with a measured tread.

'What's the matter with you, Wiley?' Mirabel demanded. 'Why are you always trying to make trouble for me?'

'Mary Flitton told me what goes on in your household. She said you was trying to prove I don't own the house.'

'What I do is no business of yours, Wiley.'

'Hoity-toity, but you'll change your tune. By the time I've finished with you you'll wish you'd never crossed the path of Septimus Wiley.'

'Why are you doing this? My father treated you well.'

'He treated me like a servant. I was as good as him, or better. I never killed no one so that I could get my hands on their business.'

'Neither did Pa. It's a wicked lie.'

Danny had been subdued and silent until that moment, but now he pushed past Mirabel, and squared up to Wiley. 'Let me bash him, missis. I'll put his lights out.'

'Don't make threats you can't keep, boy,' Wiley growled. 'I could beat you with one hand tied behind me back.'

'No one is going to beat anyone,' Mirabel said hastily. She stepped between them. 'This has to stop now, Wiley. Go back to Mrs Flitton and tell her from me that I thought she was a better person, but it appears that I was mistaken.'

'You can tell her yourself if you can find the old baggage. I sent her packing as soon as I'd got what I wanted from her, just as I did with your pa's widow. D'you really think that Septimus Wiley would burden hisself with old women like those two when he can get any amount of totty free for the asking?'

'You are a disgusting man.' Mirabel went inside and slammed the door in his face.

Edric emerged from the study. 'I heard all that. Say the word and I'll sort him out, Mirabel. Nothing would give me greater pleasure.'

She shook her head. 'Thank you, but I'll do this my way. I've been concentrating too much on the business, and to be honest I thought Wiley had moved on, but now I know to the contrary. To-morrow morning, first thing, I'll go and see my solicitor. I'll put a stop to Wiley's bullying once and for all.'

Mr Yardley was in the process of hanging his over-coat on a stand in the corner of his office when Mirabel burst into the room. His startled expression brought her to a sudden halt. 'I'm sorry to arrive so early and without an appointment,' she said breathlessly. 'But I'm desperate to know the contents of my late father's will. Have you man-aged to get a copy?'

'This is rather irregular, Mrs Kettle.' Taking off his scarf, Yardley draped it carefully over the arm of the coat stand before taking his place behind his desk. 'May I ask why the sudden urgency?'

'Septimus Wiley destroyed Hubert's orchid col-lection and now he's doing his best to make my life as difficult as he can. He won't be happy until he's ruined me.'

'Can you prove that he was the perpetrator of the criminal act?'

'No. That's just the trouble. He wheedled his way into the house in my absence by paying court to our housekeeper, a middle-aged widow who believed that he intended marriage.'

'I see.' Mr Yardley opened a drawer in his desk and took out a bundle of documents bound with red tape. 'These came yesterday and I haven't had time to sort through them.' After a brief scrutiny he selected one, and handed it to Mirabel. 'This is the last will and testament of Jacob Cutler.'

Mirabel's hands shook as she opened the document. The copperplate handwriting danced before her eyes but the intent was clear. 'Pa left everything to me.' Her voice broke on a sob of relief. 'There's no mention of Ernestine, Wiley or anyone else.'

'So this man Wiley has taken your inheritance under false pretences. That's a serious offence. Do you wish to pursue this matter through the courts?'

'Most definitely. Do what you must, Mr Yardley.'

Having left matters in the hands of her lawyer, and secure in the knowledge that Cutler's Castle belonged to her and might be used as collateral, Mirabel decided to risk investing in another, larger vessel. Alf was learning fast and Edric reckoned that he would soon be able to handle the *Beatrice* and take the anglers to fish for perch, which was in season from May until March, and much prized as a breakfast fish by those in the know. Mirabelle herself preferred a boiled egg or toast and marmalade, but there was no accounting for taste. Danny and Pip, Alf's two eldest sons, were keen to work the river and Mirabel had given them every encouragement. It would be good to keep it within the family, for that was exactly what they were now. The children, from little Kitty upwards, accepted her as a much-loved aunt, and she returned their affection unreservedly. Gertie had taken on the role of elder sister as well as a friend to Tilda and the younger children. Between them, the two girls ran the household leaving Mirabel free to concentrate on the business. She devoted all her time and effort into creating something that was both lucrative and lasting.

Christmas was a rowdy, joyful affair in a house filled with young people, and Mirabel invited Edric and Beatrice together with their brood of children to join them on Christmas Day. There were presents under the tree for everyone and Beatrice went downstairs to help Mirabel and Gertie in the final stage of preparing the turkey with all the trimmings. A near fiasco had been averted when, several weeks before Christmas Gertie had attempted to make the puddings. Everyone had had a stir of the mixture and a wish, and all had been going well until the cloth binding the mixture had split in the copper resulting in a sloppy mess of ruined ingredients. Gertie had broken down in tears, refusing to be comforted until Mirabel promised to take a cab to Piccadilly and purchase a fresh supply from Fortnum's.

The meal itself was a triumph, everyone said so, and Edric proposed a toast to the cooks. The older children raised their glasses of watered-down wine and the younger ones were treated to lime cordial sweetened with sugar. Looking round at their flushed, happy faces, Mirabel felt a glow of pride but also a degree of sadness. This was her family and she loved them all but there was a void in her heart and an ache that would never go away. She finished her wine and stood up. 'I think it's time we opened the presents.'

On the coldest day of January, Alf and Edric came across a vessel high and dry in a boatyard at Limehouse Hole. It had been abandoned by the owner, who had gone bankrupt, and no one had come forward with the money to purchase what appeared to be little more than a wreck. Edric took Mirabel to see the boat, promising her that with a bit of hard work it could be made seaworthy within weeks. The asking price was much less than she had expected, and after some shrewd bargaining she became the proud owner of a sea-going barge, capable of shipping cargo to the continent if required. Even with the cost of the refurbishment, which she decided to have done by the professionals at the boatyard, it was still a good buy, and Edric was delighted.

'It will be like the old days,' he said, looking up from the shipbuilder's plans. 'It's not exactly like the brig Jack and I used to own, but it's a start, and we can ship anything from hay to coal.'

Mirabel eyed him thoughtfully. 'We need an office close to the docks, Edric. Working from home was all very well at the beginning, but now we're expanding we should have premises of our own, and once the new boat is up and running I think we could afford to employ a clerk, so that I can spend more time visiting prospective clients.'

'You're right of course, Mirabel. You're the one with the business head. Do what you think best.' He straightened up, running his hand through his hair, which he always did when he was not sure of himself. 'What's happening about Wiley? If he's bothering you just tell me.'

'I saw him in court, but we didn't speak. He wasn't too pleased when the judge ordered him to leave Cutler's Castle. If looks could kill I'd have been dead on the spot.'

'Will he go of his own accord?'

'He was given two weeks to pack up and find alternative accommodation and he's supposed to pay back all the money he's taken. He can't draw any more from the bank,' Mirabel hesitated, frowning thoughtfully. 'I suppose some of it should go to Ernestine as Pa's widow.'

'I'd be damned if I'd give that woman a penny. Anyway, I thought Wiley had her locked away in a lunatic asylum.'

Mirabel had almost forgotten about Ernestine until Wiley mentioned her in such a vindictive manner. She had suffered at her stepmother's hands, but Ernestine had paid a high price for her cruelty. 'I think I should go and see her, or at least speak to the doctors to find out if she really is insane. Wiley had her committed but I wouldn't wish that fate on anyone, even Ernestine.'

Edric reached for his cap and jammed it on his head. 'From what you've told me about her I think she deserved all she got.' He opened the study door. 'Leave her to rot, that's what I say. She turned you out on the street without a thought.'

'But if Jack hadn't taken me to Zilla's none of this would have happened. I'd never have met Hubert or travelled to America. I wouldn't have met you and Beatrice, and we wouldn't be having this conversation now.' She smiled. 'All this happened because Ernestine hated me, and without her I might still be sitting in the attic at St

375

Catherine Court, dreaming my life away.'

'Well, I wouldn't be as forgiving. I'm going to the boat builders to see how they're getting on with the *Mudlark*.'

'The *Mudlark*?'

'It's Alf's boys' choice of name for the boat. What do you think?'

'I like it. The *Mudlark* it shall be.'

Mirabel knew that she would not rest until she had seen for herself how Ernestine was progressing. For all her faults Ernestine had been her step-mother and Pa had been fond of her at the outset. Without telling anyone where she was going, she set off one morning for Colney Hatch.

From the approach along a wide drive lined with trees, the lunatic asylum with its Moorish arches and tall cupola looked like a palace from the Arabian Nights, but inside the atmosphere was one of distress and despair. Mirabel was conducted along a corridor where the strong odour of disinfectant barely masked the stench of urine and the sound of wailing and high-pitched screams filled her ears. She was left to wait in an anteroom outside the superintendent's office, where she sat wishing that she had not come, but her conscience had been plaguing her ever since the judge ruled against Wiley. It was Wiley who had either sent Ernestine mad, or had made everyone believe that she was deranged, and he now sat in Cutler's Castle, refusing to leave. Yardley had applied to the court for an eviction notice but this, like every due process of the law, would take time.

Mirabel jumped to her feet as the door to the

office opened. 'I believe you wish to see me, Mrs Kettle.' The superintendent ushered her into the inner sanctum. 'Please take a seat.'

'I've come about my stepmother, Mrs Ernestine Cutler.' Mirabel perched on the edge of the chair. 'Can you tell me anything about her condition?'

'You obviously don't know.' The superintendent sat down at his desk, adjusting his silver-rimmed spectacles. 'I'm sorry to have to tell you that Mrs Cutler passed away two weeks ago.'

Mirabel stared at him in disbelief. 'She's dead? But she was a relatively young woman. How did she die?'

'Mrs Cutler had contracted a disease, quite probably in her youth, which sadly ends in general debilitation and insanity.' He cleared his throat, avoiding meeting her curious gaze. 'Do you understand what I'm saying, ma'am? Bad blood is a term often used.'

'I see.' Mirabel was familiar with the expression, having heard it bandied about by the girls at Zilla's. 'Have her daughters been informed?'

'They attended her funeral with their grandmother, who I believe has been looking after them since their mother was admitted here. Is there any other information I can give you, Mrs Kettle?'

'No. Thank you, sir. I'm glad the girls are being cared for, and I'm truly sorry to hear of Ernestine's sad end.'

'I'll ring for someone to take you to the gate. For their own protection we don't allow visitors to wander in the grounds unaccompanied.'

All the way back to London seated in the swaying omnibus, which jolted its passengers around mercilessly each time the wheels hit a rut or a bump in the road, Mirabel was haunted by visions of the lunatic asylum. Ernestine was dead. She tried to feel sorry, but instead she felt numb. The last link with her old life had been severed.

Throwing herself into the business with even more enthusiasm, Mirabelle secured a lease on a small office in the wharfinger's house at the bottom of Darkhouse Lane. Situated next to Billingsgate market the smell of fish permeated the whole building and boats lined up at the wharves waiting to unload their slippery silver cargo. Day and night the clatter of the boxes being hauled up onto the quay wall and the shouts of the men at work competed with the general noise of the river traffic, and the slapping of the water on the wooden stanchions at high tide.

The wainscoted room was small and draughty, and even when a fire was lit in the grate the chill from the river seemed to rise from the floorboards. Mirabel put on extra clothing and sat with a hot brick at her feet when she was working at her desk. She had to keep stopping to warm her mittened hands around the glass bowl of the paraffin lamp, and by the time she finished in the evening her toes were numbed with cold. Business was brisk but hard won. Her days were occupied with visits to prospective clients, which often made it necessary for her to do her bookkeeping in the evenings. She could not justify paying a clerk, but that would come. In the meantime it was easier to occupy her thoughts with work than to dwell on personal matters. At home Gertie made a habit of keeping

Mirabel's supper warm on the range, and she enjoyed a peaceful meal in the cosy heat of the kitchen instead of sitting in lonely state in the dining room. The younger children were always tucked up in bed by the time Mirabelle finished her long day at work, and the older boys were usually occupied with their books, studying the strict rules that bound both apprentices and barge owners as set out by the Watermen's Company. Although she suspected that Ned was reading the book by Captain Marryat that she had given him for Christmas. *Masterman Ready, or the Wreck of the Pacific* had been one of her favourites as a child, second only to *The Children of the New Forest*. Alf would not approve of such an indulgence: he was a practical man who saw little use in filling children's heads with book-reading. He spent all his spare moments doing maintenance on the *Beatrice* or working on the *Mudlark,* although sometimes he joined Edric in the pub for a pint or two of ale.

Edric had promised Beatrice that he would never set foot in Zilla's establishment again, but Mirabel made a point of calling in when she was in that area. It was a relief to share her problems over a glass of Madeira or a cup of coffee, and she valued Zilla's advice on business matters. Zilla had given her help when she most needed it, and, in their different ways, they had both loved Jack Starke. That alone gave them something in common, although his name never came up in conversation. Mirabel was resigned to a life as a single woman and the part of her life that had involved Jack was locked away in a secret compartment in her heart.

The ever-present threat of Wiley still lingered. He had so far managed to evade the bailiffs who had been sent to evict him from Cutler's Castle and had barricaded himself into the house. Mirabel could have done without the extra expense entailed in yet another visit to her lawyer, but she had just returned home from the solicitor's office secure in the knowledge that a warrant had been issued for Wiley's arrest, when to her dismay she found him waiting for her on the pavement outside her home.

'You think you're very clever, don't you,' he said through gritted teeth. 'Well, you haven't won yet, lady. I'll make sure you never live in Cutler's Castle. You'll see.' He strutted off without giving her a chance to respond and she stood very still, watching his lanky figure, all arms and legs like a poisonous spider, as he disappeared into the fog. She shivered. Although it was mid-afternoon the light was fading fast with the smell of soot and sulphur in the air, which felt so thick it might easily be sliced with a knife. She hurried indoors. The police would deal with Septimus Wiley; he was no longer her concern.

She did not mention her encounter with Wiley next day when she stood with Alf on the slipway watching the launch of the recently refurbished barge. The *Mudlark* slid into the treacly waters of Limehouse Hole with Edric at the helm and Danny working on deck, ably assisted by Pip. Ned had begged to be allowed to work with them but Edric had told him he must wait his turn. Alf had taken pity on his son and promised to take him as an apprentice on the *Beatrice,* which seemed to satisfy Ned who wiped his eyes on his sleeve, ignoring the taunts of nine-year old Jim, who told him he was a baby for crying. Mirabel had grown used to their squabbles, and she put her hand in her pocket and took out a poke filled with humbugs. She gave one each to the boys, which stopped the argument before it escalated any further.

'I've got a party of anglers wanting to go to Putney, but it looks like the fog might come down again later,' Alf said, looking up at the sky and frowning. 'We might get two or three hours in, if we're lucky.'

'If they're willing to pay then it's their problem not ours,' Mirabel said, smiling.

'They're city swells with more money than sense.' Alf patted his son on the head. 'C'mon, Ned. We'll pick our fares up and go on from there, but I'm not risking the boat or lives if the weather don't hold.'

Mirabel held her hand out to Jim. 'I'll take you home. I asked the cabby to wait for us so we'd better hurry up.'

He slipped his small sticky hand into hers. 'I don't want to work the river, Mabel. I want to write stories, like Captain Marryat. Ned reads them to me when he's in a good mood.'

She smiled down at him, giving his fingers a gentle squeeze. 'I think that's a very good idea. Have another humbug.'

Mirabel worked late at the office that evening, despite the fog which descended in a sulphurous

381

cloud as the light faded. Thin shreds of it forced their way under the door and through the keyhole. She should have packed up much earlier but she felt compelled to balance the books and leave everything ready to commence business next day. She was still buoyed-up with the excitement of launching another vessel and she gave little thought to the walk home.

When she finally decided to leave she went through her normal routine of checking the windows, and after making certain that the fire would not spit sparks and burn the place down she doused the lamp. As she opened the door she was enveloped in a suffocating blanket of evil-smelling fog and smoke, and she covered her nose and mouth with a scarf that Gertie had knitted for her.

Although she knew the way blindfold, the unusual silence was disorientating and she could barely see the ground beneath her feet. She had not gone more than a few stumbling paces when she was aware that she was not alone. Her stomach clenched with fear as she sensed Wiley's malignant presence, but before she could break into a run she was seized from behind. 'Nice night for a swim, Miss Cutler.' He held her in a surprisingly strong grip. His arms were like iron bands around her chest and her screams were muffled by the cloying thickness of the fog.

'Let me go.'

'What's the matter? Can't swim? Neither can I, for that matter, but it ain't me who's going for a dip. The tide is on the turn, so you'll be swept away by the current. It will drag you under, filling your lungs and choking you slowly. Goodbye and good riddance, I say.'

She could sense the void where the quay ended even though she could not see it, and in desperation she kicked out with her feet, catching Wiley on his shin. With a yelp of pain he lifted her off her feet and they stood poised like acrobats in the circus, but she knew if he threw her there was no chance of being caught. Then suddenly she was on the ground, gasping for breath and winded by the fall. A sharp cry was followed by a muffled splash.

Chapter Twenty-four

'Are you all right, Mabel?' Tilda's anxious voice pierced the veil of terror that had momentarily dulled Mirabel's senses. She struggled to catch her breath and allowed Tilda to help her to her feet.

'What happened?'

Alf loomed over them, his face pale and anxious in the fractured light of a gas lamp. 'Are you hurt, missis?'

'I'm all right.' Mirabel peered at him dazedly. 'What about Wiley?'

'He was going to throw you into the river,' Tilda said angrily. 'Pa chucked him in instead. Let's see if he can swim.'

'Even if he can he'll be no match for the current.' Alf tucked Mirabel's hand in the crook of his arm. 'Come along, missis. Let's get you home. You've had a nasty shock.'

'But we can't just walk away and leave him to

drown.' Mirabel looked from one to the other, noting for the first time a strong likeness between father and daughter. Alf's set jaw and implacable expression were replicated in Tilda's young face.

'He was going to murder you, Mabel,' Tilda said angrily.

'He was swallowed up by the river and weighted down by his sins.' Alf patted Mirabel's hand. 'Don't waste your pity on him, missis. He was going to kill you the same as he finished off the boss at the warehouse where he and your pa worked. Come along. Let's get you home.'

With Tilda holding one arm and Alf clutching the other, Mirabel had little option but to walk between them, but her head was still reeling. 'You're saying that Wiley killed Cyrus Pendleton?'

'That's what I heard. I've been asking around the men who worked alongside Jacob in Shad Thames. They wasn't particularly keen to talk about it, but to a man they thought that Wiley had done the boss in.'

'But why didn't anyone come forward?'

'There was no case to answer. Wiley was clever enough to cover up what he'd done and your pa never suspected anything was wrong.'

'But Wiley was blackmailing him. I'm sure of it.'

'I think that came later. Wiley was no fool even if he was a villain. Anyway, he's gone now. You might say his sins have been washed away. Justice has been done.'

The police arrived at Cutler's Castle ready to arrest Wiley, and finding him gone they seemed to assume that he had decided to give in peacefully. As far as the law was concerned the case was closed and Wiley was forgotten.

Mirabel stood on the threshold, hardly able to believe that her old home was hers to do with as she pleased. She glanced over her shoulder at the sound of Harriet Humble's shrill voice. 'Good morning, Mrs Kettle. Welcome back to the Court.'

Mirabel turned to give the gun maker's wife a weary smile. 'Good morning, Mrs Humble.'

'The tone of the neighbourhood suffered considerably while that man was in residence.' Harriet scuttled across the road to join her. 'That woman your father took up with was a vulgar harridan. I don't blame you for running away from home.' She puffed out her chest, putting Mirabel in mind of a pouter pigeon. 'You've done well for yourself by all accounts. Not that I pay any attention to gossip, you understand.'

'Of course not.' Mirabel stifled a sudden urge to giggle. She managed a smile instead. 'It's nice to be home, but if you'll excuse me I need to inspect the interior.'

'There'll be some damage, no doubt.' Harriet peered over Mirabel's shoulder as she unlocked the door and thrust it open. 'The goings-on here continued until the early hours of the morning, after your pa was taken so suddenly, God rest his soul. That dreadful person he married was no better than she should be.' She edged forward. 'I could send my daily woman over to help clean up the mess, if needs be.'

Mirabel stepped inside. 'Thank you, Mrs Humble. I'll bear that in mind. Now if you'll excuse me...' She closed the door before Harriet had a chance to follow her inside, and stood for a few moments listening to the silence echoing from room to room and spiralling up the staircase. The musty smell of stale tobacco smoke and alcohol mingled with even more unpleasant odours of blocked drains and rancid cooking fat. Dust motes danced in the pale shards of sunlight that prised their way through grimy windowpanes, and she sensed a feeling of sadness within its walls, as if the house itself had suffered during Wiley's occupation.

A rat stuck its head out of a hole in the skirting board, stared at Mirabel and emerged to saunter across the floor, heading towards the back stairs. The sight of it galvanised her into action and in a frenzy of activity she raced through the house, throwing the windows open to let in air and sunlight. Empty wine bottles littered the floor and the grates in the reception rooms spilled over with cinders and ash. Dust coated every surface, but worst of all there was hardly a stick of furniture left. Wiley must have sold everything from the china and silver to the chairs and tables. The bedrooms had fared little better, although the large four-poster in her father's old room was still there. Mirabel did not inspect it too closely, but she could see that the bedding was soiled and the sight of an overflowing chamber pot made her retch. She turned and fled, unable to stand the desecration of her childhood home. She closed the windows on the ground floor, deciding that she had had enough for now. Tomorrow she would come with Gertie, Tilda and Mrs Tweddle, the daily woman who came in to clean the house in Savage Gardens.

Next day they arrived early to make a start on erasing every trace of Wiley and Ernestine's occupation of Cutler's Castle. Mirabel had deliberately left the top floor to the last for fear of what she might find, and she went upstairs alone. Rain was beating down on the slate roof and the chill seemed to permeate her bones as she stood outside the door of her dreaming place with her fingers curled around the key. She turned it slowly and entered, half expecting to find the room in a similar state of chaos and disarray as those on the lower floors, but to her surprise it was exactly as she had left it that terrible night when her father had died. The box that had contained her small treasures lay open; the pretty gowns her father had bought her were silvered with dust but were untouched, as were the dancing slippers and her precious books. The cushions on the window seat were tumbled as if she had just risen to her feet to go downstairs, and if it were not for the festoons of cobwebs hanging like lace curtains from the rafters she might suppose that time had stood still.

A surge of relief was quickly followed by an overwhelming feeling of grief that brought tears to her eyes. She went to sit on the window seat, looking out over the wet rooftops to the spire of the church where she had been married. A sob escaped her lips as she recalled the romantic dreams that had carried her younger self to far-away lands, and the fleeting images of handsome suitors who treated her like a princess. It was all a far cry from the reality, and her dream prince had turned out to be a louche sea captain with a lazy smile, a dry sense of humour and an uncomfortable way of reading her thoughts. She leaned her forehead against the cold glass and closed her eyes. If only she could escape from the love that bound her as soundly as if she were in chains.

She turned with a start at the sound of footsteps on the stairs and Gertie burst into the room, her face aglow with excitement. 'Mabel, you must come quick. You'll never guess what's happened.' She darted out of the room without giving Mirabel a chance to question her.

Downstairs in the entrance hall Ned was hopping from one foot to the other. His wet hair was plastered down on his head and his clothes were sodden and clinging to his thin body. 'You got visitors, Mabel. They're at the house waiting.'

Gertie flung Mirabel's cape and bonnet at her. 'Open the door, Ned. Run on ahead and tell them we're coming.'

'Tell who? Why all the excitement?' Mirabel's hand shook as she struggled to tie the strings of her bonnet.

'Just you wait and see. Hurry up, Mabel.' Gertie wrapped her shawl around her head and shoulders and followed Ned out of the house. Mystified and yet apprehensive, Mirabel hurried after her.

Ned had streaked ahead and was waiting for them in the entrance hall. He thrust the door of the morning parlour open. 'She's here,' he said triumphantly. 'I fetched her like you said.'

A vision in brown velvet trimmed with sable, Jerusha emerged from the room, holding out her arms. 'Mirabel, honey.'

Mirabel walked slowly towards her, dazed and disbelieving. 'It really is you?'

'It surely is, and Ethan too.' Jerusha turned, holding her hand out to Ethan who had come to stand behind her. 'We're on our honeymoon and we just had to come to England to see you.'

Greeting her with a warm smile Ethan kissed Mirabel on the cheek. 'I feel as if you're my sister, Belle. It's so good to see you again. You too, missy.'

Gertie bobbed a curtsey. 'Ta ever so, sir. If I may say so, it's ever so nice to see you and the missis too.'

Mirabel cast off her wet cape and bonnet, thrusting them into Gertie's hands. 'I'm so shocked I've forgotten my manners. Won't you come upstairs to the drawing room?' She stopped, frowning. 'No, there won't be a fire in there. We'll take tea in the parlour, Gertie.'

'Yes'm.' Gertie scurried off in the direction of the back stairs.

Mirabel hugged Jerusha, laughing and crying at the same time. 'This is such a wonderful surprise. I can't believe that you came all this way to see me.'

Taking her by the hand, Jerusha led her into the morning parlour. 'Sit down and catch your breath, honey.'

'Of course we wanted to see you, Belle, but I also had business to transact in London,' Ethan said, moving to stand with his back to the fire. 'I've gone into the shipping business in a small way.'

Jerusha seated herself in a chair at his side,

smiling up at him. 'And I married the cleverest man in Virginia.'

'I can't dispute that.' Mirabel sank down on the nearest chair, her legs suddenly giving way beneath her. The shock of seeing them again and the memories it brought to the fore had made her feel weak at the knees. 'Bodger told me that you're a ship owner as well as a tobacco grower.'

Ethan nodded, smiling proudly. 'I sure am, and one day I'll have a fleet of steamships.'

'We're not here to discuss business, darling.' Jerusha curled her fingers around his hand. 'We're here to enjoy ourselves and spend time with our dear friend Belle.'

'It's wonderful to see you both,' Mirabel said earnestly. 'It's such a surprise.'

'And we've an even bigger surprise for you,' Ethan began, stopping suddenly. 'What is it, honey?'

Jerusha released his hand. 'Not now, darling,' she said sternly. 'We'll save it for later, because I want to hear all about you, Belle. How have you been managing? I don't know what I'd do if I were in your position.' Her expression softened as she looked up at her husband. 'I truly don't.'

Gertie chose that moment to reappear with a tray of tea and a soggy-looking cake that had sunk in the middle. 'It's not one of my best attempts,' she said apologetically.

'I'm sure it will be delicious.' Jerusha leaned closer to inspect Gertie's efforts. 'I do so love cake.'

'Thank you, ma'am.' Gertie hesitated in the doorway. 'May I ask you a question, Mr Munroe?'

'Fire away, Gertie,' Ethan said with a good-natured grin. 'What can I do for you?'

'It's Bodger, sir. I haven't heard from him since we come home. I believe he was going to work for you?'

Mirabel had been about to cut the cake but she paused. 'Don't pester Mr Munroe, Gertie.'

'It's not a problem,' Ethan said easily. 'I did find a master who was more than willing to take him on, and—'

'Not now Ethan.' Jerusha picked up a plate. 'We're going to enjoy our English tea and Gertie's delicious cake, and save our surprise for later.'

'A surprise?' Mirabel looked to Ethan for an answer but he merely shrugged and shook his head.

'I'm sorry, honey. If I told you it wouldn't be a surprise, now would it?'

'If you're not otherwise engaged we'd like to take you for a carriage ride tomorrow morning,' Jerusha said, swallowing a mouthful of cake. 'My, this is just delicious, Gertie. I doubt if our cook at home could do better.'

Despite repeated attempts by Mirabel to obtain more information Jerusha refused to give even the smallest clue. She was happy to talk about her fairytale wedding in the garden at the plantation house, but then she managed to turn the conversation around so that Mirabel found herself giving a detailed account of everything that had happened since she left Richmond. That evening she dined with them at Claridge's but Jerusha hugged her secret to herself, and Ethan was not about to give anything away. Mirabel was agog with curiosity and could hardly contain herself, but it was even worse when she arrived home and found Gertie waiting up for her, demanding to know if anything had been said about Bodger. Mirabel had to admit that she had not thought to ask, but she was too tired to go into much detail, and it was past midnight when she went to her room. At least she would not have long to wait until the secret was revealed.

She slept surprisingly well but awakened early next morning and was up and about before Tilda had risen. Breakfast was always a chaotic affair with the children clamouring for food and Gertie serving porridge as fast as she could ladle it into their bowls. Alf satisfied himself with bread and jam and a cup of strong tea. He urged Danny and Pip to make haste as they had a party of anglers booked for an early start, and he warned the rest of his brood to be on their best behaviour while he was away at work, but it was said with a smile. He ruffled Ned's hair. 'Look after Jim when you're digging in the mud, and keep an eye out for the turn of the tide.' He turned to Mirabel, who was nibbling a slice of toast. 'Will you be at the castle today?'

She shook her head, laughing. 'We must stop calling it Cutler's Castle. It wasn't meant to be a compliment, but somehow the dreadful name stuck.'

'Mabel's going out with her friends from Virginia,' Gertie said, pursing her lips. 'They won't tell her where they're taking her, but I'm sure I don't know why they have to be so mysterious.'

Mirabel said nothing, but in her heart she could

not help agreeing with Gertie. A surprise was all right in its way, but she was at a loss to know what it could be. She waited impatiently, wishing that she had something more fashionable to wear. Compared to Jerusha she felt drab and dowdy. There had been no money to spare for a new wardrobe and she had been making do with a serviceable gown made from navy-blue worsted. Until now she had not paid much attention to her appearance, but next to Jerusha, who was as colourful as an exotic humming bird, she felt like a common sparrow. Dressed for the cold weather in her mantle and bonnet, she pulled on her gloves and waited for the Munroes to arrive, which they did promptly at ten o'clock, as arranged.

Ethan handed Mirabel into the hackney carriage and she sat down next to Jerusha. 'Well, are you going to tell me what this is all about?'

Jerusha dimpled mischievously. 'We're visiting the London docks, honey. We thought you might find it interesting.'

'The docks?' Mirabel looked from one to the other. 'Oh, I see. You want me to see your boat.' A feeling of disappointment washed over her in a tidal wave. Surely they must realise that she had spent most of her life in the dock area, and now she was heavily involved in the river trade. It was hardly a thrilling prospect, but she could see from Jerusha's excited expression and Ethan's satisfied grin that the outing was of the greatest importance to the young newly-weds. She sank back against the worn leather squabs, making an effort to appear interested.

Outside the rain had turned to sleet and dark

clouds seemed to be resting on the rooftops of the warehouses and manufactories. It was a dismal day for sight-seeing but Jerusha's enthusiasm was infectious, and as they approached the docks she grew even more excited. She sat on the edge of her seat. 'We're almost there. I remember this from when we arrived.' She reached out to clutch her husband's hands. 'I can hardly wait.'

Mirabel smiled indulgently, but she remained unimpressed. As far as she was concerned one sea-going vessel was much like another. The cab came to a halt and they stepped down onto the wet cobblestones. Ethan unfurled a large black umbrella and escorted them onto the dock. 'There it is,' he said proudly. 'The *Munroe Star*. The first of many, I hope.'

To Mirabel the twin-funnelled steamship looked identical to the one tied up on the far side of the dock, but she was too polite to say so. 'It's very impressive,' she murmured, squinting through the ice-laden rain.

'It's even better on board. Just you wait and see, honey.' Jerusha seized her hand as she quickened her pace. 'Ethan, darling, run on ahead and tell the captain that we're coming.'

Ethan obeyed instantly, taking off in long strides with Jerusha and Mirabel following at a more sedate pace. As they boarded the vessel Mirabel could not help feeling let down. So this was the wonderful surprise and the closely-guarded secret. She turned her head at the sound of approaching footsteps, parting her lips in a semblance of a polite smile, which froze. Her limbs seemed to be paralysed and she could not move a muscle. She blinked, thinking that it must be a trick of the light or her imagination getting the better of her, but he was still there, standing next to Ethan. 'Jack?' Her voice seemed to float away on a gust of wind and rain, and for a moment neither of them moved.

Jerusha squeezed Mirabel's hand and released it, giving her a gentle shove. 'I told you it would be a wonderful surprise, honey.'

Ethan stepped forward. 'I guess you're acquainted with Captain Starke.'

Mirabel nodded, her gaze fixed on Jack's face as she tried to read his expression. He was smiling, but there was a wary look in his eyes. He inclined his head. 'It's a pleasure to meet you again, Mrs Kettle.'

Chilled by his formal greeting, Mirabel wished she was anywhere but here on the open deck with sleet rapidly turning into hailstones. 'I thought you had decided to stay in Florida, Captain Starke.'

Jerusha exchanged worried glances with her husband. 'We should seek shelter, honey.'

'Of course,' Ethan said hastily. 'Lead on, Captain. We'll go to the saloon first, and then perhaps you'd be kind enough to show Mrs Kettle around.'

'Certainly, sir.' Jack strode towards the companionway without giving Mirabel a second glance.

'Are you all right, honey? I hope I haven't made a terrible mistake,' Jerusha said anxiously as they hurried along the deck.

'You meant well,' Mirabel said dazedly. 'I'm not sure it was such a good idea. It's been months since I last saw him and we didn't part on the best of terms.'

They reached the saloon, which was warm and cosy. The oak panelling and leather upholstery reminded Mirabel of her father's study in Cutler's Castle. It was a male domain, uncluttered by any feminine influence. 'We intend to take a small number of passengers on each trip,' Ethan said, breaking the ensuing silence. 'It's not a large vessel but we're just finding our feet, aren't we, Captain Starke?'

'Yes, indeed, Mr Munroe.' Jack's expression was neutral.

'We have our own cabin, of course.' Jerusha looked from one to the other, biting her lip. 'And if you'll excuse me I need to find something I left behind.' She gave her husband a meaningful look. 'And you said you'd lost a collar stud, honey.'

Ethan stared at her for a moment and then he nodded emphatically. 'Yes, of course. You'll excuse us for a few minutes, I'm sure.' He hurried after Jerusha, closing the door behind him.

The air crackled with tension, as if a silken chain that bound them together had been stretched to the limit and was about to snap. 'I don't understand,' Mirabel said in a whisper. 'What are you doing here, Jack?'

He looked her in the eyes for the first time. 'Bodger returned to Coconut Grove. I think he had some crazy idea of saving me from myself. Anyway, he told me that your husband had died.'

'Hubert was taken ill when we reached Newport News. Luckily for me Ethan was staying in the same hotel and he took us back to the D'Angelos' plantation. Hubert is buried there with his ghost orchids.'

'Should I offer my condolences or felicitations?'

'That's a cruel thing to say.'

'Perhaps, but you aren't wearing the customary widow's weeds.'

The inference was plain and the insult calculated. She drew herself up to her full height. 'Hubert was a good man and I mourned his passing.'

'So now you're a wealthy widow?' The underlying sarcasm in his voice and the insolent look in his eyes hurt more than she would have thought possible.

'Don't you dare judge me, Jack Starke. I've had to earn my own living since Hubert died. You've no idea what I've been through since we last met.'

His expression softened. 'You could have sent word to me with Bodger. I would have come straight away if you had.'

'Has he come with you?'

'Yes, of course. It was Bodger who persuaded me to accompany him to Newport News where he introduced me to Munroe, who offered me a job. It was as simple as that.'

His cold tone turned her blood to ice in her veins. 'I thought you wanted to remain in Florida.'

'You didn't ask what I wanted. You were only interested in what you wanted. You chose him over me, because you wanted to return to the life you'd made for yourself here in London.'

'That's so unfair. Hubert was a sick man. I couldn't leave him then.'

His cold gaze rested on her for a moment and then he looked away. 'Now you're a businesswoman in your own right. You must be very pleased with yourself.'

'How can you possibly know what I've been doing? You arrived barely two days ago.'

'Zilla told me about your venture into trade, and your relationship with Edric.'

'So you visited Zilla first. You didn't think to come and see me.'

'I can always be assured of a warm welcome from Zilla.'

'You always go back to her in the end, and I think you always will. I don't know what I ever saw in you, Captain Starke.'

Anger flashed in his eyes and his lips hardened into a thin line. 'Zilla is an old friend, and a woman I respect, but it seems you were eager enough to go into business with Edric Hamilton. I should warn you that he already has a wife and children.'

'I know that, and I made sure that Beatrice was happy with the arrangement. Edric and I are partners. It was your precious Zilla who introduced us.' She angled her head. 'What did she tell you?'

Jack looked away, shrugging his shoulders. 'She said that he'd squandered the money I used to buy him out on women and drink.'

'That's all in the past. I truly believe he's doing his best for his family now.'

'You seem to have a high regard for him.'

Indignation replaced the emotions that raged within her breast. She faced him, glaring. 'You have a nasty suspicious mind, but you ought to know me better than that.'

'I know men, and in particular I know Edric. We parted amicably enough, but I could see that he was going nowhere. He's a weak man and you'd be better off without him.'

'You don't know what you're talking about,' Mirabel cried angrily. 'I don't need you or Zilla or anyone outside my family.' She could see that her last words had struck home and she pursued her advantage ruthlessly. 'Yes, I have a family. They're not my blood but they love me and I love them. You walked away from me in Florida. You could have tried to stop me leaving but you did nothing.' She flung out of the cabin, gulping back tears of frustration and anger as she headed for the companionway.

Jack caught up with her as she raced along the deck, slipping and sliding on the icy surface. He grabbed her by the arm. 'You can't leave like this. The Munroes have planned a special dinner for all of us.'

She wrenched free from his grasp. 'Are you afraid of insulting your employer, Jack? Dear me, I thought you were your own man, or has all the rum you drank in Florida softened your brain? It's certainly hardened your heart.' She faced him furiously, experiencing a feeling of triumph when his face paled beneath his tan. 'I don't need you or Edric or any man, come to that. I'm a free woman now and that's the way I intend to stay.' She tossed her head and stalked off down the gangway.

Chapter Twenty-five

Ignoring the hail and sleet Mirabel walked briskly, heading in the direction of home. Tears ran unchecked down her cheeks, but she was in a mood to fight the elements or anyone who got in her way. She pushed past the groups of men idling round as they waited in the hope of being hired for a few hours' work, ignoring their suggestive comments, and headed for Great Tower Hill. Her instinct was to go home, but she needed time to herself and she went straight to the office. At least here she was safe from Gertie's probing questions. She set to work balancing the accounts for the last month's trading, but the figures seemed to dance about before her eyes and she found herself staring out of the window into the uniform greyness of the sky and the water.

After a while, when she could hardly feel her fingers and toes, she decided that she ought to light a fire in the grate, but the coal scuttle was empty and when she went outside into the yard she discovered that someone had used up what was left in the sack she had bought and paid for. She returned to the office and was startled to find Ethan standing by the door. 'I'm so sorry, Belle,' he said quickly. 'We meant well, honey, but I guess we misjudged the situation.'

'I'm sorry too. I shouldn't have run off like that, but it was impossible for me to stay.'

'Jerusha is mighty upset.'

'I know you both meant it kindly, but Jack and I have nothing more to say to each other, and no doubt your ship will return to America very soon and I shan't see him again.'

'That's a matter between the two of you, Belle. As for me, I'm on my way to see a shipping agent who'll handle my affairs this side of the Atlantic, but Jerusha asked if you'd take tea with her this afternoon. She feels bad about the way things turned out, and you'd be doing her a kindness if you'd set her mind at rest.'

'Of course,' Mirabel said earnestly. 'Tell me where to meet her and I'll be there.'

'She remembers a place called Gunter's from when she was last in London. She said she'll be there at three o'clock and she hopes you'll join her.'

'I'll be there, and please tell her not to worry. It's as well I've seen Jack now and we know where we stand.'

Ethan kissed her on the cheek. 'That's settled then, honey. Goodbye for now, but I hope we'll meet up again before Jerusha and I leave for Paris at the end of the week.'

Mirabel saw him out, closing the door with a thoughtful frown. She would take tea with Jerusha, but first she had something to say to another lady.

Zilla stared at her through a haze of blue smoke as she stubbed out her cigarillo. 'Really, my dear, I don't know what you're talking about.'

'Don't play the innocent with me, Zilla. You

401

told Jack that I was consorting with Edric and he believed you.'

Zilla's eyebrows were raised in twin arcs of surprise. 'Don't be ridiculous. Why would I say something like that?'

'It's what he thought you said. What did you tell him?'

'My dear Mabel, can't you see that the poor man is mad with jealousy? I told him that you had gone into a business partnership with his old friend Edric. Where was the harm in that for a man of commonsense? But we're not talking about a rational human being, are we? No, you silly girl, we're dealing with a man who is desperately in love but won't admit his feelings even to himself. They're simple creatures, the male of the species. I ought to know; I deal with them on a daily basis.'

'You make it all sound so logical.'

Zilla leaned forward, her green eyes dancing with mischief. 'Bed the brute, Mabel.' She threw back her head and laughed. 'I'm sorry, my pet. I forgot that you are the virgin widow, and unversed in the ways of love.'

Mirabel rose to her feet. 'It's not funny, Zilla.'

'No, I suppose not.'

'I think he has real feelings for you.'

'Really?' Zilla reached for her wineglass and took a sip. 'No, my duck, you're mistaken. I doubt if Jack ever loved me, apart from in the carnal way. More importantly we've remained friends, and in my own selfish way I do care for him. I'd like to see him happy, and I think you are the only woman who's ever touched something deep inside his soul.' She held the wineglass up, gazing into its rich ruby depths. 'This is more to my liking than any man ever could be. Fine wines and good tobacco will comfort me in my old age.'

'I should go now,' Mirabel said, glancing at the clock on the mantelshelf. 'I have to be at Gunter's tea shop at three.'

'Hurry off then, Mabel. But remember what I've just told you. Jack Starke is yours for the taking. You'd be a fool to let him get away a second time.'

'I'm not sure whether you've done me a favour by telling me all this, Zilla. He made it clear that he thought the worst of me.'

'Just send me an invitation to your wedding,' Zilla said, chuckling. 'You're a capable woman now, Mabel. You can handle a wild one like Jack.'

Mirabel left the house in Tenter Street feeling more confused than she had when she'd arrived. She hailed a cab and went straight to Gunter's.

Jerusha leapt up from her seat, scattering cake crumbs on the floor. 'My dear Belle, I am so sorry for what happened this morning. I truly thought I was doing the right thing for both of you.' She beckoned to the waiter. 'A fresh pot of tea, please, and some more of those delicious pastries and two bowls of ice cream.'

Some of the tension leached from Mirabel as she sat down opposite her friend. Jerusha's kind heart was only exceeded by her love of food, especially anything sweet and sugary. 'It wasn't your fault, Jerusha. You couldn't have foreseen the outcome.'

'But he loves you, Belle. We talked about you often during the voyage across the Atlantic, and of course I knew how you felt about Jack. Then, when Ethan introduced him to me I guess I knew why you fell for him in the first place, and you seem so right for each other.'

Mirabel selected a small fancy cake and bit into it. 'People change. The first person he thought of when he arrived home was Zilla. He went to see her, and when she told him that I'd gone into business with his old partner he accused me of having an affair with Edric. I can't forgive that.'

'I guess he was jealous, Belle. Men are like that, even my Ethan.' Jerusha sat back as the waiter picked up the teapot and replaced it with another. The cakes and ice cream followed in quick succession, and Jerusha clapped her hands. 'I love ice cream. I'm going to ask for their recipe so that my cook can make it back home.' She spooned some into her mouth. 'This is so good, honey. You must try some.'

'I can't believe that Ethan was ever anything but the good-natured man he is today.'

Jerusha opened her eyes wide. 'Oh, but he can be a bear when he's angry. I danced with an old beau at the barbecue last summer and Ethan was like a man possessed.' She uttered a sigh of satisfaction. 'So you see, you mustn't allow Jack's quite natural reaction to come between you.'

Mirabel picked up her spoon. 'I'll give it some thought, but I'm not going to apologise. I'm not sure I like being married. Maybe I'll choose to become an old maid and keep my sanity rather than spend my life worrying about what my husband says and does.'

Jerusha licked her spoon. 'You don't know what you're missing, sugar.'

Suddenly the house in Savage Gardens seemed overcrowded and too noisy for comfort. Bodger had been there when Mirabel returned from Berkeley Square and Gertie was fussing around him, demanding to know everything that had happened to him from the time he parted from them in America until the *Munroe Star* docked in London. Mirabel sat and listened, trying hard to look interested although her thoughts kept wandering, and after a while Alf took himself off to the pub. The boys were bombarding Bodger with questions, and the girls were clamouring for his attention. Mirabel made an excuse to go to her room, but finding herself alone for the first time that day she could think of nothing but the fierce altercation between herself and Jack. As she lay down to sleep she could hear Zilla's words repeating over and over again in her head, and the ache in her heart refused to go away.

Breakfast next morning was much quieter than normal. The children had stayed up late and were tired and irritable. Gertie was in a hurry to get them fed and out of the way and Tilda had allowed the porridge to burn, going into a sulk when Gertie reprimanded her in front of her brothers and sisters. The sudden arrival of Edric gave Mirabel an excuse to leave them all to their own devices, and she ushered him into the study. 'You look upset, Edric. Take a seat and tell me what's bothering you.'

He remained standing, twirling his cap between his fingers and shifting from one foot to the other. His bushy eyebrows and beard were pearled with raindrops and water dripped off his jacket onto the Turkey carpet. 'I'll come straight out with it because I don't know how else to say it, but I think we should go our separate ways.'

'Why? I don't understand. What's brought this on?'

'I heard that Jack Starke is back.'

She stared at him, perplexed by his attitude. 'What difference does that make?'

'He'll tell you that I'm a bad lot and turn you against me. I'd rather we finished on a good note than go through all that.'

'Please sit down, Edric. Looking up to you is giving me a crick in the neck.' Mirabel perched on the edge of the desk waiting until he was seated. 'This is all nonsense. I've come to know you and Beatrice, and I think of you as my friends. We work well together, don't we?'

He nodded vigorously. 'We do, but maybe you'll change your mind when you hear about the way I used to behave. I'm not proud of myself.'

'Whatever happened in the past is over and done with. You've proved yourself to me, but if you're not satisfied with the way things are going I wouldn't want to hold you to our agreement. We have no legal contract and you're free to walk away if you so wish.'

'I don't.' Edric's craggy features creased into a grin. 'I'm not going back to my old ways, and I'm grateful to you for helping me out of a tight spot. I'd almost given up trying when you came along and saved me from myself.'

She smiled, breathing a sigh of relief. 'I don't want to break up our partnership.'

'Jack won't approve. He doesn't think much of me and he'll think even less when he learns that I squandered the money he gave me for my share of the ship.'

'Then perhaps you ought to take this opportunity of putting things right between you,' Mirabel said firmly. 'His ship is the *Munroe Star*, unloading in the London dock. Go and see him and set things straight.'

He stood up, ramming his cap on his unruly mop of hair. 'I'll do that. I'll go now, and I'll tell him what a fine woman you are.'

'Better keep my name out of it. Jack and I aren't on the best of terms at the moment, but don't concern yourself with that.'

Edric's brows lowered in a frown. 'I hope it didn't have anything to do with me?'

'Don't waste time worrying on my behalf. I can look after myself.'

She sat for a while after he had gone, but she had work to do and idling around the house would not cure a bruised and sore heart or put money in the bank. The office needed to be open for business and the books had to be balanced. Their reputation was growing and the need to knock on doors was lessening, although it was slow progress, but she was her father's daughter. Despite Wiley's base accusations Jacob Cutler had been a shrewd businessman and had made a great deal of money. Had it not been for his misalliance with Ernestine and the machinations of his grasping manservant, Mirabel knew that she would have inherited a small fortune. She had been robbed of a large part of it, but that made her even more determined to live up to her father's reputation in business. He might have been many things, but she wanted to believe that he had been honest and fair in his dealings. With that in mind she put on her cape and bonnet and set off first for Cutler's Castle.

Mrs Tweddle had already begun her day's work and was busy cleaning the windows in the morning parlour. The smell of vinegar and lye soap wafted in eddies around the entrance hall and Mrs Tweddle sang as she worked. Mirabel congratulated her on her progress.

'Thank you, Mrs Kettle. It's been a bit of a challenge, I have to admit, but another couple of days and you'll be able to think about putting furniture back in the rooms.'

'You've done a splendid job, Mrs Tweddle. I don't know how I would have managed without your help.' Mirabel left the house with the cleaner's words fresh in her mind. She had not come to a decision as to the future of her childhood home. It could be rented out or she could sell it, or she might decide to move in and make it her own. Now that all traces of Wiley had been removed by the application of elbow grease, soap and water, she was beginning to see the possibilities of returning to Catherine Court. Alf and his sons were earning a wage and could afford to pay rent on the house in Savage Gardens, and she had no emotional ties to the property. It had been Hubert's home, not hers. She realised with a pang of regret that she could walk away and not grieve for the life they had shared albeit for such a short time. The future was hers now to do with what she pleased. She was financially independent, and the respectability of widowhood might have been thrust upon her, but Hubert, even in death, had given her a social standing to which a spinster could never aspire. She set off for the office. The house could wait; the trade of the busy River Thames could not.

She arrived to find a small queue of men standing outside the door. Apologising for keeping them waiting she turned the key in the lock and went inside. They filed in after her and she dealt with them in turn, handing out bills of lading, taking payment for small shipments waiting for delivery and offering a quote to the last man, who had come on behalf of a brewer who required a carrier for a significant quantity of barrels of ale. As he left she realised that she had not had time to take off her outdoor garments, but it was almost as cold inside as it was out on the wharf, and she had forgotten to ask Danny to buy a sack of coal. Her fingers were blue, and it was not just the ink that caused them to change colour. She cupped her hands over her face and blew on them. Perhaps Alf and the boys were still tied up alongside and she could send one of them to purchase coal and kindling, or maybe she could attract the attention of Ned and Jim, who were scavenging on the foreshore below the Tower that morning. They often came back with bags of coal that had fallen from barges as they unloaded at coal wharves. She was about to get up when the door opened and a man entered on a gust of cold air. 'Good morning, sir. May I be of assistance?' She broke off, rising swiftly to her feet.

He stood for a moment, casting a critical eye around the sparsely furnished room. 'So this is where you hide out. You're a difficult woman to find, Mrs Kettle.'

'What do you want, Jack?'

'I've come to apologise for my behaviour yesterday.' His tone was neutral and there was a hint of wariness in his eyes.

For some reason Mirabel found his apology more chilling than his unfounded accusations. 'There's no need. I've forgotten it already.' She met his gaze with a steady look, but beneath the desk top her hands were clenched and her fingernails were digging painfully into her palms.

'I've just seen Edric. He explained everything.'

'Maybe that will teach you not to be so quick to jump to conclusions.'

'I've said I'm sorry; what more can I do?'

'And I've accepted your apology. I don't think there's anything more to say on the subject.' The words tumbled from her lips before she could stop them, but the hurt look on his face weakened her resolve to be strong. For a split second the tough sea captain looked like a small boy caught out in a naughty deed, and she had to curb a sudden desire to comfort him.

'You're right,' he said slowly, 'Then there's nothing else to say. Goodbye, Mirabel. I hope you and Edric make a success of your business venture.' He made a move towards the door.

'You're leaving?' Her voice sound high-pitched to her own ears, like the squeak of a mouse, but he did not seem to notice.

'The *Munroe Star* sails on the tide.' He hesitated in the doorway. 'I am truly sorry, Belle.'

She was left staring at the door as it closed behind him. For a moment she could not believe that he had gone. He had used the pet name that Jerusha always called her and it had slipped from his lips like a term of endearment. Her knees gave way beneath her and she sank down on the chair, staring blankly at the door – waiting. It opened as if her will had worked a miracle, but it was Sawyer the wharfinger who burst in. 'Some light-fingered bugger has pinched all my coal,' he said angrily. 'I left a full sack last night and now it's gone.'

She rose unsteadily to her feet. 'Mine too, Mr Sawyer.' She pointed to the empty grate.

He pushed his cap to the back of his head, scowling. 'We'll have to keep it inside and make sure the back door is locked. I can't afford to keep buying coal only to have it stolen from right under my nose.' He peered at her, squinting through narrowed eyelids. 'Are you all right, missis? You look a bit peaky.'

'I'm cold, Mr Sawyer. The weather has taken a turn for the worse.'

'Give us the cash, missis, and I'll send my boy out to get two bags of coal. He'll fill the scuttle for you too. The lazy lump needs a bit of exercise.'

Mirabel reached inside the top drawer of her desk and took out the cash box, selecting a few coins and handing them to him. 'Thank you, Mr Sawyer. I'm much obliged.'

He tipped his cap. 'Happy to help, missis. But if I was you I'd pop home and get some vittles and a nice hot cup of tea inside me.'

'That's good advice. I might just do that.' She

managed a smile but she sighed with relief when the door closed on him. No doubt he meant well, but he had taken up valuable moments when she might have caught up with Jack in the hope of restoring peace between them. She sat in a daze, shivering with cold and unable to concentrate on the sheaf of papers that lay waiting for her attention.

Sawyer's boy brought the coal and set the fire for her. She gave him tuppence for his trouble and as he was about to leave she called him back. 'Tommy, wait a moment.' She rose to her feet with a sudden burst of energy. 'What time is high tide today?'

He stood in the open doorway, glancing out at the river. 'It's on the turn now, missis.'

'Don't close the door, Tommy. I'm going out.' She grabbed her reticule and followed him out onto the wharf, stopping only to lock the door behind her. One look at the swirling pewter-coloured water was enough to convince her that the tide was on the turn. The *Munroe Star* was about to sail and she had only one thought in mind. As luck would have it she managed to hail a hansom cab in Great Tower Street, giving the cabby instructions to take her to the London dock. 'I'll give you double the fare if you can get me there quickly,' she said in desperation. Money seemed to matter little when the only man she had ever loved was about to set sail for America.

She sat on the edge of the seat, willing the horse to go faster and silently cursing the pedestrians who thronged the streets along with the rest of the chaotic mix of horse-drawn vehicles. In the end she called out to the cabby to stop, paid him handsomely and ran the rest of the way, elbowing a path through the crowds and ignoring the offensive remarks from disgruntled porters, sailors and warehousemen. She was breathless and on the verge of collapse when she reached the dock, only to find an empty space where the *Munroe Star* had been berthed. She came to a sudden halt, her ragged breaths tearing at her lungs and her heart hammering against her ribcage, but all she could think of was that Jack had chosen to leave. He could have stayed and made an effort to win her, but despite his apology it was obvious that he had not forgiven her for opting to stay with Hubert.

'What's the matter, darling? Left all alone by one of them seafaring men, are you?'

She turned her head and found herself looking up into the face of a man who looked and smelled as though he had not washed for months. His filthy clothes hung from his body in tatters, and his shirt sleeves were rolled up to reveal multiple tattoos. He was leering at her in a suggestive way which barely registered in her brain. All she could think about was Jack, but the man was insistent, barring her way as she started to walk. 'C'mon, love. How about it? I can pay.'

She attempted to dodge him but he was too quick for her and seized her by the arm. Fuelled by anger and desperation she aimed a punch at his jaw, catching him off guard, and she gave him a mighty shove which sent him teetering over the edge of the dock into the murky water. She gasped with horror, reliving the moment when

Wiley had attacked her. Behind her someone was clapping.

She turned to see Ethan and to her surprise he was laughing as he hurried towards her. 'I was too far away to get to you, honey,' he said breathlessly. 'But you can obviously take care of yourself.'

'I might have killed him,' Mirabel said weakly.

Ethan moved closer to the edge of the dock and leaned over. 'No, that particular animal can swim. Maybe it will teach him a well-deserved lesson.' He placed his arm around her shoulders. 'You've had a nasty shock, Belle. I'll see you safely home.'

She hesitated. 'I missed the ship, Ethan. I sent Jack away thinking I didn't care and now he's gone. I'll never see him again.'

'It's true that the *Munroe Star* has sailed, but you might be mistaken as far as Jack is concerned.'

'What do you mean? Is he in your employ or isn't he?'

'Honey, I can't speak for Jack. I've a notion how he's feeling at the moment but it's not for me to say. All I can tell you is that he asked me to find another man to captain the *Star*. He didn't sail with her.'

She stared at him in disbelief. 'But why? Where is he?'

'You're shivering and it's cold here on the dock. I have a carriage waiting to take me back to my hotel. Why don't you come with me?'

She hesitated, aware of her unkempt appearance, and had a sudden desire to be alone. 'I – I don't know...'

'Jerusha will be happy to see you. She's worried

about you, honey.'

The thought of going somewhere warm and luxurious was tempting. She wanted to get as far away from the docks as possible and to avoid the interrogation she might be subjected to if she arrived home in a state. She nodded her head. 'Thank you. I'd like that, but first you must tell me why Jack stayed in London.'

Ethan smiled. 'I think you must know the answer already, Belle. Let's just say he had business to conduct in the City, and leave it at that for now. I'm pretty darn sure he'd want to tell you about it himself.'

She allowed him to guide her towards the dock entrance but all she could think about was Jack. He had not exactly lied to her in the office when he told her the ship was sailing on the tide, but he had allowed her to assume that he would be its captain. She was confused and angry with him for not telling her the whole truth, and yet underlying everything was a huge feeling of relief. Life without Jack was unthinkable, and as she settled in the comfort of Ethan's hired carriage she closed her eyes, recalling the tender moments she and Jack had shared during their time in the Fakahatchee swamp. His kisses were burned indelibly onto her lips and the taste and scent of him still haunted her dreams. Every sense in her body had been awakened with a jolt and her whole body was aflame with inexplicable yearning. She opened her eyes. 'What is he up to, Ethan? I must know.'

Chapter Twenty-six

Jerusha was lounging on a chaise longue in front of a roaring fire, but she leapt to her feet when Ethan ushered Mirabel into the room. 'Why, Mirabel Kettle, I thought you were tied to that desk of yours and couldn't take time off to spend with your old friends.'

'She's had a nasty experience at the docks, honey.' Ethan took Mirabel's cape and bonnet from her and tossed them casually onto a spindly gilt chair. 'Go and sit by the fire, Belle. I'll pour you a brandy, and I might have one too.'

'You're very kind and considerate. You'll make a wonderful father one day, Ethan,' Mirabel said, smiling.

'I hope so.' He picked up a cut-glass decanter and poured two tots.

'Of course you will, honey.' Jerusha hurried over to give Mirabel a hug.

'And it goes without saying that you'll be a splendid mother, Jerusha,' Mirabel added hastily.

'What nonsense you talk, Belle.' Jerusha took her by the hand and led her over to a wingback chair by the fire. 'You're cold as ice. Sit down and get warm.'

Mirabel sank into the depths of the velvet upholstery. 'I'm just a bit cold, but I'm fine, really I am.'

'What were you doing in the docks anyway?' Jerusha eyed her curiously.

'I went to find Jack, thinking he was about to sail on the *Munroe Star.*' Mirabel shot a sideways glance at Ethan. It was obvious that Jerusha knew little of her husband's business dealings, and she did not want to upset her friend by saying too much. 'But the ship had sailed.'

Jerusha turned to her husband with an enquiring look. 'Is there something you aren't telling me, Ethan?'

'Of course not, honey. I'd gone to the dock to make sure everything went smoothly and was about to leave when I saw a young woman being harassed by a big brute who obviously had the worst of intentions.' Ethan handed a glass to Mirabel. 'Sip it slowly.'

Jerusha's hand flew to her mouth. 'Who would attack a helpless woman like you, Belle?'

'Helpless?' Ethan threw back his head and laughed. 'A tigress looks tame by comparison. She punched him in the face and pushed him into the dock. I've never seen anything so funny in all my life.'

Mirabel sipped the brandy and felt its fiery warmth travel swiftly to her stomach and she began to relax. 'I suppose it did look odd,' she said, smiling.

'You're both crazy,' Jerusha said, horrified. 'How can you find such a thing amusing?'

Ethan was suddenly serious. 'Of course it wasn't funny, darling. It was Belle's way of dealing with the guy that made me laugh. Wait until I tell Jack.'

'You'll have to leave it until we get home,' Jerusha said sternly. 'Maybe it won't seem so hilarious then.'

417

'You obviously don't know that there was a sudden change of plan.' Mirabel placed her glass on a small wine table at her side. 'One thing you learn is that men don't tell us everything, Jerusha. They treat us like children or pretty dolls unable to think for themselves.'

'That's not fair, Belle,' Ethan said in answer to his wife's questioning look. 'Everything changed when Jack decided to stay behind.'

'He let you down?'

'No, honey, he didn't do that. He found me a substitute to captain the ship, someone he's known for a long time.'

Mirabel's head was swimming, and not simply because of the heat from the fire and the fumes of alcohol chasing around in her brain. 'It wasn't Edric Hamilton by any chance, was it?'

'That's the chap. Big guy with a flaming red beard and a mop of curly hair. I warmed to him from the start.'

Jerusha turned to Mirabel, eyebrows raised. 'I'm getting more confused by the minute. I thought Edric was your business partner, Belle?'

'He is, or rather he was. You're not alone, Jerusha. I don't know what's going on.'

'I think Jack is the best person to answer that,' Ethan said hastily. 'I don't know the whole of it, but I'm sure he had a good reason for acting the way he did.'

'There's only one way to find out.' Jerusha reached out to pat Mirabel's hand. 'You need to talk to him, honey.'

'That's exactly what I intend to do. If Edric has sailed for America in the *Munroe Star* it leaves the

Mudlark without a master. Just wait until I see Jack Starke. I'll have plenty to say to that gentleman.' She turned to Ethan, frowning. 'You must have some idea where he's gone. Tell me, please.'

'You must, honey,' Jerusha said firmly. 'You're not being fair to Belle if you're keeping something from her.'

Ethan ran his finger round the inside of his starched collar. 'He told me he was going to Lloyd's to put in a claim for the loss of the *Lady Grace*. That's all I know, Belle. I guess we'll have to wait until he contacts one of us.'

'Then I must get back to the office.' Mirabel rose to her feet. 'Thank you for your hospitality, but I've a ship without a master and a cargo for Gravesend. Jack knows where to find me.'

With a ship idling at its moorings next morning, and Alf and his boys busy with a party of anglers, Mirabel could do little but sit in the office and wait. She had slept badly the previous night and her nerves were shredded and raw. She had even lost patience with the children at breakfast and had scolded Jim for spilling his tea, causing him to burst into tears. Gertie had frowned at her and Tilda had cleared up the mess with a cloth, but the rest of the meal had been eaten in silence.

It had been a relief to go to the office. Ethan had promised to send Jack to her if he should see him first, but he had not put in an appearance last night and she was seething inwardly. She was angry with Edric for going off without so much as a word, and furious with Jack for coming between her and her business partner. Thanks to Jack's interference Edric had shown himself to be both weak and unreliable, and she silently cursed herself for putting her trust in him. Despite her best efforts she found it almost impossible to concentrate on work, and she sat behind her desk with her pen clutched in her hand and a blank sheet of paper in front of her, but she was at a loss as to what to do next. The *Mudlark* was Edric's responsibility, but someone had to act as master in his absence, and she had a vested interest in the success of their joint venture. All would be lost if she could not find a reliable captain very soon. She wondered if this was Jack's way of punishing her for ending their relationship, but in spite of her anger she could not bring herself to believe he would stoop so low.

She was deep in thought, chewing the end of her pen and staring into space, when the door opened and Jack strode into the office. She leapt to her feet, dropping the pen, which rolled across the desk and fell to the floor. 'I don't know how you have the nerve to show your face here after what you've done.' She had intended to appear cold and aloof but the words tumbled from her lips before she could stop herself.

He held up both hands in a gesture of submission. 'I don't blame you for being angry, but hear me out before you shoot me.'

'It's not funny. You've all but ruined my business. You sent Edric to America in your stead. Why would you do that if it wasn't to ruin me?'

'We couldn't tell you because it was arranged at the last moment. Edric wasn't happy about it, but the *Munroe Star* had to sail with the tide and

I had urgent business at Lloyd's.'

'You had no right to act without my knowledge. What was so important that it couldn't wait until your next trip to London?'

He pulled up a chair. 'May I sit down? I was hurrying to and fro between the underwriters and the lawyers all day yesterday, which is why I couldn't come to see you sooner.'

'Take a seat.' Mirabel sank back onto her chair. 'Go on, Jack. I'm listening.'

'I went to Lloyd's as soon after we docked as I could, and I put in a claim for the loss of the *Lady Grace*. It's something I should have done sooner, but after the wreck I was at a loose end. That ship was my home and my livelihood, and several of the crew were lost when she went down.' He paused, eyeing her warily. 'Am I making sense?'

She nodded. 'I think so, but you never told me how you came to end up in Florida. You said that the *Lady Grace* went down off the coast of Havana.'

'It did, and I was trying to make my way home. The surviving crew were able to look after themselves, and there was a tramp steamer leaving for Florida, so I worked my passage. I fully intended to make my way back to England from there, but after a while there didn't seem to be much point.'

'You've lost me now,' Mirabel said, shaking her head. 'Why?'

He fixed her with a penetrating look. 'Because I'd fallen in love with a girl who wasn't the slightest bit interested in me, and I'd made the mistake of placing her in the care of a woman who had once been my mistress. I'm not proud of myself,

Belle. I knew I'd made a mess of things, so I allowed myself to drift. I lived in the beach shack and drank rum with the locals. If you hadn't turned up when you did I would have gone on that way until it killed me.'

She was silent for a moment, remembering how he was when they met in Florida. 'So what's changed now? Why didn't you come with us when we left for home?'

His lips curled in a sardonic smile. 'You had a husband then, or have you forgotten poor Hubert already? You were no longer the wide-eyed innocent I met in the soup kitchen. I knew I shouldn't have allowed my feelings for you to get the better of me, but you were a respectable married woman with a decent husband, and a home of your own. What had a drunken out of work seafarer to offer a woman like you?'

'It wasn't just your decision, Jack. I was involved too. You knew that I loved you, even though I wouldn't betray Hubert's trust. You and I could have stayed friends.'

His harsh laugh echoed round the room. 'You really are an innocent in the ways of men and women, Belle. Do you really think we could have gone on as we were? We aren't Romeo and Juliet, and I wasn't about to wait around for Hubert to shuffle off this mortal coil. I did what I thought was best for you and for me.'

'Then why did you change your mind?'

'Bodger changed it for me. He turned up unexpectedly and he told me that you were a widow. I knew then there was only one course for me to take. When Munroe offered me a job I took it.'

'I understand so far, I think. But why did you send Edric to America?'

'The underwriters at Lloyd's didn't throw my claim out, as I feared they might. My solicitor advised me to remain in London until matters were sorted, and Edric was the only man I knew I could trust to do a good job for Ethan. It had to be done quickly or not at all. I couldn't let Ethan down.'

'So you chose to let me down instead?'

He stood up, leaning both hands on the desk and looking her in the eye. 'I will take over the *Mudlark*, if you'll allow me to do so. I know what has to be done. Edric made me promise to work for you without pay until everything is straight. I'm at your service. I'll do anything it takes to win your trust and maybe one day you'll find it in your heart to forgive me for the way I've behaved.'

She felt herself drowning in the depths of his blue eyes, but she steeled herself to resist. It would have been easy to walk into his arms and lose herself in the passion that they had once shared, but this was not the make-believe world of a far distant shore. This was reality and she had a business to run. She was about to answer when the door opened and Alf entered the office. He came to a halt, staring at Jack beneath a lowered brow. 'Is everything all right, missis?'

'Yes, Alf.' Mirabel walked slowly round the desk, placing herself between them. 'I don't think you've met Captain Starke. He's taking over from Edric who was called away on urgent business.' She turned to Jack. 'Alf Coker is my right-hand man. He skippers the *Beatrice*, taking anglers on fishing trips, and next summer we plan to run a passenger service on the river. I don't know how I would have managed without him.'

The air vibrated like a taut bowstring as the two men faced each other. 'How do, Captain Starke,' Alf said grudgingly.

'Pleased to make your acquaintance, Coker.' Jack shook Alf's hand, but they were still glaring at each other in a gladiatorial manner.

'Alf and his family share my house in Savage Gardens,' Mirabel said hastily. 'Why don't you come home with us, Jack? You can meet my adopted family and stay for supper, unless of course you have a prior engagement.' She met his gaze with a challenging look.

'Thank you. I'd like to do that but I have to look for lodgings first, or at least a place to stay tonight. Zilla put me up in her parlour last night.' He met Mirabel's startled look with a wry smile. 'That's all it was, I assure you. I went there to say a final farewell. That part of my life is well and truly in the past.'

'The *Mudlark* has a cabin, Captain,' Alf said before Mirabel had a chance to respond. 'I'll be happy to show you where she's berthed.'

'That's settled then.' Mirabel slipped her cape around her shoulders and put on her bonnet. 'I suppose Bodger did leave on the *Munroe Star*, Jack? Or did he jump ship again?'

'Not this time. Bodger knows when he's on to a good thing,' Jack said, grinning. 'Regular trips between Newport News and London or Bristol will suit him very well.' He proffered his arm to Mirabel. 'I haven't eaten all day, so I'd be delighted to accept your invitation to supper, Mrs Kettle.'

Mirabel slipped her hand through the crook of his arm, experiencing a warm glow as if the sun had suddenly appeared from behind a bank of clouds.

To Mirabel's surprise Jack fitted in seamlessly with the noisy boisterous family who occupied the house in Savage Gardens. He knew Gertie, of course, but was soon on first name terms with Tilda and the boys, and the younger girls were shy at first, but he soon won them over. When the supper things had been cleared away Mirabel showed him the shattered greenhouse, which Alf was slowly restoring. 'There won't be any more orchids,' she said, holding up the oil lamp to reveal the damage that Wiley had inflicted. 'But Alf has plans to grow tomatoes and other vegetables under glass, when it's finished.'

Jack leaned against the staging, looking round. 'Do you intend to have them living with you permanently?'

'I won't turn them out, if that's what you mean.' She stepped over a pile of splintered wood. 'I'm seriously thinking of moving back into my old home, and allowing Alf to pay rent on this place. He's a good man and hardworking.'

'And he's in need of a wife. It can't be easy bringing up a brood like that on his own.' Jack gave her a steady look. 'You seem to have been like a mother to those children.'

She recoiled, startled. 'That's ridiculous. There's nothing between me and Alf.'

'How would he manage if you moved out? Who would look after the younger children? Tilda's little more than a child herself.'

'Gertie cares for them all, including Alf, and he thinks the world of her. I can't imagine that she'd want to live anywhere else.' Mirabel frowned thoughtfully. 'I hadn't thought that far ahead. I've had enough to do with getting a business started.' She shivered as a cool breeze whipped through one of the broken windows prodding her with icy fingers. It was, she thought, as if Hubert's spirit still inhabited the place he had loved so much and was trying to warn her to be careful. 'Let's go inside. I think it's time for Alf to take you to the *Mudlark*.' She hesitated in the doorway. 'What of you, Jack? What will you do when you get the money from the insurers? Will you buy another ship? Will you sail away and come back only when it suits you?'

'Would that bother you, Belle?'

'Hurry up, Jack. It's starting to rain again.'

Mirabel was in the office next morning when Jerusha paid her a visit. She looked elegant as usual and her presence made the room seem smaller and shabbier, but she was brimming with happiness. 'I've come to invite you to dinner at the hotel this evening, honey. It's our last night in London and we're off to Paris in the morning.' She glanced at the sheaves of documents on Mirabel's desk and shuddered. 'I declare I have no idea how you cope with all this, Belle. I wish I were as clever as you.'

'Nonsense,' Mirabel said stoutly. 'You would do the same if you had to support yourself.'

'I'm not sure I could, but that's not important.' Jerusha pulled up a chair and sat down, leaning her elbows on the desk. 'I have something exciting to tell you, but don't breathe a word of it to anyone else, not even Jack.'

'Jack and I work together. That's all there is to it.'

'Then I guess you'd have no objection to Jack being our guest to dinner as well as you?'

Mirabel shrugged her shoulders, assuming an air of indifference. 'Of course not. We're on good terms now.'

'I guess you know what you're doing.'

'I do indeed. Now what is the exciting news?'

'It's not for anyone else to know yet, but I'm telling you because you're the nearest thing I have to a sister. Can you guess what it is?' Jerusha's eyes sparkled and her cheeks flushed to a delicate pink.

Mirabel leapt up from her seat and hurried round the desk to give her a hug. 'Are you certain? Isn't it too soon to tell?'

Jerusha returned the embrace, kissing her on the cheek. 'You'll know when it happens to you.' She laid a hand on her belly, smiling happily. 'If it's a girl I'll call her Belle, and I want you to be her godmother.'

'Of course I will, but I'm so far away.'

'Ethan plans to buy another ship as soon as he can raise the money. You'll come and visit with us often, and I'll bring my children to see you.' She clutched Mirabel's hand, holding it to her cheek. 'Promise me one thing, Belle.'

'Of course. Anything you want.'

'Promise that you'll give Jack a chance, because I know he loves you dearly.'

Dazed by the sudden turn in the conversation, Mirabel stared at her in surprise. 'How can you be so sure?'

'We had plenty of time to talk during the voyage across the Atlantic. Your name came up more times than I can count. You will give him a second chance, won't you? Promise me you will.'

'I promise to think it over.'

'Wonderful. Now I can go to Paris with an easy mind.' Jerusha jumped to her feet. 'Ethan's waiting outside so I must go, but I'll see you this evening. We'll send a carriage for you.'

That evening Mirabel dressed with extra care. She wore the silk gown that Jerusha had given her and the sapphire necklace and earrings that had been her wedding present from Hubert. She picked up a fading daguerreotype of his likeness from a chest in the parlour, and his stern face stared back at her. 'I'm sorry, Hubert,' she said softly. 'I love him, but then you know I didn't feel that way about you.' She smiled sadly. 'And it was Anjuli's name on your lips when you died.' She raised the frame to her lips and kissed the glass. 'I know you'll understand.' She placed it in a drawer alongside the photograph of Hubert's true love. 'Together for all eternity,' she whispered, closing it gently.

'Mabel, the carriage is here.' Gertie's voice rang out from the entrance hall.

As she gathered up her velvet evening cloak Mirabel felt like a girl again. She left the house and made her way down the steps to where Jack was waiting to hand her into the carriage, and as his fingers closed around her hand she knew she had come home at last. It was impossible to deny the attraction that drew her to him like a magnet, and despite the drizzle that had started to fall, and the curious looks of the passers-by, he drew her to him and kissed her on the lips. As if she weighed less than a pennyweight he lifted her into the carriage and climbed in beside her. Once again she was in his arms, and as the coachman urged the horses into a walk, and then a trot, they were cocooned in a world of their own. 'I love you, Belle. Tell me that you love me.'

'I love you, Jack.' She leaned back in the circle of his arms, studying his face in the flickering glow of the gas lights as they flashed past. 'But you'll be off on your travels again the moment you get the insurance money. I know you will.'

'I'm going nowhere without you, Belle. Could you find it in your heart to leave all this behind and travel with me?'

She reached up to trace the angle of his jaw with the tip of her finger. 'Would we build a shipping line to equal the Munroes'?'

'With you at my side I could do anything, my darling.'

She slid her arms around his neck. 'I'd want equal shares in the business if I'm to invest.'

His answer was an embrace that robbed her of speech, sanity and the will to refuse him anything. He drew away, giving them both a chance to catch their breath. 'Husband and wife, lovers and equal partners.'

She smiled lazily. 'I like the sound of that.'

'How will we break it to the Munroes?'

'I can keep a secret. Can you?' She drew his head down so that their lips met in a kiss.

Jerusha was the first to spot them as they edged their way between the tables in the opulent dining room at Claridge's. Ethan stood up as a waiter appeared as if from nowhere to pull out a chair for Mirabel, but it was Jerusha who spoke first. 'I can tell,' she cried, clapping her hands. 'I don't need Mama's gift of second sight to see that you two have come to an understanding.'

Ethan reached out to shake Jack's hand. 'I guess there was another good reason for your decision to stay in London.'

Jack took a seat beside Mirabel, taking her hand in his. 'I took a chance, and I'm glad to say that it paid off. I can't believe my luck.' He raised her hand to his lips and brushed it with a kiss.

'Well, I want to be the first to congratulate you,' Ethan said earnestly. 'You'd better treat her right, Jack. Mirabel is like a sister to us.'

'And the wedding will have to be soon or I won't be in a fit condition to be matron of honour.' Jerusha blew a kiss to her husband. 'Botheration. Secrets are made to be broken. We have to fit your nuptials in before the baby arrives. There, I've said it.'

Mirabel squeezed Jack's fingers. 'I think we can arrange something. There's an empty house waiting for us, and I'll have a selection of bridesmaids from little Kitty up to Gertie.'

'Waiter,' Ethan called, signalling with his hand. 'Champagne.'

Jack leaned towards Mirabel. 'Are you sure about this, Belle?'

'I've never been so sure about anything in my life,' she said, smiling.

This Large Print Book for the partially sighted, who cannot read normal print, is published under the auspices of

THE ULVERSCROFT FOUNDATION